AFTER THE END OF THE WORLD . . .

From the hills behind the shore, if there was anyone there left alive and with enough interest, the Vindicator must have been a spectacular sight, bars of red light endlessly stabbing from it up and outwards into the total night.

Lances of fire.

They tore away and lit up the sea. The illumination spread far away over the regular swell, painting it a brilliant red with oily black moving shadows in the troughs. The distant water gleamed dully red, multiply lit . . .

Lances of fire turning the ocean into a sea of sombre blood, putting more burning blackness into the dying world.

Lances of fire.

FIRE LANCE

Books by David Mace

DEMON-4
NIGHTRIDER
FIRE LANCE

DAVID MACE
FIRE LANCE

ACE BOOKS, NEW YORK

For my grandmother,
who has had to witness too many wars.

This Ace book contains the complete
text of the original edition.
It has been completely reset in a typeface
designed for easy reading and was printed
from new film.

FIRE LANCE

An Ace Book/published by arrangement with
Grafton Books

PRINTING HISTORY
Grafton edition published 1986
Ace edition/July 1989

ISBN: 0-441-23588-3

Ace Books are published by The Berkley Publishing Group,
200 Madison Avenue, New York, New York 10016.
The name "ACE" and the "A" logo are trademarks
belonging to Charter Communications, Inc.

PRINTED IN THE UNITED STATES OF AMERICA

10 9 8 7 6 5 4 3 2 1

Author's Note

The traditions and organization of the United States Navy will have changed by the close of this century in response to evolutions in its strategic role, in military technology, and in imposed government policy. Some of these changes will be minor and some quite radical. Differences between the present day US Navy and the *Vindicator's* internal organization and its rank and command structures are thus to be seen in such terms. In this respect *Fire Lance* is an extrapolation from the present that cannot possibly be accurate in every detail.

June 1, CASAL (Command Alternate Sea-Air-Land), New Mexico

THE UPPER LEVEL tunnel was concrete lined, with curved interlocking slabs and massive reinforcing hoops. Here, only a hundred metres below the surface, the rock was less stable and less protecting, a big enough shock would collapse an unlined tunnel. The concrete slabs and rings were painted off-white, strip lights were pinned along the apex of the arch, every fourth one burning. The effect was one of bare brightness rather than prevailing gloom. The tunnel roadway serviced the surface access routes in this sector. A steady ventilation breeze blew along it.

David Drexel waited at the base of an elevator which led up to a surface lock, while at the control point against the tunnel wall an Army sergeant and a corporal checked him through. They wore fat service automatics at their hips, and looked like everyone else looked after too long in the artificial light underground. The artificial light was kept burning, the entire deeply buried command and control complex was kept alive, by long-life nuclear reactors encased in rock hundreds of metres below the flat plain. CASAL could go on unsupported for years, until the power for light and ventilation and for the deep freeze stores finally faltered and died.

All security at this fortress complex was provided by Army personnel, along with the US Air Force people who ran the air defence and the ballistic missile defence. Those systems were never used during the nuclear exchanges at the climax of the war. CASAL was only ever attacked with high-level EMP bursts, nuclear warheads that exploded way up above the atmosphere and triggered a vast energy release, an electromagnetic pulse that temporarily crippled any radar and communications equipment deployed on the surface above the fortress. Such bursts were too high even for the Skyguard system to interdict and prevent—and too high to be harmful. CASAL had got away lightly: David Drexel, too. He could have had the ill-luck to be on one of the advisement-and-crisis teams scheduled for dispersal to NASCOM, and then he would have been long dead. NASCOM had been taken out by saturation ground strikes.

The corporal finished examining his hand baggage grip, confirming that it held no disallowed contents, nothing from the list of all the precious things that the fortress administration so zealously controlled. The sergeant had inserted Drexel's machine readable ID into the control point terminal, and was checking the data it called up on the screen against the information typed onto the exit permit. He picked up the desk phone, pushed the key marked Surface Lock, and lifted the receiver to his ear.

"Time check," the sergeant said. "It's just five after twelve noon. Down here we have the transiting personnel, outgoing. Persons, one. Name Drexel, David. Date of birth September twenty fourth, nineteen sixty five. British alien, US Federal Government employee. Civilian, grade six clearance, strategic systems consultant. All checks out. His flight ready?" He pulled the ID card out of the terminal. "Okay. On his way." He put the receiver back on the hook, handed over the ID card and the exit permit. "Okay, Mr. Drexel, they're waiting for you."

Drexel slipped card and permit back into the inside pocket of his windjacket while the corporal put an emergency ration pack and then a service issue revolver and a box of thirty rounds on the little control point desk beside the grip. The gun and ammunition and iron rations for a couple of days were allowed to every outgoing passenger as a survival aid in the event of a forced landing short of the intended destination. No other weaponry was ever allowed outside because of the risk of it falling into someone else's desperate hands and one day being used against them here. Drexel put ration pack, gun and ammunition into the grip and zipped it closed. The sergeant unlocked the elevator and then handed him a parka from one of the hooks inside the door recess, a bulky quilted parka with gloves ready sticking out of the pockets. There was a shortage of winter clothing here under the New Mexico desert, and its issue was also strictly regulated.

The elevator door closed.

Drexel stood there hugging the parka and holding his hand

baggage, alone in the sealed little cage as it made its slow ascent. It rattled past the first of the blast doors that could seal the shaft, seal out the holocaust if it ever came again.

He was being sent out of this safe fortress. He was being sent northwards across the wide open awful outside to the even bigger fortress of the Cheyenne Mountain Complex, expanded ever deeper and further under its mountain range as one modification programme followed another, to eventually become the most extensive and secure of the three self-contained command centres designed to survive a nuclear war. The last and biggest modification—the last there would ever be now—had been the creation of STRACC, the Strategic Command Centre. CASAL was the backup to STRACC and STRACC was the backup to NASCOM, the National Strategic Command. The command centres were not invulnerable, not totally immune to nuclear attack, but they were expensive to erase—in progressively obliterating NASCOM the Russians had expended a vast megatonnage that could otherwise have been used on missile silos and other war material targets. It all contributed to the coherent war philosophy, to forcing your opponent to realize that your defence system as a totality had survivability and would still be there to eradicate him completely if he ever dared to attack you, the final refinement of perfect deterrence. And it hadn't worked, of course, because the opponent felt himself gravely threatened by your survivability and by his perception of your ability to attack him and get away with it, so he built himself survivability too.

The way that it went wrong was fascinating. The way the spiral of managed instability climbed higher with each new honest defence innovation, the coherent war philosophy of survivability and post-strike deterrence, the High Frontier concept of weakening an attack on its way over in space—each and every move seen by your opponent as an undermining of his honest defence, his ability to deter *you*. It had been a fascinating game, watching each side's total inability to accept that the enemy saw himself as the threatened good guy and responded to each move accordingly—we are good and therefore pose no threat to them, therefore everything they do is motivated by aggression towards us. That basic ingredient of human suspicion laced with occasional outbursts about capitalist imperialism and evil communism, and two perfectly healthy societies could wind themselves up into a relationship stabilized only by a mutual fear of destruction. He had played the game, thinking they could wind themselves up forever. He had always believed the spiral was growing steeper, not tightening in ever narrower curves. He had never realized it was climbing to a point.

But he was still alive. It wasn't quite the end of the world after all. Survivability had worked where it had been tested as lightly as at CASAL, or where high and low air bursts at STRACC had merely put all communication facilities but land line out of action for days following until new antennas could be bolted together inside the still useable deployment silos. Life was still cozy inside STRACC and CASAL. Snug and secure.

The elevator cage rattled past another blast door seal.

He was being sent from one fortress to another through the wild and lethal outside, from one haven to the next. Except that the fortresses weren't so safe any more. Policy was being run by the self-appointed committees of generals and senior Administration advisers and specialist consultants who were lucky enough to have lived through the war and its awful immediate aftermath. Now the vicious process of apportioning blame in the pursuit of power-oriented infighting had begun. Defeated and ostracized, you were as good as dead. Already the soft-liners and no-more-war people were being identified and rounded up—soon they might be shooting them at CASAL as well as at Cheyenne and at the scatter of leftover regional control centres still operational, still in contact with the policy determining fortress commands. And the fortresses themselves, secure havens of life, were turning into extremely dangerous hideaways for anyone in any kind of position of sought for or imposed responsibility. The power struggle was on the point of boiling over. And he was being sent to take part in a conference advisement where the latest and presumably most hopeless assessments of the climate collapse and the strategic situation were to be discussed and policy recommendations thrashed out. He was being thrown right into the middle of the power struggle because he happened to be practiced at evaluating what the Russians still had. He would have to tread very carefully, very carefully indeed. He had come through the worst thing that had ever happened to the world and was still alive. The name of the game was to stay that way as long as possible.

The self-driven elevator cage clattered through the third blast door ring and stopped. The cage opened.

The surface room was harsh lit, the cement walls lined with fragment-catching steel mesh. A side ladder led up to a ceiling trap, there was a control point, there was an armoured glass door at the far end and beyond it the outer portal of laminated steel. At the control point sat another Army guard, a corporal. There were two thousand Army at CASAL, around five percent of all US service personnel still known to be operational anywhere in the world. A world where most of those left alive were inside the military-political command centres and a scatter of smaller control bunkers, and where most of those few who made up the pitiful rest out there were sick and helpless and dying.

"Flight control says your aircraft is outside, engines running and ready to go." The corporal stood up and started shunting him through the hard room. "You can go right out. Follow the path right from the door. The aircraft is parked on a lighted apron a couple of hundred away. Watch out if a clearance vehicle is rolling around—they've just had to re-clear the strip again. If you catch sight of anyone standing around anywhere, don't worry. They're Army." A gesture at the ceiling. "There's even two up on top of the mound. Radars and cameras, great. But the human eye is better." The corporal opened up the armoured glass door and ushered Drexel into the lock. "Wrap yourself up well."

He closed the door and went back to the control point.

Drexel pulled on the parka and zipped it closed to the neck, all swishing nylon in the blank walled box. He pulled on the gloves, waved okay, picked up his grip. At the control point the corporal threw the door switch. The outer door moved, a massive rectangle of laminated steel and locking bolt mechanisms swinging outwards and open—

Pitch black icy iron night poured in.

He stepped out into it, stepped over the massive sill.

Ice under foot, glittering footstep-rutted in the dim lights that looked down into the slope-sided cleft in the flank of the entrance mound. Open blackness ahead, a chain of pole lights leading away to a smear of illumination shimmering around a steely drab Air Force jet, rolled up from its protected hangar ready for takeoff. Its tail engines whined across the wind, subdued but thinly piercing.

He stepped out along the path, wreathed in his own breath.

He cleared the flank of the mound and came into the razor edge of the slicing wind. Cruel cutting claws clutched at his face and ears. He gasped at the cold shock. He pulled up the parka hood, nylon fabric swished across his ears and caressed the pain. He hurried out into the freezing midday night. Blackness lay beyond the pallid light pools that danced with ground shadows as the pole lights rattled in the wind. He stumbled and slithered along the icy path, vicious cold trapping his legs, stabbing blinding at his face, at his eyes.

It is a quarter after high noon on June 1st in the New Mexico desert. It is nine weeks since the war, and this is the Nuclear Winter.

This is what has happened to the world.

June 2, USS Vindicator, 42°S 35°W

SEA GREY SHIFTING mountains slow dancing round a steel grey ship. A long and sleek-bowed ship shouldering aside foam-flecked winter-wave avalanche opponents that have followed it all the way from the bottom of the world. A half circle stormscape centred on the bleak focus of the coming sun. An empty ocean wildness.

Richard Erwin Bedford, Captain, United States Navy—forty seven, caucasian, average height, moderately overweight. Hair impeccably cropped, turning metal grey. In the enclosed environment of the ship he never wore the baseball cap with everyday service dress, so it was a hats-off ship, just a big submarine on the surface, with a couple of windows. Everyone follows the Captain's lead.

He closed the port door at the back of the bridge, stood easy on the green deck in the grey space with its line of windows. Cold light washed in. There was never any illumination but daylight on the bridge, except for instrument glows at night. The bridge was not the brain of the ship, just a monitoring station—its routine positions included only a junior officer of the watch, a seaman at the conning data repeat console, and two lookouts with next to nothing to do.

The USS Vindicator, NMSS-3 Nemesis Class. The ship was heading northeast in the desolate middle of the South Atlantic, making a steady 17½ knots through a very heavy sea state with a force nine blowing square on the stern. He stood easy: even a 56,000 tonne battleship moves and pitches ponderously in such a sea. They were—they *had been*—heading for South Africa, with the promise of a coastal anchorage, the possibility of at least some re-supply with provisions and aviation fuel. South Africa was the only country still functioning that was open and friendly to an American ship.

Everyone else in a horrendously stricken world was either
outright hostile, or else utterly wary of being seen to help
stragglers from one of the great giants that had done it to
them all and might turn out to have wiped themselves out in
the process. Only South Africa was still a friend without the
dilemma of which side of any particular fence to land on,
because without the white non-communist north to back them,
the South African racists were dead. A paradox, such a haven
for an American ship, when forty five percent of its crew
were black.

There were probably already a few warships and US merchant stragglers gathered in South African waters. The Vindicator would have been the queen of any sorry little flotilla
assembling there to await the resumption of war. There was
nowhere else to assemble. All the US and allied NATO bases
in the northern hemisphere were closed, either erased during
the war or shut down just as permanently by the Big Freeze.
The entire eastern and western American seaboard was incon-
ceivably hostile. Any war survivors that had hurried back
there before their fuel and stores gave out were locked in and
useless, helpless against future events.

Once communications with the remaining command centres
in the Continental United States were restored they had kept
him and his ship cruising around in the eastern Pacific, too far
away from Soviet possessions for its strategic missiles to pose
any immediate threat. The intention was to prevent the Soviets from getting worried enough to try taking the Vindicator
out, because the Vindicator was almost all that was left, the
only seaborne strategic system, the only operational naval
unit besides a handful of destroyers and submarines. They
had moved him gradually further east nearer home, and further south, sometimes just under and sometimes just clear of
the steadily southward spreading dust veil. And then the order
had come through to head round Cape Horn for South African
waters. The whole time he'd maintained cruising speed, using
No. 1 reactor flat out—most efficiently—with No. 2 shut
right down to slow the chain reactions in its heart and reduce
the rate of depletion of its uranium fuel. Who knew when
they'd ever get a refuelling chance, even in a year or two
years? He wanted to conserve reactor fuel and maintain his
mobility—a half-speed maximum was far better than none.
But now that priority had been superseded anyway.

The bridge was on 05 level, in the top of the narrower

forward superstructure where it tapered still further to narrow
the forward corners. The bridge was ten metres across the
front windows and thirteen metres across the rear wall, and
five metres deep. In the centre was the two-seat bridge console with the lower placed conning data repeat console in
front of it. On the right-hand chair at the bridge console sat
the officer of the watch, Lt. Judy Wigner, the Fire Lance
Target Control Officer. She wore service dress, cool in the
Vindicator's permanently cocooned interior: black shoes, khaki
pants, khaki short-sleeved shirt. No impractical skirts for the
women on board—sex was for off-duty hours, not for ladders
and companionways all over the huge ship. Khaki was for
officers, the rest of the crew wore blue denim shirts and blue
jeans; white teeshirts were worn all round. Good old fash-
ioned clothing, all cotton and no synthetics. A couple of
decades ago the British had experimented on their own men
with synthetics in the Falklands—ignited in a fire, they melted
and stuck to the skin, burning. Clumsy slow-drying cotton
was better.

Wigner caught his glance. "Morning, sir."

Bedford nodded, and started across to the console.

Out there a huge wave broke over the port bow, came
tumbling back along the ship's side. The whole vessel shud-
dered and shied off monstrously. Bedford reached the bridge
console and steadied himself with the grab rail mounted on its
side, watched the electronic compass repeater swing five
degrees, ten. Even with hugely powerful rudder drives, quick-
response pitch and speed variation on the screws, computer-
aided direction holding, even with everything that technology
could supply the ship took some skill to hold it steady in such
a sea. The helmsman one deck down in the Conning Position
below the bridge would be sitting at his console, watching the
tv screen views of the outside world and using his purely
human abilities to keep a steady course, trying to predict from
the Titan dance around them where the next stupendous shove
would come from.

The spray from the mountain wave hit the thickly armoured
bridge windows twenty two metres above the sea. A dull
slapping sound.

Bedford eased himself into the raised chair next to Wigner,
a luxurious chair, high-backed, arm rests, comfortably padded. The Navy, his father used to tell him, isn't what it was.

It had gone soft. Next thing they'd be having women on board.

Wigner shook her head. "At least it's better than it was, sir."

"About time." They were 2,000 kilometres from the Falklands now, 2,800 from Cape Horn, had been making 17½ knots all the way. They ran into appalling winter weather in the raging waste of the Drake Passage and it had stayed with them all the way—three days and four nights now. There was no way of predicting when they would outrun it. Bainbridge, the Meteorology Officer, was reduced to forecasting local area weather. She could do nothing more ambitious without weather satellite information—and there were no weather satellites any more.

There were no navigation satellites. The entire pinpoint accuracy MAPS navigation system was useless, just up-to-the-second junk. The Marine Absolute Position Satellites had been taken out in the war, along with any leftovers of the old NavStar system. Up there in orbit the High Frontier had blazed briefly, lethally. Now they were thrown back on traditional methods of finding their way, the inertial navigation system supplemented and updated by sextant readings.

The Vindicator lifted on the monstrous sea, an orange-red glow flooded the bridge interior. The sun was coming up out there at the rim of the wave wasteland, only shreds of cloud were tearing down towards it through a pallid, chilling, silver-green sky. Someone should be arriving to shoot the sun.

There were no external doors, no external bridge wings— the Vindicator had a smooth carapace, no enclosed angles and corners to catch the stupendous blast of a thermonuclear explosion. The ship couldn't survive that way. Only the bridge windows of laminated glass pierced the armoured shell, only here and from the Takeoff and Landing Control Position at the rear of the superstructure could you see the outside world directly. Four hundred and fourteen souls on board, and only eight of them looked out with their own eyes—the two lookouts and the position director in the TLCP, Bedford, Wigner, the man at the conning data repeat console in front of them, the two bridge lookouts in their corner chairs, high-stemmed and low-backed bar stool affairs. So many weak human eyes backing up the all-seeing radars.

Lt. Wigner beside him and the starboard lookout on this rotation—his father had been right, the women had arrived.

Thirty percent of the crew were female; women can push buttons and maintain electronic circuitry just as well as men. All the constant small scale social turmoil and the vastly increased complexities of personnel management had paid off after all. Not for him personally in a direct sense—for the sake of discipline sexual liaisons with the captain, with the god on earth, just had to be taboo. But one hundred twenty five women on board, not enough to go round and some of them married ashore and not interested anyway—it helped keep everyone's attention fixed on board and away from the outside world. When you considered what had happened to the world and that in spite of the psychological shock you still had to keep your crew in perfect functional order, that was all to the good.

Even the suicides had stopped. There had been five since the hot war petered out and the catastrophic hiatus hit, the only five casualties on board the ship. He had held his breath, wondering if an epidemic of psychological breakdowns might occur. He had only started to relax again after they were ordered south and left the appalling brooding shadow at the margin of the dust veil. The only losses since then had been two of the Skyhooks, the remotely piloted vehicles they flew off the ship to provide an airborne early warning radar screen. Two of the Skyhooks had crashed in wild gusts in the Drake Passage while coming in to land, writing off themselves and their SCAN radars. In such conditions it was merely unfortunate, not the fault of the pilots trying to control them from positions down inside the Air Operations Centre. Two SCAN-Skyhooks gone but ten left. It was enough. It would have to be.

They would have lost the ship if they'd been ordered to attempt a passage through the Panama Canal—if the canal was even open after the saturation treatment the Zone was reported to have received. Then they would have caught a glimpse of what nuclear devastation and spreading total winter on land looked like, a sight of what had happened to their families back home. But that would have been suicide for the ship, trapped in the canal. Whatever was left of the Soviet high command couldn't possibly have let that chance go. The Vindicator was the only major unit left.

The sun had risen clear of the restless horizon, not even dipping back during the deepest swoops of the slowly pitching ship. Brilliant bright sunlight barred the streaking clouds, bounced and glittered across the heaving waltzing spray-crowned sea. The winter iron had vanished from the ocean for a moment, it was orange-streaked and green-grey shadowed mountainsides, sliding through each other under shimmering skins.

The starboard door opened at the bridge rear. A black petty officer came through, a PO 1st class from the navigation team carrying an automatic sextant in his hand. "Morning, sir," he said to Bedford. "Morning, sir," to Wigner.

Bedford nodded. "Morning, Rutledge."

Rutledge looked out at the endless sea, looked back to Bedford. "Commander Crimmin asked me to tell you, sir. We have the course plus tactical advisements plotted all the way, any time you'd care to look at it."

Bedford nodded. He would order the course change in a quarter hour, no longer. The breakfasting ship would be buzzing with the news of the signal that had come in overnight. They might as well also feel the long boat come round to a different angle to the violent sea.

Rutledge went to the forward windows between the starboard corner lookout and the next empty chair. He stood with feet splayed on the green deck. Green decks designated the so-called safe areas during a nuclear attack. The green decks were floating decks, too rigidly mounted to respond to sea movements or the weight of walking people, but capable of bouncing through a few centimetres to absorb the very worst jolt from the slamming shock wave. The rest depended on how softly you could roll. It wasn't much, but it kept your bones from shattering. At least, that was the theory.

Rutledge shot the sun. The automatic sextant he sighted through marked the time, the compass angle and the elevation angle of the sun above its own gyroscopic horizontal plane, and stored it to be fed into the navigation computers, precious updating data that would tell them where they were more accurately than anything other than a precise landmark triangulation. Now that the satellites were gone. Shooting the sun again. They'd shot the sun clear out of the sky up in the northern hemisphere. Here dirty cloud rags were running down the wind on it, beginning to crowd it in.

The phone buzzed on the bridge console and the Engine Control talk light flipped on. Wigner lifted one of the twin handsets and listened. "Okay." She rested the handset over her shoulder, holding it hooked there. "Reactor Control have got Number Two warmed right up, sir. Now they're ready to increase turbine power any time you want it.''

Bedford nodded. ''Tell them it won't be long. We'll be coming up to two thirds power.'' Then the great ship would smash its way through the winter sea.

Wigner passed the reply through.

Rutledge had finished his repeated shots of the sun and was taking the chance to survey the spray whipped sun skimmed half-circle of ponderously dancing water. On a virtually windowless ship with at present storm swept decks, the opportunity of a view from the bridge was too good to pass.

Bedford glanced across the bridge console instruments. Three of the inset monitor screens were blank, the fourth held a picture from the camera position up on the roof of the TLCP at the rear of the superstructure. It showed a hundred metres of empty flight deck, the tops of the stern weapon mountings over the edge of the aftslope, and a hugely heaving sea beyond. More of the instruments were alive. The course indicator, the varying compass heading, the INS position readout, windspeed and direction, barometric pressure, air temperature, water temperature, bottom depth, sea state indicator, air radiation indicator, engine and service system repeaters. The weapons monitors were all shut down, there was nothing on the sonars and hydrophones, nothing on the surface, nothing on the air warning radar flying six kilometres off the bow at 2,000 metres, nothing on the Skytop search mode that watched perpetually for incoming re-entry vehicles— for nukes. No electronic warfare receiver alerts. Nothing. He was cruising in a barely abated storm in the middle of nowhere, the nearest land South Georgia 1400 kilometres southwards and who wanted it for God's sake. He was cruising around in nowhere and going nowhere like some high technology Flying Dutchman on a nuclear powered wind. He was condemned to go on lingering when he should have been dead instead, the commander of such a fearful weapon in the last of all wars. Now he had outlived the rest, isolated on an almost unsinkable, unstoppable ship. The Vindicator belonged to the Nemesis Class, it survived for the sole purpose of inflicting retribution, vengeance.

A wave mountain came over the bow, throwing up a vast curtain of spray. The ship lurched, the electronic compass repeater swung, marked the fall-off to port and the slow clawing back on to course. Flying spray doused the bridge windows and blew away. The great ship got its head up and ploughed on.

Petty Officer Rutledge let go of the grab rail under the windows and turned and left the bridge. Lt. Wigner looked round at Bedford, unsure of herself.

"Captain Bedford, sir?"

A very formal way of starting, Captain Bedford sir. He waited. A worry question was coming.

"When I came on watch I got the news about the new signal." She looked out at the tempestuous sea. Back at Bedford. "Why are they sending us up into the North Atlantic, sir?"

"I don't know." He shrugged. "They haven't bothered to tell us. And I haven't had the time to make a guess myself." In the North Atlantic, invisible under the dust veil, the Vindicator could take up a position where its weapons ranged on all of Eastern Europe and half of the Soviet Union. Or maybe the ship, a floating fortress with an air landing deck aft, could take on board anyone at all and transport them anywhere. Back into the safe south, away from the inconceivable chaos they'd made?

He stepped down from the raised seat, stood and took a last look at the storm sea before going down to Navigation three decks below inside the C3 box. The sun was being smothered in a gathering roof of clouds, this tail-chasing southern ocean fury would be with them for another day yet. He turned to Wigner. "We'll be changing course in around ten or fifteen minutes. We'll be coming up to twenty three knots around fifteen minutes after that."

"Right, sir. Be quite a ride in this sea."

He nodded.

The sun choked behind filthy fleeing clouds. The ship heaved.

June 3, STRACC (Strategic Command Centre), Cheyenne Mountain Complex

THE ROUGH HEWN cavern was dark and towering, was lightless overhead. Hints of crude slabs of rock arched up above the sparse down-glaring lights. At the nearer end, two building units away, a rock wall loomed blackly half-visible. The little line of suspended lights disappeared there into the roadway access tunnel. Above it all was the massive rock strata of a mountain range. Oppressive, not surprisingly. And it was cold in the cavern, cold air circulated through the tunnels although they were deep inside the warm Earth. The air was fed in from the surface and was fresh and clean even without protective filtering. It was weeks since the strikes now, the ground-delivered fallout was washed away or else frozen solid under ice and snow, while the stratospheric dust layer with its load of radionuclides was still up there, showing no signs at all of coming back down. Not yet. So they could feed in air direct from the surface, but the surface air was *very* cold. Cheyenne Mountain Complex nowadays had bunkered aviation fuel, diesel, gasoline, had a whole series of power reactors—it could survive for a long time still, but there was no need to squander generating capacity on heating.

Drexel left the access steps at the front of the building. It was a massive six-storey blank faced free standing box, just like all the others in the cavern. It stood on great shock absorbing springs, just like all the other building units in all the other caverns in the vast communications and control complex buried under Cheyenne and its neighbouring peaks. There used to be just NORAD here, North American Air Defence, along with its combat operations centre, the command post that would have directed the retaliatory total nuclear war. Then the inevitable move towards increasing dependence on satellites for intelligence and communication, the concomitant need to counter Soviet satellite capabilities, had led to the Space Defence Centre being added to the complex. Then came the coherent war philosophy, maintaining the ability to conduct a directed war even *after* a major strike or strike series had come in. That way you deterred your enemy by promising him you could hurt him hard no matter how heavily he hit you. So in had come the huge added extension of STRACC and all its survival infrastructure functions, all its deployable ranks of antenna dishes in silos safe from air bursts and high level EMP attacks. NASCOM, STRACC, CASAL, along with the deeply tunnelled landlines in a continent-wide network that had kept them in all-conditions contact with each other, with military bases and the local ROCC centres of the air defence Joint Surveillance System, with the DEW Line, the Pine Tree Line, the seaboard defence radars. It cost no more than money, after all, vast sums of money. But that didn't matter. There was always another social aid programme to cut.

Drexel stuck his hands in the pocket of his windjacket, hunched it about him. There was no sign of anyone on the sparsely lighted roadway running along the cavern side into the retreating darkness. This huge city of multi-storey boxes mounted on vast shock damping springs in endless dark caverns too often seemed deserted, as though only ghosts of its thousands of inhabitants lingered. Depressing. Perhaps true, in a sense.

He headed round the corner of the building and down its side, soft shoes on smooth rock. He walked beside the shoulder high casings of the mounting springs into deepening gloom. This was the second day of talks. Already one and a half days preceded it—plenum meetings, discussion groups, endless one-to-one consultations during meal breaks, during pauses between presentations, or during the late evening when the programme was finally interrupted for rest and sleep. It was intensive, it was exhausting, but this was going to be his first secretive talk. He was here as part of a farmed-out discussion group concerned with strategic options maintenance, the one who helped the group assign readiness priorities by supplying them with clever guesses as to what the Russians could and couldn't do. Swaines, a two-star Air Force general had followed him to the washroom, had picked the next washbowl to wash his hands. Lightly perfumed soap—hadn't it been nice of the Pentagon planners to provide perfumed soap to brighten the lives of the last inhabitants of the last hole in the world. Swaines had waited until they were momentarily alone, had switched on the hand dryer and spoken quiet-voiced into its breathless hum. And now he was wondering if Swaines was out here waiting for him. And what he wanted.

The general was there, half invisible in the deep shadow between the rear corner of the box and the rough rock wall. Power and telemetry cables and a bulky air duct ran along the coarse rock face; the ribbed aluminium of the duct gleamed faintly in the last touch of the lights strung along the other side of the cavern across the building fronts. It was cold here, very cold. Swaines had his coat on over his uniform. He opened it, fetched out a cigarette packet and went through the brief ritual of lighting and drawing on a nicotine fix. Sharp tobacco smoke drifted on the air. The Air Force general was one of the few people who still smoked nowadays—who still could *nowadays*, now that the last stocks were running low.

Swaines wafted the smoke away. "Sorry, David. Filthy habit. I'll kick it soon. No more cigarettes inside a month. None left."

Drexel zipped up his windjacket. "What do you want?" And so many high paid years in the States, and he still didn't like strangers allowing themselves instant possession of his first name. You got it less often from the military—Swaines must some time have done a press relations course.

"What do you make of it so far, David?" Swaines buttoned his coat closed, cigarette in hand. "Interesting to see which way the political wind is blowing, huh?" Cigarette smoke drifted off along the cavern wall. "Instructive to see which faces are missing."

A lot were missing, a hell of a lot of the moderates he'd been expecting. Those who were there seemed to have turned into ex-moderates.

"Interesting updates on the climate situation. Looks like it will be more long lasting than was hoped." A pull on the cigarette. "God help whoever's left out there."

"Do you have anyone left out there?"

Swaines shrugged. "I was on the J-3 Division. The Joint Chiefs of Staff's operational executive at the Pentagon, yeah? I was transferred out here just before it all happened. My wife and kids were still in Washington. Well, my eldest, my daughter, she was already back at Caltech for the semester.

No." A slight shake of the head. "I don't have anyone out there. Interesting summary of our strategic capabilities, huh? Interesting to see how little has survived and how little of *that* we'll be able to use once the climate collapse reverses and systems come operational again. Very interesting estimates of Soviet survivals. That's your speciality, David. What we can make out from the last look we managed with new-launched surveillance satellites, estimates from our own strike patterns and what success we think they had, what we can get out of intercepting the signals they're still sending—insofar as we still have a signals intelligence capability. What they'll be able to use on us as soon as the sun comes out again. About the only weather-immune system—apart from land silos that don't happen to be frozen up—is that Nemesis ship down in the South Atlantic. It's the biggest operational piece left on the board."

He was cold, he scuffed his shoes on the rock floor. "So. What is it you want?"

"Political groups are building rapidly among us hardline realists. Me, I'm a realist—so I can't avoid being hardline. The no-more-war people are on the way out. They're almost eliminated here, are rounded up and neutralized at CASAL. The groups are shaping up now for the big fight. Do we resume the war right now while the Soviets are least able to hit back at us? Do we finish the job once and for all? Or just make a maximum effort to be ready to wipe them clean off the face of the Earth if *they* make the mistake of trying to hit us as soon as conditions improve and what systems they still have come operational again? The positions are being drawn up, extremist war-prosecutionists against hardline war-readiness people. That's the issue. The diversion of effort and resources towards trying to help what's left of the civilian population is no longer on the table as an option. Its principal supporters have already gone to the wall."

"Which grouping do you belong to?"

"The hardliners, David. The war-readiness people. Teller's Armageddon group are overdoing it. We can still try deterring the Soviets from a resumption of nuclear hostilities. Take them clean out if they won't back down. Also there's plain common sense. Under present conditions we'd be firing half blind. We might use up what little we have but fail to eliminate the Soviet capability. Then they'd wait for clear skies and take *us* out. There'll be no more replacement of armaments until there's a replacement of arms manufacturing. Years. Generations.'' He was drawing too fiercely on his cigarette. It was finished.

"Are you sounding me out for your side?"

"Well." Swaines dropped his cigarette and stepped on it carefully in the dark. "War-readiness people are still just about in a majority at CASAL, huh? If you haven't decided which side to join you should consider the consequences, David. Pick the wrong side and you're dead. It's that serious a power game now. But if the Apocalypse people win through— well then we're all dead anyway. I consider it crazy to assume the Soviets can't do exactly what we can do if they have to. If we start hitting them, they'll hit back. Maybe they're making the same decisions right now as we are. You've heard how bad the climate situation is, with the crap crossing the equator in places. You're a strategic systems analyst, David. You know what capabilities are being talked about. If we go on with nuclear exchanges when maybe we don't have to—especially right *now*—then we'll put the lid on the climate collapse. Your Nuclear Winter turns into your Nuclear Ice Age. The war-prosecutionists are gambling on the Soviets not being able to get their act together in time to shoot back. If they *do*? It'll probably be the end of the world."

As if that frozen midsummer night out there didn't already look like it.

"Some of us are trying to organize something, David. Something to give us a firm control of some of the cards. You should keep an eye on Eileen Jenninger. Know her? Keep an eye on what she does, what she says."

Then shifting lights in their shadow recess. An electric jeep with two Air Force soldiers in it went cruising by along the half-lit tunnel roadway, headlights blazing. It was eclipsed by the next building.

Swaines hunched up against the cold. "Had enough of the discussion group. I'm heading back for the accommodation areas to get some lunch. Have fun, David." He started out for the lighted roadway, then paused, turned a moment. "Be receptive when Jenninger takes time to talk to you. Maybe after this afternoon's plenum. Who knows?"

Jenninger didn't speak to him after the plenum session. She was there, but she made no attempt at conspiratorial asides.

He left for the big canteen, ate alone, troubled, trying to think round the shadowed corners of what might turn out to be a murderous political maze. And then two people sat down at his table, and they had no food trays.

"David Drexel?" The man was a civilian in a suit. "Enjoy your little chat with Swaines this morning?"

"Teller would like a word with you tonight," the woman said. She wore a Navy uniform, was a lieutenant commander. "He'd like you to visit him at around eleven. Know where he is? Block A-eight, apartment forty two. Don't be late."

They stood up again and left.

Drexel couldn't start eating again. He looked round the crowded canteen. Who else was watching him? If they'd kill each other in their in-fighting, they'd certainly do it to a foreign national who got in the way. But you're alive, David Drexel, and the name of your game is to stay that way as long as you can. So wait and see. Wait and see.

Teller's apartment was at the end of a short box corridor leading off the stair well. A man with a gun guarded the door, knocked for him. Teller opened the door.

He was a shortish, heavy man around sixty, sagging cheeks softening a jawline set hard. His brown hair had thinned instead of going grey. His eyes seemed almost blank. He didn't look at all like a power broker. But Teller had been a senior presidential adviser, was the most important of all the advisement-and-crisis team leaders. His A-and-C team was one of three dispersed to STRACC when the nuclear balloon started to go up; now Teller was one of the most powerful—and therefore dangerous—members of the political and military caucus running the self-appointed crisis defence government.

Teller let him inside, just as far as the tiny box of the entrance lobby, and closed the door. The little living room behind him was dim and shadowed. Drexel glimpsed papers spread in a light pool on a desk, a desktop computer with its screen glowing. There was a sticky miasma of concentrated work. Teller had colourless bags under his eyes. He didn't look as if he ever slept or ever needed to.

"Don't worry about the man outside," Teller said. "Just my precaution."

Drexel shrugged. He knew Teller by sight and reputation, of course—even from advisory sessions at the White House back before it all happened. "Why did you send for me?"

"Your services are being courted. You're one of the few more highly competent strategic assessment consultants left. Funny, when you think of the selection process that governed who gets to be inside these places, but true. The big guys in your line went out with the President at NASCOM. You're useful. You're not alone in that, but you're also uniquely vulnerable. You're an alien, a British citizen. You don't have even nominal security here." Teller shook his head, a kind of parody of disapproval. "It is only nominal, the Constitution has been suspended on practical grounds. But you don't even have that amount of protection. The British Emergency Government couldn't lift a diplomatic finger to help you, even if it cared. You're threatenable, Drexel. Pressurable."

"Are you threatening me?" And there was someone else in the room behind Teller, sitting in the shadows in a chair turned half away from them.

"I don't threaten people, Drexel. I don't promise them. I tell them. I tell them facts. That's all. Such as be careful about who you let recruit you."

"No one's recruiting me." He couldn't see who it was, whether a man or a woman. He couldn't even see a uniform. Ah yes, a general officer's tabs on the shirt collar, gleaming.

"The other side is courting you. We're courting you. You're lucky enough to decide for yourself which side you join. Most people get told."

"Are you telling me?"

"It's a big responsibility. You have the choice. Don't wait too long deciding which way to jump. Any middle ground you think you're standing on is about to disappear."

"And what do you want me to do?"

"I'm just letting you know we're interested in acquiring you for the same reason that the other lobby are. Maybe you don't know yet what they're thinking of using you for. Don't worry, they'll be in touch with you again any time now. So will we."

Teller opened the door again and that was that. He was back in the little corridor again with the man with the gun.

June 4

THERE WAS NO need yet for a change of course. The new signal had come in half an hour ago, originating from STRACC, forwarded over CASAL—issued by the Nemesis Direction in NAVCOM and passed on by the backup Nemesis Direction in NAVALCOM. It had given them a more precise destination in the North Atlantic, a stationing area. The Iceland-UK Gap.

They were inside the Navigation Centre, Bedford, Boyce and Crimmin—Captain, First Officer and Chief Navigating Officer. The Navigation Centre was inside the C3-Complex isolation box on 02 level, the Navigation Centre forward starboard, the Sonar Control Centre forward port, and the Air Operations Centre aft and twice the size. The C3-Complex decks were each nine metres wide and fifteen fore and aft, eight of them stacked one above the other in the isolation box, right from the dedicated support systems for air and power down on 3rd and 4th platforms up to the CIC and the Missile Control Centre on 03 level. An isolation box was a wonderful thing: the whole structure was suspended on mighty shock dampers and return springs giving three degrees of freedom—not a lot of freedom, but enough to cushion the full fury of a close thermonuclear shock wave. It still threw you around in there, all electronic equipment still had to be additionally isolated and soft-mounted, but the key areas of the ship would survive. At least in theory. The key areas were the reactor boxes, the turbine space, the ship's service equipment space, and the ship's C3—command, communications and control. The C3 box was the narrowest and by far the tallest. It started only two decks up from the baseline, the bottom of the hull, and climbed right into the seventeen metre wide forward superstructure aft of the bridge front and forward of the much wider structure enclosing the heads of the twin main elevators servicing the flight deck. A feather-bedded isolation box suspended inside the Vindicator's massive double-walled carapace—sometimes you could almost believe you might live through a nuclear attack.

They stood at the chart table with transparent sheets spread over its internally illuminated surface, with VDU screens glowing in a row above its rear edge. Around them, running routine work at the computer consoles, were Lt. Visser, PO1 Rutledge and a couple of crew.

"No reason to change yet." Ruth Crimmin traced her finger along the planned course again. A lieutenant commander, she was the most senior female officer on board. Forty, chubby faced, blonde hair cut very short and blow-dried slightly fluffy. "We can continue following this land avoidance course until we're past the Azores. Then we should adopt a more eastward route to bring us up past Ireland into the stationing area. Ah—there's no reason to suppose that Ireland's turned hostile?"

Bedford shook his head. Twelve days earlier they had received an advisement list on who was likely to shoot at them. Ireland wasn't on it.

"Doesn't matter anyway." John Ritchie Boyce, First Officer, full commander. Son of a banker in Boston, he was thirty eight, he was tall and black and lean and textbook handsome, his khaki uniform fitted him like a tailored casual outfit, he wore steel frame glasses with large lenses and a double bridge. As a kid in the late sixties and the seventies they had always told him that black is beautiful, and Boyce had always known that it was true. He waved at the outline of Ireland on the back-lit chart. "They don't have anything that could hurt this ship."

Bedford shook his head again. "But we'll come up into the middle of the IUK Gap. I don't want to come too close to the Irish coast. Don't want to be boxed in too close to land." The Greenland-Iceland-UK Gap had been the Nato naval front line, the sea area that the Soviet Northern Fleet, coming out of its bases right round the north of Norway on the Kola Peninsula, had wanted to reach in order to interdict the sea and air reinforcement routes from the States to Europe. The GIUK Gap and the ocean northeast of it must be a graveyard now. "The further up here we go, the further we get into range of any Soviet naval remnants. And if they have anything still operational at all, then it's going to be submarines."

And submarines were bad. They might have been superseded in their strategic missile role, but they were lethal to ships.

"Speed," Crimmin said. "Can we stay at twenty three knots? That will bring us up on station on around the fourteenth."

"That should be fast enough for the folks back home. We're making enough noise as it is." Up to half speed they could use just the inboard screws, shielded in their twin tunnels under the bottom of the stern. Above half speed they needed the outboards as well, and the outboards were not housed in ducts and so pumped an enormous amount of noise into the water. Submarines hunt by sound.

"About wraps it up for the moment," Boyce said. "Maintain course and speed."

Bedford nodded. "Okay, that'll do for the moment. Ruth, I'll be calling a commanders conference in around an hour." All eleven commanders and lieutenant commanders on board. "I'd be grateful if you could see to it your people sit on this until after the conference and until I've had a chance to bulletin it for the crew. I've already asked Darius." Lt. Cmdr. Chet Darius was the Chief Communications Officer.

"Sure," Crimmin said. "No problem. I'll keep my girls and boys in line. But." She eyed the illuminated chart again. "Just what happens when we get up to the Gap?"

A captain is by the nature of things caught in a continuous public pose. All he can do when he puts on his honest face is hope that people believe him. "No idea. The only advisement on that is that the British Emergency Government will cooperate by allowing us safe inshore loiter areas if we want them. But they can't provide active air or sea support. They have no material."

Bedford and Boyce left the Navigation Centre.

They came out into a short and narrow fore-and-aft corridor, a door opposite into the Sonar Control Centre, a door aft into the big Air Operations Centre, and the tunnel door forward out of the isolation box. All the doorways were rimmed with green, the signal that this was a safe area, much safer even than the green deck areas scattered through the ship. The tunnel door was painted green round its inner end; inside it was as grey as anything else in this metal world. It was like the walk-through between railcars, except it was two metres long—it had concertina walls and overlapping floor plates that clacked as they strode across them. Bedford slid the end door open and they came out into the middle of a cross corridor. The door closed itself.

The corridor ran right across the forward end of the superstructure. Armoured steel doors at each end gave access to the 02 level external deck. In the forward side of the corridor was a pair of doors, one leading into Boyce's quarters, the other into those of Clemence, the Air Operations Controller. Outboard of Boyce's day cabin, near the corridor end, was the locked door to the small arms store. Bedford turned that way, aiming at the steep companionway leading up.

"Rick?" Boyce stopped in the corridor. "They really haven't told you what they want us to do?"

Bedford paused with his foot on the first tread, his weight thrown on the handrail. "John, if they'd told me but told me not to tell you, that much I'd tell you. It's a new ship. We've been together six months, most of the time on commissioning trials. You haven't had time to see if I do what I say. But believe me, I like my officers informed."

Boyce smiled, nodded. "I didn't even know there was such a thing as a British Emergency Government. Crazy."

Bedford started up the companionway. "Nothing. Nothing on the strategic situation up there. Soviet and Warsaw Pact potential capabilities, units presumed in the area. Goddam nothing at all." He came up in the cross corridor on the 03 level. In the forward wall at each end were narrow access doors into the retraction spaces for communications equipment mounted in the forward superstructure corners. Right in the centre was the door to his own quarters. Opposite was the centre door back into the top level of the C3 isolation box. "They've told me goddam nothing at all except there are no forces to cooperate with. Mainland Europe is out. Wiped out and frozen solid. All the British have is maybe a handful of troops hanging together ashore somewhere. Just enough to need a British Emergency Government to organize them out of snowdrifts."

"What do you think we're going to do?" They stopped in the corridor centre between the door to Bedford's quarters and the door through to the CIC and the Missile Control Centre beyond. The CIC—the Combat Information Centre—was the focus of the ship. "What do you think? Ferry this British Emergency Government somewhere safer?"

Bedford shook his head. "They wouldn't rate the Vindicator. Europe and the UK have been nuked. They're no use to our strategic defence. Only our people would get a ride on this ship. But one, they could fly themselves out. Two, they're probably safest right where they are. Three, they're not in the IUK Gap anyway."

"So." Boyce had a habit of readjusting his glasses at carefully chosen moments, just pushing up briefly with his middle finger at the upper bridge bar of the metal frame. Craze, their on-board psychologist, had told him it was probably a defensive gesture, a fleeting chance to put his hand over his face. His first officer interested him, of course. "So it's a case of pointing our Fire Lances at the Soviets and telling them not to start things up again."

"I guess so." Bedford turned and started to open the door to his quarters. "John, I want time to start thinking around this one. If we fly an air or ASW screen before we need it we'll just be throwing aviation fuel away. Can you organize everyone for the commanders conference?"

"Sure." Boyce started opening the door through to the CIC. "In one hour?"

"That's just fine."

Bedford shut himself inside his quarters. The day cabin was spacious, six metres wide and five deep. Through on the forward side was his sleeping cabin and the cubbyhole bathroom, and then the armoured front wall of the superstructure and its massive support girders. It was a quiet location on the ship, just the corridor and companionways outside, the retraction spaces port and starboard for secondary communications and electronic warfare antennas. Above the day cabin was the Ship's Conning Position with more retraction space on three sides, and then the bridge above that. You got occasional machinery noises but that was all. It was a good place to think. And only two steps away from the CIC across the corridor.

He went across his day cabin, between the work desk on one side and the little table and couches on the other. It was a place you could entertain—it even had a floor of carpet tiles and a suspended ceiling to hide all the ducting. The only thing missing was a window. He stopped at the door to his narrow sleeping cabin and through to the bathroom. He looked back across the day cabin.

In a frame on the wall beside the entrance door, always smiling out at him. Gayleen at thirty nine and Linda at twelve, thin and shooting up and not yet embarrassed about it. Thirty nine and twelve for ever now. They had died four years ago, and he had needed them every day since then. At least they had died before the war. He had absolutely no family left for the war to wipe out. Then why did it shock him, horrify him so?

Gayleen and Linda smiling out at him wherever he was in his daytime private world. He needed them now.

June 5, CASAL
(Command Alternate Sea-Air-Land)

HE FLEW BACK to CASAL through a black void world. The stratospheric small-particle suspension cloud was its official name. As soon as you put an official name on it you had it all wrapped up, neat and tidy and under conceptual control. It wasn't really real any more. An idea, not a thing.

Oh it was real. It filled the stratosphere and shut out the light and heat of the sun. All the aerosoled filth thrown up by the nuclear bursts and the huge plumes of burning that followed, a fine thin fog of micron-sized debris kicked right up above the troposphere, the turbulent weather world, into the segregated and far more stable circulation of the stratosphere. Its lowest edge was usually around 16,000 to 20,000 metres up, and it went on upward. The models that had once merely predicted it had worked on the basis of a forty percent use of weapons stockpiles, and had concluded that the sun would be variably wholly or partially obscured, with temperatures fluctuating from zero to well below until the whole mess cleared after a couple of months. A good seasonal summer would get rid of it. But when you start a nuclear war it's very hard to stop. Each side goes on escalating the size of its strikes to warn the other, until the dust closes over and the temperature suddenly begins to drop. They had hit something well over eighty percent use—much more if you counted warheads that went off inefficiently when their silos were hit. Now it was permanent night and permanent inconceivable cold. The newest prognosis was one step worse again. This summer wasn't going to get rid of it. Maybe not even the summer that would follow.

Summer up above the stratosphere. There was no summer down here.

Jenninger had given him an envelope with a slim something inside—he guessed a microdisc full of data or messages or who knew what. He should simply hand it over to whoever asked for it. The faction Jenninger belonged to had already appointed him as courier, it seemed. But apart from the package Jenninger hadn't said a word to him about his attitude, about his sympathies for the war-readiness or the war-prosecution group, the hardliners or the extremists. Like Teller, she didn't seem to want to know what he thought, but was only interested in what he did. At the end of the world integrity was worthless—only actions counted towards surviving. Or did Teller really believe it was the right thing to do for what was left of humanity, for the dead but not yet thinking corpse of America, to try and wipe out Soviet Communism once and for absolute all, to free any possible future of its evil historical threat? Did Jenninger or Swaines really believe it was better to concentrate all energies on preparing to face down or defeat a resumed Soviet threat once—and good God *if*—the dust veil cleared before the last of all lights went out in the last of all bunkers? Was that really a better way to go than trying to help any civilians still left alive out there survive?

The President hadn't survived. When the intercontinental exchanges started and the leaders fled the White House and the Defence Department to go to ground, Looking Glass, the flying command post, had done its job and brought the President and his team safely down at their new programmed destination of NASCOM. But the Russians had taken out the National Strategic Command. They sent in a single high level burst to produce a sustained EMP, an electromagnetic pulse that crippled and blanked all the ballistic missile defence radars at the fortress. For a while NASCOM would only be able to talk over land line. And they could be told just twenty minutes after the first burst that the Pine Tree Line radars could see eight warheads coming their way. They could report themselves that they had visual contacts of eight simultaneous re-entry tracks. And they still had the laser BMD system operational because it didn't depend on radars. But at least two, probably three of the nukes made virtually simultaneous ground bursts. There was no more land line contact ever again. Seismology sensors counted ground bursts going in at the fortress site every two hours for two more days. That would have collapsed every cavern and tunnel, eventually, while the ground above would be too hot to attempt an escape.

The Vice-president got it too. His aircraft was coming in to land at Cheyenne when an air burst series started taking out all the ground deployed antennas. The vice-presidential aircraft fell out of the air. And the Defence Secretary went out with the Pentagon. You could almost think the Russians were taking the war personally, but it was just strategic necessity that selected the targeting priorities. They had to reserve some of their warheads to take out the American missiles that were aimed back at them, so they took the line of command centres according to their backup sequence. CASAL merely got an EMP.

Drexel, in retrospect, was never in direct danger. The A-and-C teams had been lifted out of Washington and dispersed during the early alert phases. He'd stayed safe and secure inside CASAL, untouched by the hot war and by the freeze that followed it.

He was lucky to be alive. Almost no one else was. Just unknown numbers in groups of hundreds and tens and twos and fading away. All the hundreds of millions in the USA, Canada, Europe east and west, the USSR, Japan—the war hadn't killed all that many directly, just a few tens of millions at the most. But war or no war, the climate collapse had eradicated everything. Refineries and power facilities stopped, road transport ceased, there was no heat, no fuel, no food, no liquid water, no nothing. All the millions of Mexico and Central America, of Scandinavia, the Middle East, North and Central Africa, the hundreds of millions of India, Indochina, Malaysia, Indonesia, the one billion Chinese—almost every one of them dead and the rest dying. Someone or other in an earlier context of an earlier war had said the lights were going out all over Europe. Well this time the lights had gone out all over the world. There were only candles left, isolated and burning down.

It wasn't going to end, not in the near term or mid term. That was the conclusion of the three days at STRACC. They were short on facts and theories, there was no community of scientists to help with the scatter of data, no universities, no research institutes. But the assessments got worse and worse. The climate collapse was behaving consistently like the worst case prognoses of the old model scenarios, multiplied up to take account of the much higher use of warhead stocks and the changed targeting policies brought about by the coherent war approach. The climate collapse would last longer than predicted, all its effects would be more severe. The dust veil was crossing the equator in streamers and would envelop the southern hemisphere with a more tenuous but equally opaque shroud. And when it finally came down on the heads of the pitifully few stone age barbarians scratching some sort of existence on the coastlines of islands out in the warmer sea—when it finally came down it would bring with it the radioisotopes that were presently floating around in the stratosphere. Hard radiation, and a flood of ultraviolet from the unmasked sun because the ozone layer would have gone— that would be the end of everything.

He had no idea where they were—more than halfway through the flight and soon due to start the approach to CASAL. He looked out of the window beside his seat. Black nothing. Perhaps somewhere down there in some building, or a cave, or just a hole in the rocks, some handful of people were huddling over a propane heater and a few sacks of canned food, still alive for a few days more. Or dying from hunger or from cold. Food was no good in those conditions without heat, heat no use under such stress without food. At least it was too cold for virulent disease to spread beyond any group where it was already established. Cholera, typhoid, even dysentery or influenza would be an instant death sentence without food or warmth, with no medical care whatsoever. Perhaps some fight to the death was going on down there between two desperate packs over a crate of canned oranges or dehydrated instant cheesecake. When they ever had time to wonder any more they must want to know where the Government and its National Guard and its regular armed forces were. Where was the help they needed from the Government they'd elected which had got them into this death-trauma in the course of protecting them from a world full of enemies and alternative thinkers?

He was perfectly well aware of the psychological adjustment he'd made. A complete suppression of all temptations to *feel* what it meant, what had happened, what had been done, allowing only a purely intellectual detached consideration of the state of affairs. No closing his eyes at night and thinking of England. Others hadn't succeeded. There had been a non-stop epidemic of suicides in all the survival centres—people blowing their brains out in their rooms, or simply taking a long walk away into the ice-box cold. That way lay madness. You were still alive, you were surviving, and you had to concentrate your mind on keeping it that way.

When the plane landed at CASAL it taxied straight into one of the earth and ice heaped protected hangars. They disembarked in artificial light behind closed steel doors, and he walked down through the ID entry checks. There was even someone there to meet him, Lt. Col. Oppenheim, Army. She seemed to have driven all the way out from Signals Intelligence and up to the north air facility just to be friendly, just to give him a lift back down into the fortress proper.

He sat beside her in the electric jeep. They had left the series of blast doors behind and were descending steadily. The lighted roadway followed a gentle left-hand curve. A never-ending curve, down and round in an empty concrete tube, down and round with never a horizon line to keep your orientation, down and round mesmerizingly until the world could tip . . .

"Got something for me from Jenninger, maybe?" She was glancing sideways at him. "Package?"

He fished in his windjacket pocket and produced the envelope with the microdisc inside. She stuck it straight into a pocket inside her uniform blouse and then put both hands back on the wheel. They whirled slowly deeper around the long curve. So then that was it, an out of the way route where nobody at all would see. "I didn't know you were politically active."

Oppenheim shrugged. "It's be politically active or wind up dead. We've most of us been stalling here on the new policy concerning the softliners, the bleeding hearts. But now that has to go. Selecting and motivating the execution squads is going to be one tricky problem." They were coming to a side branch right. She slowed and pulled over ready to take it. "Now it's going to be a straight fight. Pick your side and hope."

They turned into the new tunnel. It was hardly lit. Oppenheim switched on the lights. They went down more steeply, chasing their own fleeing world of brightness. Like diving into the last dark.

He looked at her in the backwash light. "Which side are you on?"

"Oh—I've always believed there's a rationale to deterrence and credible nuclear defence. Wouldn't be in the Army otherwise. It's irrational to come this far and then turn back on maintaining a defence capability, just so the Soviets can knock us clean out when the sun shines again. So that takes care of the bleeding hearts. It's also not rational to resume fighting with all you've got when it's not even clear the Soviets want to. That isn't what I ever understood as deterrence. So that's which side I'm on.''

''And first comes the witch-hunt, then the straight fight?''

Light ahead at the end of the tunnel.

''I'll tell you about witch-hunts. They go their own way. First you wipe out the witches, then the suspected witches. That's already happened. Then you start on the possible witches and the potential witches. That we're doing now. The associates of the alleged witches. *Anyone* who's had *anything* to do with witches.'' They came to the end of the cross tunnel. She switched off the lights and then turned out onto a rough hewn roadway. A flatbed came around the bend ahead and passed them. ''You see the problem? All the witches have gone and you're into hunting associates of witches, and only the witchfinders are left. And what do witchfinders do? They hunt. And who can they find who's been associated with witches, maybe contaminated? Witchfinders. So—they hunt each other. Believe me. You can't protect yourself just by not being a witch. Not even by being a witchfinder. All you can do is pick your side and hope it turns out stronger. And you'd better hope that when the witchfinders have wiped half of themselves out—that it stops there.''

June 6

LT. GLORIA CRAZE, Personnel Advisement Officer, the ship's sociologist and psychologist-observer, sometimes almost a substitute for a chaplain. She was twenty seven and black and not all that sure she was beautiful. Gloria Craze was an escapee from Harlem, in a sense still a refugee on the run.

It was southern tropical winter, a blazing brilliant high-sun day. The wind was on the starboard quarter, and hot. It reduced the steady buffeting created by the Vindicator's constant 23 knot slicing glide through the water. She stood at the aft end of the flight deck, near the stern of the monstrous machine—56,000 tonnes, 280 metres from stem to stern, a 35 metre beam and 10 metre draught, as big as any battleship had ever been. Only some of the carriers had been bigger, the carriers that had proved so hopelessly vulnerable to direct nuclear attack. A sea monster of 56,000 tonnes and almost three hundred metres long, and it cut through the water like some self-propelled knife, a miracle of engineering technology. The ship's intrinsic power made it seem today an equal of its element, of the calm blue sea; its twin nuclear propulsive hearts helped it blend into the primal force of the wind. The wind! She wore her short sleeve uniform shirt without a teeshirt under it in this on-deck heat—it whipped and fluttered around her body, so lovely, so caressed by the living world.

She had walked the length of the ship, just because she could. Because they were heading north into the military danger zone in a war that wasn't over yet, into the appalling dark and cold whose edge they only ever skirted during the hiatus hopeless days in the Eastern Pacific. She had come up onto main deck forward and walked right to the very bow, past the mooring eyes and deck ports for the cable winches, up the smooth rake of the steel plating and out to the very point of the stem. Perched right out there over the undercutting water, she was protected only by two slender strands of cable strung wire-taught from steel stanchions. It was dizzying, delirious. The deep blue water swept down under the bow and turned suddenly translucent penetrable green in the ship's shadow—before being whipped aside in a huge silverglass rising stream that broke in tumbling foam way back aft of her cantilevered vantage point. A point hovering over the speeding sea. Such a wonderful noise, the constant rushing cleaving of the water, part of the romance of it all, the reason she'd picked the Navy once she made up her mind to try the services in search of a career. Yes, soldiers and sailors have souls, too. She had hoped to see porpoises but there were none. Either the Vindicator was cruising too fast, or else they were shunning this megatonne loaded monster of death, the guilty joint perpetrator of the sudden dark over half the Earth. Guilty without even firing a single shot.

She had looked back from the bow along the sweeping length of the main deck towards the midships superstructure and its crowning tower. A raised centreline housing bisected the foredeck for almost two thirds of its length. Aimed straight at her from its domed turret was the single barrel of the forward 155mm Automatic Gun. Beyond it was the vertical box launcher of the Seastrike area defence missile, and then beyond that further aft the vertical launcher of the Rayflex. The Rayflex-2 was their Naval Ballistic Missile Defence system, the most important of all the weapons designed to keep them alive. Mounted down on the main deck, port and starboard abreast the Rayflex box, were the twin Fire Lance launchers. Each mounting had four firing tubes, the tubes were pointed directly forward at her, their launch caps closed. The mountings were loaded from two delivery feed heads that emerged from the wall that made a break right across the ship. The steep foreslope ended the foredeck and climbed up to the 02 level. There on each extreme forward outboard corner, both deployed, were the Skyfire rapid fire 20mm cannon.

In the centre, back from the break to the 02 level, was the forward superstructure front rising featureless to the line of the bridge windows under its brow. Further aft the superstructure broadened out into the much wider box of the elevator space. Over it all rose the blank, tapered, armoured tower with its single halfway pair of port and starboard wings. The tower top, the little island of unrailed deck that counted as 13 level, was all of forty metres up above the surrounding sea. On the superstructure top behind the bridge and out over the elevator box, on the wings and on the very top of the streamlined central tower, were the domes of all the surveillance and tracking and guidance radars. The white domes of the big main radars on the superstructure roof stood up from a foreshortened forest of communications and electronic warfare antennas and camera platforms run out through armoured hatches from the safety of the retraction spaces. The Vindicator could pull in all its sensing eyes and ears, slam its armoured hatches closed, and survive the searing blast of a thermonuclear detonation.

She had walked back along the blank plates of a smooth deck armoured as massively as the last leviathans of the last total war. The Vindicator, the Nemesis Class, was the battleship reborn. The hard ship concept had taken over from the missile carrying submarine—another decade of construction and Nemesis ships would have entirely replaced the Trident boats. Such a big submarine was still hard to find, despite the noise it made, despite the coolant heat it sent slowly geysering up to the surface. But once it was found it was helpless. It was too big and clumsy and loud to escape its trackers. It couldn't defend itself against a killer submarine's torpedoes or against a re-entering nuclear warhead called in to splash down and sink right on top of its position before exploding. A surface ship, in contrast, could carry armour, could see exactly what was happening all around it, could serve as a platform for a menagerie of defensive weapons. It was visible for all to see, but it willingly suffered high observability as the price for gaining maximum self-defendability. It could survive.

She had walked the ship, right along the 02 level deck past the superstructure and out to the aft end of the flight deck. Behind her was the steep afterslope drop down to the stern apron at main deck level. Port and starboard down there were the tubes for the Mk 72 ASW torpedoes, the little short range weapons that should fend off any submarine-launched torpedo that came in too close. On the centreline housing, right above the tail, was the turret of the aft 155mm gun. Almost immediately below her at the foot of the afterslope was the second Seastrike launcher, a slightly pyramidal thing with four squared-off hatches in its top. The Seastrike missile emerged with its stub wings and control surfaces folded back flat along its body—they snapped into flight position while the booster was still flinging it vertically skywards.

Left and right of her at the extreme outboard corners of the flight deck were the aft Skyfire CIWS mountings. The Close-In Weapon System was intended to counter sea-skimming missiles fired at the ship from aircraft or surface vessels or submarines. Each mounting was half as tall as her again, capped with its own fire control radar. Each could train its six-barrel Gatling through a three-quarter circle to provide overlapping defence fields right around the ship. Each could snap down like a frightened jack-in-a-box if a nuclear strike was expected, disappearing under laminated steel hatches that would protect it from blast, from heat, from hard radiation and eletromagnetic pulse effects.

Beside her, port of the centreline, was the launch ramp for the Skycats. The ramp was flush with the deck, but it could rise to present an eighteen degree slope at the end of the catapult run, a slope that kicked the Skycat into the air in a nose-up position to generate as much lift as possible as quickly as was possible. The Skycats had vectored thrust, could take off vertically, but such a manoeuvre was drastically expensive in terms of fuel and reduced both their range and their weapons carrying capacity. The nose-up ramp and the short catapult meant that when the aircraft left the deck it was already almost flying, generating most of the lift it needed aerodynamically over its wings, and so able to use most of its thrust for gaining full flying speed within mere seconds. Of course, on its return the aircraft landed vertically, pirouetting so perfectly, setting down like a silver dragonfly reluctant to surrender its airborne freedom.

There was an F-28 Skycat parked halfway along the flight deck at the catapult head, waiting. It was a sleek twin-finned thing, silvery-grey against the steel grey of the ship, gleaming in the brilliant burning sun. Its cockpit canopy was open, the helmeted pilot seated inside. It was armed for distant air interception, drop tanks and long barbed javelin missiles on its underwing pylons and underbelly hardpoints. Beside it, one obscuring the other, was a pair of Wolfmarine helicopters, their six-blade rotors folded out and locked, anti-submarine torpedoes loaded under their hulls. Beyond the parked aircraft, the armoured doors of the elevator box were rolled up. In the shadow, on the elevator behind the port door, waited a

second Skycat. There were eight more below the flight deck
in the hangar, ten more Wolfmarines. The first line of defence.

People were busy around the aircraft—just flight deck crew
at their routine work. It was a subdued ship's company, there
was no interest in impromptu deck sports. All weapon stations were on alert routine, the entire air group was on
standby, and the Vindicator was heading for the dust veil and
for the Iceland-UK Gap. It had a quietening effect.

She looked up at the radars back above the windows of the
little forward-jutting Takeoff and Landing Control Position, at
the tall tapering tower. So many defence systems on the ship,
so many weapons. Once—until so very recently—they had
been nothing more than the physical manifestation adopted by
an abstract concept, the academic fact that the Navy was an
armed service, a war machine, that this newly commissioned
ship was a strategic unit, a deterrer of war. Weapons hadn't
really been things that killed people, that she helped to kill
people by helping the crew who serviced them. But now,
unbelievably, quite crazily, they had become killing machines. And because she was on the Vindicator and the
Vindicator was loaded with killing machines, other weapons
would be aimed at her, would try to kill her. But not because
of the 155s or the Rayflex or the air defence missiles, not
because of the Skycats or the Wolfmarines that defended a
wide area around the ship. They would try to kill her, and by
her presence on board she had accepted a legitimate reason
that they should. The reason was the Fire Lance launchers
and the four hundred missiles waiting in the belly of the ship.

In the streaming hot wind she looked up at the flawless
vault of afternoon sky. A beautiful blue sky, here in the
south. The world is too beautiful, too beautiful to kill.

June 7, Robbins Air Force Base, Georgia

NOTHING. BLACK NOTHING, and hard packed dry snow with a powdery skimmed surface that whipped round their feet and ankles in the merciless murderous wind. Nothing but a circle of near night that the wind scythed through. Over there on the upwind edge of the pressing darkness ran a line of wire fencing, most demolished, its snapped over posts iced and drift buried. Downwind was the blank black expanse of the airfield, way over to the right the leftover bits and pieces of shattered and snow-coated buildings. They had trudged for a quarter hour away from there, stumbling across the wind.

Drexel dumped his bag on the ice and stood so that it gave some shelter for his feet from the wind. The other three had snow boots—no one had thought of that for him. He rammed his clumsy-glove hands into his parka pockets and stood with his back to the wind. It buffeted him, little ice spicules spat against the back of his hood. Here near the coast the appalling wind had a whole deep-frozen continental interior to feed it with sinking subzero force. It was horrendous.

Jenninger hauled back the sleeve of her parka and looked at her watch. She had been checking her watch every two or three minutes for the whole hour since they arrived. Her face was half invisible inside the rim of her hood. She was in her mid forties, but for the moment she looked ten years older. Caufield, the Air Force colonel, stomped backwards and forwards around their little group as if he was working out some ritual dance to guard them from the winter gods. Raffles, the black woman, the Army captain, stood with her arms folded and her back to the wind, her back to everybody. She'd never said a word during the flight, and there was no incentive to say anything at all in this desolate hell of ice and night.

He was losing his patience. He was wondering how long it would take them to freeze, and was losing his patience. Oppenheim and one of her superiors and a couple of people from the complex's administration group had suddenly pounced on him with an exit permit, had stood over him while he threw clothes into his travel bag, had escorted him out through a lock far away from everywhere, and had pushed him aboard an aircraft that was there just making a refuelling turn round. And then he was up in the air, meeting Jenninger and Caufield and their silent partner Raffles. They refused to tell him what was going on, they bundled him out when the aircraft landed. It had taken off immediately, leaving them entirely alone at this corpse of an Air Force Base.

"What the hell," he half-shouted across the wind, "is going on? What the hell?"

Caufield stomped by and stopped. "We're waiting. Our people have commandeered a bird for us, a Navy ocean patrol and anti-submarine aircraft. It's coming to pick us up."

Jenninger turned half into the wind. "We'll tell you more once we're on our way."

"Suppose I refuse to come with you?"

Jenninger shuffled closer so that she could look at him without catching the vicious wind in her hood. "Wouldn't do that, Drexel. The Apocalypse People will see you got yourself in this far. That makes you unsafe. You're committed. Besides." She looked past him at the awful night. "You wouldn't want to stay around *here*. And only the one plane is scheduled to come in. And where in hell are they, god dammit."

"Got to give them time to find the place in this," Caufield observed aloud to the elements. "Is it the radiation danger is bothering you?"

"Fuck the radiation danger." Jenninger planted her back to the wind again. "I'm worried we get off before the other side catch up with what's going on. Otherwise all we get is a ride back to STRACC."

Drexel looked round as if the darkness might have started to glow. "What radiation danger?"

Caufield waved a mittened hand at the night. "Robbins here was a Pave Paws site, wasn't it? Big coastal defence radar. It was nuked. That's why there's no one here to give us any trouble. Underneath all this ice it's as hot as hell."

"CAPTAIN IN THE CIC!"

Bedford was in his day cabin, working at his desk. On the desktop screen he was running through the latest pre-war data on all Soviet and Warsaw pact sea and air capabilities in any way relevant to the Greenland-Iceland-UK Gap, together with estimated attrition rates for a Nato-Soviet conflict. He had to get together some kind of a guess on what they might have left up there. And above all else, the Soviet submarines—their design, their capabilities, the weapons they carried. Richard Erwin Bedford was an ex-submariner and he knew submarines, knew how dangerous they were. He had a pot of coffee on his desk for his morning fix. He was a coffee addict, one of the last generation to fail to kick the habit. And then the call came on the ship's address, and he left his coffee and his cabin and crossed the corridor and entered through the tunnel door in just two strides.

Redden was directing the CIC. Lt. Louis Redden was black, was the SADIS Supervisor. He was standing at the commanding officer's position just left of the tunnel door. As Bedford came in he pointed across at the main electronic plot in the middle of the rear wall of the CIC. The centre of the big screen marked the ship. Way up left near the edge was a contact light. The plot radius was set on the five hundred kilometre scale.

"SCAN contact, sir, at six thousand metres at four hundred eighty kilometres out."

Bedford nodded. He looked at the display readouts on the little console at the commanding officer's dais, grabbing his chair to climb into it but then changing his mind—too melodramatic. The Skyhook flying the SCAN radar was at 3,000 metres on a ten kilometre bow station. From that altitude it

could see out to a horizon two hundred kilometres distant.
But a moderately high flying aircraft would come up over that
horizon while much further away. Like this one had.

"We've had the contact for—" Redden glanced at the CIC
clock. "For almost a minute. It's northwest at three hundred
degrees from us, absolute heading one-two-three degrees. Its
airspeed is three hundred knots. Its course will take it north of
our track at two-twenty kilometres out. At that altitude we'll
be right over its horizon."

Bedford nodded again. That didn't matter. If the intruder
was halfway up to date it would have radar threat receivers to
tell it that their SCAN was illuminating it. So it already knew
they were there. "No radar? No IFF?"

"Neither the SCAN nor the Skyhook's own receivers are
picking up radar illumination. And no IFF response." Units
on your own side had Identification Friend or Foe transponders. When a radar with a friendly frequency hit them, the
transponders jabbered out an identification signal before the
carrying aircraft or ship got itself blown to hell. Units that
weren't on your own side stayed silent.

"Okay." The intruder was already close enough in to
launch a long range anti-ship missile to look for them. Maybe
it had. "Okay, take the SADIS. Automatic."

"Automatic." Redden was already heading for the SADIS
Supervisor's console. Only one operator sat there, PO2 Hayes
at the Air Detector/Tracker. The weapons control consoles
were half empty as well, but SADIS, the Surface and Air
Defence Integrated System, could virtually run a missile intercept by itself.

Boyce came in through the door from the Missile Control
Centre just to the right of the main plot. He walked half-
backwards to the centre of the CIC, reading the plot data. He
stopped at the centrally placed Operational Summary console
and switched it on.

Bedford glanced to his right. There was no one seated at
the Talker board just on the other side of the tunnel door to
the corridor forward. The whole of the Combat Information
Centre was only half occupied, the ship was trying to organize itself with half a brain. "John. CIC to condition one.
Weapons SCR and the AOC to condition one."

Boyce nodded. He picked up his headset at the OpSum and
started giving the order through.

He needed all the people in the CIC, just in case there was

more than one intruder coming in. He needed all the positions in the Weapons System Control Room occupied, he needed the Air Operations Centre at full alert. Just in case.

Dylong came in through the door to the left of the main plot. He must have been somewhere deeper down in the C3 box—through that door was the internal ladder up from the 02 level. Lt. Cmdr. Joe Dylong, CIC Supervisor and Tactical Action Officer. He joined Boyce standing at the OpSum. Other people started coming in, people who had been off duty but not asleep, who had been alerted by the original Captain's call on the ship's address. Lt. Stratten came in and went straight to her SADIS Systems position on the right of the CIC, reinforcing the seaman operator there. PO3 Kuroda came in, both yawning and out of breath. He must have been already rushing from his berth just in case his captain could use him. He snapped on his headset and brought the Talker board to life.

"Radar SCR can't get an identification," Dylong said. He and Boyce were both spurning their headsets at the OpSum. "They're processing the return characteristics. They get four multiscatter points. Four airscrews."

"Four props and the size is right." Boyce turned to look at Bedford, not quite ready to believe himself. "Could that be a Bear?"

A Bear was a Tupolev Tu-20, an ancient Soviet bomber and reconnaissance aircraft probably capable of packing a whole range of modern air-launched weapons. But a Bear itself would be helpless once seen. It should have dived and turned minutes ago.

"A Bear has the range to get over here from Cuba," Dylong said. "Or up from Mozambique or North Namibia. If they have any there."

Boyce shrugged. "Crazy."

"AOC, sir." Kuroda's Talker headset had a hush mike so that he could give outside orders through without other voices intruding. He had to fold it aside to speak to his Captain as long as Bedford didn't wear his own headset. "Commander Clemence wants to know if you want to scramble the Angels?"

"Tell him stand by." The CIC had filled up. That was good, that was fast. Along the left-hand side the four SADIS Supervision and tracker consoles were filled, the four weapons control consoles were occupied, LoSecco was settling himself in at the Weapons Control Officer's position. Along the right-hand side Stratten and her two SADIS Systems operators were in place, Slamon and her three anti-submarine warfare people had their consoles switched on. The whole twenty strong CIC team was there. For a Bear, for a phased out museum piece?

"Contact is turning." Chief Petty Officer Irene Jablonski at the SADIS Track Evaluator. "Coming on to one-seven-four degrees."

"Coming right down on the Skyhook," Dylong said.

"Scramble one Angel. Combat interception."

"Scramble one Angel," Kuroda repeated. "Combat interception."

In the little screen in his commanding officer's console he had a repeat of the view taken by the camera up on the roof of the TLCP. It looked aft along the flight deck. There was the little silver machine of the F-28 Skycat hooked to the head of the catapult, its canopy already closed and the external power umbilical dropped. A boiling shimmer of air started up from its tail and its underbelly engine exhausts.

Dylong, looking morosely into his OpSum. "The Skyhook is getting radar illumination from the intruder. Running it."

The ramp had come up beside the little portside Skyfire mounting. Flame heat came out of the twin tail exhausts of the F-28, and then it shot away at the ramp, went nose up out over the stern. It dwindled so quickly, passing stalling speed, then flicked away to its right, to port, over the monochrome sea. Already starting to climb.

"Got a radar determination," Dylong said. "US Navy type APGE. Thirty one or thirty one A." He said it quite impassively, without any excitement or relief. He was Chinese, and his voice was always as expressionless as his face—as if he had to live up to something.

"What carries that?" A US Navy aircraft? Where was its damn IFF? On the screen they were already rolling the second F-28 up to the catapult to be ready for launch.

"A whole list. At the right size, with four airscrews, is a C-130 ASW and maritime patrol."

That was crazy. A whole number of old C-130 Hercules transports had been taken over for maritime patrol and anti-submarine warfare work under the Saver Wise reuse programme. Saver Wise had been one of the measures that helped pay for things like the Vindicator. But a Hercules just didn't have the range to come all this way out from home and

ever get back again, not without inflight refuelling. Which in
the present state of the world you could scratch. They were
right out in the middle of the equatorial Atlantic. What in hell
was a C-130 Hercules doing flying right into them?

Bedford just shook his head. "Have Communications try
and raise them. Who are they, where's their IFF, and why
don't they have the sense to call us up?"

Kuroda started passing the order.

Boyce came over to Bedford's position from the OpSum.
"This is crazy." He looked round at the main plot, where a
bright blue interceptor arrowhead was climbing out to meet
the red intruder. "The Soviets can't pull a trick like this, can
they?"

"Impossible." Bedford looked at all the lights on his tiny
instrument desk console, looked round at the CIC personnel
all seated at their positions. All set up and ready to go. For
real. For the first time ever, on a ship that had managed to
miss the war. All set up and ready to go. For a Hercules?

Kuroda. "Sir, the Hercules is talking back. He's been
looking for us. Ah—he's got passengers who want to come
on board, sir."

Boyce's eyebrows went up behind his glasses.

"Ah—he says his IFF is zilched, sir, and there are no
spares to be had where he comes from. He says he hopes he
didn't set us crapping. That's what he says, sir." Kuroda
spread his hands, disowning the utterance.

Boyce shook his head, put his hands on his hips. "Stand
down?"

"Not yet." Bedford looked at the plot, at the closing
distance to interception. "Not until the Angel has a visual
confirmation. Then he can escort him in."

The C-130 Hercules had a team of four passengers headed by
a member of the Crisis Government on board, and their only
aim in life was to join the Vindicator. The C-130 itself was
going to fly on southeast to Ascension Island, which its pilot
confidently expected to reach just before his fuel gave out—
after all, he'd flown all the way via a set-down at Robbins
with no war load on board and next to no people, just his five
crew and four passengers. The British at Ascension would let
him land all right. The place was essentially a signals intelligence base, although it had served for a while as a staging
post to the Falklands. It had a couple of hundred personnel,

an airstrip, plenty of bunkered fuel, but not enough carrying capacity to make the move down to South Africa when the time came. They would let the surprise visitor come in if it earned them an aircraft and a crew to fly it, that was for sure. The C-130 pilot and his crew were only too glad to be abandoning the States for the duration. They had come from there. They knew.

The C-130 was in Navy colours, dark blue top surfaces, sky blue sides and underbelly. It came past the ship at only a hundred knots, all flaps right down and almost all but walking in the air. Four figures came out of the tail on short drop parachutes that were already opening before they were clear of the aircraft. They splashed into the azure sea and their chutes almost settled on top of them in the exquisite breeze. The C-130 turned like a big lumbering bird in the sky and then thundered away, airspeed increasing and flaps coming up. The pilot was in a hurry to make Ascension without waiting around and wasting fuel.

Two Wolfmarines rigged with cable winches fished the arrivals out of the water and helicoptered them back on board. They landed on the sun-stunned flight deck, carnival coloured figures in bright yellow wetsuits still oozing water, wearing brilliant orange life jackets, hefting bulky red-and-white chequered waterproof effects bags. Gloria Craze, sometimes the ship's unofficial supernumerary officer, got the job of meeting them and escorting them down below. She took them in through the elevator box, where an armed F-28 Skycat was waiting once again on the port elevator. They rode down on the starboard elevator along with an unarmed Wolfmarine going back to the hangar. She didn't give them time to look around the main deck level hangar, but marched them straight out through a forward door behind the starboard elevator, took them down two decks to 2nd platform, and turned in through the side tunnel door into the Sick Bay Area inside the C3-Complex isolation box.

Lt. Cmdr. Andrew Culbertson, the surgeon, took a perfunctory look at them while they stripped off and dried themselves, and pronounced them still alive. Boyce came down from the rarefied upper levels of the C3 box to inspect the arrivals. They were quite an assortment. Eileen Jenninger, caucasian, a civilian in her mid forties, a member of the STRACC leadership and boss of the team. Lt. Col. James Caufield, USAF, also caucasian, from NORAD's Strategic

Evaluation Team, also at Cheyenne/STRACC. Capt. Danella Raffles, US Army, black and somehow so sad looking, formerly of 6th Army HQ, the Presidio of San Francisco. And a civilian in his mid thirties called David Drexel. He was the biggest surprise of all, a British citizen but a credited Administration and National Security Council adviser plucked from one of the advisement-and-crisis teams originally dispersed to CASAL. Boyce took it all as if it happened every day.

The Captain wanted to know what was going on, what they were here for, why he hadn't been informed in advance. And while they were answering questions anyway, what about what in hell had happened during the war? Jenninger said they were tired because they'd just been flying all through the night with only relief crew bunks on board the aircraft to try to sleep in. They wanted a chance to eat, to stow their effects somewhere, and then she would be only too happy to hand out a broad briefing. Meanwhile and right away, she had a signal all drawn up and indecipherably number-encrypted on a signal sheet, and could they maybe be so good as to transmit it to CASAL immediately. Otherwise the people who had sent them would be thinking their aircraft had just dived into the sea somewhere.

Boyce was all black Bostonian charm. Synthetic, Gloria Craze thought—all synthetic. Something about John Ritchie Boyce she somehow did not like, something she couldn't identify precisely—something to do with him coming from a rich-black Boston family instead of her own Harlem ghetto. He took the signal to have it sent right out, he would arrange for accommodation right after. There was no shortage of space, after all—two officer's cabins for the extra two pilots they would have had on board had they been up to maximum plan strength of twelve F-28 Skycats, plus twin berth cabins for the missing full strength Air Group support personnel. Meantime Gloria could take them to eat in the canteen. And until after the briefing with Bedford she could keep everyone else on board away from them. Let's keep the dissemination of information under control and coming from the top down.

Americans have no style. They had an awful lot of money and all the luxury that goes with it, but they had no style. They could afford their Nemesis System ships, they could stack them full of so much computerised semi-autonomous self-deciding control equipment that the 56,000 tonne monsters, complete with attack aircraft and antisubmarine helicopters, got by with barely more than four hundred crew. They could in consequence allow enough space for around 300 modular cabins each two metres by three, two berths to a cabin for crew and junior NCOs, individual cabins for senior NCOs and officers—and of course larger cabins for the Captain and his three most senior officer commanders. Good grief, a *warship* where even the humblest seamen and seawomen, or whatever they called them, lived no more cramped than two to a cabin, cabins that ran in narrow-corridored rows out along 1st and 2nd and 3rd platforms, outboard of all the hoists and support machinery for the forward deck defence weapon mountings. Cabins like economy class on board a cruise liner, for goodness sake.

But they had no style. It seemed the senior officers ate apart in the wardroom, but the others, the lieutenants and the lieutenants junior grade, ate in the same self-service canteen as the other ranks. Of course the officers had their own mess, their segregated off-duty communal recreation area, sharing only the tiny movie theatre and compact gym with the other ranks—but they ate in the same canteen. At least it was a friendly and bright canteen. They might have no style, but they had all the money in the world.

Drexel looked around his newest home, a low-ceilinged box three metres long and two metres wide. There were two bunks right across the rear wall, a narrow worktable top and a television along one side, a table top and a washbowl in either stainless steel or aluminium along the other, and a pair of tall lockers and drawers flanking the narrow door in the other end that opened out into the corridor. There was a frame chair, there was a stool. There was no window, no porthole whatsoever. Raffles had already asked about windows. That Lt. Craze woman had said there were windows on the bridge and the Takeoff and Landing Control Position, and nowhere else. Windows were weak points.

Jenninger and Caufield had got individual cabins, unoccupied officer's cabins, up on main deck somewhere portside and outboard of the superstructure. He and Raffles had been brought the long walk here down on 2nd platform, the deck level with the water outside, and right forward to only thirty metres from the bow. Here the ship was just wide enough for the copious thickness of the massive double hull structure on each side, the depth of two cabins opposite each other, and a

corridor end between them that stopped at a narrow door.
That door led through to the anchor chain tiers, their petty
officer guide had told them. Raffles had taken the starboard
cabin, he the port. So now he sat in a neatly fitted out
airconditioned cell, no more cramped than in the individual
accommodation at CASAL, although here there was an extra
bunk over his bed which he couldn't fold up out of the way.
That didn't matter. It was the windows that were the pity. All
that time hidden away from the terrifying cold and darkness
since it had happened, and then a sudden brief reminder of
what it was like in the still sovereign tropical empire of the
sun—*still* sovereign only, because the dust veil was going to
spread across the equator and envelop the entire globe. A
sudden brief reminder of searing sunlight and a hot wind, and
then he was closed up inside another great machine.

It was the most terrifying thing he'd ever done, jumping
out of the back of an aircraft on a jolting parachute into a
deep blue sea. Much worse than sitting in CASAL watching
the war—all that had just been symbols and data on electronic
wall screens. They had made him jump into the sea, he had
been fished out deafened on a dangling wire and hauled into
the tiny interior of a two-man combat helicopter, and now he
was trapped on board a strategic unit heading for the nearest
thing to a front line. And he didn't like ships. Right forward
on the waterline, even if he couldn't hear the bow wave or
anything else but the airconditioned sigh and a faint machinery hum—here if they hit a rough sea it would be notice-
able okay.

He had already stowed his handful of clothes, his parka,
his issue pistol and its thirty rounds. Lockers and little drawers—
these modern American sailors lived in the lap of luxury. Just
time to see what the nearest washroom was like before they
were collected again to go and give the remnant of the
operational US Navy a briefing on the catastrophe that had
happened to the world.

He went out into the narrow end of the corridor and headed
back to where it split around what they had been told was the
support housing for the forward 155mm gun up above the
main deck. Round the back of the housing, inboard between
the two branches of the divided corridor, was the washroom—
neat and clean inside, white paint and stainless steel. He had
already been warned that like the rest of the ship, the wash-
rooms were not sex segregated—but there seemed to be no

one about anyway. He looked inside the shower area: there
were towel and robe hooks, and three shower cubicles. In the
main area were four toilet cubicles and a row of washbowls
with soap dispensers and hand dryers. There was a fire
extinguisher—there were fire extinguishers everywhere you
turned. There was someone in one of the cubicles. The flush
went and then the door opened and Raffles came out. She
crossed to wash her hands. She didn't seem to like him and
he didn't seem to like her. At least they were managing to be
polite about it. He picked his cubicle and disappeared inside.

That, then, was the war. Two American defence satellites
went out, and the whole world exploded. That was the High
Frontier in scenario perfection, a tripwire defence line that got
triggered.

Bedford had called the briefing in the wardroom, starboard
on 01 level outboard of the superstructure and the descending
C3 box. There was room at the table—it could seat twelve
after all, himself and his three full commanders and all the
lieutenant commanders who ran their various departments. He
took his place at the head of the table and put Boyce on his
left, then Clemence, then Steetley. Greg Clemence was Air
Operations Controller and ran the Air Group and all its support requirements. Orville Steetley was the Chief Engineer
Officer, the man who played with turbines and heat exchangers and reactors and things. Steetley's cropped hair was splendid white in contrast to his negro skin, making him look even
older and wiser than he was. After all he was at forty nine the
oldest officer on the ship, two years older than Bedford
himself.

The passengers he placed down the right-hand side of the
table—this Jenninger woman, Caufield from the Air Force,
Raffles from the Army, and this British curiosity Drexel. He
had wanted to know one hell of a lot from them, and it turned
out they had as much and more to say than he could take. It
was stupefying, just stupefying. But what else did you expect
to hear about a nuclear war?

Two satellites had gone out, one right after the other. The
probable cause was debris impacts—there was an awful lot of
junk whirling around up there nowadays—but two together, a
surveillance and a new defence director satellite, just as they
were coming over to look at the Kamchatka area was too
much of a coincidence. Because the Soviets were running a

snap missile dispersal exercise down there and had just launched something up into exactly the right orbit, and they were still foaming and spitting over the downing of their reconnaissance intruder that they claimed wasn't even over Thule anyway. So when the US Government demanded an instant cancellation of the exercise to prove that it was just that and nothing more, and when they responded by apparently putting their entire strategic forces on maximum alert and telling the world the Americans were downing their own satellites as a trick—well, the problem was the instability. The Americans were finishing up their High Frontier while the Soviets were only just starting theirs, and the perception was that the Soviets were for some reason paranoid enough not to credit American assurances of purely defensive intent. The fear was that the Soviets really thought the Americans were going to hit them with a first strike the minute the High Frontier was finished enough to thin out the necessarily weaker retaliatory response, solving the East-West problem once and for all while taking only acceptable damage in return for world supremacy. The fear was that the Soviets were really insane enough to hit first before the phantom first strike that of course would never come. The way they were so suddenly acting really and truly looked like that when you read the situation, knowing as you did that you yourselves were the good guys and they were either the bad or the mad.

So to warn them the US took out one of their communication orbiters with an Asat weapon. A tiny escalation beyond threat and counter-threat posturing, all decided in a matter of hours in one hell of a frightened hurry.

The Soviets instantly took out a US satellite. The US took out two more. The Soviets over-reacted and sent in a whole string of killers at the High Frontier arrays. That was probably a desperate move to stop the escalation by returning both sides to what they had once termed vulnerability parity, but it *looked* like clearing the way for the real thing, and they had everything on alert and were sending their eastern and Baltic and northern fleets to sea, all within a single day of the start. So the US hit a single Soviet silo in the middle of nowhere, and they replied by nuking Holy Loch in the UK. That was possibly intended to be a we-mean-it-too low escalation strike against a hard military target but not on US territory, but what it did was open up the European theatre.

Nato threw single response strikes at bases, the Warsaw

Pact perceived an attack threat and replied with heavier strikes at nuclear installations, and the whole European war was starting the wrong way around and nobody knew what to do. Nato saw itself faced with an imminent conventional roll-over and let go at Warsaw Pact tactical missile sites and troop concentrations. The other side set its troops moving to counter Nato forward pre-empter units and to get a foot on the conventional ground before it was too late, while stepping up its strikes against any actual Nato nuclear installation on land or sea. The battle for control of the Greenland-Iceland-UK Gap was already underway with a general unit-to-unit massacre and the Red Navy almost looking like winning for a day or so. Across Europe both sides started nuking troop formations and elements in the communications and route infrastructure—in other words where roads and rail and airports concentrated, namely cities. That was another of the vital misperceptions piling up on top of each other: the Soviet bloc saw a German city as not American but a Polish city as one of theirs, while Nato saw a Polish city as not Russian but a German city as one of theirs. But the British fired back at Soviet urban targets so that was that anyway.

Both the Americans and the Soviets had already wound up to obliterating each other's missile submarine forces with subs and aircraft and flexibly targeted nukes—that following attempts to cripple each other's control transmission antennas, in other words nuking military targets on home territory. Now the Soviets came back at US urban targets and the big intercontinental exchanges started and got step by step bigger—cities and economic infrastructure such as dams and power utilities, missile silos and airfields and command structure centres and satellites. For a time the command-control-and-communications networks broke down on both sides and no one knew exactly what they were doing or what was going on. There was a period of semi-autonomous unit warfare at sea while the commanders of strategic land potentials were acting on their own initiative, fighting through the corporal's war scenario for real. And by then they already had the total blackout under the dust veil, and the Big Freeze was setting in.

It was consummate crisis mismanagement. That was the consensus of all the despairing post-analysis studies that had been run. At first there was no one available to blame—the

President and the entire Administration, and presumably the whole Politburo caucus, had failed to survive.

It was already dark and the Nuclear Winter had begun to bite. The entire civil infrastructure no longer existed. Any power utilities that had survived the war were instant freeze casualties, the same for petrochemicals, all material and food manufacture, almost all food storage, all medical facilities, and all communications except portable or bunkered radio transmitters and what was left of the military land line network. An estimated eighty percent survivor group in the combatant countries and one hundred percent among the non-combatant spectators in the northern hemisphere went into the Big Freeze, and within a matter of days were down to an estimated ten percent survivor group and still dying wholesale. This collateral death hit the military in general almost as hard as the civilian population. Not a sound was coming out of Western Europe any more except for some bunkers in France and Norway and the UK, while the bulk of US Continental Forces just disintegrated and died. There remained just those Midgetman and Miniman silos which hadn't been hit and managed not to freeze, plus some Air Force and Navy cruise missiles stored in bunkers or on board ship and waiting until it all cleared and any leftover carrier platforms could deploy them again. There were a few scraps and shreds of conventional forces, a few submarines, and the Vindicator. And of course CASAL and STRACC and the whole Cheyenne Mountain Complex.

The priority should have been to re-establish communications and reconstruct some sort of governmental authority, regaining control over what was left of the strategic military potential and at the same time mobilizing conventional forces to support the surviving civilian population. That's what the game plans had always said. But what conventional forces? And support the poor civilians in what way—the Nuclear Winter had hit far harder than it was supposed to do, and the assessments were getting dramatically worse with each new one that was made. It would be absolutely all they could do to keep an operational strategic potential together. Any hopeless attempts to consolidate the civil situation and help more civilians survive than the few who could somehow help themselves—that would only wreck any chance of maintaining a viable military defence posture. While the soft-liners argued and even tried their hand at passive and active sabotage, the transmitters out in the dark were going silent one after the other.

The problem was that the Soviets had survivability, too. They would have just as much of a leftover strategic potential to string back together. Further, they would know that the Americans did as well, so they would put all the efforts they could muster into getting ready to resume the conflict as soon as the Freeze broke and operations became possible once again. Whether they were planning to continue the war or just to be ready to do so was immaterial. They would have the capability, and if America emerged from the Nuclear Winter without any effective counter-threat—well the Soviets would be fools not to use it. Obviously they weren't going to have *that* happen to their country without wanting to get something back for it—namely the eradication of the enemy that had done it to them—if they thought they could get away with it.

So that settled the problem of the softliners and the decision as to which policy direction. The softliners turned obstructionists and saboteurs and started getting themselves shot. It was sickening but it was necessary. Wanted or not, this was a war for Christ's sake, and the continued existence of the United States, sole effective survivor of the free Western world, was at stake. It made horrible, unavoidable sense.

And it didn't stop there, unfortunately. The lesson of assuming that the other guy was a bad guy and forgetting that he assumed the same of you—the lesson of what that led to was as bitter as it could be. But it made no difference at all. Even if the Soviets weren't inherently dangerous, they were a deadly danger because they couldn't *know* for sure that we weren't inherently dangerous to them. They would have to distrust us because they would know that we knew that they had to think exactly the same way about us.

So did you have to hit them after all before they hit you?

You got two power groups forming around the issue, the people who argued for maximum possible war-readiness, and the extremists who wanted a unilateral prosecution of the war to eliminate the Soviet threat while the Soviets were still down and disorganized, before they could make any comparable attack themselves. The last, the ultimate pre-emptive strike—a kind of Armageddon, if you went for biblical plunderings.

The war-prosecutionists were more than just a splinter group. They included some members of the Crisis Government at STRACC, and they were a minority that was literally prepared to do anything at all for their version of the ultimate good of the world. There was a real risk that they would make serious trouble right in the controlling heart of the command and control system responsible for coherent defence, the very last place you could afford any kind of disruption. If your executive centres put themselves effectively out of action for a while, then the Soviets might really take the risk and hit you first, bringing the same unnecessary wave of further destruction that would certainly follow if you suddenly started throwing nukes at them.

It might very well not come to an open attempt at a coup by the extremists, but the danger had to be taken seriously. Which was why Jenninger and her little support team were here. The Vindicator represented a major proportion of the entire surviving nuclear potential, and all in one place; it was being moved right up to the strategic front line from where its weapons could range on a whole concentration of potential targets in the western USSR, just right to deter the Soviets from doing something ultimately stupid, but unfortunately also just right for immediate pre-emptive use. Without the Vindicator there was too little left for an effective defence against any Soviet threat, and without the Vindicator there was no possibility of even contemplating a sudden erasing attack to which the Soviets would have no chance to reply.

The presence of Jenninger's team solved two problems. It defused the power struggle issue back home before it could ever blow. The majority consensus would prevail and there would be no wild and possibly bloody action by the war-prosecutionists: if they couldn't count on the Vindicator, then there was no point in even trying. At the same time effective defence was secured against all eventualities. This was no encroachment on Bedford's tactical and ship-command competence, now, but they really had to avoid the all too thinkable situation where he was faced with the impossibility of having to take independent *strategic* decisions. With a credited political-strategic controller on board, then even if the Soviets really did start something themselves and there was a temporary wipe-out of communications with STRACC and CASAL at a critical moment, the Vindicator's deterrent value, its ability to respond with protective destruction strikes, was secured. That guarantee was vital in itself, and it further helped to calm the extremists and to prevent them from simply boiling over. To that end Jenninger had with her a little microportable, the cassette recorder sized thing she kept slung over her shoulder now she was on board the ship. It was battery powered and had a hard memory—a store that didn't wipe every time the power was switched off. With it she could encrypt and decrypt her own private signals that would travel ship-to-shore over the Blue Talker domain, she had a data store to help her with any decisions that might become necessary, and for the worst eventuality she had legitimating command codes and the Permissive Action Codes that were needed to launch a nuclear strike.

And that was God awful it.

They would give more details any time on anything upon request. There was plenty more—God knows, there was plenty more. The mechanism of the Nuclear Winter, for example, and how bad the prognosis had become—it was going to hold through the northern hemisphere summer and the ensuing seasonal winter, and might or might not weaken wholly or only partially in the course of the following seasonal summer. It was also definitely spreading to envelop the southern hemisphere—streamers were crossing the equator both over the Indian and over the Pacific Oceans now. How severe and how long lasting the effects in the southern hemisphere would be couldn't yet be predicted, nor to what extent a redistribution of the stratospheric dust might or might not modify the climate catastrophe in the north. But the real alarmists were speculating that it would hold long enough for the huge heat stores of the oceans to be depleted significantly, so that the global climate would flip right over into its statistical norm in this geological epoch: then the Nuclear Winter would turn into the Nuclear Ice Age. It was only wild speculation, but they weren't being laughed at any more.

There was plenty more to pass on in an endless series of briefings, but that was more than enough to absorb right now—much more than enough. Just one question: it had to do with maintaining the safety of his ship. What had happened to the other Nemesis Class units?

The NMSS-4 Defender was destroyed in the fitter's yard. The NMSS-5 Peacemaker and the NMSS-6 were demolished on the slips. The Protector and the Consolidator were both sunk. The Consolidator went down in the Mediterranean to concentrated air and sea and eventually nuclear attack. The Protector was destroyed in the North Atlantic by repeated nuclear attacks—at the very least twenty warheads coming in before the defences were worn down and the attacks came too close. That left just the NMSS-3 Vindicator. And if the Vindicator hadn't only just arrived at Honolulu when the war blew up, but had been in a position to be deployed direct towards the Soviet Pacific coast, maybe the Vindicator wouldn't be afloat. No, the Nemesis ships were not and of course could not be unsinkable. But they were extraordinarily hard to kill.

Jenninger and her team left.

They left Bedford and his three commanders sitting silent in the wardroom. Eventually they would have to tackle on-board politics, deciding what to bulletin for the crew, how much to pass on personally and via officer briefings, and how much they could just leave to filter out without fear of distortion.

But for a moment there was nothing to say.

The sunset was a fearful thing, more exorbitant than any normal end of a tropical day. It was like the blood of the world.

It was no cloud. It was the tenuous edge of the dust veil so high up there that caught the light of the sinking sun, that smeared it right across the sky, that burned with it. The spread of luminous colour was amazing, breathlessly beautiful and awesomely wrong, brilliant crimson in the west and arcing over in a vast scarlet dome to a sombre magenta on the vanguard of the coming night. The ocean turned blood red like some sea of splintered rubies, the grey ship glowed a ruddy, bloody pink.

Off-duty crew gathered all along the port side, on the flight deck, along beside the superstructure, forward down on main deck from the foreslope break right out to the bow. Gloria Craze went up to the Takeoff and Landing Control Position jutting out from the rear of the elevator box up between the two huge roll-down doors. She didn't have the place to herself, of course. The two duty lookouts were there, as well as Warrant Officer McCune, the man who ran the TLCP at Condition 1, and Seaman Wendy Springer, one of the TLCP Assistants. They crowded the two small windows on the port side, and didn't say a word. From the windows she could see people up on the rear corner of the elevator box roof, but she didn't want to go out there, not exposed under the awful fire-sky. This was the edge of the dust veil at 8°N, much closer to the equator than it had been when they last saw it twenty two days ago in the eastern Pacific. No, she didn't want to go out under the burning vault of the fire-sky.

If something was going to go wrong up there in the North Atlantic, this fearful deathly splendour would be the last sunset any of them would ever see.

Bedford went on working in his day cabin. He sat at his desk in a shallow pool of light, the computer screen aglow and charts and tactical summary printouts spread in front of him. The problem was the tactical situation in the Iceland-UK Gap, the assigned stationing area, with all its islands, its shore-lines, its varying water depths. And that problem, at its core, was submarines. Any Soviet surface ship he could hit back at just as hard as it could hit him. He had the F-28s as a first line of defence, then the Fire Lance anti-ship mode tipped with a half-tonne warhead, and if something somehow got closer still there was the Seastrike on anti-ship instead of anti-aircraft mode, and finally the automatic 155s. And no Soviet surface vessel he encountered would be hard armoured like the Vindicator. Ships were not the problem. It was submarines.

A sub would be helpless if he could get it pinned right down. He had twelve Wolfmarines to send against it, and although these days a sub with the right armament could knock an attacking helicopter out of the air, it would never be able to take down twelve in a row. Not even two or three. But a submarine could sneak around the Vindicator despite the ship's own sonar and hydrophone capabilities—even the Soviets had finally learned how to build quiet boats. And a sub could lie in wait. It could make a mess of even the Vindicator if it got in close with a nuclear tipped torpedo or tube-launched anti-ship missile, or if it got a chance to drop a deep water nuclear mine. What would one or two or three or more submarines do to try to catch him, where would they patrol, where would they loiter, how would they coordinate? He tried to activate all his own knowledge of tactics as you ran them from beneath the waves. But his experience was on Trident boats. He knew what it *felt* like down there to know that you were the quarry of everything and that you were potentially helpless, to imagine that the sectioned-off boat was holed somewhere and you were trapped inside, still breathing and still waiting as your tomb sank down and down and down. He knew what that felt like. But he didn't have experience on hunter-killer boats, the predators of ships and other submarines.

What he really needed, what he desperately needed, was a full support group, frigates and destroyers that he could use to deploy a forward and flanking screen. But the Vindicator was alone, just as if a nuclear strike had wiped out all the support units—the extreme contingency for which the designers had developed the ship. Starting your war with the backstop option was a frightening way to begin.

His desk phone buzzed.

"McGready, sir, in Communications." Senior Chief Petty Officer McGready, the woman in charge of the Communications Systems Control Room on this rotation. The Communications SCR was inside the C3 box on 01 level. "Two signals just come in, sir. One is addressed to you, sir, from Naval Alternate Command over Naval Command. Came in on the Blue Talker cryptographic domain. I can fax it straight through."

Bedford keyed the printer on his desk terminal. "Okay, my printer's on." The matrix printer started to run. Blue Talker was one of their secure communications links. Any signal text was coded into a string of number cyphers, and then each number was multiplied by another from an endless list of discrete numbers—each used only once, hence the term one-time pad. The partnered receiving decryption computer had to possess the same one-time pad run down to exactly the same next number on the list. Without the right one-time pad you couldn't crack the signal with all the computer time from here to eternity.

"The other signal's a problem, sir. It's on standard Blue Talker, it has the STRACC code, and it's addressed to Jenninger on board. But decrypted it just comes out as a string of five digit groups. It looks like something intended for a further decryption. I doubt we can handle it at all."

That would be a job for Jenninger's own microportable, keeping her signals private. "Okay, McGready. Hold on a moment while I take a look at this one." He tore the sheet out of the printer.

ORIG: CASAL NAVALCOM NMSS DIR 1011 JUNE 08 1330
FWRD: STRACC NAVCOM JUNE 08 1509
INCOMING: JUNE 08 2210
NMSS-3 VINDICATOR CPT BEDFORD CO

1. Advise command authority retained NAVCOM/NAVALCOM.
2. Seek other-source command confirmations from NAVCOM/ NAVALCOM.
3. Advise cooperate with Jenninger at own discretion.
4. Confirm alert station assignment IUK Gap. Require deployment June 13 latest.
5. Advise possible Soviet hostility. Defensive engagement at own discretion.
6. Adopt Fire Lance LAM readiness on station.

That was exactly the reply he had expected to his inquiry. Most of it, at least. "Best thing to do is just print up the signal for Jenninger and have someone take it along to her cabin with my compliments. Put it on store but don't waste time trying to crack it. She has her own decrypter for the job."

"Okay, sir. Hope I didn't disturb you, sir."

"Thanks, McGready. You didn't disturb me." He put down the phone.

The signal. The apparent time delay between forwarding at STRACC and receipt on the ship was an illusion, an artefact of the time difference around the world. But the delay between issuing at CASAL, going out via its local Nemesis Direction communications facility, and the forwarding by STRACC was different. As if the people at STRACC had taken their time approving the signal—but he couldn't read any more out of it than that. Maybe it had something to do with the two power groups being more evenly balanced than Jenninger had hinted at, being in a position to check up on each other. Who knew? All the first four points were just what he'd expected, especially that points one to three confirmed his doubts about the legitimacy of Jenninger's claim to absolute command authority. Five and six were different— they pointed out that there was still a war going on.

Require deployment in the IUK Gap June 13 latest. That was a matter of mere mental arithmetic—he'd been using navigation data half the day and had all the figures. From their present position it was still 5,800 kilometres to the IUK Gap, that vaguely delineated ellipse laid onto the sea between Iceland and the northwest of Scotland. At their present 23 knots that would take 137 hours. That would be—that would be the afternoon of the 14th. Which was too late.

He picked up the phone. Now who was on the bridge—he

didn't have to keep all of Boyce's computerized sliding duty rosta in his head, but he made a point of knowing who was running each key position without having to consult his desktop. Lt. junior grade Alan Villman, Damage Control Officer. He punched for the bridge.

"Bridge. Villman."

"Bedford. I'd—"

"Evening, sir."

"Evening, lieutenant. I'd like a speed change. Come up to thirty knots, balanced power on all four. No course change."

"Thirty knots, balanced power on all four screws, no course change. Right away, sir?"

"Right away. Thank you, lieutenant." He put down the phone.

At 30 knots, with the two outboards threshing the water at almost full power and without the partial sound screen afforded by the inboard tunnels, any reasonably up to date submarine lying within two or three hundred kilometres of their course should be able to hear them go by. But orders were orders. And Orville Steetley wouldn't be happy at his reactors and turbines having to run almost flat out for days on end even though he was inordinately proud that his babies could do just that. Again, orders were orders.

Orders. Point six, adopt Fire Lance land attack mode readiness on station. Land attack mode was the strategic mode, meant the four hundred nuclear tipped missiles with their four thousand kilometre range. It made him cold. It frightened him.

The bridge was pitch dark but for the instrument glows at the central consoles. Hardly guessable, all but invisible, there was a lookout perched on a stool at each forward corner, there was a seaman at the conning data repeat console, there was Villman at the bridge console running the watch. The slow acceleration up to 30 knots was already over, the ship was still riding motionlessly smooth over a flat calm sea. It was so utterly dark outside that the blast shutters might just as well have been lowered over all the bridge windows. There was no gleam of starlit sea, no sense of motion at all. Lt. Susan Bainbridge, Meteorology Officer, could see the Vindicator in her mind, silently sliding in under the dust veil.

"I can't see any stars at all now," the starboard lookout observed out of the blackness. "Not even the brightest."

"Same on this side, sir." The port lookout.

"That's it, then." Bainbridge walked across to the bridge console, homing on the instrument lights. "That can count as official. We're under the dust veil." Without aircraft, balloons or rockets to sound the stratosphere and give precise data on the density and thickness of the shroud, there were only two absolute measurements you could apply, two contours you could map. Given a cloudless troposphere beneath the veil, you could mark the point where you could no longer see the stars. And further in, where you could no longer see the sun.

She noted the position readout.

Villman's hand tapped the glowing figures in the dark. "That's five or six degrees further south than it was in the Pacific. It's going to cross the equator?"

"That's what they tell us. That's what it looks like." She turned away and left the bridge by the starboard rear door.

She ducked out through the blackout curtain and stood blinking in the cross corridor that ran between the rear of the bridge and the big retraction box for the main SPY-X12 radar. She crossed to the stairway head and paused. She would write in the meteorology log: at 2319 June 8 at 9°57'N latitude, Vindicator entered under the dust veil. It sounded final.

June 9

BOYCE GOT THE job of taking Jenninger and her team of three on a tour of the ship; it made an excuse to cancel his morning office hours and escape from the confines of his little day cabin. He decided to start at the bow and work aft: the first few things he would just tell them about, not show them.

The bow sonar. It was a water-filled and sound transparent bulge under the bow with an all-round sonar transducer inside that could send its sound pulses out and down into the surrounding sea and listen for the return echo from anything that was there—a wet radar. The transducer itself could be retracted back inside the hull proper to protect it from the shock wave of a nuclear blast. Being most of three hundred metres forward from the screws it had a good local area response— the churning propellors didn't drown it out. Then, just aft of the sonar housing, the twin bow thrusters that helped manoeuvre the long and slender vessel in port, and that ensured she was still steerable even if some close water burst smashed all three stern rudders.

They walked aft from the bow on 3rd platform, one deck down below the waterline. They passed the mounting supports and magazine feeds for the forward Mk56 155mm Automatic Gun, walking along accommodation corridors all the way. The assignment of cabins—that was done basically according to the wishes of the prospective occupants. With a mixed sex crew you couldn't rationally attempt any regime other than freely allowed sexual relationships. Only the Captain lived fully above all that in splendid celibacy—which really wasn't so much of a disadvantage, because with a two-to-one sex ratio there was always a little healthy tension in the air. The only place where a single sex machismo lingered was inside the little world of the aircrew. All 10 of the F-28 pilots and all 24 Wolfmarine pilots and observers were male.

They passed the hoist for the forward DPAD Seastrike mounting. Dual Purpose Area Defence—the Seastrike was more than three tonnes of missile and booster with a range of 140 kilometres. It flew at Mach 2.8—almost three times the speed of sound—against either air or surface targets. It was self-homing, using the self-contained radar in its nose: it had to be, since at anything much above forty kilometres away either a very low flying aircraft or a tall-towered ship would be right over the horizon as seen by the Vindicator's radars.

Every twenty metres the already narrow corridor squeezed right down to an open doorway piercing a massive bulkhead, one of the crosswalls dividing the ship into sections. The doors could be closed manually, at Condition 1 they were closed remotely from Damage Control. They were watertight, smoke tight, fire-proof, blast-proof. If they ever had to pass through one of these doors when it was closed, *check it closed again behind them*. Each door was electrically powered and should close and dog itself automatically—but look round and make sure that it did! You could be saving the ship, and your own life.

They came to where the useful deck area was pared right down between the port and starboard Fire Lance hoists outboard and the vertical hoist for the centreline mounted Rayflex-2 NBMD, the Naval Ballistic Missile Defence, the thing that protected them against re-entering warheads during a nuclear strike. It was six and a half metres long, it flew at a maximum Mach 5.5, it took off at a terrifying thirty gee straight up. It could intercept a re-entry vehicle by the time the thing had plunged down to a mere forty thousand metres—up there in the high stratosphere. The idea was to blow the attacking warhead apart before it could trigger its own thermonuclear charge.

They went down onto the Fire Lance storage decks.

On 3rd, 4th and 5th platforms the storage decks ran aft for sixty metres, flanking the support box for the C3-Complex. On each deck, six ten-metre bays one behind the other, in each bay twelve of the Fire Lance vehicles with launch booster ready attached, sleeping in long shock-cushioned cradles, wings and tail fins folded, waiting. Seventy two missiles to a deck, three decks port and three decks starboard, a total of four hundred and thirty two Fire Lances. Sixteen of them were adapted as vehicles to carry a Mk72 anti-submarine torpedo, could fly out to one hundred and fifty kilometres and then drop the torpedo into the water right on top of a located submarine. Sixteen more could carry half a tonne of high explosive out to five hundred kilometres, searching for and then attacking any enemy ship they found. The rest were for the land attack mode, the strategic mode. The Fire Lance wasn't fast, just a jet propelled cruise missile with a subsonic speed of one thousand and fifty kilometres an hour and a range of four thousand kilometres. But it flew almost down on the ground, it was packed with electronic countermeasures to help it evade radars that tried to locate it and weapons that tried to bring it down. It had real survivability, it was nothing like its simplistic Tomahawk predecessor at all.

The missile storage decks made an awful brooding place. They left them, going down on 4th and 5th platforms on the centreline forward of the C3 box. That was where the nuclear warheads were stowed ready for vehicle assignment if a strike was set up. Four hundred thermonuclear warheads with yields ranging from 100 to 250 kilotonnes, a total yield of seventy megatonnes, each warhead due to be delivered to within half the length of a tennis court from its designated target by a Fire Lance vehicle. The warheads had to be stowed separately from their carriers because the steady radiation they produced would over time degrade and damage the microcircuits in the Fire Lance's guidance and control systems—the computation that gave the missile both its survivability and its accuracy. Fire Lance lived on its electronics.

Down on 5th platform they turned aft into the support box for the C3-Complex, the ship's isolated vertical stack of command and control and communications functions. They walked in line, heads bowed, through a dense regimented forest of gleaming hydraulic cylinders and fabric shrouded suspension springs. The C3 isolation box itself sat inside a support frame on this massive array of shock dampers and return springs which allowed it to make a retarded bounce up or down of at the most one metre either way, and then brought it back to its rest position. The support frame was in turn mounted on bearings and surrounded by lateral shock dampers and return springs, so that it could displace a metre in any direction sideways or fore and aft. Not that the C3 box in the middle of its giant suspension actually displaced in its own right. It was the whole ship that would bounce around it if a close nuclear air burst or water burst came in. The suspension was there to smooth out the horrendous shock of the input energy, thus maximizing the chances of survival of the people and the key computer and control equipment inside the box. Elsewhere on the ship the only safety was to be found in the green deck areas—that had already been explained to them, hadn't it? When the ship closed up at Condition 1, they were to run direct to the canteen on 1st platform forward of the C3 box. The whole canteen was a green deck area, was the place where the damage control parties would assemble.

Here underneath the box they were standing on 5th platform, and 5th platform was really the inner skin of the double hull. Below them was only the baseline, the forty centimetres of outer hull armour, and then just ocean rushing past. The whole of the double hull, bottom and sides, was built up in a box-cell structure for maximum toughness and rigidity. The entire structure from stem to stern, from baseline to tower top, was designed to withstand the most enormous forces without collapsing. Some box-cells in the baseline were used for water and aviation fuel storage, but their function was strength, and to ensure only the most limited flooding if the outer hull was ruptured. They made the Vindicator essentially impregnable to conventional weapons. They made for an incredible labyrinth down there inside the baseline—all the box-cells were interconnected. You could get lost in there.

They came out from under the C3 box aft and passed the Midships Position Sonar. The MSP Sonar was fully retractable, transducer and streamlining dome and all, making it even more likely to survive a nuclear burst than the bow sonar. But it was only half as far away from the noisy screws, and so didn't hear so well in the water. The ship had its own hydrophones, too, line arrays all along the sides and bottom of the hull, listening microphones that could produce a fantastic sensitivity when coupled with a computer to clean up their response signals.

They went through under the Air Group weapons stores decks between the after ends of the Fire Lance decks, climbed up two ladders and went further aft through another tunnel door. This time they were in the centreline corridor that divided the reactor isolation box in two. This isolation box took up the full width of the ship under the hangar, it contained No1 reactor port and No2 reactor starboard. They looked through inspection windows into the containment rooms, saw the twin silent hearts of the ship. It was so utterly unspectacular, the reactor vessels, the pump housings, the heat exchangers. Two hundred atmospheres pressure and two hundred degrees centigrade inside those cooling circuit pipes. It looked too peaceful, too clinical for such forces.

They went aft through the crosswall bulkhead and into the next isolation box, the turbine room. It was a clean and gleaming space barely populated by technicians—all the controls were far away inside the C3 box on 1st platform. There were the huge series turbines humming unmodulated songs of power, there were the steam condensers and return pumps, the standby gas turbines with massive reduction gearing, the header ends of the transmission trains. They went through the last crosswall into the last isolation box, the service equipment space. It was a much narrower box because they were so near the stern and because there were more Air Group stores decks port and starboard. Here there were electric generators hooked to the transmission trains, plus standby diesel generator drives. The place was packed solid, but they could see that the floor was much higher than the other boxes. Underneath it were the twin tunnels for the inboard screws.

The Vindicator had four screws, the outboard two regular water screws, the inboard pair housed inside huge six metre diameter tunnels. The arrangement had two advantages. First, when they were cruising at 17½ knots or less, they could let the outboard screws idle silently and use the inboards to do all the work. Being enclosed in ducts, those generated far less noise and made it difficult for a submarine to hear the ship at long range. Further, the tunnels could be closed off at both ends by armoured louvres. A close water burst that might shear away the outboard screws would leave the inboards untouched—the ship could still manoeuvre freely at up to half speed. The Vindicator had three rudders, a pair right aft aligned with each of the outboard screws for maximum turning effect, and a centreline rudder extending behind the openings of the paired tunnels. Even if all three rudders were lost the ship could still steer with the aid of the bow thrusters. The Vindicator had as much survivability as you could build.

They went through into the stern area, getting lost among the huge actuators for the rudders and between the magazines for the stern weapon mountings. They came up onto the stern deck at main deck level.

There was wind and there was no sun. It was a dull and gloomy light under a uniformly dull grey sky—an absolutely featureless sky, not like a cloud roof. It was around midday in the northern tropics in summer, it wasn't exactly cold because of the cushioning effect of the heat stored in the ocean surface waters and continuously given up to the air, but they felt it in their on-board clothing, Boyce in shirt and teeshirt, the others in jackets or tunics and shirts. The wind was coming in over the starboard bow. They needed the shelter afforded by the near vertical afterslope up to the flight deck.

Above them on the stern deck was the aft Mk56 155mm gun mounting. Its single barrel could fire a round every three seconds out to a maximum range of 27 kilometres, and put one round neatly on each corner of a baseball diamond. It was for use against attacking aircraft and against any surface vessel that somehow got that close. Squeezed in between the 155 and the afterslope was the aft Seastrike launcher. Because it was a vertical launch system it could fire missiles to engage targets anywhere around the ship, just as the 155 could train through a full circle and fire its shells over the top of the tower. They merely had two of everything for added security. On each side of the stern was a set of four tubes for the Mk72 ASW torpedoes, little three-metre things, each weighing just three hundred kilogrammes. They weren't there to engage submarines. Submarines weren't supposed to get that close, submarines should go down to 72s delivered on top of them by Fire Lances or by the Wolfmarine ASW helicopters. The Mk72s on the stern were to intercept torpedoes. A long range torpedo running deep and armed with a thermonuclear warhead would sink even the Vindicator if it got to within a few hundred metres. The 72s had to be capable of making torpedo-to-torpedo intercepts and kills.

They went right to the stern, to the flimsy double strands of safety wires strung taut between steel stanchions. Below them boiled the monstrous churning wake. 56,000 tonnes of ship travelling at 30 knots—it moved mountains of roaring water. A black line trailed down from a stern port below them and cut into the foaming white water. It was the Surtass line, the surface towed array. It trailed hydrophone lines down deep in still water far astern of the ship, super-sensitive ears untroubled by the drowning tumult of the ship's screws; it was the Vindicator's main anti-submarine area defence in open water where sound travelled through the ocean for as far as you could hear.

Above them on the outer corner of the afterslope was one of the Skyfires, the Close-In Weapons System. It would engage attacking missiles that came inside its range, one thousand five hundred metres down to just five hundred. A supersonic attacker would cross that gap in just a second or two, allowing minimum time to destroy it. The Skyfire's Gatling cannon fired sixty rounds a second to do the job, each a subcalibre bullet of pure uranium—*uranium* bullets, maximum density so as to do maximum kinetic damage when one hit a missile head on.

They went through an armoured door in the afterslope and into the aircraft hangar, a single space a hundred metres long and more than thirty wide. It was busy, there was constant maintenance and servicing activity here. They walked between the rows of parked aircraft, eight F-28 Skycats on one side with their outboard wingtips folded up, ten Wolfmarines on the other with their six rotor blades bundled together and their tail pylons folded double. The Skycats were beautifully ugly-sleek things, the Wolfmarines just mean machines. They walked right forward to the twin main elevators blocking the width of the ship. The port was up, the starboard down. They rode the elevator with one of the remotely piloted Skyhook helicopters, a little thing complete with spider legs and the huge can of a SCAN surveillance radar fitted under its belly, on its way out to relieve the Skyhook presently flying airborne early warning station on the bow.

The big elevator brought them up inside the elevator box, the hollow rear half of the ship's superstructure. An F-28 waited armed on the port elevator, its pilot already in the cockpit. The two giant roll-up doors were open on the gloomy darkening day—they needed the doors and the whole armoured box around them to protect the elevators against the shock wave from an air burst. The elevators weren't secure, they would either buckle and jam or else collapse and let the ripping blast into the ship.

A tractor towed the Skyhook out onto the flight deck, they followed and stood beneath the overhang of the TLCP. Two Wolfmarines were armed and ready to go on the starboard side aft, halfway back port was a waiting F-28, already hooked up to the catapult and pointing at the takeoff ramp. The Skyhook came to howling little life and hopped up into

the sky, into the dark and gloomy sky. Far away from the
ship the world was dim, too dim to make out the horizon.

Boyce led them forward, round the port side in the lee of
the elevator box. The free deck was only two metres wide,
was narrowed to half that by the locker boxes containing
inflatable life rafts, was lined by the same flimsy two strands
of safety wire, with a twelve and a half metres drop over the
side into rushing water. Thirty knots—the water down there
was going past faster than the surrounding street when you
drove in a city. If you went over the side you wouldn't have
time to drown. You would be sucked into the screws.

They came to the broader deck apron beside the forward
superstructure, stood inside a towering angle of blank grey
steel. Up above was the edge of the rooftop forest of radomes
and communications and electronic warfare antennas. Everything could be pulled back inside the armoured roof for
protection, everything was doubled and trebled in case a
system was wrecked. The main radars, the SPY-X12s up
behind the bridge and the TLCP, the SPY-X10As fore and aft
of the tower base, were multimode phased array antennas
each capable of scanning and simultaneously tracking and
illuminating multiple targets across ninety degrees of sky—all
done by the miracles of frequency discretion and computerized beam scheduling, all in the service of the SADIS in the
Combat Information Centre.

They stopped at the lopped pyramid of the port Arrowflash
launcher. The Arrowflash was for point air defence against
missiles and aircraft, it had a ten kilometre range, it hit three
and three quarter times the speed of sound. In the overlapping
defence fields system built around the ship, it was the outer
ring against anti-ship missiles with the Skyfire as backup and
the 155 gun as supplement, and it was the inner defence
against nuclear warheads reentering from space and dropping
down on them, backing up the Rayflex. It was the oldest
system on the ship, the one scheduled for replacement by the
Hilite laser. That wouldn't happen now.

The port forward Skyfire CIWS was being put routinely
through its paces by someone in the Weapon Systems Control
Room. It popped down under its protective hatch and then
popped up again, it trained and elevated, whipping round and
stopping dead, tonnes of metal and mechanics as agile as a
ballerina, a supreme machine.

Jenninger was looking at him wryly. "Commander, you really like this ship, don't you?"

Boyce adjusted his glasses, middle finger pushing briefly at the bridge. He smiled. "I like it. It's the most wonderful possible toy any kid ever imagined, and I get to play with it. I like it."

Forward, right at the bow and marching slowly aft towards them, the washdown sprays fired fountains. Curtains of sea-water cascaded down on the forward deck, spray plumed out past them to port. On a real day it would have made bars of rainbow colours like some magical aurora stolen from the Northern Lights.

"That's the washdown starting a test," he said. "We can swill off every square inch of the ship, wash off fallout deposition. It's going to get wet. Better get inside. Pity."

Raffles looked around her at the gloomy awful midday, darkening. She hugged herself. "It's cold out here. It's getting cold."

The Navigation Centre, on 02 level inside the C3-Complex box. They stood at the chart table with transparent sheets spread over its internally illuminated surface, Bedford, Ruth Crimmin, and Lt. Jud Visser, the Navigating Officer with Fire Lance Support responsibility. The problem was navigating accuracy. The MAPS system was out, its satellites all dead or downed, and now that they were under the dust veil they were denied sun and moon and star sightings. They could do wonders with the inertial navigation system, of course, but they needed checkpoints—either land or ocean floor features—to correct the cumulative error that inevitably arose. And the course taking them up towards their stationing area in the IUK Gap had been deliberately chosen to keep them out in the middle of the Atlantic Ocean, out of range of any routine radar fixes on passing shorelines, well away from any remnant inshore navies belonging to who knew what newly unfriendly nations. The Vindicator had no surface or submarine or air support. If he ran into a Soviet surface group or submarine group Bedford wanted to be able to turn away rather than being forced to fight his way through. He wanted sea room, a big demand in modern war. Sea room used to mean enough open ocean so you could disappear over the horizon as seen from the top of a thirty metre mast, plus enough wind to get you out of sight. Nowadays, with radar and sonar and air cover it meant hundreds of kilometres.

Unfortunately, the inevitable cumulative error had to be corrected once they got up into their stationing area. The Fire Lances needed to know their launch point exactly if they were to ever enter their programmed-in courses from the initial timing control point right to the target. If they didn't know precisely where they started from, they would never find their initial timing control point and would automatically abort—drop out of the air.

"There's no problem when we get to the Gap?"

Crimmin shook her head. "Not once we're there, there isn't."

"There's no shortage of fixed points." Visser waved his hand over the back-lit chart. "The Orkneys, the Shetlands, the Faeroes, Iceland. Lumps of rock like Rockall. Up there we're okay."

"Would you prefer an interim ocean floor fix? Timewise we can afford a detour to a feature to put the sonar on it."

Crimmin tapped the chart. "There's this seamount coming up just to the east of our course right *here*. But I don't think we need it. Jud?"

Visser shook his head. "Our error's still less than a couple of kilometres. Too small to matter."

"We can pass that up okay."

Bedford nodded. "Good. I don't want to shout through the sea with the sonar unless I have to. Okay, we'll go straight for the Gap." He caught Crimmin's eye and nodded towards the door.

They went out, leaving Visser to fold away the charts. They stopped in the narrow little corridor leading forward from the Air Operations Centre towards the outer tunnel door. No one else in the little space squeezed between Navigation and Sonar. Bedford glanced at his watch: twenty after six.

"Just a word, Ruth—Culbertson and Craze will be waiting outside my quarters already. Just so you know why."

Ruth Crimmin finished closing the Navigation door. "Yes?"

"The check is because—when we reach the stationing area we go to Fire Lance readiness."

"Oh." She looked along the little passageway, then back at his face. "The Russians haven't started anything again?"

"I don't believe so. Not from what I know."

"Are we starting?"

Bedford shook his head. ''The United States of America doesn't start wars. You don't mess with us, but we don't start first.''

He went out of the C3 box into the 02 level cross corridor, and up one level to where they were waiting outside his day cabin.

''No,'' Gloria Craze was saying, ''I haven't picked up any untoward reactions. I've been snooping around the ship all day, eavesdropping in the canteen. The main topics of interest seem to be Jenninger and her team, the conditions outside, and the fact that we might be heading for action. Which is what you'd expect.''

''How do they feel about it?'' Bedford had his legs crossed, had his left arm stretched out along the back of the couch. Funny how he always adopted that position when he sat on one of the paired couches in his day cabin, as if he wanted to demonstrate how relaxed he really was. For the sake of everyone else on the ship, the Captain has to be visibly at ease with the situation. ''How are they reacting to the prospect?''

''They're not exactly thrilled, if that's what you mean. They're taking it seriously. But I get no sense of gloom or discontent. The only thing that surprises me is that no one's going out on deck to look at the dust veil. We never went this far in under it while we were up in the Pacific.''

''Surprises you?'' Andrew Culbertson was the ship's Medical Officer, was a lieutenant commander, one rank higher than Craze and two lower than Bedford. He was forty one, compact and solid looking; he seemed to fend off a latent gloominess with perpetual good humour. You almost had the impression he might be one of those doctors who got merrier the sicker you were. ''We never had any real daylight, and since noon it's just got darker. Now it's pitch dark outside.'' He waved a hand happily at the painted metal walls. ''And the temperature's dropping by the hour. Some time tomorrow we're going to have to issue the flight deck crews with winter clothing.''

Bedford smiled, patted the back of his couch with his outstretched left hand. ''John's already taken care of that. Parkas, boots and gloves. There'll be a general issue tomorrow.''

''Andrew won't need any,'' Gloria said. ''He never goes on deck any more anyway.''

Culbertson shrugged. "I might have to. Who knows? Accidents happen. Sick call was more eventful than it's been for days. A seaman bruised his fingers shoving sea-to-air-missiles around on the armaments decks. Otherwise nothing."

"You haven't picked up any worries?" Bedford asked.

"Nothing at all. There's never anything to get excited about. The most use I am is for giving contraceptive advice and checking people's teeth."

"You're really worried about suicides recurring, aren't you, sir?" Gloria Craze shook her head. "I don't think there's a risk of that. The previous five were all one after another in a quick rush, and they were because people were suddenly having to absorb what had happened. The real, the unbelievable—the great big God awful nuclear war. But now that shock is over. The climate situation will depress them, but they've had plenty of time to adjust to it. No one will be shocked into unstable acutely depressive responses. And they all have real work to do again, full defence readiness inside a war zone. Keeping busy is the best thing."

"Good," Bedford said. He stood up, and that was the end of the interview. They followed him to the door, which he opened in impeccable style for them, and Culbertson decided to play gentleman and send Craze out first. Then Bedford planted his afterthought. "Oh, lieutenant. There's still one thing I'd like to check with you. Just take a couple of minutes."

Culbertson smiled, departed. Bedford closed the door again, nodded towards the two couches. Gloria resumed her seat once more, Bedford sat down again, crossing his legs and adopting his relaxed posture.

"Sir?" It couldn't be about Andrew. The Captain was far too skilled to let someone know that he was going to ask the ship's psychologist about them.

"Boyce," Bedford said. "I'd like to ask for your assessment again. The crew's only been together for a few months. I haven't had the chance to really get to know my people, to predict how they'll behave under pressure. How do the behaviour experts assess him? How will he hold up under stress, or if we get a launch order for the Fire Lance? Firing those things can kill an awful lot of people. It's a terrifying responsibility."

Gloria shrugged. "Boyce is a technician. A super-technician. He's job dedicated—about as dedicated as possible. If we got a firing order he'd go right ahead and do it. I don't think he has no imagination or no political awareness, but he doesn't seem to be interested in all of that. He got his promotions and this posting on the strength of his pure unshakeable technical efficiency. He's the perfect man for the machine. Ah—you should be careful on how I report on his assessment. How I phrase it, I mean. I should admit I don't find him particularly sympathetic, don't completely like him, somehow. That might always colour what I say. He's an utterly reliable first officer, I believe. Certainly as long as he isn't given anything way out to do without the chance to think through how it works first.''

''Oh that's fine, just fine. The first officer's job is to hold the fort coping with the expected while the captain tries to figure out the unexpected. Otherwise one or other of them is a waste of taxpayer's money. And me. What about me?''

''Sir?''

''What are my weaknesses?'' He was looking right at her, as if pretending they were talking about someone else.

''Weaknesses, sir? They had an awful lot of captains to choose from when they appointed one to this ship. They'll have picked what they wanted. An exact fit.''

Bedford shook his head. ''No individual matches ideal parameters exactly. So what are my weaknesses?''

Dammit, in a moment she was going to shift uncomfortably in her seat like some kid in school. ''Well—if anything you're a potential depressive, and any creeping depression would undermine your motivation and therefore your dedication. But all good captains are potential depressives. A captain has to have a highly developed sense of responsibility, and to get that he has to be capable of sustained worry about everything under the sun. Which isn't possible without introspective and potentially depressive tendencies. A captain has to like worrying. That's normal.'' No, it wasn't like being some kid in school again, it was like college. The class had played through group therapy, and when she was on the receiving end all the whites had started grilling her on whether she thought her reactions to her were primarily influenced by the fact that she was black.

''Did the fact that I'm a potential depressive show as a consequence of the death of my wife and daughter?''

She glanced at the framed picture on the wall beside the entrance door—a smiling woman with her arm round the shoulders of a smiling skinny girl. ''No. That was known from the start of your career. Personality tests, observation and so on. But the tragedy did show that you can *control* the potential depressiveness. The test scores a year after the crisis and right through the last three years show no significant changes. Not on my assessment, anyway.'' Why were they there on the wall? Gayleen Bedford, died aged 39 and Linda Bedford, aged 12. Both killed in an air crash right after takeoff at San Diego. Bedford's cruiser was due to put in at Seattle and they were on their way to meet him as a surprise. Four years ago—it was all in the file on her office computer. But why were they on the wall? Why not in his sleeping cabin or standing on his desk over there and facing him as he worked, private glances between himself and the lost dead past. Why did they hang on the wall, watching over and policing the whole space of the cabin? She looked at Bedford. ''Why are you asking me, sir?''

Bedford stroked the back of the couch with his left hand, watched his hand stroke the couch, fingertips catching the fabric. ''Like everyone else in this position, I've necessarily had to face up to what nuclear weapons can do. That is, collateral effects beyond the taking out of military targets. Suddenly it wasn't theory any more, was it?'' He patted the couch in apology, looked round at her again. ''Sometimes I wonder if I'll hold up and cope with doing my duty here if it ever comes to it. Defending the ship is no problem. But launching a nuclear strike is something else.''

Something else altogether. ''You believe in deterrence?''

''If I didn't I could never have countenanced spending my entire career nursing nuclear weapons. If they didn't have a deterrence value they would be unthinkable.''

''And then it didn't work in the end. It finally happened after all. That's a shock to have to accommodate, isn't it?''

''Oh it worked. Nuclear deterrence kept the peace longer than ever before, gave the politicians time to at least try and sort things out. Maybe the politicians failed. At any rate, the crisis management skills obviously broke down for that critical little bit too long, and we got the God awful war. But the inherent deterrent force has still worked. The war has stopped again with plenty of weapons unfired. Because, for instance, this ship is still around and backing up the missiles in silos ashore. Deterring further madness.''

So that was what was helping him go on despite what had happened to the world, helping him keep sane and under control. Keep alive. He was certain, to his own satisfaction, that by doing his ready defined duty he was helping both to prevent things from getting any worse and even to lay the necessary groundwork for them to ever get better—a cessation of hostilities that would permit both sides to try and do something about the mess. His ship and his running of it, and therefore *himself*, were a counter in the strategic game of peacekeeping, were serving the world. The ship and its functioning were as valid as they had been before the war. The war was a ghastly mistake and that was that.

"One thing I always used to think, sir. All those other people—on the other two Nemesis ships, in the Trident boats, the old Tomahawk system cruisers, the Army people in their silos and the Air Force people in their delivery aircraft. People exactly like you and Boyce—and me, because I'm part of the machine. All the Russians in all their ships and silos. I never really could bring myself to believe they'd do it, they'd press all their buttons when the order came through. Not normal people like you and me. I still can't believe it. It happened, and I still can't believe we didn't have more sense."

Bedford just looked at her, quietly.

The phone buzzed. It buzzed on his desk, and it buzzed faintly beyond the closed door to his sleeping cabin.

Bedford stood up and crossed to the desk. Standing, he picked up the phone. "Bedford."

"Korsyn, sir. In the CIC." Lt. Cmdr. Ray Korsyn, Chief Weapons Officer, taking a turn at directing the Combat Information Centre. "A few minutes ago Communications picked up a transmission from our vicinity. We only have a poor triangulation on it from the ship and the bow station Skyhook because it came from an inopportune direction. The signal came from two hundred ten degrees, range about one thousand kilometres."

210° put it at 30° west of their course, back the way they had come. "Identification on the transmission?"

"Electronic Warfare think so, sir. It's on a frequency band used by the Soviets for naval traffic. The carrier frequency and modulation and the sideband characteristics—EW are fairly sure it was a Sparker Box."

Sparker Box was Nato's name for one of the newer communication systems the Soviets had put into some of their surface ships and submarines. There would be no chance of deciphering the signal, of course—it would be encrypted as securely as was their own communications traffic. So a ship or sub carrying Sparker Box, a thousand kilometres behind and around five hundred off to the west of their previous course. A submarine could have laid quiet and heard them thundering past at thirty knots, a ship could have picked up their SCAN radar while itself out of sight over the horizon if it had been flying passive antennas on a balloon or even a small RPV like a Skyhook. Then whatever it was that had caught them would have made distance out from their course and waited until they were far away again before risking a signal. For a small ship, the Vindicator was an overwhelming danger.

"Sparker Box." He said it for Craze's benefit, who was standing there now and wondering what to do. "We'll assume we've been picked up and are being tailed. If they happened to have a unit down here available, they'd certainly put it on our course to wait for us. There's been enough signals traffic from us to let them predict where we're heading. Okay, we assume we're not entirely alone any more."

"Yes, sir," Korsyn said. "Do you want to take any action?"

It was a long way out, a thousand kilometres—way beyond the maximum action radius of the Wolfmarines. He could still launch a strike with the F-28s, of course. That would make a mess of or even sink any Soviet surface vessel, but it might also cost aircraft and it would certainly cost time. And if it was a submarine that had just surfaced long enough to transmit, then the F-28s would find themselves burning fuel uselessly over empty sea. The only sensible offensive action would be to turn the ship around, but he had an urgent appointment in the north. "No, no action as yet. Just keep an eye on it from now on. Thanks for the call, Ray." He put the phone on the hook.

Gloria Craze had made for the door. "Better leave you to it, sir." She paused with the door open, a surprisingly sympathetic expression on her face. "Another worry, huh?"

Bedford gave her a weary, slightly theatrical smile. He was still smiling at the door when it closed. Gayleen and Linda smiled back at him, sideways out of the frame. The job in hand.

The oceans might be devoid of merchant shipping. Every vessel that could do so in time had scuttled back to port in the north, and was now either destroyed along with the harbours and docks, frozen in, or laid up without fuel oil or other supplies. Ships caught out at sea had fled south, harbours and anchorages down there were choked with impounded vessels owned or chartered by northern hemisphere companies. All of the northern navies not involved in the war were equally immobilized, while most of the Nato and Warsaw Pact warships had shot each other out of the water. The Vindicator was sailing a huge expanse of benighted North Atlantic, virtually devoid of shipping.

But not entirely empty.

June 10

JENNINGER AND CAUFIELD were hunched over coffee at a table in the corner of the canteen, talking quietly, earnestly. Cpt. Danella Raffles was with them, listening gloomily. They looked up at the interruption from Lt. Barbara Spirek, Senior Electronic Warfare Systems Officer. The Captain wanted to speak to them in the officers' mess right away. Spirek stood there and waited, obliging them to drink up their coffees and follow her immediately.

They went up from the canteen on 1st platform, through the main deck and onto 01 level. The officers' mess was forward of the wardroom on the starboard side. It was a large enough space, penetrated by heavy steel pillars supporting the armoured outer deck above. It had close little chair and couch groups like a very cramped and slightly VIP airport lounge, plus a pocket-sized pool table. There were altogether eighty two officers on the ship, but not many of them were to be seen relaxing during the shipboard morning. Department chiefs were busy in their hardware spaces or control centres or offices managing their territories, junior officers were on watch duty or else overseeing the never ending maintenance and servicing checks. There were just four pilots sitting around together, waiting on standby. Two of them had so many leads and tube connections sprouting from their flying suits that they had to be from the high performance Skycat jets. In the forward outboard corner was a boxed intrusion complete with access doors—the retraction space for the Skyfire CIWS starboard forward mounting. The only real bit of luxury was a hard carpet laid in tiles, and some cladding around some of the ceiling service ducts. Not much cladding—it tended to be plastic, and plastics spew toxic fumes when they burn.

Sitting at one of the three-sided couch groups were Bedford

and Boyce, together with Lt. Cmdr. Warren Lister, the Missile Control Officer—the man who ran the Fire Lance functions. Jenninger and Caufield and Raffles joined them: so it wouldn't be crowded Spirek hauled up a couple of free standing chairs. Drexel appeared at the door to the officers' mess, delivered by a petty officer. Boyce beckoned him to join them.

"The ship has been located by a Soviet vessel and the information passed on to their command," Bedford explained flatly. "We intercepted the signal and got a triangulation on the source—around a thousand kilometres approximately south-southwest behind us. The transmitter type confirms that it was either a submarine that surfaced to send the signal, or a small surface ship. We're making thirty knots due north, so at that distance and position the vessel is no danger to us. Not directly."

"A surface ship?" Jenninger looked sceptical. "I suppose a submarine could hear us go past at a distance. But wouldn't we have seen a surface ship if it saw us?"

"Not if it was right over the horizon as seen from our SCAN. Say at least two-forty kilometres further out to make sure even its tower top was out of sight."

"How would it see us, then?"

Bedford glanced at Spirek, so Spirek answered. "Basically by picking up our SCAN radar. For that they'd need a Red Balloon—that's the Nato designation. That's a tethered balloon made of synthetic fabric with a carbon-fibre reinforced cable, so it's radar transparent, so our SCAN wouldn't see it. Otherwise they'd need a Fat Fly, an RPV just like our Skyhook, all synthetics except the motor so it also produces a very small radar profile indeed. On both of those things they can fly a Hanging Basket, a surveillance radar like our SCAN, but we'd have noticed that. So instead they must have been flying a passive EW receiving antenna. Then they'd have no problem spotting us, especially if they knew we were due to pass by."

"I have to assume other units will now try to pick us up," Bedford went on. "They have no visual or radar-equipped surveillance satellites left that could have tracked us across open ocean, with or without a dust veil. But we've been sending enough outgoing signals for them to have marked and predicted our approximate track, and they'll have had time to figure out exactly what we are—even though neither STRACC

nor CASAL have as yet sent us a single signal on Nemesis
reserved frequencies. They'll know how dangerous we are
and exactly where we're heading, so the next thing waiting
for us might try to engage the ship. To avoid the interception
I can neither turn back nor shut down the radars. We have to
get to the IUK Gap, we have to see what's going on around
us. What I have done is up our airborne early warning cover.
We now have three Skyhooks on station flying SCANs, one a
hundred kilometres on our bow, one each a hundred kilometres
out to port and starboard. At three thousand metres up they
can see a sea-level horizon at two hundred kilometres, so now
we can look ahead and on both sides out to three hundred
kilometres. My first question, Jenninger, is do you know of
any reason why we can't go right over to the western, to the
Iceland end of the IUK Gap? That way we can put a big
westward zag in the course and hopefully get around anyone
trying to line up and wait for us. The biggest worry is a
submarine lying stopped so we can't hear it dead on our
course. I'd like to avoid the risk."

"The Fire Lance," Jenninger said. "What does that do to
its effective range?"

"Warren?"

Warren Lister was a lean man in his later thirties, with
sandy hair and wrinkles around his eyes—wrinkles made
from narrowing his eyes in concentration, not from laughing.
"They have a four thousand kilometre range. From Iceland
they could penetrate into the USSR as far as Odessa, Gorky,
or the North Urals almost down as far as Sverdlovsk. All the
big western targets."

Jenninger nodded. "Then I see no objection to heading
towards the Iceland end of the Gap. Ah—you know there's
no possibility of friendly support. Keflavik was taken right
out."

"I know." Bedford turned to Spirek. "Tell the bridge I
want an immediate thirty degree turn to port. Then let
Crimmin's people know what's going on. The course adjustment we'll set up later."

"Okay, sir." Barbara Spirek stood up and left.

Bedford's eyes swept over Drexel, Caufield, Raffles, and
back to Jenninger. "My second question. Would you care to
tell me exactly what is going on? I need to know whether I
can expect the other side to watch us and get ready to pounce
at the first sign of our making trouble, or if they're just going

to hit us right off as soon as they get the chance. We're tough as hell, you understand—but we're not entirely unsinkable."

"What's going on is fluid, Captain." Jenninger settled in her seat as if most comfortable when implicitly challenged. A challenge meant she was worth challenging, was to be taken seriously. "Signals intelligence, such as it is these days, indicates that what's left of the Soviet command, control and communications structure has been doing its best to consolidate itself. There's also an apparent maintenance of the operational readiness of what forces still remain to them. Signal intercepts don't usually allow of decryption and translation, but the Soviets are sometimes a little backward and sloppy. It seems there's been some sudden changes and shake-downs in their command bunkers—something of an upheaval at some levels among the command personnel, including what few purely Politburo elements are known to be still in existence. It seems almost as if an internal purge has been going on."

"More or less the same as our side back home." Drexel smiled at Jenninger's expression. "Well I'd call it a purge."

The officers' mess tipped slightly, perceptibly around them, as if to emphasize how insecure the world can be. The Vindicator was heeling gently, coming slowly round at an implacable thirty knots.

Bedford found himself disliking Drexel. No one seemed exactly fond of him: the Englishman had taken to wandering round the ship wearing an old wind cheater and shabby cord jeans, out of place and remarkably defiant about it. Weren't the British supposed to have style or something? "So—ah—so the Vindicator is being moved up to remind the Soviets we still mean business. Because it looks as though they have every intention of emerging from the climate collapse with all the strategic potential they can put together still intact."

"Exactly, Captain." And Jenninger said it as though he'd done well to understand. He was getting to dislike her, too. "The posture they've adopted is a threat we can't possibly afford to ignore."

"Just like our posture," Drexel said. "For them, of course."

"Our posture is readiness." Caufield wanted to neutralize the remark, as if he saw himself as a mediator or moderator. "The idea is to be ready to knock them to hell if they try as much as whistle, but to exercise some common sense. We don't do anything if they don't start."

"Which brings us back," Jenninger said, "to why we're

on board. We're here to ensure that the Vindicator's Fire Lances can be fired to warn off any Soviet attack series if they really do try it—even if communications with both STRACC and CASAL are completely blacked out. We're also here to ensure the war-prosecutionists aren't tempted simply to order their pre-emptive Armageddon as soon as they have the means for it moved up into range. That is, this ship in the IUK Gap.''

"Armageddon?" Boyce asked. "Didn't we just have that?"

"No." Caufield shook his head. "Everything up to now has been your wars and rumours of wars all rolled into one. But the world hasn't quite come to an end yet and the opposing armies are still there. Only in bits and pieces, but still there. Armageddon is the absolutely final battle between good and evil, isn't it? The one where evil gets wiped out once and for all, if you believe any of this Christian crap.''

"The war-prosecutionists belong largely to those people who used to equate Soviet Communism with incarnate evil." Jenninger shook her head. "I doubt that's very respectable theology. But they want to go for their final eradication option—the final solution, you might say. They even call it the Armageddon option now.''

Bedford waved his hand dismissively. He no more wanted to get into a discussion of Moral Majority or Heritage Foundation theology than he was interested in the wranglings of crisis politics. He had more immediate worries. "I'll assume the Soviets are more likely to try taking us out the nearer we get. Is there anything you can tell us about their naval and air capabilities in the North Atlantic theatre?''

Caufield shrugged. "They won't have much. That's for sure.''

"During the conventional European phase they came round North Norway from the Kola area," Drexel said. "I don't mean the Northern Fleet just deploying forward to the GIUK Gap to interdict the transatlantic ferry routes. I mean land forces hopping down the Norwegian coast with sea and air support.''

"They'll have needed forward bases fast," Boyce said. "Support for their naval units.''

Drexel nodded. "Exactly. Our forces were operating close to home, and theirs weren't. They came round in force on land and got as far as Tromso before the big carve up in the North Atlantic really got under way. Then they managed to leapfrog some forces further down the Norwegian coast, at least as far as Bodo and probably a little further still. All that was achieved in just a few days. Then the nuclear balloon went up in Europe. Norway tried to arrange its own ceasefire and even threatened to turn what was left of its forces against Nato if Nato went for the Soviet presence along its coast with nukes, because then the Soviets would nuke *them*.''

"They were fuck all use when it mattered," Caufield muttered.

"Perhaps." Drexel shrugged. "Pity nobody else but the French caught on to the idea. We might not have had a global war after all."

"Did they establish forward bases?" Bedford asked.

"That we don't know. They overran positions by force in just a few days, so the places where they tried to establish themselves will have been badly war damaged—airstrips and harbour facilities bombed out, and so on. They were certainly trying to move supplies into a few places by sea and air, but they took an awful lot of interdiction from our forces, and then the Big Freeze closed in and all significant supply movements will have stopped immediately. All we can say for sure is that they probably still have a few toeholds on fjords up there and that the North Atlantic Drift is still probably delivering enough warm surface water to keep them ice free. If they managed to move in a few bits and pieces of stores anywhere—beyond what they'll have needed just to keep the troops there alive—then there's always a chance that they've managed to establish some aircraft in the area. They might even be able to keep one or two naval units supplied or at least ready for sea without having to rely on what's left of the bases right back on the Kola Peninsula."

Bedford nodded. Vague but at least of some help—so the Englishman had his uses after all. "And the Baltic Fleet?"

"I think that's no threat. All the Baltic Fleet bases were destroyed, almost all its units were confirmed sunk in the Baltic or out on forward deployment in the Atlantic. There weren't many of those—the war blew up so damned unexpectedly that most of the Baltic Fleet was lost trying to fight its way through to the Atlantic theatre. Anyway, our information is that the Baltic is now frozen over right out to the Kattegat or whatever it's called between Denmark and Sweden. The only thing that might come from that direction

would be any aircraft they could get their hands on that still
happened to work.''

Bedford nodded again. If there was going to be no support
from US or other Nato forces, at least it was a comfort to
know the other side was in just as much of a mess. More or
less.

"Was that it, Captain?" Jenninger looked satisfied.

"One more question. You wouldn't care to tell me what's
in these coded signals you're getting every twelve hours or so
now?''

Jenninger shook her head. "Just purely political situational
updates, Captain. That's all. Strategic or tactical intelligence
will always be passed direct to you.''

Gloria Craze had a cabin on main deck, starboard side, one of
the identikit single-berth officer cabins. That was her private
world where no one was allowed: the intrusion of the phone
was often resented, but the ship's address was always toler-
ated, even when it woke her in the night. After all, the
broadcast announcement might suddenly turn out to be the
foreplay to her own death.

Her office was her professional hideaway, open during the
morning to anyone who called—not that there were all that
many callers, a couple a week at the most. Her office was on
1st platform, starboard side, outboard of the C3-Complex
box. You came along the corridor there from forward, went
past the access door to the Arrowflash hoist on the outboard
side, past the Chief Engineer's Office on the inboard side,
past the entry door to the C3-Complex—labelled Engines,
Reactor, Service Systems Control, Computer Area, Damage
Control—and the next door inboard was her office. Well,
box. It was the same modular size as the standard cabins, just
fitted out with cupboards and chairs and a tiny desk instead of
with a bunk and lockers and so on. It was where she worked
on the running record of the psychological state of the crew
so that Pentagon analysts could keep a monitoring eye on the
way the new professional crew-structuring principles worked
in practice—in this case in the maintenance of a strategic
system—and so that someone in the system could sound an
alarm if stress related abnormalities ever started to show in
the behaviour of, for example, the senior officers. It was also
the place where she spent a lot of the time reading and
studying, because her function was largely redundant on board.

And it was also the place where people could look her up if they ever wanted to talk about their worries or problems in private. That service wasn't much in demand—all personnel records went to a higher authority for assessment, didn't they.

Danella Raffles came in cautiously, sat down awkwardly. It isn't easy bringing your own private mess to display it to a stranger.

"You're the—ah—Pesonnel Advisement Officer? You look after the psychology on board?"

Gloria shrugged. "The psychology looks after itself. I just look on while it does so."

Raffles nodded, looking at the floor in front of the desk. Two black girls, one very obviously acutely unsure of herself and the other hoping she hides her insecurity well enough to get by: Danella Raffles in the Army's loose olive drag field uniform, Gloria Craze in the Navy's tailored khaki service dress. Gloria in short sleeves, Raffles with her sleeves rolled matter-of-factly to her elbows—with her forearms crossed over her stomach, defensively. And Raffles was miserable, visibly quite utterly miserable.

Well, you're supposed to do personnel advisement one way or the other, and you didn't study psychology and sociology specifically to reduce your level of human sympathy and understanding. So do something for the woman.

Gloria pushed back her chair from her desk and turned it half round. She let herself slump in it, one hand stretched out on the surface of the desk, the other hooked in the belt of her pants. It made her posture more welcoming, more relaxed—a standard trick. "Well—what can I do for you?" And smile.

Raffles shrugged, was still looking away at the floor. "It's kind of—it's kind of stupid. I keep getting these—dreams. I keep getting dreams."

"Dreams?" Remember that an adult has to get pretty upset before she or he runs to tell you about dreams. The embarrassment threshold is enormous. "They disturb your sleep?"

Raffles nodded.

This wasn't going to be easy unless she could get the woman to talk, make an officer's report or something. At least an Army captain ranks equally with a Navy lieutenant. There was an age difference, Raffles was three or four years older, and that might be problem enough. But she'd come along to talk in confidence, and that was the lever to pull. "I'm not a clinical psychologist, you understand? Not any kind of analyst. And no way am I a Freudian, someone who goes around interpreting dreams in terms of his own and Freud's sexual hangups and childhood traumas. I'm not any kind of *counsellor*—though I guess I'm the nearest thing there is these days to the old idea of a chaplain. I can't analyse dreams or cure problems. But I can listen. That's one of the jobs I'm here for.'' The woman still wouldn't look at her. ''So?''

''I don't need analysing.'' The voice was tiny and far away. ''I don't need the dreams analysing.'' Then she pulled herself together, quite literally pulled herself upright in her chair and threw a straight look across at Gloria. ''The dreams aren't really the problem. They're memories I don't want to see. They're not symbolic dreams or something. They're bits and pieces of things all jumbled up, real scenes or scenes just like the real thing. Things I experienced myself, or else bits and pieces put together from those experiences. They're just memories coming up again. Only I can't bear it. I can't bear to see it any more. And I don't know what to do. I'm afraid of going to sleep, but you have to sleep, don't you? You have to sleep.''

''How long have the dreams been going on?''

''Oh—for around three weeks now. They started up a while after I was brought inside to STRACC—to the Cheyenne Mountain Complex. They only came once in a while at first. But now they come more and more. Every night and now more than once every night. I always have to fight my way awake out of it. I—'' She shook her head, looking up at the narrow ceiling almost as if there might be a way out of the world. ''I can't bear to be made to see it all again. I just can't.''

''And they're—factual dreams? Basically memories, or closely based on memories?''

''Memories. What happened when the real war started. And after, when the Freeze set in and everything fell apart. All the time that I was still outside after the big events—it didn't seem to matter so much. Maybe I was under too much of a shock, at having to work too hard just to keep up with the job and stay alive. But it all started surfacing once I was inside. As if I was safe enough to react, almost.''

''And these memories—these things you don't want to have paraded in front of your eyes every night, as it were—they're from the period before you were posted into STRACC?''

"From the time when I was still outside, yes."

"And you know what they probably are, don't you? If an experience is sufficiently unpleasant for you to want to suppress it consciously, for you to want to escape from it—well then it's also sufficiently important for you to *have* to come to terms with it. People who've gone through really rough times sometimes find they have to suffer years of—well, mental torture—as a follow on. Disturbed sleep and insomnia, difficulties with interpersonal relationships, depression and so on. The only real help is to talk about it, to gradually accept it as a part of your own personal past—precisely so that it doesn't have to stay quite so alive in the present the whole time. Have you talked about it with anyone?"

"Some. Just a little. Everyone has their own story to sweat over. Or they're up to their eyes in work and worry."

"Well—how about making a start, Danella? That's your first name isn't it? I'm Gloria. How about making a start?"

Raffles drew a deep breath. She was looking at the anonymous floor again, getting ready to report. Another breath.

"I was attached to 6th Army HQ, the Presidio of San Francisco, California. I was in the contingency planning command. There'd been those renewed scares about civil defence measures, and since the HQ wasn't going anywhere in any war anyway, we made some civil defence support preparations. We even had winter kit stockpiled for some units so they could keep mobile and provide action backup for the National Guard in the event of an unusual cold spell—helping them with their primary job of maintaining order and supplying the civilian population. It was all based on any Nuclear Winter being a couple of cloudy weeks with a light frost day and night. Crop failure in summer and nothing worse. Well, when the nuke exchanges started up in Europe we went on dispersal alert, and I found myself attached to a couple of companies detailed to an out-of-town transport and supply park. Then of course the nukes came in over a whole string of days, and we sat tight ready to close up in huts and vehicles if fallout rolled over. But we were lucky with the winds and stayed clean. Then when California had taken its treatment and the strikes moved off east, we got back into the communications net that was being patched back together between the surviving units. That's when we learned that all major military installations and all the major cities in California had been taken out. There was confusion, there was chaos, and just a general lack of any information on the net.

"The CO decided we should try to get back into the big centres and see if we could help, so he detailed one of his companies, and since I was from HQ I tagged along. At first we'd seen a constant stream of people coming out from the big urban areas through the National Guard routes—controlling where they could go and how they behaved—but that had stopped. Now—this was a couple of days after the nuking—we found lots of people strung out along the roadways, fighting over any gas or food or water that was left. Some of them were obviously burned, or had radiation sickness. We kept having to shed troops and supplies at small towns along the way that were more or less intact, so as to keep them safe from damage and so as to force the inhabitants to take up and house the refugees. The people were terrified and shocked out of their wits, and were only interested in trying to look after themselves.

"We got north of San Jose, and were seeing more and more injured people, and above all dying and dead. The nukes had been going in all around the area and the initial fallout levels had been really high there. It was still warm then, and the bodies were pumping up and rotting. I've never seen such a thing. Thousands and thousands of dead. Men, women, old, young, kids, and dogs, cats, everything—lying in cars, near cars, under cars, or right in the middle of nowhere. And in houses, motels—hundreds of them clustered round looted motels. And everywhere just a few left alive, either injured, or sick and dazed with radiation sickness—right into the debilitating stages and starting to haemorrhage all over. And we had nothing to give them because there just wasn't the medical supplies available to waste on people who weren't worth helping.

"We never got near Frisco or Oakland. We came up on the hills about level with Palo Alto. We'd seen the huge roof of overcast rolling eastward days before, and now we saw where it was coming from. The whole area—the whole area was burning as far as you could see. Nothing but smoke curtains streaming slowly upwards, and more rising from the south towards San Jose.

"The thing is, a nuke creates so much blast from an air burst that it flattens things for kilometres around, just explodes them and sweeps them away. From the blast wave you get an enormous overpressure and then a split second later an enormous underpressure—wood frame houses disappear, the toughest concrete and steel buildings burst and disintegrate. People—well, people shielded from the flash and the thermal shock—they get their chests pulped and drown in their own blood. Close to ground zero—that's according to Japanese experience—I mean, we never went in to look for ourselves— closer to ground zero a person gets vaporized by the flash radiation, and a bit further out gets totally incinerated by the thermal shock. But that's all inside a few kilometre radius where the blast wave and the thermal wind are so intense they just demolish and incinerate and flash burn the air itself, and the oxygen goes and all you get is glowing rubble. Further out you still get gross and then gradually diminishing demo- lition, breaking things up nicely into ready made piles of firewood. Whatever material you have—even steel or concrete —it all burns and it burns *hot*. At a greater distance the flash radiation is still so intense it sets everything alight. Every- thing burns. And there's no water, because the ground- transmitted shock has smashed open all the mains and the stuff is flooding into the ground, and the pumping stations are out anyway, and there's no one in the least state to do anything about it. So you have raging fires and all the com- bustible material in the world—an entire outer city and sub- urbs, and orchards and woodland and everything, and dormitory commuter centres.

"And because the heat at ground zero is so intense, and because after the collapse of the fireball you get an extreme rising wind—all mushroom clouds go upwards—because of that the dynamic after effect of the blast is a strong surface wind blowing in towards the centre. And it gets heated all the way because of the fires, so it rises faster at the centre, so it pulls in oxygen-rich air faster and faster from the outside. *Everything* burns. You get a firestorm that makes Hamburg or Dresden or Tokyo look like a kiddies' bonfire, if you put a big enough nuke on a big city. The whole area, the whole city and outskirts, burns for days, for weeks until there's nothing left to burn. Except that the centre drawing in the wind, which gets heated all the way—it gets so hot that *everything* burns. I heard afterwards that observations taken by God knows what kind of dedicated people on some of the big-city burns confirm that it was so hot and so long lasting that eventually even the ground must have been burning. And that, this incredible furnace fed by what ends up close to like tornado winds, is what produces the plume.

"When you've seen that—when you've seen that. It's so broad and so high you can't see its shape at all. It's not like a *column* of smoke, it's like a wall. Some sort of wall of darkness—from close to sort of reaching halfway across the world. All you can make out is patterns of smoke clouds boiling up the face of it, and then you get some clue to the scale and you see just how big the patterns are and how fast they're rising. And it goes up and on up under this huge dark roof, until you can't see the detail any more as the stuff gets higher.

"And that's not even why you have your Nuclear Winter. The Winter would happen anyway. You can't explode a few thousand or more nuclear warheads all around the northern hemisphere—a few thousand of them in the lower atmosphere so they pick up millions of tonnes of debris and kick it right up into the stratosphere like the finest of dust, so it spreads on the winds up there and stays floating around and blocking the sun. You can't do that without getting one of your middle-severity climate collapse scenarios for real. But now the plumes from the big cities and such, they get so hot and energetic that a lot of the stuff they spew up as smoke particles also gets pumped right out of the troposphere where the weather is and up into the stratosphere to join the rest. So all the experts sitting in their deep command centres away from it all, they explain to you that's the reason why it gets worse and worse every time they get hold of any new data. There was far more stuff fired off up there than they originally predicted. They predicted! They knew basically it would happen, and they let it. They knew more or less how bad it would be, even if they miscalculated some effects. And they let it happen. They went right ahead and did it.

"We pulled back, because there was nothing we could do there. We tried picking up our own troop detachments we'd left along the way, but most of them had just disintegrated under the shock at the state things were in. Or else they'd been overwhelmed by bands of looters who could see the advantage of having some military equipment to help them survive at the expense of others. We pulled right back to our original dispersal base, where the CO had kept one company back to run the transport and supply park. We got ourselves into three firefights on the way—we lost lives when they attacked us, but then we always cleaned up against amateur civilians. What were we doing, *shooting* our own people? Had we been defending America and the whole Free West so we could shoot down our own people in the end instead of someone else doing it for us? They had to try to take us. They had no gas to get anywhere, no drinkable unfouled water supply, and disease boiling up all around. They had no food because all the food supplies went up with the stores and warehouses in the cities. They needed to get hold of our firepower so they could take what they needed from anyone else trying to get their hands on what was left. If I'd been in their state I'd have done it to us. What goddam use had the Army been to them anyway?

"We got back to the dispersal base—about a platoon strength of us left, along with the vehicles—and joined the other company there holding the perimeter and trying to cope with the people camping around outside. Those people were dying of starvation and disease, and they weren't going to wait much longer before they rushed us and tried to eat everything up at once instead of letting us portion it out. Whenever they had a turn at murdering each other there wasn't even anything we could risk doing about it. There'd be a fight and maybe a hundred left dead or dying—and sometimes someone would try dragging off the bodies, but first they always robbed them. They needed clothes, food, and it was cold at night. Most of the fights happened when new groups tried to join at the outskirts. They knew that the more there were, the less there'd be to go round. In the end we were just handing stuff out to those who could keep in the best positions—we didn't dare try going outside to distribute stuff more evenly.

"We tried to tell ourselves we were at least keeping some of them properly alive. Alive—you don't know. Upwards of three thousand people squatting right on the spot for fear of moving and getting squeezed out, and no sanitation, nothing. Upwards of three thousand people with dysentery. You can't imagine. Worse than pictures of the worst Third World refugee camp without the doctors, and all happened overnight. You just can't imagine the total collapse of all services, of the entire infrastructure of a society like ours. No food because no gasoline or people to farm the fields and such, and all the nation's food stocks gone with the cities. No water or sanitation. No doctors or nurses because they and their hospitals and practices were all burned in the cities. No medication for the same reason. They couldn't believe it outside, we couldn't inside. We had to just watch them dying and getting ready to take us with them. Our unit medic said he thought there was typhus and cholera out there, and any time we'd be coming down with it as well. Some of our guys were getting sick. The whole time we kept asking, begging for support—for supplies or whatever else they could arrange—and it was always nothing doing. Some signal stations started disappearing off the net. That lasted until the ninth day after the end of the big nuking on the West Coast. Apparently it was still going on elsewhere, and our side hitting the Soviets as hard—but all kind of petering out. Then the veil started coming over.

"It started with the sky all hazy and a kind of pale sun, with blood red sunrise and sunset. It was more pronounced every day. At first we thought maybe the wind had changed and it was the edge of the plume from the Los Angeles area coming over us, but we got plenty of information over the net. For a while people somewhere important were even taking notice of us, wanting weather reports and sky observations data so they could map what was going on. What was coming over us was Europe, or several million tonnes of it all spread out on the stratosphere winds, and as many millions of tonnes of the Soviet Union, all having got halfway round the world or more in a couple of weeks, and much more coming. Within three days you couldn't see the sun in the daytime, and it was getting gloomy right from sunup to sundown. And it was getting cold. The people outside made a first attempt to rush us, and we killed hundreds. Our CO yelled for 'copters to get us out and was told no dice. He was a major and he was the third highest ranking officer known to be still alive in California, and he could just stay put and do his duty. Then we got night frosts and some freezing rain. Then some daytime snow. We got cloud overcast, and it was really dim and a half dark under that underneath the dust veil.

"The CO decided we'd better get out before we couldn't even shoot our way clear. We loaded food and fuel for ourselves onto the rough-terrain vehicles and kitted up with winter clothing, then we rolled out of there and left the thousands of people storming in to grab what they could. I guess we murdered them. I remember sitting up front in a truck looking out at a flood of starving freezing savages rushing the other way and thinking, my God, are these Americans? Are these Americans? And my only feeling was to be glad to get away from the fear and the stench of them and to get as far as we possibly could.

"The CO set off across Nevada heading for the Rockies. Up until then the best information we had was that Salt Lake City hadn't been hit, and over in Colorado the Rocky Mountain Arsenal was supposed to be intact, and of course there was the Cheyenne Mountain Complex from where STRACC seemed to be running things. I thought he was crazy. We shouldn't head inland and uphill in worsening weather—the continental interior always gets much colder than the seaboard, doesn't it? We should have been trying for the coast. But so would everyone else who could move, and one day we'd have all died out there for sure.

"By the time we'd crossed Nevada there wasn't any daylight at all any more. People who'd still been moving were dead on the roads, frozen in their cars. The townships were dead—had no power from anywhere for heating or for pumping water. And who has heavy winter clothing in Nevada nowadays? Our gear wasn't good enough. Too light. We had frostbite cases, influenza, dysentery. We got as far up as Provo and were seconded by the local colonel who was trying to hold things together there. We got blizzards and drifting, and it was permanent subzero. I was there for two weeks about. Then I was given a four-truck convoy and told to go all the way over to Fort Carson to pick up some supplies and some diesel tankers ready for us. Carson was the base for the 4th Infantry, and had never been nuked because the division had long ago been packed off to reinforce the 7th Army in Germany. They were well organized, the Russian strategic command. Once they knew they had the 4th Infantry—or what bits were left of it—on the ground in Europe, they didn't go wasting a nuke on its home base.

"I didn't do so well. Two of my people who were sick just died in their sleep in the cold. We got into real winter like I've never seen and just didn't make any progress any more. At a place where we couldn't even find the road in all the ice and drifts one truck turned over and exploded—most of our fuel reserve gone. I abandoned another truck that had been playing up so as to conserve fuel, and prayed we'd get to the next town. The next town was an icebox with everyone left in it dead. So was the next, and the next. One truck lost an axle going out of control on a down incline and ending up over an ice ridge. One more soldier died, and I just had me and one truck and three guys. Then we ran out of fuel and started walking through the Rockies in early May in pitch darkness round the clock in Arctic conditions, and not one of us dressed or trained for it. We got down to lower land where we found an iced up farmhouse where around a dozen people were huddling inside. The place had been a poultry farm, and they were living on the thousands of frozen chicken carcasses from the battery sheds. Only thing was, the chickens had all died when the power first failed and they suffocated in the sheds before it even started to get cooler, and they hadn't been frozen before some of them started to rot and they all got diseased. And there was nothing to heat the carcasses with and you couldn't pluck or bone them, and you could only smash them apart with an axe and suck and swallow the pieces. The people there were all sick with something and it stank like a dry sewer. But there were no flies. Cockroaches and mice everywhere, but no flies.

"We got walking again—figured it would be far better to die in the cold than to go like that. They'd told us that a couple of soldiers had been by a week ago and told them that even Fort Carson was running out of everything just trying to keep up power and heating, and was closing down. We couldn't go back over the mountains, so we tried to make the highway. Something had to be moving there. Another guy died on the way. The highway was out, just a flatter strip on the ice sheet. By then we had better winter clothing than we'd been given to start out with, because we'd taken gloves and socks and jackets and such from the ones who'd died and didn't need it any more. Only one of the three of us had frostbite. We just sat down on the highway in the dark and didn't know what to do. About ten or eleven hours later a big Air Force transport helicopter came by, navigating by following the highway line. They spotted us and took a look at us, then took us on board. Nobody had room for us along the way, so we ended up right at STRACC. We got warm, we got fed. I felt like I was saved. Then I started learning from the general talk and from the assessment jobs I was given to do just what was going on in the world and what was going on in STRACC and CASAL. Some people were getting ready to fight the war some more, and the ones who were calling loudest for support for the surviving civilian population were being accused of defeatism and communist subversion and were getting put out of the way.

"Then the dreams started up even though I wanted to forget it all, didn't want to think about it. Later I heard that both of the guys who made it through with me, one over in NORAD and one somewhere inside STRACC, had shot themselves. There were a lot of suicides. So many that when the executions of the softliners started, at first word went around that the weaker willed defeatists were just killing themselves in an epidemic. It took some of us a few days to catch on to the—to what was really going on. What they were really doing. I mean—oh. What the hell."

Raffles stopped.

That was just the basic story, without the awful details. Told in a snug little metal room inside the armoured bulk of the ship of ships, the last word in warships, almost the last of ships, tearing sedately through a benighted sea at thirty knots, heading for the north, for weapons range of Russia.

Snap out of it Gloria, girl. She's stopped. She's laid herself open to you. Now don't let her feel it's been taken cold. It hasn't. Oh it hasn't.

"Look—would you like something to drink? Tea? You're not one of the diehards who still take coffee, by any chance?"

Raffles shook her head. Her eyes were closed.

She only had to go along to the canteen just forward on the same deck, but if only she could just phone through to the galley and get them to bring a pot along the way the Captain always could. Raffles might run away during the couple of minutes she was out. She got up to go. "I won't be a minute. Okay? I'll get us some tea. Just you wait here." She started to go past the woman's chair.

Raffles had her eyes closed tight. She was silent, she was still. And finally—finally—glistening tears were starting to squeeze out between her dark brown eyelids.

"Captain in the CIC!"

Lt. Cmdr. Joe Dylong, CIC Supervisor and Tactical Action Officer, was taking his turn at directing the Combat Information Centre and thus, basically, the entire ship. He was standing at the Operational Summary console in the centre of the half-populated space, looking at data displays combined from the Sonar Track console and from the Sonar Control Room one deck below. He was wearing his headset and had been talking to Sonar. It had been time to page the Captain and possibly spoil his day.

Boyce got there first, coming up the C3 box internal ladder and entering through the left-hand door beside the main plot on the internal wall. He came around the OpSum and looked at the displays.

Dylong settled the headset round his neck. "You weren't far away."

"AOC. Chatting with Ted." Ted Marcovicci, the Air Group CO and Greg Clemence's number two. "Sub?"

"Looks like it."

Bedford came in through the tunnel door behind them and strode straight up to the OpSum. He looked down at the displays combined on the cathode ray tubes. "Off the port bow. Fuck."

"Three-two-four degrees," Dylong said. "Extreme range. Sonar has it as an intermittent hydrophones source with the hull line arrays. There's no useful triangulation from the line arrays, but the Surtass had it for around a minute."

"Both strings?"

"Just the intermediate. That's at—" He called up data. "Right now that's at one hundred metres down and five hundred astern. The deep string hasn't heard a thing. The triangulation from the Surtass put the source at four hundred sixty kilometres, plus or minus thirty."

"Depth determination?"

"They think it's near the surface, probably not more than a hundred metres down. They're guessing it's a surface layer transmission we're picking up."

The ocean arranges itself in layers characterized by differences in temperature and salinity. Sound transmission across layer boundaries can be poor, can lead to partial internal reflection: the layer acts almost like a two dimensional waveguide, reducing the dissipation of sound energy with distance. That would be why they had heard the submarine at all, if submarine it was. That would be why the line arrays on the Vindicator's hull had heard it repeatedly while the Surtass line down at 100 metres had heard it only once and the deep line hadn't heard it at all.

"How definite is it?"

Dylong shrugged his shoulders—almost. "It's been very intermittent for around ten minutes. It's hardly above background. We were lucky to hear anything at all at that range."

"Could it be a surface contact?"

"Met say from the radar they can see a weather front passing out there with precipitation. There'd be too much wave noise for us to hear something on the surface."

"And as it is," Boyce said, "we can't make out either speed or heading. Can't identify it."

Bedford stared down at the combined display on the OpSum. It was vague, but it was solid enough to be a real submarine—to be a *possible* submarine. It was something like two hundred kilometres west of his course, and around four hundred kilometres ahead. It could easily close on his course and get it ahead of him. In fact if it had its own towed array strung out from a reel inside the top of its sail tower, then it had probably heard the Vindicator already and was moving to close the distance. Within a couple of hours it would hear the ship anyway, unless he ordered a change of course. *If* it was a submarine and not some figment.

If it was a Soviet boat it could engage him with torpedoes from fifty kilometres, and with tube launched anti-ship missiles from at least six times as far away. So after just five hours, that was the end of his zag out to the west. "Call the bridge. Course change forty five degrees to starboard." That would bring the contact round to 279°, just forward of the port beam, making it difficult for even a fast boat to close the range. To chase the Vindicator it would have to make a noise.

Dylong put his headset over his ears again and started talking through to the bridge.

Bedford moved away from the OpSum towards the CO's position, and Boyce followed him. "Think it's solid enough to send out a Wolfmarine?"

Bedford frowned. "Four sixty kilometres out." At 450 kilometres and carrying a standard ASW warload, a Wolfmarine would have only around thirty minutes loiter time in which to find the submarine—less, if it spent many minutes drinking fuel by hovering so as to use the dipping sonar, instead of just dropping a pattern of sonobuoys into the water to listen to the sea. At the efficient cruising speed it would have to adopt in order to reach the search station, by which time the submarine could be too far away to find in a mere thirty minutes. If it was a submarine. "What do you think, John?"

The deck heeled under them, slightly but perceptibly. The huge ship was coming round at thirty knots.

With his middle finger to the bridge of the frame, Boyce

touched his glasses into place. "I guess one wouldn't hurt. Just to be sure."

Bedford nodded.

Nothing. Nothing at all for twenty minutes now.

The Wolfmarine was the first one out so its call sign was Watchdog 1, but it was the only one out so they could drop the number when talking to Vindicator. The pilot was Lt. Joseph Selrose, a Washington black, the observer Petty Officer 2nd Class Rick Garwin, a caucasian from Burlington, Vermont. The machine was carrying the standard load of three Mk72 ASW torpedoes under its fuselage and four advanced short range air-to-air missiles for self-defense—two AIM-320 ASRAAMs on each side boom pylon. It carried a dipping sonar which deployed out through a hatch in the port side of the fuselage, it carried mini sonobuoys dropped from an internally mounted dispenser, it had marine markers and smoke flats. It had the standard fit air and surface search and tracking radar, and self protecting ECM—electronic countermeasures—and decoys. The observer in the right-hand seat had a tactical display which was able to integrate sonar contacts with radar and navigational information. Both crew wore helmets with face mikes.

When they were scrambled they had come running through the dim lit elevator box and out into the darkness and freezing wind of the flight deck, past the first of the parked helicopters to the second one waiting aft of the Skycat hooked up to the catapult. The machine was parked with its nose forward towards the TLCP; before they reached it the battery of lights up on top of the elevator box had come on to ease the TLCP's view of them at takeoff. Selrose climbed in, half ducked, through the starboard side hull door—you had to watch you didn't rip your suit on the noses of the two AIM-320s hitched to the side boom. Head down inside, he slid between the two hip-high racks of sonobuoy dispensers bolted to the floor, got forward into the pilot seat and started up the twin motors overhead. Garwin closed the hull door and squeezed through forward and slid into his right-hand seat. They pulled on their helmets and plugged in the intercoms, and were able to communicate again despite the screaming of the twin Minxette turboshafts. While Garwin began the basic checks they allowed themselves in a scramble takeoff, Selrose clutched in the six-blade rotor, keeping the pitch set for negative thrust to

clamp them safely to the deck for the few seconds until the
rotors came up to speed. The TLCP said go. The Wolfmarine
took them up, and they turned off to port away from the ship
while still going through the transition from hover to forward
flight. They turned away into the blank daytime dark, and the
flight deck lights over the TLCP snapped off.

They flew for ninety minutes at 162 knots maximum continuous speed, 100 metres above the darkly gleaming waves.
After one full hour they went over the horizon of the port
station SCAN-Skyhook and were suddenly completely on
their own. They had just their own search and tracking radar
and the threat receivers to tell them if anyone else—a ship or
low level aircraft or incoming missile—was there.

They reached the search position far too far from home and
slowed right down to 20 knots to drop the first sonobuoy. On
hitting the water it deployed its telemetry antenna and spooled
its hydrophone down to 15 metres to listen to the sea. The
Wolfmarine circled away.

They were under cloud, which made the night dark joke of
a day almost pitch black. They were in rain and a high wind
that was whipping up the waves into a moderately heavy sea
state, making faintly visible spray tops on the dark-oil half-
guessed moving surface below. Up in the smooth wind the
flying wasn't so bad, but down where the wind had lifted and
dipped and bounced over the waves it had been tricky keeping
level even with the flight computers stabilizing the ride.

The first sonobuoy turned up nothing. Neither did the
second one they dropped twenty five kilometres away. There
was no trace at all of a Big Fish moving below the surface.
Which was worrying, because a sub had sensitive ears and
could hear the sound put into the water by a low flying
aircraft or a helicopter from a long way away. A sub could
hear the Wolfmarine approach and lie stopped down there.
And nowadays the Soviets, like the Americans, had a subsam,
a self-homing anti-aircraft missile that could be pre-instructed
and then launched up to the surface in a quick rising buoy.
You didn't want to confirm to the Vindicator that there really
was a Soviet sub by blundering right on to it and being taken
out by its Flying Fish.

Nothing at all after twenty minutes out on the nighttime
nowhere sea. If any sub was really down there it was lying
quiet until they had gone, not wanting to call down yet more
searchers on its head. The Vindicator told them to use the

dipping sonar, so they went down to hover. It wasn't nice, in the darkness under the cloud under the dust veil, in the erratic bouncing gusts of the surface wind, in the rain that took away the last ghost of vision, and all just up above a broken and big-wave sea. Selrose had the AFCS, the automatic flight control system, to help with the tussle of plan position holding and altitude maintenance, but it wasn't exactly a pilot's dream.

The sonar went down on its cable and drank through the up-and-down surface of the sea. It came on okay and Garwin started searching for a contact, scanning around and switching the beam angle to probe increasing depths. The sonar worked perfectly, picking out the wave sinused surfaces between deep lying thermal layers. Vindicator told them optimistically they should assume any Big Fish they found was a Red Whale and could engage it immediately if feasible. But there was nothing there.

They went on searching for more minutes. Hovering was expensive, the twin Minxettes drank the precious fuel reserve far more thirstily when the Wolfmarine balanced itself on their thrust instead of flying around in slow circles. The flight computer steadily counted down the time that was left until at this distance out they had only enough fuel plus a ten percent reserve to get home. The time margin stood at six minutes.

"Nothing," Garwin said over the intercom. "It might be lying stopped further off, but it ain't here."

Five minutes. If they waited around any longer they would have to dump one or more of their torpedoes to lighten the load in order to get home. Going home meant reaching the ship, not ditching short. "Want to make another sweep? Move ten klicks and try one last time?"

"What for?" You couldn't see Garwin shrug in the pitch darkness, but you could hear it in his voice.

Selrose switched channels. "Watchdog. There's no Big Fish around here. He's gone."

"Copy, Watchdog One. How's your loiter time?"

"Four minutes. Coming down to three. We're calling off and coming home."

"Copy, Watchdog. Come home safe now."

"We will." Garwin was already winching up the dipping sonar. Selrose brought his machine from hover through to forward flight, turned on to 130° true heading and picked up height and speed. The Wolfmarine went whipping through the rainstorm dark.

She'd spent the rest of the day in a daze.

The Vindicator had run into the rain front and the active sea, and was riding uneasily over the long underlying swell and made little hesitational shudders every time it ploughed at 30 knots straight into one of the bigger waves. Gloria Craze went up to the blacked out TLCP to watch the Wolfmarine land after its four hour round flight. When she arrived the lights above the TLCP and out on the outboard corners of the elevator box were already burning, showing rain that lashed through the lightwash and swilled on the flight deck. Ill-lit over the sides port and starboard, the angry foaming sea wake rushed by, thundering to itself. The Wolfmarine set down with the help of the TLCP director's talkdown—the everyday little miracle of a pilot landing his machine precisely on a circled number painted on the windswept deck of a fast ship cutting through a roughening sea. The 'copter was hooked up to the squat little tractor and hauled inside through the big door left under the TLCP to be elevatored down below. The changeover of the duty pilot waiting patiently in the cockpit of the F-28 Skycat out on the deck was due. The relief pilot and someone from the flight deck crew went hurrying out in parkas against the wet and cold. The flight deck crew member had a light ladder to hook against the side of the bird while the canopy was opening. The duty pilot came stiffly down after his two and a half imprisoned hours, the relief handed him his parka and then scrambled up into the cockpit and lowered the canopy against the unnatural light. The two figures came back, heads down against the wild wind. She realized that it was mostly sleet she was watching whirling past from overhead and down onto the deck. The heat stored in the ocean made a buffer against the Nuclear Winter out here in the middle of the Atlantic, but the weather could still produce sleet and snow and freezing air at the end of a seasonal summer day. A seasonal summer, somewhere up there above all the roiling radioactive filth that's been wrapped around the world.

She went down inside the warm and bright and humming ship.

Andrew Culbertson was still in his office in the Sick Bay Area. The whole facility had the generous entirety of the 2nd platform deck inside the C3 box at its disposal. Squeezed in there was an eight bed ward aft for the care of intensive cases, a pharmacy and an X-ray/dental/pre-theatre room and the compact operating theatre forward, and fitted between the two ends and surrounded by access ways you could wheel a bed through, the Surgeon's Office. And the office was tiny—a desk and a chair, shallow wall cupboards, and an examination couch. Almost room for Culbertson himself and a visiting patient.

It was late in the ship's day—already evening. Gloria sat herself up on the side of the couch while Culbertson started to clear off whatever work he'd been doing from his desk. He shuffled a stack of papers roughly together. "Gloria, you look like the end of the world."

"Huh. Who says it isn't the end of the world. When did you last go upstairs to look at it?"

"I've better things to do."

He was hiding from it. That was it—hiding from it. "It's pitch dark, wind, heavy sea state coming up, and sleeting. By now it's probably snowing."

Culbertson nodded. Then looked at her a moment, turning the tables on her. "Something I've always wanted to ask you. How does someone like you end up here on a Nemesis ship? You don't quite fit, Gloria."

She just shrugged. "What else was there to do? Me, a psychology and sociology graduate fresh out of college. Psychology and sociology were out of fashion at the time for management philosophy, so they were taking on very few new people there. And when that happens they prefer males and preferably whites. And there am I, female and black and out. A university career would have been fun, but the soft sciences were taking another funding cut right then. So that left only social work, with my qualifications. But there's these two cycles that run there, isn't there? City administrators switch around between utilizing social workers as a political alibi and regarding them as a financial liability, and State and Federal penal policy swings from punishment to correction and back. And it just so happened that the city cycle was at financial liability and the penal policy was at punishment when I needed a job. They weren't hiring social workers, they were firing them."

"So you ran off to join the Navy."

"Andrew, they took me in with open arms. Liberal studies

graduates don't come knocking on their door every day—the military has this little right wing image problem you might have heard of.''

''What did you pick the Navy for, the adventure?''

''And the material. Fascinating. Closed communities on long duration voyages, precisely defined social hierarchies, the personal responsibility of command, the control of strategic and deterrent weapon systems. Would you believe it took a couple of years before I finally realized that no research I ever did would get published outside? And I didn't like all of what I found out about the Navy—about the military in general, I guess. Sometimes you all have a very disturbing way of thinking. And you live in a closed environment in informational terms, where all the external inputs are screened and filtered by precisely those same social and political structures that define your closed world. I'm not really suited to Navy requirements, I suppose.''

''Really?'' Culbertson finally put the papers away in a drawer. ''You're twenty seven and a full lieutenant. That's not so bad.''

''No, it isn't. They don't seem to have noticed, do they? Here I am snooping on the fitness of the crew on board a key strategic unit. I suppose it's just not possible to study psychology and sociology and then not be able to give them the answers they want at interviews and attitude screenings and so on. The irony is that I'm really nothing more than a virtually redundant social worker with upwards of four hundred well adjusted and functionally role-oriented people as my case load. Sometimes I think they should have reintroduced military chaplains instead.''

''Bless those who're about to kill and die?'' Culbertson shook his head. ''Now. What's the problem? You look sick.''

She looked over at her feet dangling clear of the floor. ''I am sick, Andrew. I'm sick to my stomach.''

''What at?''

''The mess we're in. The whole mess.'' She glanced across at him. ''I've had a talk with Raffles. You know—the one who never says anything.''

He nodded. ''The Army captain. Looks like she's seen a ghost the whole time.''

''Yes. I guess she has. She came along to see me and we were talking for a couple of hours altogether. She has real problems. She has real problems and there's nothing I can do for her. She wasn't inside any of the command centres when it all happened. She was outside in the open.''

Andrew Culbertson didn't say anything.

"She saw the after effects of the nuclear strikes. She saw what happens to people when the entire social structure is blown clean apart and there's no way left to do anything about it. And she was still outside when the climate collapse and the Freeze had wiped everything out.''

He still didn't say anything.

"You see, I thought I was coping with it rationally. I thought I'd got my reaction to it under control. But that's just because I haven't seen the *reality* of it. It happened somewhere else, didn't it? Not here, not right where we are. But now I've had my face rubbed in it. I don't think I'd really been believing it had happened. All we've ever had is a little bit of information. Not anyone's experiences to borrow.''

"I haven't woken up to it yet.'' He sounded quite harsh, as if guarding himself. "I doubt I really believe it at all. I don't think I will even if I ever have to see it for myself.''

"It's hearing what it was like, Andrew. What it *did* to people. My parents, most of my friends, my brother and his family—they all lived in New York. I've managed to realize that they're all dead and to more or less cope with the fact. At least, I think so. I think I've assimilated that. But—'' She looked at Culbertson's flat expression. "But now I know *how* they died. In the attack or afterwards. I know *how* they died!''

Andrew Culbertson's expression hardened. He managed to find a pen still lingering on his desk and put that away in a drawer. He looked at his watch, checked it against the clock on the wall behind Gloria. "It's late. I hope you weren't wanting to talk to me about it.''

"Andrew?'' She came here for a different reaction. "Andrew, I don't quite—''

"I'd appreciate it if you could refrain from unloading onto me any of what Raffles unloaded onto you.'' He stood up, pushed his chair in under the desk. "I had a wife and two kids at Oceanside just up the coast from San Diego. Remember? I'd really rather not hear about it.''

Oh. Oh goddam it. You really ought to know better. You have a personal file on every last man and woman on board, and you have more than enough skill to read their reactions and to steer your own interactions with them. But you get upset yourself, and you hurt someone. "Andrew—I'm sorry. I'm sorry."

He just shrugged. And then dredged up some medical jollity from somewhere. "Just imagine how my patients feel when I make a slip with my scalpel. Terrible scene. Come on, let's close up here. I want to eat!"

The little light glowed over the door in his narrow sleeping cabin. He fumbled for the phone while trying to focus on the time. A quarter to midnight. He'd been sound asleep. "Bedford."

"McGready, sir, in Communications. Sorry to wake you, sir."

"That's okay, McGready. Signal?"

"Yes sir. Just come through on Blue Talker. It's addressed to you, sir." She still sounded apologetic, the senior CPO running the night shift down there. "So I thought I'd better disturb you."

"That's okay." He was already propped up on his elbow ready to leave his bunk. McGready would have seen the signal as it was decrypted—she wouldn't wake him for nothing at all. "Stand by to fax it through. I'll pick up the phone in my day cabin. Please stay on the line."

"Yes sir."

He hung up the phone and hauled himself out of bed. He went straight through into his day cabin, switching on the light and blinking. A picture of a commanding officer, in his bare feet and his underpants and a little overweight. That would inspire confidence in his crew. He yawned at his desk for being there. He switched on the permanently on-line desktop and keyed the matrix printer. Text started to roll out of it immediately. Roll. The Vindicator was moving more now than when he went to sleep. The sea state was rising.

ORIG: CASAL NAVALCOM NMSS DIR 1012 JUNE 10 1455
FWRD: STRACC NAVCOM JUNE 10 1635
INCOMING : JUNE 10 2340
NMSS-3 VINDICATOR CPT BEDFORD CO
1. Reaffirm NMSS DIR 1011 June 08 except following:
2. Alert station assignment IUK Gap south of 63°N east of 10°W
3. Advise one or more Soviet units possibly at sea.

They were boxing him in. The people back home were boxing him in, deliberately ordering him into a limited area of sea and without arranging for any support units to help him stay alive there. They were narrowing his stationing area to the eastern side of the IUK Gap, hardly letting him go north or west of the Faeroes, bringing him just that little bit nearer to the European mainland. To the Soviet Union. It worried him. It really worried him. And the naval intelligence advisement was next to useless. At least one Soviet ship or submarine *might* be at sea. A lot of use. One hell of a lot of use. But then the folks back home had next to nothing left around the world with which to eavesdrop on the enemy's signals traffic.

He picked up the desk phone. "McGready, I don't suppose there's been a signal for Jenninger?"

"Came in a couple of minutes earlier, sir. Direct from CASAL. Same as usual, sir. We put it through the Blue Talker and out came a string of one-time pad numbers. The difference is this one's much longer. About three times as long as all the others she's received up to now."

He didn't *like* this situation—secure and undisclosed communications going to an undefined superior authority on board his own ship. It was hardly the same as carrying an admiral or some such. "Well if it's so long, maybe it's important. Get someone to send it along to her right away. And my apologies if we've unfortunately woken her up."

"Right, sir. Again, I'm sorry about waking you, sir."

"No need, McGready. I have to think about a course change."

He put down the phone and went back to his sleeping cabin to dress. Asking himself: what do I do if the firing order comes through? Do I do my job? Because I believe in credible deterrence? Outside was the unnatural dark and cold of the ultimate night, asking him what is a credible deterrence, when using it to prove it credible does this? Does this.

June 11

THE VINDICATOR WAS rolling. The stabilizers killed a good half of it, but the huge ship was still leaning slowly, almost sedately over from one side to the other and then back again. It was soothing, once you were used to it. Neither Caufield nor Jenninger nor Drexel seemed quite used to it yet. Eileen Jenninger, Lt. Col. James Caufield USAF, Capt. Danella Raffles U.S. Army, David Drexel—Bedford had hauled them all up to his day cabin. He'd called Boyce, and Craze was there as well—as the ship's spare officer she could be detailed to miss out on her own breakfast in order to drag the visiting team away from theirs. All because Bedford had been told the four of them were sitting eating in the canteen—wearing sidearms.

With his desk chair included he could seat just six people in his day cabin. There were seven of them filling the place, so he didn't invite anyone to take a seat. What in hell were they doing running around carrying guns on board his ship? Jenninger and Caufield and Drexel had belts strapped round their hips which were fitted out with an ammunition pouch and a leather or else leather look holster with a closed over flap. Drexel seemed to feel faintly ridiculous in possession of a gun—British and all that, maybe. The Raffles woman wore a webbing belt with an ammunition pouch and a bulky button-down holster—it looked huge on her, but somehow she fitted the part better than the others. Professional Army. He had demanded they show him the things they were carrying and was almost surprised when they did. The three of them had .38 Service-Six Ruger revolvers, proper killing weapons, none of your snub-barrelled police detective toys. Raffles, of course, had the standard issue Colt .45 automatic pistol, a huge and murderous thing. So, what was the sudden show about?

"Safety precautions, Captain," Jenninger said.

"In case of what?" And she looked so tired, as if she hadn't slept at all since he'd let them wake her up with the midnight message. Caufield and Raffles looked grim as well.

"Captain, where are the ship's small arms stored?"

"Just one deck below here." He growled the answer.

Boyce pointed at the deck. "Right next to my cabin. M16s, pistols, grenades. All safely under lock and key."

"Just want to be sure, Captain."

"To be sure of what?" She was going to make him boil over. "That there's no backsliding if and when it comes to any firing enactment order?"

"From what I've heard, not everyone on board accepts the use of nuclear weapons as unquestionably as you might expect."

That was too much. It was an almost explicit criticism of his crew and thus an implicit criticism of himself as the crew manager. "They're human beings, not rabid animals. They can be in the armed services and do their duty when they have to without actually being of the opinion that war is a good idea!"

"I'm also anxious in view of the delicacy of the situation and the apparently growing ascendency of hardline attitudes. I also want to ensure there'll be no precipitate action."

Precipitate action—as if they'd go firing a strike themselves? "A Fire Lance launch requires cooperative control key action by the Launch Control Officer, the Target Control Officer, the Missile Control Officer, First Officer Boyce, and me! Like everything else on this ship, it needs me!"

"Nothing happens without the Captain." Boyce almost smiled. "Not even the end of the world."

"Jenninger, will you be so good as to explain yourself! You might be a halfway credited representative of command authority, but you don't run this ship. I want to know what makes you parade around wearing sidearms in front of my crew?"

"All right, Captain. All right." Jenninger looked as if she might have just fallen into a seat if there'd been one right behind her. She was very worried indeed, and was trying not to show it. "If you must know, there's trouble back in the States. It's started at STRACC but apparently not yet spilled over to CASAL. The extremists, the Apocalypse People, have started taking one-sided control of various command elements and policy committees. They've moved fast, now that it's come to it. The war-readiness people haven't managed to secure such a hold on the military support staffs and thus the personnel in general.''

"You shouldn't have helped execute the softliners," Craze snapped at her. "You shouldn't have set a precedent."

"Are you trying to tell me," Bedford said, "that there's some sort of a *coup* going on at STRACC?"

"Not a coup. A purge, Captain. A purge. That's the political reality we live with now."

"That's ridiculous!"

"You don't know!" Raffles almost yelled back at him. "On this ship you're isolated. You don't know what's going on. You're warm and comfortable and well fed. At least as long as your stores and power last. You haven't even *seen* the land. You haven't seen a city that took a nuclear strike. You haven't seen the bodies and the mess and all before the Freeze started. You haven't experienced the Freeze. You haven't been *outside* in the dark. You don't know what's going on, so you don't know what's happening with people now they're having time to react. You just don't *know*."

Bedford bit back something he was going to say, took a deep breath, and turned to Jenninger again. Yes, it was possible. Oh dear God above, in a nightmare anything was possible. "Is it conceivable that opposing power groups might establish themselves, one in STRACC and one in CASAL? The procedure is that as long as both are operational I take orders originating from Naval Command in STRACC or originating from Naval Alternate Command inside CASAL and forwarded by STRACC and therefore confirmed by STRACC. What in hell am I supposed to do if I get contradictory orders?"

Jenninger shrugged. "Can't tell you, Captain. You'll have to follow your conscience, perhaps. I possibly don't envy you. At least I know where I stand if things start to happen."

That was enough. Dammit, that was quite enough. Just one other question and then he could let them all out of his cabin. "Okay. Another problem. Can you give me any advice on the weather?"

Jenninger was surprised. "The weather?"

"There's been snow all through the night," Boyce explained. "Now there's a force eight blowing outside, a steady gale from due east, and it's air at minus eight centigrade. We know there's a climate collapse and a Big Freeze on land, but that doesn't make any sense at all at this latitude this far out over open ocean. Our Met Officer can't explain it."

Everyone on Jenninger's team turned to look at Drexel.

The Englishman shrugged. "It's the cooling mechanism reorganizing the climate patterns. An ocean-continent division is stabilizing. With no solar heating at all, you get a major cold descending circulation over the continental interiors, and with the thermal reservoir of the oceans you get a general rising circulation over the water masses. That's on a large scale, of course. The local story is always variable. The descending air over the continents gets immensely cold in contact with the ground and basically spills downhill. It's not much of a gradient on average from the interiors to the coast, but it's a long way and there are no thermal disturbances to disrupt the flow patterns by re-heating the air. You get a gradually accelerating katabatic wind of immense proportions—a cold sinking wind getting steadily colder and faster all the time. Which eventually is going to make all the coastal peripheries as utterly uninhabitable as the deep interiors."

"And you think that's what we're getting?" Bedford asked.

"The wind would have the momentum, that's for sure. Of course, it would be twenty degrees or more colder when it first left the land—it's that heat taken up from the sea surface that's going to drain the ocean reservoirs in time. Of course, you wouldn't expect the outflow to be stable this far out because of ocean generated weather effects, but the outflow tongues should be getting gradually longer where they're starting to establish themselves. That must be what we're going through at the present moment, some particularly strong katabatic flow out from Western Europe. Perhaps it's reinforced by the Pyrenees. It's the fact that such a mechanism is establishing itself that frightens some people without a depletion of the ocean heat stores. If they run down then the climate collapse will last longer, and when the dust veil comes down the sun won't be able to warm things up again. Not enough for us, anyway."

He said it all as if it was interesting. Just interesting.

Bedford sent them away, just waved them out of his cabin. He turned to Boyce and Craze and shook his head. "That's as much bad news as I can willingly take right after breakfast."

For a moment his pose was cracking, she thought. A captain has to maintain a permanent show of confidence. But for a moment it had slipped.

• • •

Allan Villman, the Damage Control Officer, was given the job of organizing off-duty personnel into deck parties to clear off the overnight accumulation of snow. Gloria Craze joined in voluntarily—it was always reassuring to feel useful. She worked wrapped up in her teeshirt and shirt, a sweater, her service dress blouson jacket, and an issue parka. And she was still cold in the hideous icy black buffeting wind that ripped across the ship from starboard to port.

The Vindicator was rolling in a huge cross sea, a long and giant swell that came in beam on from starboard as the ship ploughed tirelessly northward. The parties working down forward on main deck were six metres above the sea surface: for one long minute they were balanced up above two valley sides of ocean, and the next they were down in a trough with night-glimpsed water walls looming above them out in the surrounding darkness. One party had to clear the unrailed top of the tower at 13 level, seventeen metres over the superstructure roof and forty above the monstrously flexing sea, and then come down to sweep clear the two radar carrying wings. Gloria mixed in with the people clearing the superstructure roof, huddled and miserable victims almost chased on their sweeping and scraping way by armoured hatches opening on test as soon as they were free of the accumulated snow, by antennas and radomes sliding up and down out of the safety of the retraction space. The huge forward SPY-X12 radar and its SPY-X10A backup in front of the tower base needed no clearing: they had been alternating throughout the night, and their beam energy was intense enough to melt any snow that landed on their streamlining domes.

The blank superstructure roof was a staggering purgatory of cold and dark and wind. The 02 level exterior deck to starboard and in front of the forward superstructure was little better. But then finally they were working down the port side in the lee of the blank metal wall. Of course, there the snow was deepest—the overnight deposit, plus most of the piled up top weight they'd thrown down from above. She finally found herself alone with two crewmen and an empty deck. They decided to take a break, retreating through the access door in the front wall of the elevator box. They dogged the massive armoured and hermetically sealed door shut, and were cocooned by the unbelievable luxury of the unheated and half-lit elevator space. They could throw back their hoods, pull off their gloves, unzip their parkas.

The great roll-down doors aft were closed. Both armed and ready Skycats had been pulled back inside and waited one on each elevator, parked with their outer wing sections folded up. They had full de-icing strips, but it didn't exactly help aerodynamic profile or takeoff weight to sit parked out in the blizzard that had swept the ship during the natural night. The elevators, being mounted on lifting mechanisms, counted as green deck areas, but the aircraft had no need of that safety feature. High performance aircraft are designed to bounce around in the air and so their airframe structures are tough while their sensitive electronics are soft mounted and shock resistant, and they stand parked on undercarriages equipped with powerful shock absorbers. Parked on the narrow strip of deck between the two elevators, jammed between the Skycats and the space-dividing tongue of the closed-in support structure for the tower up above, was a single Wolfmarine with its rotors folded. It couldn't be scrambled as fast as the Skycats, jammed in like that, but then it was the air interceptors which had to be ready to go within a matter of minutes to engage an aircraft that could be approaching at more than twice the speed of sound.

They walked round the gaping tail ducts and the long underwing loaded missiles of the portside Skycat and went to the deck access door down below the TLCP between the pair of rolled-down aircraft doors. They propped their brooms against the vertical ladder going up to a ceiling hatch just behind the TLCP, and got used to the idea of going outside again. The flight deck would be awful—a hundred metres of wind blasted flatness. They stood there right in front of the meanly curved radar housing of the Wolfmarine's nose, its two empty windshield eyes staring at them.

"The end of the world was never like this," Seaman Reyhook said, an air radar systems mechanic. He rubbed at his ears, glowing after the cold. "I seen all those old films, the sci-fi and disaster stuff. Aliens invading the Earth, mad scientists blowing it up, the Moon or a comet or something crashing, the day after and all that crap. Half the time they rescued it at the last minute and got the President back on the phone, the other half it went up like every Fourth of July you ever saw. All those crap old films. The end of the world was never like this."

PO3 Woolstead, a reactor control technician, shook his head. "You know what's going to survive all this? If it lasts a year, or just half a year. You know what? Mice, cockroaches and microbes. That's the future of life on Earth. Mice, cockroaches and microbes. And if it lasts more than a year you can scratch the mice."

Reyhook looked at Gloria Craze. "You think it's the end of the world, sir?"

She shrugged. "Not yet. We're still doing fine, and we're not the only ones."

"But it sure looks like it, sir," Woolstead said. "What have we got—mid morning, June, at forty four or forty five degrees north. And that out there. It sure looks like it."

Villman came hurrying round the starboard side Skycat with half a dozen of his victims in tow. He joined them at the deck access door and someone started turning the central wheel to undog it.

"Leave that," he said. "We can go through the hangar." He looked at Gloria. "I want to get the stern deck cleared before the cold and spray together compact the snow there to ice. There's icing right forward on the bow, even on the forward one-five-five mounting. We can leave the flight deck until last. But icing on deck on a ship this size. That's crazy." He started heading along the side of the Wolfmarine for the door to the companionways inside the tower support structure. Everyone started to follow.

"Lieutenant Craze!" Someone shouting down through the hatch at the top of the ladder that led to the TLCP. "Lieutenant Craze there? Captain wants to see her in his quarters right away!"

She was hugging her parka and uniform blouson, and still too hot in the airconditioned warmth. She was standing in her boots on the carpet of his day cabin. "Oh, I'm sorry, sir. I guess I should go and change before—"

"Sit down, lieutenant." He was standing beside his desk and pouring himself a fix of coffee from the pot whose presence meant that he was working—thinking or planning or worrying, or running through data or scenarios or tactical options. Three months ago, before the war, it would have been just performance reports. "Sit down. Dump that stuff on the couch."

She heaped her parka and blouson together and sat down

beside them. He came over with a cup of coffee in one hand and a signal sheet in the other. He sat down opposite her and handed the sheet across the little intervening table. A signal it was.

"You got all that earlier about the risk of finding ourselves under a divided command? It seems to have happened."

She looked at the signal.

ORIG: STRACC NAVCOM NMSS DIR 1013 JUNE 11 0420
INCOMING: JUNE 11 1130
NMSS-3 VINDICATOR CPT BEDFORD CO

1. Legitimate command authority retained NAVCOM.
2. Disregard as of now signals originating CASAL NAVAL-COM. Temporary dysfunction at CASAL.
3. Advise Jenninger no longer represents legitimate command authority. Is potentially obstructive influence in critical situation.
4. Achieve position 50°00′N 12°00′W by June 11 1800 for rendezvous with on-board control party. Party to be airlifted cooperation British Emergency Government.
5. Acknowledge this signal.

"I just sent the acknowledgement." He was adopting his confidently relaxed posture, legs crossed, left arm stretched out along the back of the couch. "The signal came in over Blue Talker, so it was automatically decrypted in Communications and will be no secret on the ship. Question: should I tell Jenninger right away, or wait until she finds out for herself. How will she react?"

Gloria put the signal sheet down on the little table, reaching over and putting it next to his coffee cup. "I've never even talked to her, sir, so I can only guess. Probably calmly—after all, she's a fairly tough politician. On the other hand she's potentially trapped on the ship."

"This is an active service unit, not STRACC or CASAL. There'll be no political purges on board my ship."

"No sir." She was far too hot. "Excuse me, sir." She pulled the sweater up over her head, pulled her arms free and dumped it on top of the parka and jacket.

Bedford was watching a woman shed a layer of clothing in the privacy of his cabin. A young woman, an attractive woman whose trace of negro insecurity intrigued him so. Gayleen and Linda were behind him on the wall, smiling.

"Where exactly is fifty north twelve west?"

"Southwest of Ireland. It's near enough four hundred fifty kilometres due west of the western tip of England. Cornwall. I toured there on vacation years ago. It's within feasible helicopter ferry range—if they have the machines for it. I've already got a course modification from Navigation. We'll be there dead on time."

"What's an on-board control party?"

"Who knows? Same as we've already got." He reached for his coffee cup. "But from the other side. And with warning."

"And what's a temporary dysfunction at CASAL supposed to be?"

"Anything up to and including fighting in the tunnels and the command centres." He sipped his coffee. "I just can't get to grips with the idea of a physical power struggle going on inside the central command complexes back home."

"We've been told it's suspected that something of the sort happened inside the Soviet command structure. Why not ours?"

"But *Americans* for God's sake?"

"Why not? They'll be subject to the same psychological pressures as the Russians. Without a Congress they'll be as totally deprived of a moderating constraint as the Russians are without a party or Politburo. There's no Capitol Hill, any more than there's a Kremlin."

Bedford put his cup down again. "What psychological pressures? Tell me that."

That would teach her. Now she was faced with having to work a string of intuitive ideas through without having formulated them properly herself. "Imagine you're one of the people responsible for the war. Well, you are one and I am—without people like us it just can't happen. But at a higher level—imagine you're responsible for the initiation and conduct of the war. No one started it, but the reactions they produced to the developing situation went on escalating until *that* outside there happened and they had to stop. Imagine that at some acknowledged or deeply suppressed level you have to know that the whole mess is in no small degree *your* fault. *You* helped to do it. How many people are there in the world? Six billion or thereabouts, wasn't it? Most of them in the northern hemisphere, two billion in India and China alone. Almost all of those people will now be dead and the rest dying—because of you. Virtually all of your own national population wiped out because of the decisions you helped take in order to defend them—all those escalatory steps that were supposed to deter the other side but only frightened him into escalating to try and deter you. Imagine *that* if you can. I can't, not really. And exactly the same will be true for the surviving Russian leadership as for our people because they're just as responsible. The war was just as much their fault and their mistake. Well now, no one is going to act any more like the normal well-adjusted human being they used to be, not under that load of guilt. People do the weirdest things when they're under extreme psychological stress. One of the most typical syndromes, and also the most dangerous, is hysteria. The scientific use of the word, I mean—not a cheer leader at a football game."

"I know what hysteria means."

"Sure." And bad tactics, to sound like you're talking down to your superior. "Basically, because a rational appreciation of themselves and their circumstances is in some relevant way no longer bearable, they switch it off. They erect a solid screen of belief—that is, a construct made of alternative realities that they *want* to be true—and then hide from actual reality behind it. And the more either you or reality hammers at their defence, the stronger they build it up. They are no longer open to objective reason."

"So?" He was clearly sceptical of psychological theorizing.

"So you've just done *this* to the world. How can you cope with the truth? Only a very few people will be psychologically tough enough to face it and somehow to hold themselves together long enough to try and find *something* to do to alleviate the consequences of their own actions. Paradoxically, it's precisely those people who'll go to the wall first because their attitude will be a direct threat to the stability of the belief structures set up by the others. They are the softliners who want to help the civilian population survivors, and they've been labelled as saboteurs or whatever and been eliminated. Another whole group will neither be able to face the truth nor to build themselves a defence against it. They'll all have shot themselves by now. Then in between we have the group who kind of detach themselves from reality. Up to a point they're the real survivors. It goes something like this, I'd expect. This awful thing has happened to the world, and you helped do it. You cannot possibly have done such a terrible thing without an externally imposed reason so imperative that you couldn't have acted otherwise. What you really need is that the enemy be an utterly evil, vile and monstrous creation that has made it all happen through its own horrifying actions. In the case of our people, individuals who were never particularly right wing turn into rabid anti-communists. On the Soviet side some individuals who were once normal rational entities will have turned into fanatical anti-capitalists.''

"Extremist polarization.''

"Extremist polarization. The point is, the only way to cope with what's happened is to make it *necessary*, to make it a supreme sacrifice for the good of those few who can hopefully survive—to make it into your own private vision of Armageddon. And once you've got that far, the only way to justify that alleged immense sacrifice in order to defeat an alleged evil will be to eradicate any lingering presence of that evil force. In other words, go ahead and finish the war once and for all, and to hell with any rational assessment of the need or of the consequences. After all, once you've convinced yourself at some aware or suppressed level that the enemy *is* evil, then you're absolutely certain they're going to wipe you out once and for all at the first chance they get, so go ahead and get in first. And then every fact you hear, every action you see others perform, will be interpreted exclusively in terms of the protective schema you've constructed for yourself. Everything will confirm you in your belief—because any belief is necessarily a closed system, which is why it's so dangerous. It's because of belief that people have been able to torture heretics to death—a screaming human being right there in front of them. It must be considerably easier to bring yourself just to press a button and kill invisible people half a world away.''

She stopped, suddenly surprised at her own eloquence and upset to find individual thoughts she'd been entertaining for some time fitting together so neatly to form such a fearful picture.

Bedford wasn't relaxed any more, although he hadn't changed his easy posture. "And you're saying it's these—crazy people who appear to be getting hold of the power at the top both on our side and on theirs?''

"I'm not saying they're crazy. That's an empty term. Nor am I saying they're not sane. That's a relative term. They're individuals producing a perfectly understandable reaction under an extreme of psychological stress. And I'm not saying it's necessarily the same kind of people who've won through on the Soviet side. After all, they're not throwing nukes at us right now, are they?''

Bedford shook his head. ''I can't buy it. Not all at once, anyway. We'll just have to try and sit it out, maybe.'' He uncrossed his legs, sat hunched forward towards his coffee cup. ''I'll tell Jenninger myself and work something out to stop her panicking. Or else with guns on board that's going to be a mess. At least we don't need to worry about Soviet intruders for a while. They don't need to risk getting shot at trying to locate us while we're giving them radio fixes for free.'' He reached out for the cup.

''Sir?''

''The acknowledgement signal I was ordered to send.''

50°N 12°W, the wind had veered southwesterly and the air temperature risen to –2°C, and as the wind had steadily abated the sea state had eased to a low and broken swell that hardly affected the motion of the charging ship. Not charging through the sea any more—he had brought the Vindicator down to five knots to keep the rendezvous with the British helicopters.

Sea Kings—the British were coming out in ancient Sea Kings, built decades ago by Westland under license to Sikorsky. Sea Kings—the British armed forces had always been the same, the best personnel in the world but not enough money to keep them in modern equipment. The two machines were coming out from somewhere near the tip of Cornwall, from RAF Camborne, a rescue station or something of the sort that had never got hit in the war. All the majority military installations and most economic centres had been nuked to hell, creating the inevitable utter chaos and mass death as the entire social infrastructure disintegrated, but the British Isles were on the warmer eastern edge of the Atlantic Ocean and at first the Big Freeze and had not bitten quite so hard. There had been a few extra days of grace in which the British Emergency Government could attempt to organize itself and its shreds of remnant forces before everything had disappeared under mountains of snow piled up by the endless blizzards coming in over the cold land from the wet ocean realm. Now the blizzards had mostly abated and the country was frozen solid and sinking into the iron grip of the incredible cold marching out from the vast continental interior. The immobilized handfuls of survivors and the British Emergency

Government that claimed to be watching over them were as doomed as all the rest. This ferrying job for its big ally would be one of the last acts of Britain as a political entity.

It was deep late twilight gloom at the end of the afternoon on what was supposed to be a brilliant summer day. From the darkened bridge you could see nothing but a ring of black and foam flecked ocean fading into total dark. Not even that much seascape would have been visible if the troposphere hadn't been clear of clouds between the frozen world and the obscuring dust veil.

"There, sir." In the gloom the starboard lookout pointed out on the beam. "Leading one about ten degrees high, second one about half of that."

Bedford spotted them, two black specks out against the night dark of the eastern horizon. They were already growing visibly and swinging aft. Two machines for safety, presumably. They had to come out to the ship across 480 kilometres of open sea, and absolutely nothing to help them if they got into trouble of any kind. One crew had to be ready to pick the other out of the water. They weren't even going to pause at the ship, just touch down to let their passengers jump out and then head straight back home again without wasting any fuel. Bedford wasn't going to refuel them: a Sea King could just make the round trip with a light load, and he was going to keep all his helicopter fuel for the Wolfmarines for anti-submarine defence.

Lt. junior grade Ellen Mendes, Mk72 ASW Torpedo Systems Officer, was running the watch from the console in the almost impenetrable shadow at the back of the bridge. She answered the phone when it buzzed. "AOC, sir. They've handed the Brits over to the TLCP for talk-in. Seems they both want to touch down, sir. They've got their passengers split between them."

He nodded, if a nod was any use in the dark. Boyce was at the bridge console using the other phone to talk through to the wardroom. That was Bedford's eventual solution. He had Jenninger and her team waiting down there with Korsyn, the Chief Weapons Officer, to keep them company; he and Chief Warrant Officer Kusatsu and two crewmen ready inside the elevator box to meet the new arrivals and escort them along to the wardroom. He was going to bring both groups together where they were to some extent protected by the presence of neutral shipboard personnel and where he could box them in

if there was trouble. He was going to require that they all
surrender their weapons into his keeping, and if they refused,
then before they knew what was happening the small arms
store would have been broken open and a dozen of his crew
drawn up issued with firearms, and they would be forcibly
disarmed. And it had to be both groups at once—Jenninger
had already declined to give up her own guns until and
unless the new people let go of theirs.

He crossed from the windows to the bridge console. At
least there were instrument glows here. One inset display
screen traced the static display combined from the SCAN
radars flying on the trio of Skyhooks, each one hundred
kilometres out. It was all empty sea except at the upper right
where the extreme southwestern tip of Ireland intruded, showing the coastline and the low Caha Mountains and the radar
shadow behind. They would have nothing to do with Ireland
any more than the Irish, however many of them were left
alive, would want to have anything to do with them. It hadn't
been Ireland's war. But it had been Ireland's planet.

The second display screen showed a view aft along the
flight deck from above the TLCP. The lights were blazing
there now, showing the empty deck immediately below
the TLCP, and then the F-28 Skycat parked once again at
the head of the catapult track and pointing away towards
the stern, and beyond it on the starboard side a single
Wolfmarine parked nose forward with its windshield reflecting the lights. They were getting nearer to the waiting Russians every hour—he wanted aircraft out on the deck again
ready for an instant start now that the weather allowed it.
Even the takeoff ramp at the end of the flight deck port was
deployed and ready.

Boyce put the phone on the hook. "They're watching on
the monitor in the wardroom."

The big Sea Kings came into view on the screen, visible as
pairs of landing lights and a halo shimmer reflected down
from their rotor arcs. One hung back astern while the other
came in lower and nosed forward until it was hovering above
the clear deck in the wash of the floods, matching speed
exactly with the moving ship. It was a beautifully smooth and
crisp manoeuvre, holding position perfectly above the deck of
a ship moving still on an uneasy sea while an unsteady wind
came in over the port quarter. The British knew how to fly.

It was a silent world inside the little screen, no thundering roar from the descending machine.

Dark coloured, it set down on its own fanning shadows conjured by the battery of floods. You could see the pilots inside the nose canopy. Figures appeared, jumping out of the obscured cargo door at the rear of the helicopter's fuselage on the starboard side. Ducked, they ran towards the edge of the deck to escape the immense downwash from the rotors. There were three of them, a fourth, a fifth, dark figures in bulky clothing with heavy packs, all tiny on the screen. A sixth, a seventh, an eighth. The helicopter suddenly hopped up into the sky and the second started to come in. ·

There were eight figures gathered on the deck, walking down to the access door beneath the TLCP. They had heavy packs on their shoulders, they had steel helmets slung at their sides, they had guns in their hands.

"What in hell?" Boyce said. "The *marines?*"

The second Sea King set down on the deck. Six more figures spilled out of it and it went straight up into the sky and vanished from the screen. Fourteen figures on the deck, most of them with rifles.

The phone buzzer went. Boyce lifted one of the handsets, listened. "Jenninger and her people just quit."

"What?" That was the end of his peaceful solution.

"They took one look at what landed and bolted." Boyce went on listening.

The phone buzzed again. Mendes took the other handset, listened. "Okay. Sir, it's Kusatsu in the elevator box. He wants to know should he open the door and let them in?"

"Tell him to stall," Bedford snapped. *Soldiers,* goddam it. "Has Korsyn got after Jenninger, at least?"

"He sent people after them," Boyce said. "Three of them have gone, the British guy is still there."

"Okay. Get down there to the flight deck and try and find out what in hell's supposed to be going on." He intercepted the handset that Boyce was replacing and punched for the CIC. Armed people running around on board, for Christ's sake.

"CIC director." Marcovicci answered, the Air Group CO, taking a turn at running the Combat Information Centre.

"Bedford. We have three armed people loose on the ship. They have to be regarded as potential saboteurs. Alert every sensitive station—the entire C3 box, reactor and engine spaces, armament stores, the Fire Lance decks. They're to close up and sit tight. There's no need to panic but we take this seriously."

"Right sir. Okay to use the ship's address, sir?"

"No. Talk to the stations individually." If it went over the ship's address Jenninger would be convinced she was being hunted, and then the shooting really might start.

The big aircraft doors were still rolled down and closed against the preternatural night, the space was cold and half lit. A dark sea-camouflage Wolfmarine was parked on the starboard elevator, a silver-grey Skycat bird on the port. Boyce had come from the bridge through the retraction space under the superstructure roof over the top of the C3 box, and down the ladders inside the tower support. He hurried along the deck to where Kusatsu had the little access door open and people wrapped in parkas were coming through.

"These are the leaders of the group, sir." The chief warrant officer was waving his two seamen across the entrance in order to block it. He could have done the job himself, he was squat and solid and as immovable looking as a karate master. "There are ten more soldiers outside."

The four he'd allowed inside were unzipping their parkas and throwing back their hoods. Three of them were bareheaded, one wore an Army forage cap and had a steel helmet slung from his belt. The oldest looking male, a white somewhere around his mid forties, pulled off his gloves and clapped them into his left hand, standing there with all the self-assurance of a leader.

"Kylander," the man said. "Bradford Kylander, STRACC Crisis Committee. This is Arlene Rimmington." He turned to the woman, a redhead civilian, then pointed his gloves at the older of the two blacks, the one without the forage cap. "Major George Dresher, United States Air Force. And this is Second Lieutenant Gittus, 101st Air Assault." That was the black Army officer with the forage cap and helmet.

Boyce ignored Kylander and the others, spoke direct to the Army man. "Those guys outside belong to you?"

"They do, sir." The expression on Gittus' face made it clear that the tone in Boyce's voice had killed any hope of black brotherhood. "Don't you think they could wait around inside, sir?"

He looked out through the door at the winter-kitted soldiers

standing around in the floodlight wash. Each of them had a
short weapon slung over his shoulder or dangling in his
hand—a short assault rifle, a snub-barrelled Colt Commando,
the handier brother of the M16 carbine. Ten real killers and
their officer dredged up from somewhere to back up the
on-board control party. He looked at Kylander. "Don't you
people back home trust us any more?" Then he turned to the
phone at the foot of the TLCP ladder.

Susan Bainbridge, the Meteorology Officer, was standing in
the wardroom doorway. Lt. Cmdr. Ray Korsyn was talking
on the phone to the Captain. "That's right, sir. They found
her sitting at the bottom of a ladder near the portside Fire
Lance hoist on third platform. Bainbridge brought her back up
here. She doesn't have her gun, sir. Must have given it to the
others. Guess they think they'll need the firepower. No, she's
not saying a word about where they went." She wasn't
saying a word at all: Raffles was just sitting hunched up at the
big table, staring at nothing. No one had ever looked less like
running away. "Okay, I'll try asking. Does either of you
know who Kylander is? Or Rimmington?"

No response from Raffles. Drexel, the Englishman, shrugged
his shoulders. "Kylander was somebody minor on the National Security Council. He was on the backup A-and-C team
dispersed to STRACC. I don't know a Rimmington."

Raffles stirred herself. "Rimmington was on Teller's team."

"Kylander was on the National Security Council and on an
advisement-and-crisis team dispersed to STRACC, sir. Rimmington was on Teller's team, whoever Teller is."

"One of the people who've come out on top," Drexel said.

They came out from underneath the service equipment space.
They had turned in under the C3-Complex on 5th platform
and then run the whole of the way through the squat steel
forests under all the isolation boxes right to the stern. They'd
had time to grab parkas and gloves from their cabins and that
was absolutely all. Raffles had run off forward. God alone
knew why.

They closed the door to the suspension box base behind
them before anyone anywhere could notice a door state telltale and guess where they were. They paused in the narrow
space between the door and the huge actuator drives for the
centreline rudder. All they had to do now was to get up past

the magazines for the stern defence mountings, through the Surtass stowage and machinery decks, and they would come out on the stern apron. Then they could climb up the ladder rungs bolted onto the near vertical aftslope, and they would be on the flight deck. If the lights were out again up there, they might get all the way to a parked helicopter before anyone saw them. And then they would have a chance to get to France. Which was probably an illusion, but an illusion was better than an execution squad.

"You're sure you can fly that helicopter?"

Caufield was checking his revolver again. "A helicopter, yes. *That* helicopter, I don't know. I've never flown a Wolfmarine myself, though I've sat beside the pilot a couple of times. But it's loaded up and fuelled and ready to lift. We'll just have to hope I can start it up first try."

At least he'd managed to get some of them together in the wardroom. Korsyn and Bainbridge had Raffles and Drexel sitting there quietly, and Boyce had brought the new arrivals along. Kylander and Rimmington, Dresher the Air Force major, and Gittus formerly of the 101st Air Assault Division at Fort Campbell, Kentucky. Bradford Kylander pulled off his parka and threw it over the back of one of the wardroom chairs, really making himself at home. Dresher and Rimmington did the same. Gittus just stood with his hands on his hips so as to hold his coat open. He had a huge webbing holster encasing a service automatic at his hip. The other three all had heavy revolver holsters. The usual display.

"Jenninger and Caufield are dangerous people, Captain," Kylander announced. "They belong to a group that's been acting to obstruct the prosecution of measures essential to the effective defence of the United States. Sabotage at command level. They're political criminals during a state of war. I can't tolerate them running around loose on this ship."

"Let me bring my people in to search for them," Gittus said.

"What?" Bedford couldn't believe it. "Are you crazy?"

"Been on this ship before?" Boyce asked. "Fifty six thousand tonnes, something over forty thousand square metres of deck area. We'd have to waste our time trying to find you. Leave it to us."

Kylander simply turned his attention to Raffles, still sitting there staring at the table. "She didn't try to run?"

"She came back voluntarily," Bainbridge said.

"Where is there to run to?" Raffles said to no one. "What's the point?"

"You don't have to run from us." Kylander seemed intensely aware of his own magnanimity. "You're only a junior in the obstructionist hierarchy. Just change your ways and we can use you. In the present state of the world we need every man and woman who'll pull their weight. As a precaution in the meantime you can surrender your gun."

"She doesn't have a gun," Korsyn said.

Kylander seemed surprised, but let it pass. He turned to Drexel, sitting there and most visibly wearing his holstered revolver. "I'll have to ask you to surrender your gun as well. A gesture of good faith. You've created an ambivalent status for yourself. I'm not at all sure whether I can trust you, but I can use you if you'll cooperate as fully as I expect."

Drexel smiled an unreadable smile. He unbuckled his gunbelt and reached it across the table towards Kylander. Dresher reached out to take it, but Korsyn intercepted it and took the thing instead. He fastened the buckle and slipped the belt over his shoulder.

"When weapons are being impounded on my ship, I'll do the impounding," Bedford said. He still wanted a peaceful resolution of events. If he could get Raffles and Drexel safely under his protection there would still be a fair chance of getting Jenninger and Caufield to give themselves up without further trouble. They wouldn't try any sabotage, he just couldn't see them thinking like that. But if they got down below 5th platform into the box-cell structure of the baseline they would be almost impossible to get out if they decided to shoot, and they could stay down there as long as they could hold out without food or water. It was about time he talked to them over the ship's address. "What happens to the other two? Do you want to disarm them and place them under open arrest?"

Kylander shook his head. "Hardly appropriate. They're senior members of a top level group which has been attempting to sabotage the readiness of the United States for war and to obstruct the enactment of measures necessary for national survival. They are, I repeat, extremely dangerous."

"I can't slap them in irons for you. We don't damn well have any."

"It's not a matter of arrest, Captain. They'll be disposed

of. We're at war and in a state of severe crisis. All normal measures are suspended.''

The wardroom phone buzzed and Boyce turned to take it. Raffles put her head in her hands. Bedford was going to say something.

''Jesus!'' Boyce said. ''There's shooting on the flight deck.''

Boyce ran from the slanted light under the TLCP, chasing swarms of his own eager shadows along the freezing flight deck. He ran past the F-28 waiting at the catapult head and on towards the Wolfmarine parked with its nose forward on the starboard side, its tail towards the blank night out astern. He ran past the helicopter to where its overlapping shadows started to cloak the deck, and stopped. The sound of the freezing wind across his ears all but drowned the noise of the wake rushing along beside the ship. The wind cut through his shirt and teeshirt and wounded him.

Soldiers were standing around, shadows with assault rifles in the long shallow light. Lying on the deck aft of the Wolfmarine, half in its shadow fan and half in the pallid gleam coming from the TLCP floods far away, sending its own long darkness pool along the deck, was what was left of Caufield. He was twisted over onto his face as if someone had thrown him there, and blood was slowly spreading darkly out around him. Just a mess on the deck.

Kusatsu was there with a couple of the flight deck crew anxiously circling the helicopter looking for damage to the precious machine. The flight deck crew, like the soldiers, were dressed for the cold. It was a vicious cold.

He yelled at the nearest soldier shadow. ''What in hell's going on!''

No answer.

Gittus appeared at the run against the floodlight wash. ''Eslon! Report!''

''Sir! Two people were trying to make it to the 'copter. Looked like they might be attempting a takeoff. We got this one and the other disappeared back over the edge that way.'' The soldier pointed aft to where the takeoff ramp and the two flanking Skyfire mountings stood up against the blackness. ''Sergeant Hawley's taken three men after the escapee.''

Boyce intercepted Gittus. ''Are your men *crazy*? Opening fire out here! This machine's loaded with torpedoes and air-to-air missiles and around twelve hundred litres of fuel!

And the Skycat—my God, the Skycat! Sixteen missiles and around six and a half tonnes of fuel!''

"The aircraft didn't go up." Gittus waved his men with him and headed aft.

Boyce grabbed the nearest of the flight deck crew, a woman half-anonymous behind the microphone of a talker headset. "Thorne, tell the AOC to get the aircraft rotated below to check them out."

"Already done, sir. Lt. Jennesten's coming to take a look at them first, sir. I think he's already on deck."

"What in hell happened?"

"Dunno, sir. I think it was the Skycat pilot saw figures come up over the aftslope and told the TLCP. They asked the soldiers if it was any of their people outside and the soldiers just went out and started shooting. Then Kusatsu brought us out."

He looked round. The soldiers had all gone, the deck was dark despite the wash of the floods eighty metres away. The pool of blood beside Caufield picked up highlights from the TLCP floods, little dancing highlights because the wind sweeping the deck was making ripples in the blood pool, pushing back its edge and stopping its advance. Back there more figures were congregating round the looming Skycat. He ran.

Jennesten, the Aircraft Management Officer, was shivering violently in his short sleeve shirt in the icy darkness, giving orders to the people around the aircraft and himself peering at the three missiles mounted on the outboard wing pylon. He'd already organized a ladder to get the pilot down out of the cockpit.

"Damaged?"

"Don't think so, sir." Jennesten was having to run his hands over the shafts of the missiles in the dark. "The pilot says the systems didn't register anything. But I'm not taking this bird down inside until I'm sure there's nothing smouldering inside the aircraft or a missile. Bullets are hot when they hit. We can't risk all this lot going up in the hangar or it'll be the end of the entire air group."

Jesus Christ, trigger happy soldiers down in the aircraft hangar or the armament decks. "Kusatsu!"

Kusatsu was coming anyway. "I think the 'copter's all right!" He skidded to a halt. "What do we do with the body?"

"It's not going anywhere, man. Get down inside and try and round up the goddam soldiers."

"Those fuckers don't listen, sir."

"Well keep our own people up with them so they don't blow us all to hell!"

Kusatsu nodded and ran towards the side of the flight deck, making for the nearest deck hatch down into the hangar. Boyce headed for the aftslope down to the stern.

They caught her down on 2nd platform forward of the starboard supply elevator which serviced the aft air armament decks. Another few seconds and she'd have been through the inspection hatch and inside the double structure of the hull. She could have gone down through the interconnected box-cells and got into the labyrinth of the baseline. Then let them catch her with a gun to keep them at bay. But they caught her and that was that. She hadn't been injured in the shooting but she was as shook up as hell—wild and frightened but too damn full of self-respect to show it. The officer and his sergeant and their troopers hauled her up to the hangar deck and started to march her aft, one of the bastards half dragging her by the arm. She had a far better idea of what was going to happen than did the startled onlookers running around between the aircraft. A far better idea.

Among all the naval technicians she spotted Drexel, looking stunned and aghast. Come to see for himself. Bastard. The bastard. "What did they promise you, Drexel? A seat in the last bunker?" They were marching her past the last few aircraft. She yelled over her shoulder at him. "Want to come and watch? Over there! There's a ladder goes up to the flight deck! Go take a look at Caufield! Go on! From up there you'll get a great view!"

They reached the armoured access door at the rear of the hangar on the starboard side, two steps up to it right beside the support structure for the Skyfire mounting. Her legs were going from the fear. They had to haul her up the steps and out into the freezing darkness.

Boyce had come down the outside ladder onto the stern deck. "Why in hell are you bringing her outside!"

"Guess!" she hissed.

He could guess. He ducked through the narrow door, bumped straight against Gittus. "Now hold on, lieutenant." He outranked the man by four grades. "Just hold on!"

Gittus went outside with the last of his soldiers. Boyce went for the nearest phone, pulling off his glasses as they steamed over. To stop this Bedford had to issue guns.

One of them had hold of each of her arms. They marched her straight aft past the torpedo tubes and got out past the end of the centreline base for the weapon mountings. Out into the icy wind. They stretched out her arms and marched her right up against the two strands of the guard wire. Held her there. The stern wake creamed and mounded dimly, deafeningly, dizzyingly, boiling up and rushing away into the blackness of the surrounding sea. She could just make out the line of the Surtass tow cutting down into the water. She was shuddering with the cold and fear. They pressed her over the wires. This world was coming to an end anyway and another day didn't matter. The noise of the stern wake was a huge swallowing roar.

Gittus nodded. The soldier's assault rifle went off with a clatter like iron bars tumbling on the deck. Jenninger pitched double over the top strand of the safety wire. One of the soldiers who'd been holding her grabbed her ankle and tipped her clear over the stern. Up on top of the aftslope in the dark beside the skyfire mounting Drexel was standing, shivering. Trying to make himself believe what his eyes had just seen.

KYLANDER AND HIS team had flown the Atlantic in a C-5 Galaxy transport aircraft. An entire giant C-5 just to ferry fourteen individuals across to the UK, the last C-5 in the world carefully nursed on what was left of Miami Airport in the vicinity of the slightly warming influence of the Caribbean Sea, the only place anyone could have parked it and hoped to keep it serviceable for just a few more days. Now it had been used to fly three controllers and eleven troops clear across the Atlantic, putting down on the ice desert that used to be some inland Royal Air Force base or other without any hope of ever finding the fuel to fly back home again. Wasting such a giant bird—the rulers of what was left of the United States must really have wanted to get their hands firmly back on the Vindicator. Perhaps the aircraft was the price paid to the British Emergency Government for their cooperative effort in flying Kylander out to the ship. If they could somehow get enough fuel together before the machine froze solid out there unprotected in the twenty four hour night, perhaps they might be able to use it to ferry themselves down to Ascension and then on to a brief reprieve in South Africa.

It would be brief. The dust veil and the climate collapse was moving south. And even if it wasn't so catastrophically severe in the southern hemisphere, the destruction of white South Africa was only a matter of time. The regime was too unstable to survive without its northern supporters. White racism and the kind of government prevalent in Central and South America—was that the image of freedom America had killed itself to defend? Was that what his service of deterrence had always been about? What did Craze say—he was a potential depressive. But a captain can't let go and retreat into depressive gloom, not when he's failed to prevent a piece of butchery on board his own ship—a butchery he couldn't possibly anticipate and which moved too fast to prevent anyway. If he retreated into the swarming cloud of his darkening thoughts he would be wilfully destroying the fragile morale of the crew.

Accommodation had been no problem. Raffles and Drexel could stay out of the way right forward on 2nd platform, Kylander and Dresher could take over the officer's cabins vacated by their victims. The infantry lieutenant and the woman Rimmington had wanted to share, and the ten men of the troop detachment fitted easily away into five of the spare twin berth cabins. There was still room for a few more guests on board. Clearing Jenninger's handful of effects from her cabin had turned up the decrypted version of the last signal she had received from CASAL. It was just a long list of names, with a postscript that they had all gone at STRACC and that the sender expected to lose access to an authorized transmitter at any time, because now the same thing was starting at CASAL. Just a list of the names of the dead sent by someone who expected to die.

"At least both our command centres speak with one voice again as it were, sir." Lt. Cmdr. Jason Hosky, a black governor's son and the Vindicator's Chief ASW Officer. He'd arrived late for his breakfast, had been directing the CIC for the past couple of hours.

Bedford nodded. A signal from STRACC had come in during the night confirming that the undefined dysfunction at CASAL had been cleared and legitimate command authority restored to NAVALCOM.

"Would've been one hell of a mess." Lt. Cmdr. Chet Darius, Chief Communications Officer, son of a poor black from Chicago. "Two opposing command centres telling us what to do."

"No problem." Lt. Cmdr. Warren Lister, Missile Control Officer. "NAVCOM has precedence over NAVALCOM. That's procedure."

Breakfast in the wardroom. Six of them and their Captain preparing for the day, the other senior officers already out and about around the ship.

Ruth Crimmin put her breakfast tray back on the side shelf and sat down again. "Now we know what an onboard control party is. An execution squad. Do you think Caufield and

Jenninger were really saboteurs, or just political dissidents?''
The question was addressed to no one in particular, and no one
volunteered to answer.

"What do you make of Raffles?" Darius asked. "Didn't
run, did she?"

"Where were they going?" Lister said. "France? They'd
just freeze to death there."

Hosky nodded, swallowing to speak. "Gloria Craze says
Raffles already had one spell outside in the Freeze and had
one hell of a time. She wouldn't want to go through that
again."

"What about the English guy?" Crimmin asked. "What do
we make of him?"

Cmdr. Greg Clemence, Air Operations Controller, shrugged.
"Seems he's been playing both ends against the middle and
got away with it so far. Maybe he's just trying to survive."

"Think Raffles is a potential danger to the ship, sir?"
Darius asked.

Bedford shook his head.

Cmdr. Orville Steetley reached for the coffee pot he shared
at wardroom meals with Bedford. Two years older than his
immediate superior at forty nine, he was another incurable
coffee addict. He would have fed his reactors and turbines
coffee. "Ruth, aren't we at fifty six north, thereabouts?"

Crimmin nodded. "Around five hundred kilometres west
of Glasgow."

Steetley refilled his cup and replaced the pot. "Nearest I've
been to Holy Loch for years. Started out on Poseidon-modified
Polaris boats stationed there. Where are we aiming for,
exactly?"

Steetley could only be asking Bedford, and Bedford couldn't
just grunt at one of his three full commanders. Good mood or
bad, it was necessary that he spoke to them beyond a formal
good morning, and Steetley was senior enough and subtle
enough to achieve it.

"Sixty north ten west," Bedford said.

"And then?"

"Then we loiter in the stationing area."

"The Russians won't like it."

"If we hang around long enough," Clemence said, "they'll
do something. They must have more to throw at us than just
one tailing ship and one possible submarine. And we're a big
threat to them on station up here. We'll be getting our war yet."

Lister nodded. "One way or the other."

That put a pause in the conversation at the table. Clemence ran the ship's first line of defence, and Lister's department was its main offensive capability and thus the reason for attacking it.

"And we go to Fire Lance readiness," Crimmin asked, "when we achieve the stationing area?"

Bedford nodded. "That's been ordered since four days ago."

"Give the crew something more to do," Steetley said. "How's morale after yesterday?"

The wardroom phone buzzed. Hosky got up to answer it.

"Craze will pick anything up," Crimmin said. "Her only job."

"John's out walking the ship," Clemence added. "See if he hears anything."

Hosky handed the phone on its stretched cable towards Bedford. "Sir, it's for you. Chet's department."

Bedford pushed his chair back from the table so that he could comfortably take the phone. "Bedford."

"Caro, sir." Elise Caro, one of Darius' communication systems officers. "Signal just come in from STRACC, NAVCOM. It's in the Nemesis cryptographic domain, sir." A pause. "And it's got the Dark Mirror command code."

Dark Mirror was the Fire Lance command instruction code— Dark Mirror from STRACC, Shadow Glass from CASAL.

"There's also an encrypted signal for Kylander, sir. Shall I send it out to him?"

That would be Kylander's private advisement that the Dark Mirror signal had been sent. "Yes, do that. Thanks, lieutenant." He held the phone out towards Darius. "Your people."

Darius took the phone. They had stopped talking, they were waiting for his response, watching his face.

Bedford stood up and pushed his chair under the table. He looked at Lister. "Dark Mirror, Warren. Looks like our war may already have started."

The Missile Control Centre was inside the C3-Complex isolation box on 03 level aft of the CIC. It was a much smaller space, sharing the deck area between the CIC and the aft tunnel door leading out of the box with the narrow room containing the support computers of the CIC/MCC Administrative Area and also the internal ladder to the next deck

down. The Missile Control Centre contained the control instrumentation and planning direction facilities needed to prepare and launch a strike with nuclear armed Fire Lances
against designated land targets. The ship's reason for being.

All of Lister's officers were there: Target Control Officer
Lt. Judy Wigner, Launch Control Officer Lt. Vince Lewy,
Guidance Functions Officer Barbara Vogt, Vehicle Systems
Officer Debra Stothers, Armaments Officer Paul Milgrom.
The lieutenants and the lieutenants junior grade, the commis-
sioned rank members of the team that did the big killing. Two
of the others were there, the duty crew on this rotation: PO2
Charles Gowlett who worked on the Target Navigation Com-
puter and missile tasking, and Seaman Alice Jackman who
worked on the Target Listing File.

The signal had gone through the Nemesis cryptographic
computer down in Communications, and now it was running
through the MCC's own decrypter that handled the additional
one-time pad cryptography for both Dark Mirror and Shadow
Glass codes. The text readout was on the signal screen.

ORIG: STRACC NAVCOM NMSS DIR 1015 JUNE 12 0015
INCOMING: JUNE 12 0720
NMSS-3 VINDICATOR
FIRE LANCE COMMAND CODE: DARK MIRROR SACI 01
1. This is a Strike Allocation Command Input for strike series
   preparation.
2. Advise possible Firing Enactment Instruction within 20 hours
   from this transmission.
3. Advise strike launch points will be in plan box 57°–64°N
   5°E–5°W.
4. List of TLF PD-targets and Supplementary Target Coordinates
   appended.
5. Acknowledge this signal SACI 01.

Warren Lister looked round. The decrypter was still churning
out target designations—reference indexes for predetermined
targets listed in the Target Listing File Computer, geographi-
cal coordinates for supplementary targets not available in the
TLF store of potential targets all over the globe. "How many
targets do we have?"

PO2 Gowlett was watching the designations transfer into store
ready for processing. "Hundred so far and still coming, sir.
There's the break. One strike list closed and another running."

Lister nodded. "Someone get Navigation to send up map data so we can look at the plan box."

Vogt went to the phone to call through.

Boyce arrived through the tunnel door from aft—he had been right at the stern on the Surtass decks when Darius had tracked him down by phone. He looked at the signal readout and the target list, now totalling 120 and still growing. He glanced at Bedford. Bedford was looking away, staring at the commanding officer's control point on the wall just to the left of the door through forward into the CIC. It had a slot where you inserted and locked the firing key and a little number keyboard through which you entered the Permissive Action Code into the Firing Signal Verifier, when the code came. The first officer's identical control point was up on the wall to the right of the CIC door.

"Map data's ready," Vogt called. She had a bare coastline map filling one of the Target Navigation screens. Overlaid on it was the plan box, a trapezoid tapering into the narrowing north. One corner cut into the Scottish coast from Cape Wrath round to just south of Aberdeen, then the box ran on for three quarters of the way across the North Sea before angling up due north on the five degree eastern meridian. It grazed the Norwegian coast north of Bergen, then went a little further up into the Norwegian Sea, ran back west along the sixty fourth parallel, turned south just short of the Faeroes and ran back down to Cape Wrath. The launch points for the strike series would be fixed inside that box of sea.

"Well, we can reach the whole of the western Soviet Union from there," Lister said. "From getting on for a thousand kilometres east of the Urals up in the north, right round to the border with Turkey. We could hit the whole of Europe and just about the entire Mediterranean area. Dammit, we could reach Greenland and Labrador."

"We could, sir," Vogt said. "Take in most of New-foundland and clip the Gulf of St. Lawrence."

Stothers shook her head. She wore her hair braided in little Afro plaits, about the limit of extravagance the Navy permitted, and they jiggled round the tops of her ears. "Those won't be the targets. We're aimed at Russia."

Wigner was looking at the target designations transferred into store. "The supplementaries all have coordinates east of here. They all look to be Soviet, I think."

"How many?" Lister asked.

"Three hundred and four, sir," Gowlett said. "In three lists."

"Possible Firing Enactment Instruction in twenty hours." Boyce looked round at Bedford again. "Around oh-three-hundred tomorrow. We could never reach the northeastern corner of the box by then."

Bedford nodded, slowly. "We'll get Navigation on it."

"And it's a lousy launch area. More than half surrounded by land, and right on the doorstep of any Soviet capability that might be operational in north Norway."

Bedford nodded again. Turned to Lister. "Warren, you can get everything set up within twenty hours?"

"No problem at all. Although having so many supplementary targets complicates it some."

"Around half are supps," Wigner said.

"Okay, Warren. Might as well get started."

"Right. Jackman, page personnel."

"Sir." Alice Jackman took one of the console phones and punched into the ship's address. "All missile systems personnel stand to. All missile systems personnel stand to."

Now the whole ship knew.

The door through to the CIC opened. Andrea Stratten, the SADIS Systems Officer, looked through. "Captain Bedford, excuse me, sir. Lt. Redden needs help. This Kylander is wanting to get into the CIC, sir."

Bedford went through immediately, Boyce following. The CIC was half occupied at readiness stations. At the forward end, between the Talker board and the commanding officer's position, Redden was physically blocking the tunnel door. Fuming in the narrow tunnel beyond were Kylander, Dresher and Rimmington.

"Sorry, sir." Louis Redden was black, was the SADIS Supervisor. "They want to go through to the MCC. I thought I shouldn't let them in here without your permission, sir."

Kylander started. "Captain Bedford, I think you should inform your officers that—"

"Exactly right, lieutenant. Exactly right." Bedford started past Redden into the tunnel. "John, let's escort these people outside." And then with Boyce behind him he was all but pushing them through the two metre tunnel and out of the door at the end.

They were in the cross corridor between the tunnel door and Bedford's own quarters. Kylander started again. "I've received an advisement concerning the strike allocation and I demand to see that the allocation order is correctly carried through.''

"Let's get something straight, Kylander." He almost stabbed the man in the chest with his forefinger. "This is a warship and the CIC is its nerve centre. It's an informational system and it's what keeps the ship alive and serviceable. It keeps me alive, you alive, and our missiles alive. *No* superfluous persons are permitted in there at any time. I repeat, *no* superfluous persons. The CIC is forbidden territory under all circumstances. The same goes for the entire C3-Complex. Every control centre is crucial, and I will not have passengers standing around getting in the way and disrupting the functioning of those control centres. Is that clear?''

"I represent legitimate command authority—"

"External command authority. That authority gives orders *to* this ship, not *on* this ship. Inside the on-board control centres you are *in the way.* You are not competent to interfere in the internal running of this ship. Is that clear?''

Kylander could change course quickly when he wasn't going to get anywhere, that was for sure. His decision not to get angry in return was quite visible. Instead he nodded. "Very well, Captain. The internal running of the ship is not a part of my competence. That is clear. However, I have my own job to do here. I am required to verify that strategically relevant orders coming through from STRACC or CASAL are correctly prosecuted.''

"And how do you want to verify it?''

"That would be possible if I was allowed access to the Missile Control Centre. That's all I need.''

Think. Meet him halfway on that and keep the peace. If you let him in on a tight enough rein he won't interfere once he's inside. "Right. Under restrictions. You can't possibly go into the MCC now. The real work is going on and will be for hours. They need to be left in peace for the setting up of a strike. You've read procedure manuals?''

"I have.''

"Then you'll know why. They have their hands full.''

"There isn't the room in there," Boyce added. "No deck space for visitors.''

"What you have to—verify—is that a strike is correctly launched. Yes?''

"Exactly, Captain." Kylander was waspish.

"Very well. I'll permit you access to the MCC if and when we are ordered to launch a strike under the following conditions. Only for the duration of a launch. The enactment you can verify, the surrounding management work is none of your business. Also, only yourself and either Dresher or Rimmington. Either or. There isn't room for more than two without being in the way. And neither of these two here are allowed in except in your company. I hope that's acceptable."

Kylander nodded. "That will be acceptable."

Good. "John, will you help Mr. Kylander and his friends find their way back down to the accommodation decks? And then can you make sure all senior officers are briefed about the strike allocation?"

Boyce nodded. "Also a bulletin? Officers' mess and the canteen? Or is it worth the ship's address?"

The ship's address went everywhere, but off duty personnel would be trying to sleep. "Just a bulletin. Keep it low key."

He went back through the CIC and into the Missile Control Centre. It was full. Stothers and Milgrom had gone, Stothers to the missile storage decks and Milgrom down to the nuclear warheads magazine, but all the MCC personnel had assembled and were busy at their stations— ten of them, including Lister.

"There's going to be something of a problem," Lister said quietly. "The PD-targets are fine, but the supps aren't going to be easy."

"Routing?" PD-targets were listed in the TLF complete with an entourage of courses in from any feasible launch area—you just had to pick one out ready made and add an initial route to connect it to the actual launch point, then the Fire Lance could fly to its target. But supplementary targets had no predetermined routes. You had to loan out a route from a nearby PD-target and add a new terminal phase. All of which took time.

Lister shook his head. "Routing should be okay. But what about the target type? They haven't sent us any data through. We just have latitude and longitude and a map. Do we select for ground burst or air burst? What altitude? What yield? That's going to be tricky."

Bedford nodded. What did the people in STRACC expect them to do, guess? "Either they send the data through sometime soon, or this guy Kylander can tell us, or we fire the things without heads. Warren, can you spare me someone to take a signal?"

"Sure." Lister looked round. "Jace. Signal board."

PO3 Kelly Jace, black and beautiful, left the launch coordination console and crossed over to the signal encrypter/decrypter. She tripped the keyboard switch. "Okay, sir."

"NMSS-three Vindicator," Bedford dictated. "Captain Bedford CO. Let Navigation put the date and time on it. STRACC NAVCOM, Nemesis Direction. Fire Lance reply code Dark Mirror. Okay, now the signal text for Nemesis encryption."

"Ready, sir." Jace's dark hands hovered. She could probably type faster than he could talk.

"One—acknowledge SACI oh-one, received June twelve oh-seven twenty. Two—urgently require precise data on Soviet local-area capabilities. Three—what possibility of tactical support from British forces? Right, send it down to Communications to go right away." And he was thinking, my God is this it? Is this it after all? The whole war, the ultimate awful nuclear war, happens and by some miracle of chance and timing manages to happen without you. You begin to believe you've got away with it after all. You've had the sheer thrill of independent command at sea— submarines, nuke systems cruisers, and now a nemesis ship—and all of it without ever having to confront the reality of the weapons you've carried.

Until now.

Some problems supply their own solutions. Not knowing where the final launch points would be inside the prescribed plan area, and still being on the wrong side of the British Isles, the decision about where to head for next was easy: round the top of Scotland and on into the middle of the delineated box. He decided to put the Vindicator on a north-easterly course that would bring the ship through the Shetlands-Faeroes Gap north of the Shetland Islands. But they would follow that course only as far as 59°40'N, and would then turn due east to pass through between the Orkneys and Shetlands and head direct for the Norwegian coast. That course would take them straight across the centre of the plan box.

There were hazards. Not oil installations—the huge production platforms were a thing of the past, most of the fields had been bled dry, and the remaining wellheads were automatic stations down on the sea floor that fed their hot crude direct into a pipeline network focussing at the big shore terminals. The shore terminals would have gone the way of

the war, and the production net would have choked and
stalled. The hazards were the dry land, and the nature of the
sea. He called Boyce and Clemence to his day cabin to
discuss tactics.

The land, to put it crudely, got in the way. It made for
obstacles you had to sail around and that others could possibly hide behind, that defined and narrowed the web of possible routes in and out of the box. It made you both easier to
intercept and easier to shut in. It formed a trap. Any enemy
unit, air or surface or subsurface, would have an easier time
trying to guess which manoeuvring option you might take in
any given situation, was more likely to outguess you and
catch you. The only compensation was that the same con-
straints made it less of a problem to prepare yourself against
any such countering moves by your opponent. You also had a
better idea of where he might happen to be.

The sea was shallow and cluttered. The Shetland-Faeroes
Basin running out northeast into the Norwegian Sea was
deeper than a thousand metres, parts of the Norwegian Trough
went down to more than three hundred metres, but all the rest
was shallower than two hundred. A submarine could bottom
with engines stopped almost everywhere in the area. Making
no noise it would be impossible to detect with hydrophones,
and on an uneven or rock cluttered floor, it would be difficult
to detect by echo-locating sonar until you were almost right
on top of it. Worse still, a profusion of shallow-sea water
layers and irregular bottom-to-surface bouncing of sound would
completely degrade the long range discrimination of even the
most sensitive hydrophones, while the shallowness made it
impractical to deploy more than a single Surtass line at around
fifty metres down a few hundred metres astern of the ship.

So they needed a Wolfmarine screen. A constant patrol by
three machines would do, sweeping a perimeter one hundred
and sixty kilometres out from the ship, just a fraction further
than the maximum range of the Vindicator's own anti-submarine
mode Fire Lances. Only three patrol sectors were needed,
forward and port and starboard. While they were making
thirty knots, no submarine in the world would be able to close
from astern without making enough noise to be heard forever
through any sea. The Wolfmarines could sacrifice two of their
self-defense AIM-320 missiles in order to carry a Magan on
one side boom, a long and slender magnetic anomaly detector
that responded to the slight distortion imposed on the Earth's

magnetic field by the presence of a mass of metal—a submarine. Carrying a Magan would reduce the frequency with which they would have to hover to use the dipping sonar. Hovering drank fuel, and at 160 kilometres out they were already reduced to two hours on station plus an adequate action reserve. At two hours on station plus one hour out and another back, the machines would be in the fair for four hours at a stretch. With out-and-back time the same as loiter time, there would be six Wolfmarines in the air at once, three on station and three transferring. Each one of the twelve helicopters and each of the twelve crews would have to spend four hours in any eight flying. It would be a cumulative strain.

Did Bedford want a CAP, a combat air patrol? A solitary F-28 could be kept in the air at all times, ready to engage an intruder and above all able to survey the surrounding sea and air space—at its service ceiling of 18,000 metres an F-28's radars could watch a circle of sea more than nine hundred kilometres across. But no, it wasn't necessary as long as they had enough Skyhooks to provide airborne early warning. They would begin to lose the Skyhooks if nuclear strikes came in. Then they would need the precious fuel for CAPs.

A new signal came in while they were still discussing: a response to Bedford's transmission.

ORIG: CASAL NAVALCOM NMSS DIR 1016 JUNE 12 0145
FRWD: STRACC NAVCOM JUNE 12 0150
INCOMING: JUNE 12 0900
NMSS-3 VINDICATOR CPT BEDFORD CO

1. Soviet in-area air and naval capability unknown but assumed minimal. Advise signals intelligence indicates one or more Soviet units at sea, also increased command signal traffic.
2. British Emergency Government cannot provide tactical support due to lack of forces.

"Huh," Boyce said. "It's starting to look as though they think of us as expendable. You'd expect they would have brought a destroyer or sub across the Atlantic to rendezvous for support. We can't really be the only thing the US Navy still has operational. And if we are we sure aren't expendable."

"The air strike potential," Clemence said. "Land forces are out, all the big carriers went down to tactical action or nukes. With ten F-28s we probably represent the single most powerful concentration of air power in the northern hemisphere.''

"The F-28s are expendable," Bedford said. "The ship's expendable. Only the strategic war load isn't.''

"Reminds me.'' Boyce adjusted his glasses, forefinger lifting the middle of the frame. ''This problem of assigning warheads to the supplementary targets. Kylander was suggesting we should use Drexel's expertise. Soviet strategic capabilities is his speciality. What do you think?''

"Assigning warheads." Bedford thought for a moment. It was the same difference as having a strategic expert working on the problem back in the States. ''He'd be working for Wigner, wouldn't he? Okay, see what Warren says. If he's happy with the idea, and if he can arrange for the guy not to be left alone for even a moment, then we'll give it a try.''

"I'm Judy Wigner," the lieutenant said, smiling. It was just about the first time that anyone on board had been friendly to him. ''Target Control Officer. Welcome to the MCC.''

Missile Control Centre—MCC. It had to be, of course, but don't tell the Americans because they wouldn't understand. ''This is where you control the Fire Lances.''

"In land attack mode, four hundred of them, yes. The launches of vehicles assigned to anti-ship mode and anti-submarine mode, the tactical modes, are run from the Weapon Systems Control Centre under direction from the CIC. Okay now, what do you know about Fire Lance?''

"I know what a cruise missile is. I don't know Fire Lance in too much detail.''

"A-BMG 119 Fire Lance," she recited. ''Sea Launched Advanced Cruise Missile. Seven metres long—eight with the launch booster. Total launch weight two and one quarter tonnes. Standard warheads one hundred to two hundred fifty kilotonne yield. And it's the best cruise missile there ever was. Familiar with the guidance principles?''

Drexel nodded. ''Inertial navigation with terrain comparison.''

"Right. Terrain contour matching aided inertial navigation system. Primary guidance is through the gyroscopes and accelerometers of the INS. It follows a preset course from the launch point to the initial timing control point, then it enters into the preset course to the target and descends to as low as fifteen metres off the ground to keep it as invisible as possible. The route programme is generated on the basis of data supplied by the US Defense Mapping Agency and the US Defense Intelligence Agency—exactly what the ground is like and just where the targets and defences are. The missile could fly the whole way blind, but that isn't accurate enough when you want to hit the target on the button, so the terrain contour matching is added.''

''The missile periodically looks at the ground it's flying over with its radar, compares it with a map stored in its computer, and corrects its course accordingly.''

''Right. There are up to twenty eight course control points programmed in for the longest routes—that including the terminal map on approach to the target. All the preset events have to be passed—the control points, the launch events from booster ignition through booster jettison to turbofan start—before the warhead can arm itself on target approach. If the vehicle somehow gets lost no harm is done.''

''And the Fire Lance is subsonic. About a thousand kilometres an hour.''

''A thousand fifty. Four hours to a target at maximum range, near enough. It's not much faster than the old Tomahawk, but the real improvements are in its observability and survivability. The observability is low. It flies so low over the ground, and it's pretty well stealthed so that it gives only a very small signature even on an airborne look-down radar. And then for survivability it has electronic countermeasures. The ECM includes crude incident radar jamming—saturates and blinds a missile guidance radar and can switch frequencies as fast as the attacker—and it also has position faking or position multiplying. That's all done by phase shifting on the radar transponder so that an attacker's radar either thinks it's where it isn't, or else can't tell which of several echoes is the real target. Unless the steering computer is *very* good, any attacking missile just hits the air and then the ground right after. Also, the on-board electronics are all hardened against electromagnetic pulse effects. It's estimated that with a fully functioning Soviet air defence, eighty percent of the Fire Lances would get through to their targets. Against a Third World target country it should be one hundred percent. Never been politically necessary to try that out.'' Wigner stopped and looked round the MCC. ''Well, I'd better show you how this place works. Then we can get you started.''

Drexel surveyed the consoles lining the room. There seemed to be work stations for nine or ten people, most of them occupied. There was another female officer in khaki like Wigner, and the rest were lower ranks in denim blue.

"Okay, over here. This is the Launch Control position." A three seat console where two petty officers were working. "Lt. Lewy runs this function, but he's down on the missile decks with the boss right now. Here we have the Armaments Disposition Invoice, the Missile Tasking Control Position and the Launch Coordination Computer. It all starts out with the Armaments Disposition Invoice. The ADI is a computerized listing of all the vehicles and all the warheads—where each and every one is at any time on the storage decks or the magazine, or which warhead is fitted into which vehicle, and what readiness state everything is in. It provides continuous data on what's where, and if it's ready to go, and where it's supposed to go if it is. Without the ADI we'd just lose track down there."

Wigner turned to the other side of the room. Another three seat console where two people were working. "This is the Target Control position—my department. This here is Chief PO Jonathan Deevers." The black petty officer looked up briefly from his work and nodded. "And Seaman Alice Jackman." Jackman barely glanced away from her computer screen.

"I'll be working here?" Drexel asked.

"Right. Here we work the Target Listing File. The TLF is a computer listing all the predetermined targets all over the globe. Thousands of them in every country. *Everywhere.*"

"That's where the name Nemesis comes from, isn't it? Naval Mobile-response Strategic System. Because the Fire Lances can be targeted absolutely anywhere. They're not dedicated warheads."

"Right. You know your way around okay. Your job, I guess. So—the PD-targets. Each one is stored as a location, an end point map, a type description with the warhead assignment and such so that we know what to put on a vehicle going there. There's also a priority determining key and a listing code-complex for strike series generation if we're told to put together our own launch, but we don't need to worry about that because we've been given nice and simple fixed lists from STRACC. More important is the way we handle supplementary targets, which by definition aren't already in the TLF. The first problem is routing the missile from its launch point to the target location. What we do is to attach the supplementary target to a geographically appropriate PD-target already in the file—tag it on, you might say. Doesn't matter whether the supp is a site of something or just an open field where the enemy have set up a missile launcher. The principle is the same. We associate it with a PD-target so that we can tell our Fire Lance how to get there by borrowing most of a ready-made route in to the PD-target. We just have to generate a new end phase.''

"But you still have to assign a warhead.''

"For which they haven't given us the data, so that's where you'll come in. Okay now, this here is the Guidance Control position.'' Another three seat console with an officer and two crew working the keyboards. "This is Lt. Barbara Vogt who runs it, with PO2 Charles Gowlett and Seaman James Broglie. They run the Target Navigation Computer. It generates the routes from the launch points to the targets, all complete with the necessary contour maps for the course control points, and sets them up ready for input into the individual missile guidance computers. In general the PD-targets all have ready routes reaching in from one or several feasible launch areas—that is, routes from an initial timing control point onwards. Then the TNC just has to fish out the appropriate route, add on an initial phase to take the missile from its eventual launch point to the initial timing control point, and the route is ready. Basically it's just the same for a supplementary target but with the added on terminal phase specifically generated.''

Vogt looked up. "Don't make it sound so easy. It isn't.''

Wigner shook her head. "Okay now, once we have a route complete with launch point it goes back for the TLF to tag on the warhead requirement, then it goes over to the Launch Control position where they arrange for a vehicle to be tasked with the route and fitted with the correct yield warhead. Once the vehicle is tasked and pre-armed it's only necessary to launch it from the correct selected launch point and it will fly all the way to its target, arm its warhead, and engage the target by detonating right at its aiming point. Then the only thing Lewy's people have to do is coordinate the launch. But now that's an art in itself. Each of the launchers fires four missiles every two minutes. That means that down on the missile decks on each side of the ship they have to deliver four missiles every two minutes to the hoist, and it has to be exactly the right missile in the sequence. The missiles are spread over three decks and back through six bays—the furthest aft have to be rolled sixty metres to get to the hoist, and you can't have the gangway jammed by a team coming back the other way with an empty car to collect their next missile. The ship is sailing the whole time and you miss your launch point and the Fire Launce can't go. If Lewy doesn't get it right up here they have utter chaos down there.''

Wigner ended her summary of the Fire Lance system and grabbed hold of one of the spare chairs. She towed it across to the Target Control Position where Deevers and Jackman were working, sat down in her own chair and pulled the spare in next to her. Deevers rolled his seat to the side to make space. Drexel sat in the chair she'd arranged for him.

"Nice chair, huh? Rotates, is fully adjustable, and you can lock the rollers. Look, down here. Yeah. That lever's important. We're in for some rough weather ahead—a real storm coming down in front of us. You want to be able to sit secure instead of rolling across the deck. Okay now.'' She tapped instructions into her position keyboard and the screen in front of her lit up. "The supps we've been given are all just coordinates in space. I figure what we should do is call up map data and see just where they are." A full colour mapscape was suddenly skidding across the screen as she typed. "Then maybe you can tell us what's there and we should be able to figure out what size warhead to put on them. I guess it's going to take some time. There's a lot of them.''

Noon in the canteen, forward of the C3 box on 1st platform—a bright space divided by steel pillars supporting the structures above, laid out with rows of paired four-seat tables to accommodate a maximum of slightly more than half the crew. And the whole of the canteen a green deck area, one of the places you were allegedly safe.

Outside it was blowing a gale and rain mixed with snow was lashing the sea and the ship. Even in the advanced state of climate collapse the heat store of the ocean could pump enough energy into the weather world to generate low pressure systems up over Greenland, huge swirling whirls of winds and fronts that came roaring down eastward in full fury. The Vindicator was running northeast at the perpetual 30 knots and overriding a following sea by main force. The waves were too short and sharp to pitch the great ship, although they could jolt it and send dim shudders through the armoured leviathan, but the long underlying swell was rocking the ship slowly bow up and then bow down.

It had still been calm at breakfast and the whole of Kylander's team had turned up to eat. Now only Gittus and half his soldiers were on show. She hoped, she most fervently hoped, that Kylander and all the rest of them were seasick. What had surprised Gloria was that the crew hadn't noticeably shunned the troops after what had happened. But then they were so isolated on the ship and desperate for word of the conditions back home. Word had got around about the fate of the 101st Air Assault. It was a division assigned to the strategic reserve and had never been sent to Europe in the train of the 7th Army reinforcements because Europe was over too quickly. The 101st had been dispersed out of Fort Campbell as soon as the first nukes started coming down on the DEW Line and Pine Tree Line early warning radars, and had simply disintegrated during all the chaos that had followed. Gittus and his detachment were part of a scratched together company that had finally found its way inside STRACC and the Cheyenne Mountain Complex. Their sole job since then had been guard and execution details. The only people Gittus and his men had ever killed in the defence of America during the entire war were fellow Americans. It seemed that like anything else, you got used to it quite quickly.

There weren't many people in the canteen, even at midday. The Fire Lance teams were working at full stretch, the Air Group and the full air support departments were fully occupied, and the ship's defensive systems were at readiness stations. On-duty people were breaking in rotation to eat, and then not lingering long—almost half the tables were completely unoccupied. But she sat down opposite Raffles just the same.

Raffles was just picking at the stuff on her tray. The ice cream was already melting as it waited.

"You're not seasick?"

Raffles shook her head. "No, I'm not sick."

Just isolated and shocked, fearfully unhappy and desperately alone. Gloria tried a touch of vengeance humour. "I heard Kylander and the others are puking their guts. Don't suppose it happens to be true?"

Raffles shrugged. "Fine with me if it is."

"Drexel's had time to get used to the sea. I wanted to ask you about him. You know he's helping set up the strike series—doing target value assessments? What do you make of him?''

''Hardly know him.'' Danella Raffles looked straight at her, a surprisingly steady glance. ''Why don't you talk to him yourself?''

That was an accusation, just a small one. By listening to Raffles you've intruded into the *privacy* of her horror and she's still uneasy about it. Slowly coming to terms with that is all a part of the gradual readjustment the woman has to make. Keep her talking and hope you can help her help herself. ''What do you make of the fact that we're preparing a strike? I mean, you've seen what it does on the receiving end. Next to no one who's ever been around when a nuclear missile is fired has had firsthand experience of its effects.''

''That's why they get fired.'' A terribly bleak smile. ''It isn't real. It's just a procedure you run through. Just a conceptual game. That's why the people in control now in STRACC and CASAL are going to order the launch, and that's why you people on this ship are going to do it. Because not one of you knows.''

''There won't be any launch.'' There couldn't be. There just *couldn't* be.

The ceiling speakers all over the canteen clicked as the ship's address came on. Everyone stopped to listen.

''Captain in the CIC! First Officer and Supervisor in the CIC!''

''What's that mean?'' Raffles looked almost frightened.

''It's started,'' Gloria said. ''They've found us.''

BOYCE HAD BEATEN him. Boyce had been just through in the MCC, while he had to come up the ladders from two decks below where he'd been talking with Korsyn in the Weapon Systems Control Room. Dylong made it in just after him, coming in through the forward tunnel door. Then the CIC's three heads stood together while Marcovicci explained the situation. Lt. Cmdr. Ted Marcovicci had been directing the nerve centre; he was short and compact like any ideal pilot, he was Air Group CO and no longer an active flyer—the Vindicator's requirements didn't include squadron operations against distant targets.

There were two air contacts on the forward SCAN-Skyhook, down on the sea and three hundred kilometres out and closing. The line-up from ship to Skyhook to contacts was almost a straight line. The Vindicator was at 58°30′N 9°W and heading directly northeast on 45° at 30 knots, the Skyhook was at one hundred kilometres out dead on the bow, and the contacts were two hundred kilometres further on bearing 41°. They were due west of the Shetlands, they must have come down through the Shetland-Faeroes Gap. They had to be Russians, making a perfect intercept on the basis of the Vindicator's morning signal transmission. For a confirmation they just needed the radar echo characteristics.

The CIC was half full. CPO Irene Jablonski was running the SADIS from her Track Evaluator/Scheduling Operator position, while PO2 Hayes had moved to his Air Detector/Tracker console. Jablonski was waiting for the identification to come through.

"Got it." She didn't even turn her head from her board. "Fanners, both contacts."

Bedford nodded. And Dylong was already plugging in to the

OpSum, and Marcovicci was making for the internal door and the ladder down to the Air Operations Centre on the deck below.

Fanner was Nato's name for the Yak-236, a vertical/short takeoff and landing fighter normally deployed on Soviet warships.

"CIC to Condition One," Bedford said. "Weapons and AOC to Condition One."

Dylong talked the order into the ship's address.

Hayes was hunching forward in front of his screen. The black petty officer had a way of crouching in his seat when something was starting to happen. "Bandits holding course. Climbing."

The Fanners could afford to come up off the sea. Their radar threat receivers would tell them they'd been picked up by the SCAN, and now if they climbed they would widen their horizon and be able to look around for themselves. Find the Vindicator.

"Scramble two Angels on intercept." Bedford strode to the commander's dais. "Bring two more up ready on deck. Rotate the Wolfmarines down out of the way."

Boyce passed the order to the AOC—he had already plugged in beside Dylong at the OpSum. Bedford slipped onto his raised chair on the little dais, pulled on his own headset and switched in to the CIC open circuit. The telltale light on his console's comm panel came on. He leaned on the little desk console and watched the CIC fill up around him. Forty seven years old and a lifelong career in the Navy. And this, oh God, was finally the real thing.

Lt. junior grade Conrad Birkinshaw, runaway son of a black fundamentalist preacher in Tuscaloosa, married with a wife and a baby boy in Oakland—dead now, of course.

The F-28 was rolling out of the elevator box on a tractor tow, the one-piece forward canopy and windshield was already down and locked. No bow frame breaking the smooth acrylic and interfering with the excellent all-round view—not that visibility was going to count for anything in this. They had the floods over the TLCP dimmed right down so they could see what they were doing without unnecessarily wrecking the night vision of the pilots. Shadow figures on the soaking deck around the catapult head, and nothing beyond but a ring of stormy night. Rain lashed the canopy.

He'd kicked out the power umbilical and gone to internal battery power the moment the TLCP passed the scramble through. They had the big door rolling up so fast that he saw Chad Lovins in Angel 1 leaping off the ramp and disappearing as a double flare of tail jet exhaust into the surrounding darkness. The power check ran okay, all systems loads covered for all computers and all actuator drives for the aerodynamic surfaces—no warning lights on the autocheck panel. He was checking that the accommodation air and heating and pressurization was okay, and that his suit was correctly connected up in case the main system failed. He had his feet up ready on the high heel-line of the reclining seat. You needed that aid with the gee force the wonderful bird could throw in a manoeuvre.

Rain lashed the canopy and the wind rocked the rolling aircraft. Birkinshaw looked over his left shoulder at the retreating elevator box and TLCP. The TLCP slipped back behind the port fin of the twin finned machine. The outboard wings were folding down, came right down and locked.

"Catapult is returned," said the voice of the TLCP into his ears. "We're going to get you off on the next good swell. Wind is sixty six dead astern." A force 8 in kilometres per hour.

The parka-wrapped woman driving the squat tractor down in front of the bird's nose had lined him up perfectly first try. He had 225° on the inertial compass as he faced dead astern at the head of the catapult.

"Take flight level fifty metres. Circle right. Make that close-in to avoid a tired Skyhook coming in on the stern. Your intercept heading will be forty one degrees."

The tractor swung clear. Flight deck crew were locking the catapult connector to the front wheel leg. Fifty metres away the ramp waited at the edge of the dark.

"You're on the catapult. Clear to start engines."

He gunned up the two huge turbofans in the fuselage behind him. A roar rising to a shuddering shriek penetrated the canopy and the snug-fit helmet and the built-in earphones. Switch the autocheck to power plant readouts: no lights on the constant systems monitor.

In the shriek of the jets in his ears: "Your load factor is good, ramp fully deployed. Vector forty degrees at forty eight percent."

All flight systems were engaged. The bird had quadruplex

redundant flight control systems, computers that governed all manoeuvring through the fly-by-wire and the controlled configuration vehicle trimming operations. He set for catapult assist, ramp full, thrust vector 40°, vectored thrust 48%—the CCV computer automatically deployed the leading and trailing edge flaps to give optimum lift at the angle of attack and airspeed with which he would come off the ramp. He could feel the ship slowly pitching stern up. Power was increasing smoothly. The F-28 was waiting to be flung into the night.

The catapult would throw the bird at the ramp and up and off it. The advantage of the ramp wasn't any upward thrust it might give while the aircraft travelled its fifteen metre length and the catapult disengaged and slammed into its hydraulic brakes. It was the fact that the aircraft's nose was tipped up at 18°, increasing the angle of attack and packing more air under and over the wings. The aircraft left the ramp with the speed imparted by its own power—52° of the engine thrust directed aft plus a half-component of the 48% directed down through the vectored outlets—and by the huge kick of the electromagnetic catapult. It was going fast enough to be able, at that favourable attack angle, to support half its weight by aerodynamic uplift on the wings alone. The downward vectored thrust only had to balance half the total weight in the air, so that most of the engine power could go into accelerating the machine to attain true flying speed in seconds. It mattered. Aerodynamic lift was efficient flying, hovering on downward directed jet plumes was a gross squandering of fuel. The sooner you attained true flight, the more war load you could carry and the further you could fly it. He had nine tonnes basic weight of aircraft, with five and one half tonnes of internal fuel and one tonne of external in a centreline drop tank, and four tonnes of missiles. The F-28 Skycat could manage another four and one half tonnes more before it reached maximum takeoff weight.

Through the jet shriek in his ears: *"Okay, Angel Two. Ten seconds to launch. Wheel brakes off."*

He unlocked the wheel brakes, and only the catapult was holding the quivering bird. He took hold of the control stick with his right hand. A little thing with limited displacement and force sensors to do the job of conveying pilot instructions to the aircraft—another of the advantages of fly-by-wire, effortless.

"Angel Two, standby to launch. Go!"

A mighty thundering kick. Lift. Nose up and out over a black waste of sea just below. Undercarriage straight up and closed, airspeed winding higher. Stable, with enough lift to drop the nose and begin the gentlest turn. The CCV computer automatically adjusting the vectored thrust and the flaps—you see the stabilizers flicking through angle changes just down forward of the canopy. Airspeed 80 knots, better than stalling speed and zero vectored thrust. *Flying.* He threw the control stick and banked into a steep turn, dark wild waves sloping up on the starboard side of the canopy. Following Angel 1 into the near night, waiting for the AOC's mission briefing.

The CIC was full, all twenty people at their stations. Bedford sat on his dais to the left of the tunnel door and watched the lights on the main plot past the OpSum on the opposite wall. The Wolfmarines in the ASW screen were in danger, out beyond even the 140 km protective range of the Seastrike mounted on the ship. Watchdogs 4 and 5 on the port and bow sector were down low and heading full speed back to the ship; Watchdog 6 on the starboard sector was at the aftermost end of its sweep and far away from the area of possible action. Angels 1 and 2 were racing away northeast, keeping low so that the Bandits didn't see them any sooner than could be avoided. Not for safety's sake—the F-28s carried snap-up capable missiles which neutralized any possible height advantage enjoyed by the Bandits. They just wanted to get as close as possible before the Bandits saw them and turned to run.

The Bandits were still climbing, were at 4,000 metres and heading straight for the SCAN-Skyhook, which was trying to escape at its crawling maximum speed. They were 250 kilometres from the ship, 150 from Skyhook. They were approaching at Mach 0.8, 960 kilometres an hour, sixteen kilometres a minute.

Dylong's voice over the headset. "They should just about now be able to see our tower on their radars."

"Our radars are quiet?"

Redden answered, the SADIS Supervisor. Everyone in the CIC could hear the commanding officer over the open circuit even though most of them usually spoke not on the same circuit but privately within their own departments. "All radars shut down except Skytop mode."

Chief Petty Officer Irene Jablonski at the SADIS Tactical

Evaluation position: "Watchdog Five is in missile range of the Bandits, sir."

And the Bandits would have been seeing the Wolfmarine skimming the surface of the sea for several minutes now. Watchdog 5's survival depended on the arrival of the Angels. The main plot marked them as making Mach 1.4, 1,680 kilometres an hour and their maximum possible sea level speed.

PO3 Kuroda spoke from his Talker board just across the other side from the tunnel door. "Sir, AOC wants to arm a second pair of interceptors for a larger action radius. Two drop tanks under the wings instead of one centreline."

That would mean 2,000 kilogrammes of external fuel instead of just 1,000. But it meant that although the centreline station was freed to carry up to two medium range air-to-air missiles, both inboard pylons under the wings would be tied up with a loss of altogether four medium range missiles. Balancing fuel and war loads for missions was an art in itself. "Whatever they like."

PO2 Hayes from the Air Detector/Tracker: "One Bandit is turning. Heading for the position of Watchdog Five."

"They're flying without radar." Dylong's voice. The crew of Watchdog 5 were hoping to escape notice, and failing. "AOC are warning them they're under attack."

The Bandits were at 200 kilometres, at 4,500 metres altitude.

"Bandits chattering the whole time," Kuroda relayed. "Communications and EW are getting Russian on Crackler Twos." Crackler 2 was the tactical communications transceiver fitted to the Yak-236. "They've also been talking on Buzzer Box. Encrypted. Talking back to their base, sir."

The Russian pilots were high enough to see everything on their radars—the ship, the Skyhooks arrayed around it, the scuttling ASW helicopters, and the intercepting Angels racing in. They would have told their home base what they could see. That was their job.

Hayes. "Bandits turning. No longer climbing. They're turning through onto oh-four-eight degrees. Steadying on that heading. They're accelerating."

Heading back almost exactly the way they'd come, trying to get the hell out of there with a pair of Skycats coming in on their tails. On the plot the leading Skycat was around 110 kilometres behind them, with the second about another thirty to forty further back. The Bandits' speed markers were coming up to Mach 1.5—from now on they would accelerate right through to the Fanner's maximum Mach 1.8, outrunning the Angels still down on the surface of the sea.

"Tell the Angels to climb so they can gain speed." They could fly faster the higher they went. At real height the F-28 could make Mach 2.4—one of the several ways in which it outperformed its Soviet equivalent.

"Do we assume they've launched missiles?" Boyce asked from his position beside Dylong at the OpSum.

"We do." Little missiles. Modern missiles that produced hardly any echo on the radar screen until very close indeed, that fired their own radar pulses to home in on a target without external guidance, that could be instructed on launch to fly an invisible intercept course before switching on their radar and announcing their presence as they sought their target on final approach. Fire-and-forget weapons, FF mode. Fuck off mode, the British called it, because you could launch your weapons and then turn and fuck off out of there and away from danger as fast as possible. "How close was the Bandit to Watchdog Five when he turned?"

Hayes: "Forty kilometres, sir."

"Watchdog Five report radar threat on their tail." That was Kuroda relaying from the AOC. "Trying to turn to get off a missile."

The Wolfmarines were each carrying a pair of short range AIM-320s for self-defence. They were designed to engage an aircraft but also had a reasonable chance of knocking down an incoming missile.

"We have an ID on the missile radar over the SCAN," Dylong reported. "It's an Axhead." A Soviet medium range air-to-air missile, very up-to-date.

Hayes: "The Axhead and Wolfmarine tracks have coincided. The radar echo just hit the sea, sir."

Just like that, a helicopter and its two crew killed.

"The AIM-320 is circling, sir." Circling on target search with no target to find.

"Forget it," Dylong said, quite gently. "We only need commentaries on action tracks."

"Bow position SCAN has a small contact coming in," Boyce said. "Heading dead for it. That will be an anti-radiation missile." Standing at the OpSum, he and Dylong could combine displays direct form the AOC and the Radar

Systems Control Room. "SCAN shut down. Trying avoidance and ECM."

One deck below in the AOC Clemence's people were not only trying to raise a distress beacon from any ditched survivor of Watchdog 5 while directing the two Angels on to the fleeing Bandits, they were also trying to save the Skyhook whose SCAN radar was looking the way things were happening.

Kuroda: "AOC say do we want to fly two more Angels?"

Two more Skycats to help in the chase, to be up there already to intercept any new intruders coming down from the north. That still left six on board. Both Boyce and Dylong, doing tactical evaluation, had glanced round and nodded, so no objections occurred to them. "Yes," Bedford said.

"The Skyhook is taking radar from the incoming missile," Dylong said. "Got an ID. A Sneaker." Sneaker was a very low-observability anti-radiation missile that homed on a radar source, and that could switch to using its own active homing radar if its target suddenly shut down. "The Skyhook is firing chaff. It's beating the Skyhook's ECM." In the AOC a pilot at the remote vehicle console was losing to a too-clever missile. Soviet technology had caught up in some areas. "The Skyhook's gone."

Now the Vindicator was blind out to the northeast after the retreating Bandits. They would have to rely on what the chasing Angels relayed back to them.

Kuroda: "AOC will put up another Skyhook as soon as they've flown both Angels."

Bedford nodded. Kuroda was watching him and that was enough.

Boyce unplugged from the OpSum and came over with his headset slung round his neck and the lead dangling. The padded earpieces didn't quite sit comfortably over the sides of his glasses—you could see little red marks right in front of his ears just under the metal. "The killing's started and the first thing we do is lose."

Bedford shrugged. A Wolfmarine couldn't fight a Yak-236 under any circumstances. "What's worrying me is where they've come from." The Yak-236, the Fanner, was essentially a naval aircraft just like the Skycat, intended for flying from ship platforms where its short or vertical takeoff and vertical landing facility were of most advantage.

"Could be they've come down from those little bases they're supposed to have established along the north Norwe-

gian coast. It's just the right aircraft to put there. Need next to
no runway, don't need concrete, and a naval attack capability
is just what was wanted up here.'' Boyce shrugged. ''On the
other hand they can operate from a carrier or a little ASW
helicopter cruiser. They *shouldn't* have any of those still
afloat.''

''But if they're operating from a ship they're operating
from a mobile platform that can stay out of sight but still
come in close enough to launch concentrated strikes.''

''Preferable if they're coming down from Norway.'' Boyce
looked across at the main plot with its blank northeastern
area. ''Right at the end of their operational range with no
time on target to play with. Let's hope they don't have a
major surface unit up here.''

Bedford nodded. He switched to the ship's address. Time
to tell his people what was happening.

The F-28 Skycat was at 6,000 metres, up above the low
pressure system's cloud and weather. The sandwich world
was an infinite panorama of deep gloom under a smooth and
sombre roof, was a sightless circuit of emptiness.

Conrad Birkinshaw was not alone. The stylized display on
the horizontal situation indicator told him where the Shetlands
and Faeroes and Norway were, where the Vindicator was 700
kilometres behind. On the vertical situation display set, the
cathode ray display mounted high in the centre of his instrument board, he had Chad Lovins' Angel 1 out in front of him
and both Bandits further out and running, plus indicators for
Angels 3 and 4 following 500 kilometres behind. On the
combining glass of his head up display right in his forward
line of sight he had basic course, altitude and flight data
glowing gently against the distant dark. He switched to his
AOC control channel.

''Angel Two. Bandits One and Two at one hundred five
kilometres, altitude five thousand. Heading steady oh-four-
eight at Mach 1.8. Angels One and Two at five thousand.
Making Mach 2.2. Closing range.'' Closing it at eight
kilometres a minute after nineteen minutes of chase.

''Vindicator. Copy, Angel Two. Break off at eight-five-oh.''

''*Angel One.''* Lovins, the boss of the two of them, talking
to him on the tactical channel. *''Conrad, we'll go to nine
hundred to launch if necessary. We can fly home half the way
at economy speed, dammit.''* At Mach 0.8, at 520 knots,

using less than half as much fuel per minute. And by 900 kilometres out from the ship they would be only 60 behind the Bandits, close enough to fire the AIM-300 medium range missiles.

Both birds were carrying eight AIM-320 short range missiles, four on hardpoints under the nose and two on each outboard underwing pylon. They were carrying eight AIM-300s, one on each outboard pylon, one on each offline hardpoint station under the fuselage. They were carrying two Long-arm anti-radiation missiles, one on each offline hardpoint station aft of the AIM-300. Each bird had a 20mm rotary cannon in the nose back of the radar housing for if it had to dogfight. But there would be no need for dogfighting—just launch AIM-300s and break off for home. Coming up to 800 from the ship.

The radar contact tone bleeped in his ears. On the vertical situation display two new indicators had appeared, two contacts at 142° right—due south. He selected a format change to see more detail. They were right down at sea level and coming in at Mach 1.1, they were in a perfect position to cut off Lovins and himself. The radar threat receiver flashed an alarm, wrote out a Soviet air search radar. The IFF reply evaluator clicked up no reply claiming friend or foe.

Tactical channel. "Angel Two. Chad, I have two Bandits at one-four-two degrees, range two-seven-oh and closing."

"Angel One. I have the new Bandits. I'm launching against Bandits One and Two now. Break off left."

His tactical computer had determined an identification from both his own radar return characteristics and from the radars flying on the Bandits. Two more Yak-236s. He tipped the little control stick left and the aircraft banked in a turn. The gloom world canted over, deep darkness out on his left and nothing-grey on his right. The display revolving on the vertical situation set showed the new Bandits in a perfect position to make an intercept—the F-28s only had enough fuel to fly straight back the way they had come, no avoidance courses. He came round 180° according to the heading indicator and levelled out straight. On the display Angel 1 was turning, all of seventy kilometres behind. There were also indicators for two AIM-300s racing after Bandits 1 and 2 who were still retreating northeast at maximum speed.

Control channel. "Angel Two. We have two new Fanners at plan position six-one north oh-three east. Heading—" they were turning now for a cut-off intercept "—turning onto heading three-two-nine. Altitude zero. Am returning at six thousand on two-two-eight degrees. Angel One following at eighty-five behind me." Lovins had lost extra distance on the turn.

"Vindicator. Copy your new Bandits Three and Four. Will vector Angels Three and Four on to them. Can you avoid or will they intercept?"

The new Fanners were climbing and gaining speed. Mach 1.2 now. "They can intercept in three and one half minutes. We have zero combat time. When can Angels Three and Four intercept Bandits?"

"Three and Four can intercept in six minutes."

"Copy." He changed channels. "Angel Two. Chad, we have to fight the Bandits ourselves."

"Copy, Conrad. My Bandit targets just disappeared in a mush of ECM and chaff back there. My arrows got lost, no hits."

So the first two Bandits had escaped. Didn't matter. He and Angel 1 were flying down the long side of a triangle while the new pair of slower Soviet aircraft were flying in to meet them across the much shorter base. The separation distance was now only one hundred kilometres and dropping rapidly.

"Angel One. Conrad, they're closing on you to attack range. Break right, man."

"Angel Two. Copy." He was pushing instructions into the tactical computer. Targets 3 and 4, AIM-300s 1 and 8. The computer immediately pumped heading, altitude and range data into two of the AIM-300s. Ready lights. He pushed the launch buttons. Left and right a missile dropped from each outboard wing pylon and streaked red-trailed on a left-hand curve. He tipped the control stick right and turned through 60°. The Bandits had swung slightly, were trying for Angel 1. His own missiles on the display were racing away towards the Bandits, radars locking on to them. "Angel Two. Chad, they're coming for you."

"I see them. I have a radar threat warning. Correction, two radar threats. Two missiles coming in. Axheads. Flipping head on to launch AIM-320s."

On the display his own two missiles were going down behind him towards the Bandits. And there were not two but four missiles climbing up towards Angel 1. And the bird had already flipped head-on and then away again. There wouldn't be time for another defensive launch. "Chad, there's four missiles coming for you. Both Bandits have launched at you."

"Copy, Conrad." Angel 1 was turning sharply away on the display.

The first two climbing contacts disappeared, hit by Angel 1's own AIM-320s, intercepting the interceptors. Two more were coming on. Angel 1's format blip on the display started streaming out ECM. The Bandits were streaming ECM. His own missiles slid in and took out both Bandit blips one after the other. The first of the climbing Axhead missiles coincided with Angel 1. The Bandit blips faded.

One last missile went flying on northwest, too unintelligent to search for a new target.

Control channel. "Angel Two. Angel One's a goner. Both Bandits killed. Bandits One and Two escaped. Am diving to keep speed and conserve fuel."

"Vindicator. Copy, Angel Two. Angels Three and Four have you on radar. Your heading for home is two-one-eight degrees. Did Angel one eject?"

"No chance, Vindicator." No chance. He eased the stick over. That was a first taste of high speed war with automated weapons.

A hectic, distant and short-lived situation that had so suddenly lost any immediate threat and any immediate relevance. A deadly little flying game that had never placed the Vindicator in direct danger. Angels 3 and 4 were passing the returning Angel 2, 550 kilometres northeast of the ship. He had ordered the fresh birds up to 15,000 metres from where they would be able to see a circle of ocean more than 800 kilometres across, almost from the Norwegian coast out past the Faeroes and on half the way to Iceland. That would safeguard the northeast sector against more attacking Bandits. The two F-28s could stay up there a good 120 minutes at economy speed.

He had his head set laid on the desk console. It made your ears sweat after a time. The tracks of all four Fanners fitted the interpretation that they had come down from some base somewhere northeast, somewhere up north on the Norwegian coast. The first pair had found the ship while right at the limit of their range, had turned to run home and called in the second pair for support. It was consistent, it explained why the first pair didn't even attempt to fight the Skycats. But they *could* have come from a ship. It would depend, perhaps, on how quickly any more came. If there were any more that could come. And it had cost one Skycat and one Wolfmarine, plus one Skyhook.

Kuroda had the hush mike on his Talker headset folded aside so that Bedford, without his own headset, could hear him. "Sir, AOC have the names through. Lt. Lovins in the Skycat, Lt. Sing and PO Rowland in the Wolfmarine. Communications are still listening, but there are no distress beacons from Watchdog Five."

He nodded. With sheer kinetic energy coupled with its warhead detonation, the Axhead missile would have blown the helicopter to pieces.

Kuroda was listening intently again. "AOC says Angels Three and Four have a surface contact."

Dylong was bending over his OpSum immediately, keying displays on the inset screens. "Three and Four are on loiter at five hundred out, circling and climbing. They're at twelve thousand metres. The surface contact is at—is at four hundred ten kilometres north of them."

It was in the wrong place, too far west, not the direction the Fanners had run. But it *could* be the big ship, the carrier or the cruiser-sized ASW helicopter platform they were flying from. Were there any more aircraft on board, and was the range low enough to fit Yak-236s with heavy anti-ship missiles with which to attempt a stand-off attack on the Vindicator? "What's the range from us?"

"Almost dead on eight hundred kilometres."

"AOC, sir," Kuroda relayed. "They're already bringing armaments and tanks up to fly two F-28s at the contact. Do we want a third Angel to fly with them to provide air-defence support?"

Clemence was fast as hell. "Wait on that. Do we have an identification on the ship yet?"

"It's certainly a Pirate," Dylong said. "No IFF response triggered by the aircraft radars. It's looking back at them with a beam-switching phased array. The computer's searching. One moment."

Boyce had just been talking through his headset. "Communications and EW say it's talking to someone with a Sparker Box. It's a destroyer or a sub."

"Found the radar type," Dylong said, not an ounce of satisfaction or excitement modulating his voice. "Bugeye Pair."

Bugeye Pair was a naval back-to-back air surveillance radar group. Fixing the radar and the transmitter type narrowed down the possible classes of Soviet vessel.

"Has to be some kind of destroyer," Boyce said.

It would carry no Fanners. At the most it would have a pair of anti-submarine helicopters and maybe a Fat Fly robot or a Red Balloon on which to fly a Hanging Basket airborne early warning radar.

"Okay," Bedford said. "Tell AOC to go ahead preparing a strike, but we'll wait until we have a better identification." And now Clemence would really have his hands full, rotating tired Wolfmarines and Skyhooks, replacing the lost Skyhooks and Watchdog 5, receiving Angel 2 as it returned and getting ready to send two more F-28s off from the flight deck. Literally keeping everything in the air at once.

It was a Chenin class destroyer, and he had sent off the strike—two aircraft armed with standoff missiles flying down flat on the ocean and watched over all the way by Angels 3 and 4 on high altitude air observation station.

The identification of the Soviet vessel was achieved by an analysis of the radar return characteristics being observed and relayed by the pair of loitering F-28s. The Chenin's double-box superstructure was clearly discernible, the single semi-lattice stepped tower, the foredeck echo-clutter produced by its gun and the vertical missile launcher array. The Chenin carried a SAN-60 missile system for area air defence corresponding to but with less range than the Vindicator's own DPAD Seastrike, and it had twin rotary cannon CIWS mountings for anti-missile defence, but its main armament was that foredeck array of missile launch boxes. The Chenin class carried at least twelve, probably sixteen Skimmer Poles, SS-N-100 cruise missiles with up to 450 kilometres range. Skimmer Pole was almost like the Fire Lance in its anti-ship mode. It was a sea skimming missile with low radar observability and good ECM defence once it was spotted and engaged; it was difficult to see the thing coming and it had a good chance of getting in close—and it quite possibly carried a nuclear warhead.

He didn't want that ship to come anywhere near him.

Its position suggested that it was on its way towards the Faeroes, probably coming down from northern Norway or even from around North Cape. Once west of the Faeroes it could have plugged the Iceland-UK Gap, taking air reconnaissance information and launching its Skimmer Pole missiles over the horizon at any ship—in other words the Vindicator—that tried to pass through. If the Vindicator had been half a day later the Soviet destroyer would have been ready on station, possibly with other units gathered in support, and the trap would have been laid.

But now he had seen it and he was going to try and take it out. The only question was, what would they do if the Skycats succeeded in sinking or crippling the destroyer? What did the Soviets have left, what other dregs of conventional forces? If the Vindicator, with a nuclear strategic purpose as its sole reason for being, were to fight its way straight through a scratched together defensive screen and come in as close as possible to deep Soviet targets, wasn't that an open provocation for them to go nuclear and fire high-path re-entry ballistic missiles down on his head?

He looked at the CIC wall clock. 1330. Angels 5 and 6 were already on their way, and inside a mere hour his war had turned deadly real. All hell would come visiting yet.

F-28 Skycat Angel 6, in the pilot seat Lt. George Sindow, caucasian, son of a family of Navy fliers with a tradition going right back to the Battle of the Coral Sea. The bird was carrying two external tanks, one on each inboard underwing pylon, and had started out with 7½ tonnes of fuel. It was armed with one Talon supersonic anti-ship missile on the centreline hardpoint station under the fuselage, plus four lighter Seaflash supersonic anti-ship missiles, two on each offline station under its belly. On each outboard underwing pylon it carried a single Longarm anti-radiation missile, and on the hardpoints under the nose were four short range AIM-320s for self-defence against air interceptors. Almost four tonnes of war load. Lt. Todd Bryson, flying out ahead in Angel 5, was carrying two Longarms and three of the heavy Talons.

He was speeding along at fifty metres above the sea, flying blind through darkness and snow and spray at Mach 1.4, heading for the Pirate at maximum low level approach speed. Only a combination of his own attention to the attitude control indicators glowing on the head up display, together with the flight computer's monitoring and constant automatic ride stabilization, was keeping him and his bird in the air. At that speed and that low, dropping the nose by just a couple of degrees would fly him into a wave in a second or so.

Six hundred kilometres from the Vindicator, out past Angels 3 and 4 still at high level on air observation station, ready to warn them of any sudden intruders, any Bandits coming down to intercept the sea level attackers. The Pirate had got a Hanging Basket AEW radar up over his position. It had gone up so quickly he must have flown it on a remotely steered helicopter, a Fat Fly. He knew he had been located by the high level Angels and wanted to see the ocean around himself as he waited for an attack.

The tactical situation on the vertical display showed nothing except Angel 5 ahead and Angels 3 and 4 high up behind. The horizontal situation indicator told him where he was and where the coastlines of the Faeroe Islands were, all worked out by inertial navigation—he never saw them on the radar from this low even though he flew right past their eastern flanks 250 kilometres and nine minutes ago.

The radar contact tone bleeped in his ears, on the vertical situation display a blip appeared representing the Pirate's Hanging Basket. The radar threat receiver flashed alarm as the Hanging Basket's searching pulses found the F-28. Like Angel 5 ahead, he was now inside the horizon ring of the Pirate's airborne surveillance radar and had no more need to hide down low on the sea. He eased the bird up to one hundred metres, more than high enough to launch missiles.

Sindow watched the new format blip on the vertical display. He watched it go out. Bryson in Angel 5 had fired both his Longarms further back on the approach and now the first one had struck home, zeroing straight in on the radar antenna with an observability so low that it couldn't be seen in time for the Pirate to do anything about it. He broke sharp left, black sea surface spinning out beside his canopy, he straightened up, making a course change to ensure that he came in on a bearing different from the one the Pirate last saw. Angel 5 would have broken right.

A voice in his ears on the tactical channel. *"Angel Three. Todd, confirm the Hanging Basket is out of the sky. Can't tell if your second Longarm actually hit the Pirate."* The second missile had been fired in the hope of taking out the air surveillance radar on the Pirate's tower.

"Angel Five. Copy. All three Talons launched. I'm turning away." Angel 5 would be turning at 90 kilometres from the Soviet ship. The Pirate's SAN-60s could reach out beyond that range, were self-guiding fire-and-forget weapons—they could already have been fired over the ship's horizon on an intercept course aimed at the F-28. Now Angel 5's three Talons were heading for the Pirate at Mach 1.6, would scream over its shipboard radar horizon and test its close-in defences.

Sindow flicked the stick over in a right turn, the daytime night sea angled spinning out of the right side of the canopy. Straighten up again as the heading comes round, flying direct for the target once more through a blind of dark snow. Only instruments and trust keep you on line in such conditions.

"Angel Three. George, you're heading straight for the Pirate at Range one-four-five."

"Copy." Time to launch the Longarms. He instructed the computer—port and starboard outboard pylon, heading straight, munition on search-and-home mode. They would fly away looking for a radar to zero in on, but if the Pirate had no senders operating they would switch to their own active homing radars, lock on to the echo of the ship and dive in. He launched port, and the Longarm dropped clear and then streaked red-tailed past him and disappeared into the obscurity ahead. Its reflected rocket trail called up a brief blood gleam from a writhing waste of water. He launched starboard and the second missile whipped away with the same brief eerie vision of hell.

He turned to circle in a long curve to give the missiles a good lead time, and then came back on heading racing for the ship. He eased back the throttles to drop speed— Mach 1.3, 1.2, 1.1, 1.0, Mach 0.9, 0.8 and steady. If he was a hundred metres off the sea, the Pirate's Bugeye Pair back-to-back air surveillance radar group should see him when he was around 55 kilometres out. But he didn't want to close the distance that fast.

"Angel Three. George, Angel Five's Talons got right in to the Pirate. Maybe no hits, maybe a couple. You are coming up to range one-two-zero. Mark."

"Copy, Angel Three." Over the armaments computer he selected the centreline station munition—the Talon he was carrying. The computer fed in heading and range to target. He fired the Talon. Seven hundred and twenty kilogrammes of missile dropped free and the bird lifted and corrected perceptibly. No hell light on the sea this time—the Talon was a turbofan driven supersonic cruiser. At a mere ten thousand metres out from the position of its target it would switch on its radar and home in. Minimal warning. Sindow banked round in another gentle delaying turn.

"Angel Three. George, your Longarms put out the Bugeye Pair. He's wide open to your Talon."

"Angel Six. My Talon's already flying." The missile was so near invisible that 3 and 4, hundreds of kilometres away and up high, wouldn't see it at all until they got reflections coming off the target from its radar.

He straightened up again, still heading for the target, well within range of its SAN-60s if it only knew he was there. Now that its main surveillance radar was out he could risk going in to fifty kilometres to launch the Seaflash missiles—they might have 70 kilogramme warheads compared to the Talon's 200, but they were more destructive than a naval shell. The idea was to make damn sure the Pirate was taken out or hurt so bad he had to run, point anti-missile defences or no point defences. Four Seaflash supersonic arrows streaking in at once should overload him even if he was still relatively undamaged. The trick was to open the way and get in close enough despite the Pirate's SAN-60s. He instructed the computer and the computer instructed both pairs of missiles on the offline stations under the fuselage, giving them the heading and the range to radar switch-on. He fired all four in rapid sequence, the Skycat lifting in steps as each third of a tonne dropped away. Blurred ocean was lit by vanishing moments of red reflected exhaust glow, a strobed and heaving mass of waves in a sparse slow slur.

He turned and circled again, him and his beautiful bird alone in the dark, four hundred kilometres from the nearest friends and twice as far from his floating home.

He came round onto a second circuit, watching the fuel. There was still plenty to take home again—on an attack mission the F-28 had a maximum 1300 kilometre operational radius even on fast approach. He could afford to head back to the Vindicator at Mach 1.4 if he wanted to, a thirty minute journey. Angels 3 and 4 would have to start back for the ship in thirty minutes anyway, and he wanted to be well inside their protective screen before they turned away.

Sindow came round again and levelled his bird right at the Pirate. He wanted to see if there was any clear indication that the target really had been hit hard and that no second mission was necessary. Mach 0.8, sixteen kilometres a minute.

"Angel Three. George, that's close enough, we think. Turn out of there."

He could see it! A fuzzy glow spread out ahead, some filtered light seeping through the snow flurries and reflecting faintly off the clouds and coming all the thirty kilometres from the ship. A red light of burning.

His radar threat receiver clicked. A naval search radar. The Pirate wasn't completely dead and it had seen him. He turned sharp right, dead away. He pushed up the throttles and put on speed. The radar warning blip vanished. Escaped back over the horizon of some low-mounted antenna. Mach 1.1, 1.2, 1.3, up reluctantly to 1.4. Escaping.

The radar threat receiver lit up. Down on the bottom of the vertical situation display a format blip appeared. A SAN-60 coming in on his tail. Dammit. The readout lights said his automatic ECM was running, trying to keep the radar on the incoming missile saturation jammed as it switched frequencies to beat the jamming.

"Angel Six. Pirate is burning badly. Have a SAN-60 on my tail."

"Copy, George."

The radar threat receiver again. A second SAN-60 following him. Why'd they have to launch two?"

"Angel Six. Now have two on my tail."

They were almost twice as fast as his bird down low, little format lights on the situation display, down below centre and hurrying up one behind the other. Their altitude data said they were higher than his bird and starting the up-and-over dive to the kill. Can't outrun them, can't take the precious time to turn and fire off a pair of AIM-320s, not with them coming right up your ass. So close despite all the ECM can do. Fire the chaff dispensers—up high it would give a radar blanketing screen of reflective metallized strips, down here most of it spits straight into the sea.

Avoidance manoeuvre. This bird can whip around the sky. Not too soon, not too late. The SAN-60 is right up on you on the situation display, diving right on your tail—

Snap the stick left. Big slamming gee pressure. Snap centre to straighten up immediately.

Some *thing* streaked brilliant past his starboard side and dived into the sea. Gone.

The next one coming down behind, a slight angle off to the left. Don't turn right or you'll cross its flight line. Left again. Not too soon. Not too soon. It's coming—

Now!

"AOC says no, sir. Angel Three Saw Angel Six go right into the water when the SAN hit. No chance the pilot ejected."

Not hitting the sea—in pieces—at more than the speed of sound. Bedford took off his headset again and laid it on his little desk console. He was aware of an icy cold cruel thought. It was preferable that the pilot had not survived somehow and was floating for a little while still, alone in a survival suit and a life jacket on the stormy skin of the sea—not so far away in the wrong direction. He didn't have to reject the impossible rescue, almost twice a Wolfmarine's there-and-back range and nowhere near the Vindicator's planned course. He didn't have to let the man die.

"The Pirate is heading away," Dylong said. "Heading northeast. Probably taken serious damage."

Boyce wandered over, also without his headset, and half leaned on the front edge of Bedford's console. "Figure he's out?"

"We got his main radars—his Hanging Basket and his Bugeye Pair. We probably hit him with two more Longarms. He's hit by at least one Talon and probably two or three, plus anything up to four Seaflash. He's out, even if he still had some air defence to fight back with when Sindow approached."

Boyce nodded. "But whatever happened to one-hit ships? The Chenin doesn't carry any armour."

Upwards of two hundred lives—if they were all of them still alive now—out there in stormy nowhere on a hit and burning ship. A light ship of destroyer type burned like a bonfire, burned right down to the waterline from end to end once the fire caught hold. One way or another the Pirate was completely out of things as far as the Vindicator was concerned.

John Ritchie Boyce smiled. "He may or may not have a hope in hell, but we don't have to worry about him any more."

Bedford looked at the smile. Two Russian aircrew and four of their own dead, and over two hundred condemned lives on a blazing ship isolated from all assistance in the middle of an empty ocean. What made Boyce tick?

Bedford shook his head. "We'll keep the CIC and Weapons at Condition One, but we can allow rotation breaks. Greg can do whatever he likes with his AOC. You, me and Dylong—from now on at least one of us is going to be in here the whole time.''

''You're worried about what else they have? The units following us up here?''

''And what they don't have. If they're down to a couple of aircraft and maybe a pair of subs too far behind to stop us in time, they'll have to start throwing nukes at us.'' He glanced at the wall clock—1400. All that had happened in just one and a half hours.

''Modern war moves fast while it's happening,'' Boyce said.

''It does.'' Damn fast.

June 12, 2145–2210

DAVID DREXEL HAD missed it all. He had been working nonstop until he had lost all track of time and was dizzy with target designations and small-screen slipping large-scale snapshots of land maps. He had been working through so intensively they only let him out to visit the washroom—they even brought him drinks and a tray of food to his console in the Missile Control Room. The only thing he noticed as it all happened right next door in the CIC were the sparse and terse ship's address announcements and the long delay through midday before they finally brought up his food. Whatever had been going on, he had missed it all.

He had also ceased to notice the gradually changing motion of the ship on a wind lashed rising sea. The repeated mugs of tea they kept bringing him served as strange spirit levels, the brown liquid tipping lazily to one side and then the other, vibrating all the time with a pattern of concentric ripples as the huge ship quivered to the thrashing of its own screws. The Missile Control Room stayed still. Only the magic liquid level moved, a changing dance of little tides as the wind slowly changed and the cyclonic storm in the world outside ran over and around the ship on its own southeasterly course. He had only noticed the motion of the ship once, at about 1800, when the Vindicator turned due east to head direct for the seaway between the Orkneys and the Shetlands, changing its orientation to the waves and the wind. For an hour or so the Vindicator rolled hugely. And then the rolling eased and the pitching resumed—the wind and the sea had changed again.

They had let him go at 2125, after more than twelve hours of uninterrupted work. Not so bad really: the people who ran the Missile Control Room had been working just as intensively and for longer, and they were still working when he left.

He left through the tunnel door at the rear of the MCC and went down three ladders inside the massive support structure under the armoured tower. He came out on main deck at the forward end of the aircraft hangar, passed behind the vertical guide rails of the main elevator on the port side, and went through forward along the side of the C3-Complex box. In a couple of the cabins there Kylander and Dresher were hidden away, nursing their own plans. He dropped down one more ladder onto 1st platform and entered the canteen. It was quiet, few of the tables were occupied. He collected a tray and loaded it up from the service hatch without really thinking what he was choosing. He went over to a side table away from everyone else and sat down. Exhausted. He was exhausted. They should all just leave him alone.

They left him alone until he had almost finished eating. Then Gloria Craze appeared. She put her drink on his table and sat down opposite him. Damn the woman.

"Your eyes are red. They been working you hard?"

He looked at her looking back at him. She wasn't going to go away. She was pretty, now he noticed it, dark brown skin and close cut hair and eyes much deeper than he'd realized. She was pretty and he was lonely. Pity he didn't go so much for girls in uniform, and a pity she obviously disliked him so. He scooped up some more of the good American ice cream, paused with it halfway up to his mouth. "Where are we, anyway? What's happening outside?"

"We're approaching the zero meridian. We're at fifty nine degrees forty minutes north, heading due east at thirty knots as ever. A little less than an hour ago we passed Sumburgh Head—that's the most southerly tip of the Shetlands—at about fifteen kilometres distant. You know, that's the first land we've been in sight of since we put out from Honolulu three months ago when the all-units alert was given, right back at the beginning of the war. Except we didn't see it at all except on radar. Driving snow in a force ten gale—which is why the ship is moving—in pitch darkness late on a June evening under solid overcast under the all-concealing dust veil." She played with her cup for a moment, as if thinking of something. Then looked up again. "The wind is coming from the northeast now, right on the port bow. The storm centre has passed us but it seems to have a whole complex of fronts trailing round it and one is coming over us right now. Did you get anything of what happened earlier?"

"Some of it." He shrugged. "There was air combat way off north."

She sipped from her cup, put it down. "Yes there was air combat. It came only around two hundred kilometres away at the closest. A total of four Soviet aircraft. Yak-236s, if that means anything to you."

"It means something to me." If she wanted to make him angry she was wasting her time. He was too tired. "The Yak-236 is the Soviet equivalent of the F-28. It has a lower performance and only about two thirds of the weapons carrying capacity. Its avionics are approximately five years behind contemporary American designs, but it adds up to an effective up-to-date system. It's capable of engaging six air targets simultaneously." Now he was needling *her*.

She didn't like that at all, but wasn't going to change her view about who was controlling the situation. She stayed cool and collected. "Our Skycats got two of them but they brought down one Skycat. Also a Wolfmarine. Also one of the Skyhooks. There was also a Soviet destroyer way off north, a type armed with Skimmer Pole, with SS-N-100 missiles. Those can carry a nuke and would blow even us out of the water if they got in close enough. Two Skycats attacked the ship and hit it and set it burning, but it downed one of our aircraft. Balance, two Fanners—that's Yak-236s—and probably one ship for two Skycats and a Wolfmarine."

"Any of the aircrew survive?"

"No." She was playing with her cup again. "Makes you think. A handful of aircraft—maybe only those four we saw, who knows, but still a handful—and then that unconfirmed submarine contact, and the unit that signalled from somewhere behind us three days ago. You wouldn't have thought they had so much left, would you, considering that the good folks back home don't seem to think we rate the assistance of any support units. You would never have thought they had so much left."

He shrugged—the good folks back home weren't his fault, either. The political view of strategy tends not to coincide with the specific mix of goal-orientation and protective caution that usually characterizes the military standpoint. "It seems they have plenty left to hit. You know the strike list is for a total of three hundred and four targets, I suppose?"

She nodded. "I know."

• • •

Gloria Craze knew right enough.

She had been down on the missile storage decks, down on 3rd and 4th and 5th platforms starboard of the C3 box, where the missiles lay batch behind batch in their twelve-cradle bays back along sixty metres of deck, from the hoist loading area right aft to the solid crosswall closing off the isolation box of the reactor spaces. All the narrow aisles running through the bays were blocked somewhere along their length by busy technicians, Paul Milgrom's people fitting the thermonuclear warheads into place in their assigned vehicles or Debra Stothers' girls and boys checking through the systems on the vehicles themselves.

She had watched a team checking a Fire Lance vehicle through all its mechanical functions—they had hoisted it out of its longitudinal cradle in the bay and laid it on one of the narrow delivery trailers that they could run back and forth to shuttle the missiles forward in the correct pre-planned sequence to the loading hoist. And then the hoist lifted them up and back-loaded them into the launcher tubes where they received the automatic firing signal, and they sped out under the thrust of the automatic booster rocket, automatically swung onto their flight path and droned turbofan powered all their automatic way to their automatically designated targets—to deliver death that was equally automatic except to those who died. But could there be any truth to the feeling that automated weapons are a less human or humane way of killing than twisting a knife with your own hand? Wasn't it just that their thoughtless functionality merely brought home the dread awfulness, undiluted by any warrior mythos?

She watched as the stub wings folded outwards, as the tail control surfaces snapped out from folded flat to flight deployed. The Fire Lance was a round nosed and streamlined thing, sixty centimetres in diameter and seven metres long—eight, including the solid fuel booster. It weighed two and one quarter tonnes at launch. It was a blind thing, the blank radar housing of the nose didn't look remotely like an eye. It flew mostly blind, only checked its position occasionally by taking radar snapshots of the ground and comparing them with the stored computer representation of the return echo it should receive at precisely *that* time point after launch. It flew a narrow inertial imaginary world, with an end point that was only so much time and so many turn and height manoeuvres after its beginning, an end that was defined as a count of seconds and confirmed timing points after the instant of electronic initiation at launch. An end that was merely an instruction to fire a current surge into the initiator and into the primer—into the neutron generator that would spew thermal neutrons into the plutonium, and into the hollow shell of high explosive that would instantly compress the concentric spheres of fissile uranium and plutonium to supercritical mass and density. That was the little fission bomb that would detonate the lithium-deuteride pencil of thermonuclear fuel. And that would generate in an instant and at a point in fragile space the unimaginable heat and energy that can cauterize the world.

She had watched a man and a woman fitting one of those slender axial units into the bay behind a missile vehicle's guidance electronics. She watched deft and skilled hands securing precise connections. We all have our little bit to do. The complex task of preparation is broken down into an endless series of little steps, each of which an individual can encompass, none of which by itself can kill. Even the firing of a missile is merely a trained response to an order coming in from outside, while the final act of task execution is done for the giver of the command by soulless little microcircuits in the machine itself. It becomes manageable, contemplatable, someone else's—*something* else's—doing. From the politician to the commander to the operator to the servicer to the manufacturer right back to the voter, it was always someone else's fault—at the last resort the fault of a personified purely obedient machine. We all of us, we all of us will do it to ourselves. Such is human psychology.

She watched for a while. Since first she came on board she had never liked these decks with their impersonal sleeping machines. They had always reminded her uncomfortably of just what kind of power she was supporting through her commission in the Navy, through her peripheral role in the machine that was the Vindicator's most crucial component—its crew.

Slumbering cargoes of death, and all that. Except that they weren't slumbering so soundly any more. One by one and silently, they were waking up.

Drexel looked utterly exhausted. He was blankly watching the gyroscopically tilting surface of the tea in his cup. He was sore-eyed and tired-faced and washed out. As a fellow human, he called forth sympathy at the moment. You could forget his oh-so-English shabbiness and his effortless switch from Jenninger's to Kylander's team. You could almost forget. "What have you been doing? Helping assess targets that weren't already given in the TLF?"

He nodded. "Out of the three hundred and four targets, a hundred and forty nine are these supplementary things. Open field sites, to steal a phrase. They assigned warheads to the predetermined targets according to the codes in the Target Listing File, then they got down to playing with me at shuffling what warheads were left to fit appropriate ones to the unlisted targets."

"And you've finished now?"

He leaned his elbow on the table and laid his cheek on his open hand. "I've finished."

"And what were the supplementary targets?"

"Oh, villages. Forested areas. That sort of rural site where trees or buildings might afford some sort of protection against the cold. Which must be *really* intense in the middle of a northern continental heartland."

"Villages?" Was he trying to make a fool of her? "Forests? Are those supposed to be strategic targets? What's the idea—bomb the last farmer and the last country doctor out of existence to guarantee the Russian people is exterminated once and for all?"

"No, no. The last farmer and the last country doctor froze to death weeks and weeks ago—if they didn't starve or die of disease first. The Russian people are already exterminated, essentially, just like the American or the European people. Or the Chinese, or anyone else where the cold has got to yet. And when it's spread right south round the world and when the dust settles—literally—we'll have the combination of a high radiation dose and high ultraviolet penetration everywhere, and then *everyone* will be exterminated. There'll be no infrastructure left which could possibly have coped. No, no. The targets are selected for quite genuine strategic reasons."

He enjoyed it all. The white English bastard enjoyed it all. "What strategic reasons?"

Drexel sighed. "The Russians have always liked mobile land based missiles—yes? Old SS-20s and bigger things rolling around on go-anywhere tracked vehicles. Great big motorized monsters sometimes, and quite capable of coping with normal Siberian winter conditions. So *some* of the ones that survived the big strikes could even be functioning in this—

which inland will be much worse than a normal Siberian winter. Some of their land mobile weapons are probably still fully operational, if not exactly mobile any more, *if* the vehicles and crews have managed to find somewhere to hide—some sort of enclosed or enclosable shelter with enough food and enough fuel for heating.''

"A farmstead, an iced-up village.''

"Exactly." He started drawing cryptic little lines and pictures for himself on the surface of the table with his finger. "Well, an SS-20 wouldn't interest anyone any more. Multi-warhead missile. After the peak with the MX with its ten warheads, the move—in the States first of all—had been back to light ICBMs carrying single warheads, small missiles you can put in little automated silos scattered all over the place. When you do that it means that to knock out one of your warheads your enemy has to expend one of his own. One warhead hitting the silo, one warhead inside the silo. That means your enemy can no longer even contemplate a first strike to try knocking out your retaliatory capability. He can't possibly take out all the warheads you would reply with, and he has to use up virtually all of his own in trying. And that leaves him with no leftover backup deterrent potential to frighten you out of your retaliatory strike. Now that situation frightens *him*, because he still has his warheads bunched up on big delivery vehicles—three or six or ten warhead on top of one missile inside one silo. He sees that you can threaten him with an endless rain of little single warhead missiles, you can take out *his* retaliatory potential with your first strike if you want to. So he goes ahead and builds his own little single warhead missiles as well, and all you get is rearmament with a new dispersal of strike potential on *both* sides, leading to a reduction in perceived security felt by both sides. A lowering of the crisis threshold."

"Destabilization."

"Exactly. Destabilization. Just the same with the space defence systems. Once your side looks like being able to thin out the other side's retaliatory strike on the way over—that is, weaken his retaliatory threat, which is his only perceived insurance against being attacked by you—he's more likely to panic in a crisis and fire his first strike before you have a chance to do the same. And as he doesn't actually want to start a war himself, when you build your High Frontier he has to go ahead and build his own system, and the result is *two* sides feeling less secure as a result of introducing a purely non-aggressive defensive system. A system which doesn't work anyway. The High Frontier collapsed the instant its control satellites were taken out. Any fool could see that would happen.''

"Really? You people—the strategic specialists. You told them to do it.''

"No, we never told them to do anything. We analyse and we tell the politicians and the generals what will happen in any real or hypothetical situation they ask us about. Then they pick their options. We just do our best to make sure they know what they're doing, and we all hope they can cope with it. Everyone has always known that the only sensible thing was to change the situation by getting rid of the nuclear weapons. But you just try getting the nice people to throw away their big sticks. They never do.''

"The psychology of human aggression," she said. "Convenient scapegoat. And what's all that got to do with you selecting warhead yields for farmsteads and villages?''

"Ah yes, back to the point. Back to the little single warhead ICBMs—the Midgetman and the new Miniman and the Soviet answers. Well, the Russians put quite a lot of theirs in silos like you Americans did, but they always had this love of big tracked vehicles revving through the snow with a huge long missile on top ready to stick up in the air. Probably phallus worship Siberian style—you'd know that better than me.''

"I'm no Freudian.'' Why did people persist in confusing Freud with psychology? Come to think of it, penis envy was junk from Freud, but was phallic worship from him? What the hell.

"My apologies. Back to the missiles. Some of these land mobile missiles were last seen in particular sites before the last of the reconnaissance satellites were brought down, before the veil closed in and the cold started. The assumption has always been that those few of them that weren't nuked in the very last phase, and that weren't too far from anywhere still fairly intact, would have tried to move into the nearest suitable village or forest farm or whatever for shelter and fuel for heating—timber is good for both—and for food. A village's shops and domestic larders would keep a small troop detachment going for months, once the unequipped villagers had died off, and a farm full of frozen livestock would be almost as good. So those are all the supplementary targets. Sites where it's assumed one or more mobile ICBMs might be and just might still be operational.''

"And you've been assigning the warheads. How?''

"I just have to look at the map and see what the shelter possibilities are and at the same time try to remember what is supposed to be possibly there. How many missile units were known to be in reasonable transit range of the place before the Freeze would have made all movement impossible, and if there's likely to be enough food there to support them all. I just have to remember all the discussions we were having back there in the States and then try to apply the probability ratings we worked out. Then you choose your warhead—a hundred kilotonnes for a point shelter, two hundred and fifty for a scattered village where three or four tractors might be hiding and making a bigger warhead worthwhile. As simple as that, basically.''

"Places where one or more missiles *might* have been driven to or parked. Where they *might* be still functioning and pose a potential threat. A *potential* threat only. Or else where they aren't. Where some farmer and his family are eating their frozen pigs and trying to stay alive, or a few villagers are burning the last piece of the last house apart from the one they're sheltering in. For God's sake, what kind of targeting is that?''

Drexel shrugged. "Contingency targeting.''

"And the PD-targets? What have they selected there?''

"A hundred and fifty five predetermined targets.'' He stifled the beginnings of a yawn. "About a third are leftover missile silos that were never hit in the main exchanges. Most of the rest are small civilian airfields with enough of a shed to house a long range strategic bomber and a few maintenance crew and support equipment—places they might have dispersed such an aircraft to before it all closed in. Then there's a handful of small communications centres known to have self-support facilities. There's a few naval depot stores areas on the Kola Peninsula—the whole region got saturation strikes but there's still *some* military signals traffic coming out of there. A dozen or so small power stations that were never hit and are assessed to be sufficiently cold-resistance to be still working—normally all the auxiliary plant would have frozen up. And one single big target—the underground command complex at Narodnaya-Chobeyu in the North Urals. That's one of their twin backup centres. The other is in the Cherskogo Range way over to the east.''

''One Fire Lance with a maximum two-fifty kilotonne warhead isn't going to crack that.''

''Ah, our people have learned from the way the Russians took out NASCOM. Spread through the three strikes of the series the target comes up twelve times. You just have to route the four missiles assigned to it in each strike so that their flight times stretch out the arrival times of the missiles at the target. It's only about two thousand eight hundred kilometres away from the launch points, plenty of spare range for stretching the routes. The missiles in each group of four will come in thirty five minutes apart. When one detonates at the target the next one is still over five hundred kilometres away, so it survives. With twelve missiles coming in, first all the communications equipment will be destroyed, then the repeated ground shocks will collapse probably the whole place. Just like NASCOM.''

''And what's the control centre over in the east going to be doing all this time? The silos and the *maybe* operational mobile missiles, everything over there outside our range?''

''Oh there's very little useable stuff left in the Eastern Soviet Union, and what there is will be taking coordinated strikes from the surviving missiles in the United States. Kylander tells me the Russian capability will be wiped clean out once and for all—so that in his terms the Free World can get back to picking itself up free of the Communist Threat.''

''Picking itself up! Picking itself up with what? And who says our Fire Lances are going to get through?''

''A cruise is vulnerable to in-depth air defence, isn't it? High-level aircraft with look-down radars good enough to see it and snap-down missiles good enough to hit it. There is no in-depth air defence any more.''

''And the intention is—the intention is to wipe the Soviets out once and for all?''

He looked slightly amused by her disbelief. ''Know what they've apparently decided on as a code name for this operation as soon as they got complete control back in STRACC? Armageddon. Really—no kidding at all. Armageddon. The final battle between good and evil when evil is totally destroyed. They're actually calling it Armageddon.'' He shook his head. ''Jenninger kept calling them the Apocalypse People, and now they're having their Armageddon.''

"And this strike series." It could not be. It just could not *be*. "This—Armageddon is really going to be *launched?*"

"I assume so." He shrugged. "The launch points came through during the afternoon—all close up against the Norwegian coast. I assume the strike is going to go. Don't know, of course."

"And are the Soviets hitting us again? Are *we defending* ourselves? *Have they started nuking us again?*"

"Not that I know of."

She stared at him. My God, oh my God. It simply cannot be. It cannot be. "You've just been helping. Actually *helping* this happen. What about morality? Don't you have any sense of *morality?*"

Drexel was looking at his empty tray. And she thought, that's dumb of you. Drexel is just the nearest target to attack, and it isn't his unique fault any more than Warren Lister's or the Fire Lance technicians or any other single individual on the crew. And the weapon of attack—morality. That isn't user-friendly, it's a two-edged sword. A psychologist should know better than to divert shock with aggression, but you're still human after all.

"Morality is a fiction," he said. "Common sense—the slim chance of the world and the human race surviving at all, and the sheer idiotic stupidity of pumping up the climate collapse and the long term fallout with yet more megatonnage— that I could understand. But morality!" He glared at her. "I'll tell you about American morals. Military and financial aid is poured into any government that practices torture and political murder—by political murder I mean killing people, with or without due process of law, when they don't share the government's politics—just so long as that government is fanatically anti-communist. All aid is refused to any country with a communist government, even the ones that don't practice torture and political murder. All aid is refused to any country that practices abortion for any reason, even when it's drowning in an exploding birthrate. That is American morality, so beautifully and blindingly simple. Communism and abortion are works of the devil, torture and political murder are the province of angels. Some morality."

That went too far! "What kind of an attitude is that, Drexel? Goddammit, you work for the US Government as a military specialist."

"Oh—it's just a job." He spread his hands disarmingly, as

if signalling that he didn't want to fight. "You've got to have a job, haven't you? Why not one you can do well and that you find absolutely fascinating? After all, jobs have been in short supply in your country and in mine for a quarter of a century. What about you, now? Black, female, with liberal academic tendencies. And there you've been all this time, willingly working inside the armed forces—the *strategic*, the *nuclear* armed forces—of a white, rich-constituency, strongly conservative government. So what's your excuse?"

She didn't have one, of course.

He looked round at the nearly empty canteen. It was 2200 and he was tired as hell, and he had the prospect of trying to sleep in a closed-up cabin just back from the bows of the ponderously pitching battleship. "I really don't care any more. An awful lot of people have killed themselves because they cared too much about what's happened. A lot of the others seem to have gone crazy in an attempt to make what's happened make sense in terms they can understand. I don't care. I just want to stay alive as long as they'll let me, one way or another, and I'd like to stay sane. So I've decided I don't really care."

Ducking out. The apathy way to survive what you've helped do to the world. Each to his own, then.

"I keep remembering something I heard when I was still at school," he said. "Must be more than fifteen years ago now. Back then when Reagan was standing for his second term. Remember Ronald Reagan? The man who came out and said what half of America and half of Western Europe really thought and thereby created the Reagan Doctrine—that Moscow is the heart of an evil empire threatening the Christian Capitalist world. From that to believing the Kremlin is the citadel of the Anti-christ is only a small step for a diseased mind, I suppose. And they all conveniently forget that the United States developed and deployed the hydrogen bomb all by itself—the most evil thing in the world—and was the first to *use* the atom bomb—the second most evil thing in the world. Anyway. Anyway. I remember hearing a speech he gave reported on the radio. He said something or other like: casting my mind back to those days when we used to say better dead than red, would I say that for my little girl, I asked myself. At first I thought no, but then I thought, I'd rather my little girl died now, still believing in God, than that she lived under a communist regime and died later, no longer

believing in God. That's really what he said—it's not the sort
of crap you ever forget. I thought at the time, if you believe
that you'll believe anything. And there were roars of ap-
plause. They believed it. They always have.''

Gloria stood up. That was it and she'd had enough of the
British bastard with his superiority and his hypocrisy and his
apathy. Talk to him yourself, Danella Raffles had said. Well
she'd talked to him, and that would do.

· ''One of the several university courses I studied,'' he went
on, not in the least disturbed by her intention to go, ''was
computer situation-modelling at Sheffield. Depressing place,
Sheffield. Just near the centre of the university in a back
street was a gate with graffiti sprayed on it—'When you've
seen one nuclear war you've seen them all.' The idea being
that a nuclear war would be the end of the world. I never
believed it, was always sure people would manage their
affairs better than that. Well—now it looks like they were
right after all, doesn't it? Anyway, I've seen my nuclear war
already. I'm not in the least interested in this new one.''

That was really enough. She'd found out more than she
wanted to about what made Drexel tick. ''You're really something else, aren't you? Really something else. Why don't you
go to hell!''

Drexel nodded. ''See you there.''

She grabbed her cup from the table to take back to the
service hatch. The ship's address clicked on.

''*Captain in the CIC! Supervisor in the CIC!*''

BOYCE HAD COMBINED the ASW situation display with navigational data on the OpSum console screen. The result was a selective version of the central area of the representation on the main plot, but with the addition of water depth contours. Bedford and Dylong stood there beside him, looking down into the OpSum display.

The Vindicator was 55 kilometres east of the Shetlands and a little to the south, was heading east at the never varying speed of 30 knots. At a distance of 150 kilometres from the ship, the Wolfmarine on ASW screen station searching the port sector flew a sweep that took it out to the north and west of the Shetland Islands into the Shetland-Faeroes Gap. It was comparatively safe there, even on the wrong side of the islands, because it was well inside the warning sweep of the newly deployed Skyhooks. With only nine SCAN-carrying Skyhooks left, they were flying three at a time, one of them fifty kilometres due south of the ship and a pair two hundred apart on an east-west line one hundred kilometres north of the ship. Any further air or surface attacks would come out of the northern sector, that was for sure.

"Watchdog Seven is here." Boyce pointed on the display. "Some thirty kilometres northwest of the tip of Mainland. Stupid name for a little island, that is. They've picked up very indistinct machinery and screw noise on the dipping sonar on listening mode. Stress, *possible* machinery and screw noise. A possible Big Fish. They've dropped a sonobuoy and they're traversing to drop a second to get a triangulation."

One hundred fifty kilometres away, plus the distance to the actual finalized position of any submarine that really was there, while the Vindicator's eastward course was opening up the distance by an additional fifty five and a half kilometres an hour, and additional twenty minutes at efficient cruising speed when the helicopter had to give up and come home. "What's their endurance on station?"

"They've been out there over an hour. We're moving away. Say maximum one more hour."

Bedford nodded. "So—do we send another 'copter?"

Boyce shrugged. "It's in a perfect position to close the box and get us on the way out."

"If it has Skimmer Pole it's in range," Dylong said. His perfectly expressionless face was comment enough.

Bedford turned toward the ASW control consoles along the side of CIC to the right of the OpSum. "Send a support to join the search. Immediate launch."

At the number two Weapon Control and Air Ops Coordinator Console, Seaman Belle Jastrow started to pass the order through to the AOC. CPO Cavanee was at the Sonar Track position, the number one Weapon Control Console was vacant while PO2 Stacey took his rotation break, and the ASW Supervisor was waiting with her seat turned to watch them at the OpSum. Lt. Anthea Slamon was black and very tall, and wore her hair in enough of a back-combed Afro style to have got her into trouble with some commanding officers.

"Run the operation direct from here, sir?" she asked. For an anti-submarine operation it was easier to work from the CIC than over the AOC. ASW operations took time.

"From here," he said. "What's the weather at Seven's position?"

"Clear, no precipitation, wind six to seven, temperature minus six degrees and falling. Reasonable flying."

They would need it if the search took very long—the tension and the strain of flying drained an aircrew's nerves.

"Ship's address?" Boyce suggested. "Just to calm everyone down before they get the idea something serious is happening." He smiled, because it was a joke. Because a submarine was very serious indeed.

"Watchdog Seven has a triangulation, sir." The ASW control station was taking telemetry direct from the Wolfmarine over the nearest Skyhook: Cavanee's Sonar Track display could show the same readout as the observer in the helicopter had on his screen.

Bedford leaned in between Cavanee and Slamon to look at the screen. The readouts were poor data—in fact poorest data, only just better than junk. It was a noisy sea there, with mixed up water layering, with irregular bottom in places and turbulence noise coming up from bottom currents.

"Intermittent and indistinct," Cavanee said. "But it keeps coming back. Machinery traces on both buoys."

Slamon was listening to the relayed sounds on her own headset; the headset band was imprinting a cleft across her hairstyle. She nodded. "I think it's real."

Cavanee was tapping a calculation through. "It's around forty kilometres north-northwest of their position."

"Something deep moving slowly," Slamon said. She pulled off the headset, the divide in her hair filled out again. "I think that's definite enough, sir. I think we can cut the telemetry."

Constant telemetry meant constant danger for the Wolfmarine out there away from the protection of the ship, meant that anyone who was listening could hear it and swoop on it or else stay safe on the other side of the horizon and send a long range searching missile to hunt for it. Transmitting tells them you're there.

Time moves slowly while you watch it, while you wait.

Watchdog 7 had picked up indistinct sounds again ten kilometres nearer the approximate location of the source—a very approximate location in the sound slurring sea. The sounds had been no clearer and no louder, as if the submarine —if submarine it really was—had either slowed or dived deeper, or both. The helicopter had listened for six minutes with its dipping sonar on listening mode, and then dropped a sonobuoy at the position and moved on. The sonar served as a more sensitive ear, but at hover you used up precious fuel too quickly. Hovering is staying up in the air by brute force, and you pay for it.

You pay for it in terms of noise as well. Hovering or sliding around low over the sea, helicopters are noisy machines—and submarines have extremely sensitive ears. They have great spherical sonar transducers filling their bow sections, they have line arrays along their hulls, they have hydrophone assemblies mounted like great stabilizers out on their wide tail hydroplanes—a pair of assemblies mounted symmetrically left and right of the submarine's own screw so that they cancel out its relatively deafening noise and can hear the faintest whispers propagating through the black deep. And most modern subs have long towed arrays deployed from winding drums in the rear of their sail towers. Submarines can hear helicopters.

Maybe the sub had heard the helicopter and was going to lie low and play safe, just like the one out to the west of their track two and a half days ago. If that had been a submarine at all. Maybe it was one and the same boat that had gradually closed the distance while matching the Vindicator's north-ward progress. Several classes of Soviet sub could comforta-bly do over thirty knots while submerged without making too much of a noise. Maybe it was the same boat falsely inter-cepting the Vindicator's predicted course through the Shetland-Faeroes Gap, while the Vindicator had turned east and passed south of the Shetlands. Or it was another boat altogether, but that didn't matter. What did matter was that the ship had escaped a second potentially lethal trap by sheer luck—last time the luck of timing, beating the Soviet destroyer to the Iceland-UK Gap, this time the luck of actual course instead of intercepted course. The controllers back in the States had to be half crazy sending the Vindicator into an enclosed area of sea without any support at all while the Soviets still had any units they could mobilize. It wasn't only a show of force, it was a gamble.

It made Bedford uneasy. Uneasy about the motives and plans of the people playing with his ship.

The sea floor at the contact location was very uneven and was four hundred metres down. The depth itself was no problem, neither to any up-to-date Soviet boat which would be able to go much deeper, nor to the little Mk72 ASW torpedo which could operate down to one thousand metres. But four hundred metres down was continental slope and was the descending flank of the Shetland-Faeroes Basin, which went down towards twelve hundred metres midway between the two island groups and which ran out northeastwards into the really deep waters of the Norwegian Sea. Deep uneven bottom at four hundred metres and descending—if the sub sat still down there with its motors stopped the hydrophones in the sonobuoys would never hear it. Even active echo-location with the sonar set dipped into the water might not find it, might have the greatest difficulty identifying even the bulk of a submarine standing up like a rounded wall from the surrounding floor.

Uneven and fractured or scoured bottom might be a jumble of such walls.

"No more hydrophone response at all now, sir," Slamon reported. "They're going to close in on the last-guess position and try with the sonar and the Magan."

The Magan was the magnetic anomaly detector the helicopter was carrying. It had only a very short effective range and it worked best of all over deep open ocean where deeply buried rock deposits and magnetite intrusions were far enough down not to interfere too severely with its fragile sensitivity. The Magan searched for the slight knot tied in the Earth's magnetic field by the metal bulk of four or five thousand tonnes of submarine.

"The Big Fish is either lying stopped in mid water or he's bottomed." Slamon shook her head. "He's cautious, that's for sure."

Bedford could see it from the other side, the submariner's side, with an armed helicopter prowling around somewhere overhead. Helicopters frighten submariners.

"Communications, sir." Kuroda was holding the hush mike on his headset folded aside. "They're picking up Sparker Box and broadband transmissions. They have a good triangulation from the Skyhooks. It's coming from a little further north of the last position we heard from the damaged Pirate. They're giving it through the EW to see what they make of it, sir."

"Okay." He looked across at Dylong. Lt. Cmdr. Joe Dylong was standing impassively in front of his OpSum, an image of perfect patience, an ideal calming influence for the rest of the CIC crew who were reduced to mere spectators during this game. Boyce had gone through to the MCC to talk to Warren Lister.

The clock on the wall said 2240. Watchdog 9, the support machine, had already arrived on station and was searching an adjacent area. Soon it would have to take over entirely—Watchdog 7 had used up so much fuel on hover that it would have to turn for home in twenty minutes.

"All finished through there." Boyce leaned with his forearm on the front edge of Bedford's desk. "All three hundred and four missiles fully tasked from launch point to target, the firing sequence list fixed for each launch."

All those mathematical lines laid out from the three launch

points off the coast of Norway, a mesh laid over southern
Scandinavia and over the frozen Baltic, spreading out across
the entire Western Soviet Union to end at a scatter of deathlisted
locations reaching out to an arc from the Kara down to the
Caspian Sea.

"The launch points they've given us are just lousy." Boyce
shook his head. "Right up on the Norwegian coast. They
could have let us stay out west of the British Isles and only
lost a couple of hundred kilometres range. Why'd they have
to put us inside this box?"

"Don't know, John." The signal conveying the second
Strike Allocation Command Input had merely given the three
launch point coordinates, three points in space laid out along
the 4°E meridian.

"Just so long as they let us back out of here fast." Boyce
adjusted his glasses with his middle finger. "Think we'll get
the firing enactment?"

Bedford shook his head. "They're showing the Soviets
we're ready for them. That should do the trick. Nothing's
going to happen." Hopefully. My God, hopefully.

"Sir! Seven think they've found it." Slamon had unhitched
her headset again; this time it left a cleft across the top of her
hair. "They have a positive on the Magan and are going in
with the sonar to see if there's something down on the
bottom. It's four hundred and sixty deep where they're
looking. Nine is on station around seventy kilometres east
of them. We're sending Nine in right away because Seven
only have ten minutes loiter time left."

"Good." It would take well over ten minutes for the
second Wolfmarine to close the distance. Watchdog 7 was
alone with the Big Fish right up until it had to turn for home.

"Sir." Kuroda this time. "Communications and EW have
an evaluation on the signals traffic. They're both on the line,
sir."

Bedford pulled on his headset and switched through to
the channel whose call light was showing on his private
board. Boyce crossed over to the OpSum to listen in with
Dylong.

"Darius," announced the first voice, Lt. Cmdr. Darius,
Chief Communications Officer. "There's encrypted Sparker
Box plus Russian voice transmissions coming from the Pirate.
That's still going on. There's also a lot of traffic coming
from the direction of North Norway and also over from the

northern USSR. Lt. Spirek has an analysis which I'd support entirely, sir.''

Lt. Barbara Spirek, Senior Electronic Warfare Systems Officer. ''I'm pretty sure of the analysis, sir. It looks like the Pirate is going down. They're abandoning ship.''

Abandoning ship in the middle of the open ocean in Arctic conditions, and no chances at all that anyone would ever come to pick them up. ''Okay, we'll consider the Pirate as sunk. Thank you.'' He removed his headset again. God help the poor bastards. All they had ever done wrong was try to defend what was left of their country from the Vindicator, which was trying to defend what was left of its country from them. Such a stupid, stupid circle. Not a bit like the ethos he grew up under, that was reflected expressly in the Navy orientation courses, that had formed the consistently maintained force and focus of his career. Twenty years as the son of a superpower and then twenty seven more as one of its servants working at the numbers games of the tactical and strategic models. The reality of war, conventional just as surely as nuclear, was different.

''Sir! Trouble.'' Slamon jammed her headset over her ears again, turned back to Cavanee's neighbouring console.

Jastrow was talking to the Wolfmarines over her own headset. ''It's a missile,'' she said. ''Came out of the water.''

''Watchdog Seven have a missile coming in from close.''

''They're firing ECM. Chaff. Everything.''

Across the other side of the CIC, PO2 Hayes suddenly hunched in front of his Air Detector/Tracker screen. ''Watchdog Seven has a homing radar track closing right on it.''

''The SCAN has a good view.'' CPO Irene Jablonski at the adjacent Track Evaluation position. ''Feeding the radar type to the computer.''

''Seven say they—Seven say—I lost them. I lost them.''

''The missile track has coincided with Seven's track, sir. Seven's gone down into the water.''

''Fuck,'' Slamon said.

''Quietly,'' Dylong said. ''Quietly.'' He was peering into the OpSum, setting up an assessment.

Boyce was standing behind Slamon and Jastrow. He turned to look at Bedford. ''The thing came out of the water around four thousand metres from the machine.'' He shrugged. ''No chance.''

Dammit. God dammit, why did that have to happen? Why

couldn't the Wolfmarine find the sub first? Why couldn't it see the boat in time to launch a torpedo and turn away? "Anything left of Seven on the surface?"

"Not a thing, sir." Jablonski peered over at Hayes' screen. "The sea state's not so bad out there. The SCAN could see it sitting on the water."

"The computer's identified the missile radar." Dylong looked round from his OpSum. "It was a Flying Fish."

Flying Fish was a submarine-launched surface-to-air missile, a short range active-homing weapon. It wasn't as good as the American system, but it was obviously good enough. A Subsam was launched either from a special dispenser or from the submarine's torpedo tube, it consisted of a rising buoy which broke surface and a missile which leaped from the buoy into the air, already seeking its target in the direction fed to it before launch.

It could kill Wolfmarines. "Who was crewing Seven?"

"Lt. Selrose, PO Garwin, sir," Slamon said. Two more names on the day's list of the dead. "We have the Red Whale's exact position now, sir. We can direct Watchdog Nine right onto him. Nine can be there in—in eleven minutes, if they keep at max speed."

"Tell them to take it easy. Get to the area fast before the Red Whale can move away, but take it easy closing on the position."

"Will do, sir."

"Problem," Boyce said, coming over. "Do we send out another machine in support? It's a long way."

It was over 250 kilometres out to the position and the distance was opening further all the time. He couldn't turn the ship around and close in for any more elaborate hunt— NAVCOM in STRACC had given him a deadline of 0300 to be ready to take the first launch point on the 4° eastern meridian. Any machine he sent out in support would take one and a half hours to reach the area, by which time the distance back to the ship would have increased to three hundred and twenty kilometres—two more costly hours deducted from its precious flight time. And anyway, by the time it arrived on station Watchdog 9 would have either killed or thoroughly lost the submarine.

"No support," he said. "Nine has three torpedoes on board. They should be able to handle it."

•   •   •

This was their second time out since the screen was first set up. Last time the weather had been disgusting, this time it would have been easy night flying low over the waves, despite the wind and the icing risk. The air temperature was nine degrees Centigrade below freezing, and still falling. Some God awful summer.

Lt. Matt Baes in the pilot seat of the Wolfmarine, estranged third son of a retired lawyer and a circuit judge from Sacramento—not that there was still a Sacramento or a pair of never understood and never really understanding parents any more. He looked up through the canopy roof window, through the invisible rotor arc. It would have been a clear starlit or even moonlit night, there were no uneven cloud patterns in darker black against black. There was just the utterly light-smothering blanket of the dust veil up high.

They flew low over a rough and windswept sea in pitch blackness, like a flight simulator with a total power failure. Except for the awful noise of the twin turboshaft engines and the thundering of the rotor, except for the bounces in the ride made by wind deflected up off the sides of the invisible waves. It was blind instrument flying, following a heading on the inertial compass and the navplan chart tube, keeping the level as displayed by the automatic flight control system. They were racing at maximum speed, at 160 knots, for the reference point on the open sea where Watchdog 7 went down. They had to get into the area fast because the Red Whale was probably making speed away from the scene before something else came in to catch him. The nearest of 7's sonobuoys had heard fading machinery noise for more than a minute. They had to get there fast, but then they had to slow down and move in cautiously and play cat and mouse with the hidden quarry. If they ran right down on top of it, it would take them out of the air.

In the observer's seat PO 2nd class Tom Cline, a black boy who had managed to break out of Watts into the big wide world. Still a white world, really. He had the readouts from the Magan and from the still transmitting sonobuoys to watch, glowing figures on the tactical display down inside the tube that screened them away from the pilots night vision. He had the job of identifying their Red Whale when they came down on it. To find it he had the dipping sonar, five of their original eight sonobuoys, and the long pipe of the Magan detector bolted to the starboard side boom. And when they found the Red Whale—then he had the three Mk72s.

On the wall it said 2340. And he was tired.

A Soviet submarine was lurking out there somewhere north or northwest of the Shetland Islands. He only had one machine on station and it hadn't found any telltale magnetic anomaly where the other Wolfmarine had been downed by the sub forty five minutes ago, it was still searching but it was probably going to lose the sub. That boat's commander was too careful. There had never been any giveaway machinery noise bouncing through the sea. He must have started to move out, heard the helicopter approaching, and bottomed again. The Wolfmarine would only find him by stumbling right over him again, and then the same thing might happen. At least it wouldn't repeat a third time. If the sub downed the second Wolfmarine there would be no point at all in sending a third. The Red Whale would be long gone before it got there.

Bedford looked round the CIC, three quarters full. Everyone looked tired, everyone showed the effects of the long tense time since noon. Joe Dylong looked impassive but tired, steadily surveying the functional heart of the ship, the people and the positions that he supervised. Even Boyce, usually a picture of smooth self-confidence, looked tired. He was at the SADIS Systems monitoring position, half sitting on the edge of Lt. Andrea Stratten's instrument desk, his arms folded, his head bowed. Thinking what? What made his First Officer tick? Sheer technicianship, Craze had said. The reasons for and the consequences of an order didn't interest him at all, just the optimal execution of the task. Boyce was the man to launch a nuclear strike, not Bedford himself. Boyce would do it whatever happened.

Strattan was as silent as Boyce. Was he waiting there next to the woman for some sort of emotional support? She belonged to the casual sexually socializing group of which Boyce was a member, a fact about himself which he'd reported perfectly per regulation. God, he could sometimes wish he wasn't the Captain screened away in shipboard purdah for the sake of discipline. If dear dead Gayleen would forgive him the thought, sometimes when the strain and sheer loneliness mounted he wished he wasn't the Captain. Even in this armoured giant, an armed enemy frightened him. And the triple strike that was all set up and ready to go frightened him

sick. If only he could talk to her, wherever she was, why ever
she'd died. Why ever she'd had to set off with Linda and take
a plane up to Seattle to meet him, a plane that had fallen back
out of the sky on takeoff.

"Sir. Watchdog Nine has a slight Magan response. Plus
one-eight. They're staying out and are going to try a sonar
search."

Hovering over the invisible kicking sea. The Magan response
was so slight it couldn't be a real one. How could you tell if it
was evoked by a point source collection of submarine hull
and machinery without going in to see how the response
climbed and peaked? And if you did, and it was, you got a
Flying Fish to prove it. Instead you hover like a thunderbird
just above the waves, and if it is the Red Whale he can hear
you.

"Any sonar response, Watchdog Nine?"

"We're checking the bottom now." Baes clicked to the
intercom channel. "Got anything?"

"The bottom's all hard echoes and shadows," Cline's
voice said in his ears. "Must look like a field ploughed by
some giant. Pluto and his trident or something."

"Neptune and his trident."

"Okay. In Watts we got no classical education. Ah but one
of the teachers! She had the best pair of—" Even in pitch
darkness punctuated by nothing but instrument glows, even in
the thunderous howl of the turboshaft engines inside the
quivering machine, you could sense the sudden tension in
Cline. "We got something. Got a real hard echo. We got
him. He's just sitting there. Range twelve thousand on the
bottom on two-zero-two."

"Winch up the sonar." Baes switched to Vindicator's
channel.

"Is already coming up. Is out of the water—now."

He tipped the nose down and started to ease the Wolfmarine
into a left curve. "Watchdog Nine. We have a hard echo on
bottom at range twelve thousand. Closing to engage."

"Copy, Watchdog."

He switched to the intercom. "Tell the torpedo where he is
so it can go straight. He's heard our sonar and he can hear us
coming in." He would know the attack was coming down
there.

"Port munition is activated. Feeding target bearing and depth."

Heading direct for the target location at airspeed 30 knots,
barely clear of the waiting waves. "Tell me when we're at ten
thousand." The Mk72 had a range of 11,000 metres, but you
had to come in closer to give it a margin in case the target
started to move away.

"Another minute. Less. He's got to do something down
there. Or is he going to sit it out?"

They would find out. You glide like the very voice of hell
across the water, and the man down there has to decide what
to do.

"Range ten thousand. You want a confirmation with the
sonar?"

"The fuck I do. Let it go." Watchdog 7 got a different
confirmation.

Cline pushed the button. The helicopter lifted unevenly as
300 kilogrammes of torpedo dropped from the port underbelly
station.

"Sonobuoy."

"Sonobuoy gone. That leaves just one."

He turned away left and flew on slow, watching the automatic flight control's height line, blind above the black sea.

"Buoy is transmitting. Torpedo is running straight. Its
sonar is firing." The little underwater weapon was hunting
for the sub, going in straight and gradually deeper at 60
knots, at 2,000 metres a minute. "I just heard something
else. Something."

"Machinery noise? Screw?"

"No. Something. It's gone. Torpedo is running straight
and down. It's got to pick him up. He was so clear at twelve
thousand out, it's got to pick him up in close. Now I hear
machinery noise. Screw turning. Strengthening. He's turning
away and trying to move. That won't do him any good.
Torpedo running straight and down. Hey, I do hear something
else. Like a splash on the surface."

A splash on the surface. Or a little missile surging out of its
carrier buoy into the element of air?

The radar threat receiver lit.

"Jesus. Missile coming in on nine-zero."

He looked at Cline in the blackness. He saw out there, past
him somewhere, a pinpoint red light climbing, weakening.
Not going away. Arcing over and down. He spun the 'copter
round in the air and pulled out the throttle, nose down and

flying forward. Vindicator's channel. "Watchdog Nine. Got a Flying Fish coming in."

"*Copy, Watchdog.*"

"It's coming. ECM firing. Jesus. Try firing a missile?"

Intercom. "Too low. Too close." Far too close. A flight time of seconds.

"Jesus. It's right on our tail!"

He cut the rotor pitch to zero, killing the lift. The Wolfmarine fell vertically out of the air.

It *slammed* into the water. A hard shock crunching his whole body together. A red fire streaked down right overhead and hit the sea in a brilliant flash.

"Jesus. Jesus. Jesus."

The tail rotor response was still there. The stabilizing blades hadn't hit the water and sheered off. They could still fly. Ease the lifting pitch back on the main rotor. The sea will try to hold you, sucking. Ease on the pitch, power up and engines screaming.

The sea held.

Then they were nose down and swooping deeper on a wave side roller coaster. All in a black nightmare in a hell battering rotor and engine roar. Something at his feet at the pedals.

"Hey! That's water round my ankles. We've split the hull."

And the stink. The stabbing sudden stink—aviation fuel from the underfloor tank. Hit the water too hard, too hard. "Jettison the other torps."

"We can instruct them." And they levelled out in a wave trough and then started to sail up again nose high. "We can use them."

"Man, we're sinking! We're too heavy to fly! Jettison the torps! The Magan! The missiles!"

Cline hit the switches. And he had maximum contingency power, he had the rotors at full pitch and shaking themselves out by the roots.

The Wolfmarine jumped up out of the sea. It wanted to go nose down straight back in again. The trim was fucked. The underfloor space was full of water. It was slopping around the cabin. If it didn't drain he couldn't hold her. Faster and faster forward to prevent the steep nose-down attitude flying them straight into the sea. If they dropped now they wouldn't ditch, they'd disintegrate. Climbing, altitude increasing slightly. His feet still in the water piled up forward in the cabin. It must be draining out of the underfloor space. It came in. It must go out!

"I can't hear the torpedo. It must have hit by now."

"Fuck the torpedo!" But the nose is coming up. Ease back the power, just a little, just a little. Just a tiny little bit. The nose is coming up. It's holding! Flip the channel selector. "Watchdog Nine. We nearly took a missile. We hit the water but we're airborne again. We have damage."

"Copy, Watchdog. Can you make it?"

"No idea." Intercom. "What you say about the torpedo?"

"I can't hear it. It must have hit. There's no more machinery noise from the Red Whale."

Vindicator's channel. "We think we might have hit the Red Whale. We did not, repeat not, hear the seventy two go home. The Red Whale was making machinery noise but isn't now. The seventy two was running straight at him."

"Copy, Watchdog. Can you check it out or are you in trouble?"

"We're in trouble. Hold on." He switched the channel out.

The nose had come up, the water had gone from round the pedals. It was just his feet that were wet. It was suddenly cold as hell. The heating was still on so there had to be holes or cracks right through the bottom and the cabin floor, letting in a sub-zero wind. There was still a stink of aviation fuel. Pray to God the vapour wasn't collecting somewhere and no electrical component was shorting.

Pray to God. "Give me a course towards Vindicator."

"One-three-oh. That's good enough to start out."

"Okay. Coming on to one-three-oh." Speed steadying at 90 knots, the efficient cruising speed, using least fuel per kilometre. "Let the last buoy go. It's dead weight."

"It's gone. I'm looking at the fuel. The underfloor aft is empty. Underfloor forward reads sixty litres and steady. We can't risk using it in case it has water in it. It was reading ninety before we hit, so it got some sort of hole."

"Okay, so it's just the mains. How much?"

"Port one-fifty-five, starboard one-seventy. Total three hundred twenty five."

"How far to Vindicator?"

"One moment. Ah—two-nine-nine kilometres. By the time we get there it will be—three-eight-two. That's if they maintain course and speed."

"Okay." Christ, that was close. "Okay. We're carrying no extra weight." He switched the channel. "Watchdog Nine. We look like we can nearly make it to you. Can you drop speed to wait for us?"

"Wait on that one, Watchdog. There is an alternative. You can land on the Shetlands and wait until we can pick you up."

"No deal. It's minus nine—minus ten out here. We need you or we're dead."

"Understand, Watchdog. We have a decision for you. We cannot drop speed and make our date as ordered. But you'll have another Watchdog with an empty cabin and lights and a winch out to meet you if you have to ditch short. We'll see you get home. No sweat."

"Copy, Vindicator. Can you give us an exact heading? Our airspeed to you is six-oh knots."

"Can do. Coming up. Hold on, Watchdog."

Baes clicked off the channel.

"Huh," Cline said over the intercom.

"We should be okay. We should make it without ditching."

"Huh. If we don't freeze first. Jesus."

An icy whirlwind was whipping round the cabin. Baes turned the heating up to full.

HE WASN'T ASLEEP. He was only dozing in the dark.

It was the submarine. It was or it wasn't a kill. The torpedo had been running straight at a clear target: the target had been making machinery noise beforehand but not afterwards. Only the confirmation of the strike was missing, because at the time the Wolfmarine had been sitting in the water with other things to worry about. The torpedo carried a fifty five kilogramme warhead. It would have hit a clear target and holed it. In action a submarine closed up into watertight sections. Only the holed section would flood, and the boat would sink until it hit bottom—over deep ocean, until it went down below its depth limit and the whole hull crushed and everyone on board died. This submarine was holed over ocean floor at 460 metres down. It was moving slowly just off the bottom when the torpedo struck. It wouldn't have split with the impact when it downed on the mud and rock. It would still be lying under the huge weight of water, helpless.

The boat would have been turning away and the torpedo would have struck aft. The machinery spaces would have flooded and the people in there would have died. The forward compartments would be intact. Most of the crew would be forward. How many lives? Sixty lives, eighty lives? One hundred lives? Trapped down there with battery power to drive their lights and their emergency air systems. Trapped down there in their curved-shell coffin, waiting to die. When he was in the Trident boats he had always thought of it. Now it had happened. He wasn't asleep, he was dozing. It was the submarine.

"Sorry to wake you, sir."

"That's okay, McGready. Wasn't asleep, just dozing." He

hauled himself up into a sitting position, fumbling the phone. "Signal?"

"Just come in, sir. From STRACC, in the Nemesis cryptographic domain. It's got the Dark Mirror command code. Lt. Caro is just sending it up to the MCC for decryption. I'll call Commander Lister now, sir."

"Fine. Thanks, McGready." He put down the phone.

It was 0225 by the glowing clock. He got up, putting on the low light. He pulled on his shirt and shoes, splashed water over his face in the box of a bathroom, straightened his hair, went out into his day cabin and blinked in the bright light. He went across the cabin, out through the door, straight across the corridor and into the tunnel door to the CIC.

The CIC was three quarters full, of course. Dylong was spelling Boyce at directing. "Morning, sir." In the middle of the night.

He managed more or less a smile. "Morning." He stopped to look at the CIC wall plot to check the position: 59°59'N 03°51'E. They were almost there and STRACC was exactly, inevitably, on time. "Did the Watchdog Nine crew get back okay?"

"Around twenty minutes ago. Just made the ship. Jennesten's taken the machine down below." Jennesten was the Aircraft Management Officer. "But he doesn't think he can get it fit for operation flying with the facilities we have on board. It needs more than black box maintenance. We're officially down to nine Wolfmarines."

He nodded. He went through into the MCC.

Warren Lister was already there, wearing his blouson jacket as though he'd been asleep and felt the cold on waking, even in the unchanging ambient warmth inside the airconditioned ship. Lewy, the Launch Control Officer, had been looking after the station. With him were Deevers, the black chief petty officer who worked on the Target Listing File, and PO3 Kelly Jace who worked on Lewy's station. Lieutenant and both petty officers—an all-black night shift in the MCC. Jace was already running the signal through the Dark Mirror and Shadow Glass cryptographic facility. Text was starting to appear on the screen.

"Anyone know," Lister asked, "what the weather's doing?" The ship was still moving, but only slightly.

"Clear, sir," Deevers answered. "Wind force six and falling. Temperature was minus five an hour ago and falling."

There was too much text on the screen to ignore.

> ORIG: STRACC NAVCOM NMSS DIR 1018 JUNE 12 1910
> INCOMING: JUNE 13 0220
> NMSS-3 VINDICATOR
> FIRE LANCE COMMAND CODE: DARK MIRROR
> SACI 03

1. This is a Firing Enactment Instruction for strike series as SACI 01 launch points as SACI 02.
2. Permissive Action Code for each launch: 130602 231251 060845.
3. Launch times (Vindicator): June 13 0310 0910 1510.
4. Acknowledge this signal SACI 03 with repeat of PACs and launch times.

Lister looked at Bedford. A long little pause. "It must have started up again," he said. "The Russians must have done something after all."

Bedford glanced at the MCC clock. 0235—just thirty five minutes to go.

"Better call our people to stations," Lister said to Deevers.

Deevers picked up the nearest phone and punched into the ship's address. "All missile systems personnel, stand to. All missile systems personnel, stand to. Fire Lance launch in thirty minutes. All missile systems personnel, stand to."

"Repeat the call in five minutes." Lister was looking again at the text of the Firing Enactment Instruction on the screen.

The first launch point was really a line of points along which the Vindicator would cruise for twenty five minutes heading due north at 9 knots. The line began at exactly 60°N 4°E.

Bedford borrowed the phone at another empty console and punched for the bridge. Lt. Phil Cole, Radar Systems Officer and current chief of the bridge watch, answered.

"Bedford. Make the following change. Speed down to nine knots, inboards only. Stop both outboards." While they were cruising slowly they could use just the two screws in the huge underhull tunnels and let the outboards idle, pushing far less noise out into the surrounding sea.

"Nine knots, inboards only. Helm setting, sir?"

"I'll get Navigation to send one up." He depressed the hook and then phoned through to Navigation.

"Navigation." That was PO1 Rutledge's voice.

"Bedford. Manoeuvre for you to work out, Rutledge. I want a course to take us round in a sweep and bring us out exactly on zero-zero-zero at exactly sixty north four east at exactly oh-three-ten."

"Zero-zero-zero at sixty north four east at oh-three-ten. The speed, sir?"

"Nine knots. Give it through to the bridge and conning position."

"Yes, sir."

Communications this time. Lt. Elise Caro came on the line.

"Bedford. Did we also get a signal for Kylander?"

"We did, sir. Just come through. Send it to him?"

"Right away please, lieutenant." He put down the phone. Let Kylander come and watch the deadly fun.

Lewy and Jace were already seated at the launch control consoles bringing systems to life. Barbara Vogt, lieutenant junior grade and Guidance Functions Officer arrived and went straight to her position. Didn't she even want to glance at the FEI—a real FEI and not a drill? But the real thing would go exactly like a drill. That was what the drills were for, to ensure that a real order was executed with emotionless mechanical precision, so that in a reflective sense the people never thought about what it was they were doing.

He turned to Lister. "Warren, you have time to dictate the acknowledgement for me?"

Lister nodded. "Sure."

Bedford turned to the CIC door, and stopped for a moment. Up among the wall instrumentation to the left of the door was the control point where he would have to insert and engage his firing key and enter the Permissive Action Code into the Firing Signal Verifier. If the code matched with the one stored in the Verifier's computer memory, the firing signal was verified and the launch could go ahead. Each code was used once only for each launch, and only NAVCOM at STRACC and NAVALCOM at CASAL knew the codes in the Vindicator's computer. The people on the ship couldn't launch a nuclear strike on their own initiative. They, at least, were fail safe.

He went through into the CIC. Dylong was expressionless, waiting. They'd heard the ship's address in the CIC.

"Tell AOC to get their Skycat and the Wolfmarines back inside the elevator box. We don't know how soon there's

going to be a reply to our launch.'' The aircraft would be safe
inside the closed up elevator space—outside they would be
toys in a thermonuclear wind.

Dylong picked up his headset and started punching through
the connection.

Bedford looked at the clock. It was 0240. ''Bring the entire
ship to Condition One in ten minutes. I'll be in my quarters.''

Dylong nodded.

Bedford took the bunch of keys from the pocket of his pants
and unlocked the safe. The safe was nothing more than a
tough metal-lined cupboard in one side of his desk below the
drawers. Inside was his firing key, was an automatic pistol
complete with holster and box of ammunition, was the thin
sheaf of faxes of all the personal signals he'd received ever
since they were rushed back out of Honolulu on all units alert
almost before they had arrived from the commissioning voyage out of San Diego. Tucked in at the side was his own
handwritten log, almost redundant now that a commanding
officer had his own secure computerized secretary. The handwritten log was nothing more than a diary, and Bedford had
never been much of a diarist.

He took out the firing key and looked at it. The key was
an old-fashioned mechanical metal thing that couldn't possibly be accidentally damaged, couldn't be destroyed without
throwing it overboard. He put it in his shirt pocket and
buttoned the pocket closed.

The gun. He was required by regulation to ensure that a
legitimate Firing Enactment Instruction was obeyed; he was
required to prevent any obstruction of the execution of a
legitimate FEI. But he was not prepared to mistrust his crew
to the extent of wearing a gun ready to shoot down anyone
who might attempt to sabotage a launch from inside the
MCC. If anyone failed to comply he would ask them to leave,
and replace them. They would have to face a court martial
later, if ever another court martial was held anywhere on the
Earth, but he was not prepared to act as pre-emptive executioner. He would not even contemplate wearing the gun.
Boyce could do so if he wanted to. Boyce would wear his gun
because the first officer's instructions recommended that he
did so. Bedford wouldn't wear his.

He locked his safe and straightened up. On the wall was
the picture of his wife and daughter, both smiling, both

watching the whole cabin. Wherever Gayleen was, wherever Linda was, he hoped they couldn't see him now.

The bridge was Gloria Craze's Condition 1 station. It gave her the appearance of being useful while keeping her out of the way. The bridge was an observation position and a backup to the Ship's Conning Position on the deck below, as well as serving as a backup damage control coordination point for Allan Villman's Damage Control Centre down on 1st platform inside the double safety of the C3 box.

The bridge counted as a safe area in the event of a nuclear attack. It was inside the Vindicator's laminated armoured shell, it had armoured shutters that slid down over the outside of each window to keep out flash radiation and the monstrous hammer blow of the blast. It had a green painted deck, floating deck, a deck to which the bridge console and the conning data repeater console and all the tall-stemmed chairs were bolted. A deck mounted on high restitution springs that didn't give as the ship moved on the sea, as a group of people crowded to one side, not even as you jumped on it—but a deck that could displace eight centimetres and take the worst, only the very worst, snap out of any shock wave that hit the enormous ship.

You could still get thrown around by a nuclear detonation too small or too distant to damage the ship. There were grab handles on the centre consoles, grab rails right along the rear wall and along under the windows. In one of the chairs you could brace yourself against the footrest and the grab handles, and hope that the floor and the seat's suspension spring together would protect you from a spinal compression injury. Otherwise you had to take up the shock posture—leaning forward bent half over, hands apart holding the rail tight, feet planted wide on the deck, elbows and knees flexed so that you could take and hopefully absorb vertical and lateral forces. The fifty six thousand tonne armoured and double-walled ship was supposed to be able to take it, and you were allegedly able to survive inside. The first two ships in the Nemesis series, the Protector and the Consolidator, had gone down.

Her Condition 1 station was on the bridge, apparently useful and out of the way. Chief Petty Officer Will Holicek in the seat beside her—he ran the bridge and the bridge team of four seamen and one other petty officer. There was no need for an officer on the bridge even when the Vindicator was manoeuvring and fighting in company—except that the bridge was where an officer traditionally used to be, and she was spare and got put there. The watch officer backed up the officer directing the CIC at all other times, but the Personnel Advisement Officer on the bridge at Condition 1 was just a passenger. She was even allowed to absent herself at her own discretion, to get in the way of damage control teams sent out from their assembly point in the green deck canteen, or to calm down some hypothetically crazy crewman.

The lookouts and observers were little better than passengers either. It was three in the morning, it was a clear tropospheric night out under the uniform black blanket of the dust veil. There was absolutely nothing to see. From her high seat behind the console on the totally blacked-out bridge she could sometimes make out a faint gleaming glimmer forward. There was ice on the bow and on the foredeck to well aft of the 155 automatic gun—spray ice, tonnes of it. It was cold out there. She eyed the instrument readouts glowing on the console: air temperature –12°C, wind force 5 and still dropping, coming out of due north, almost straight on the bow as the ship came around a slow and gentle curve. The sea was settling calm, the ship was riding at exactly 9 knots across a low swell almost as if it wasn't there. There was only the barest of pitching movements perceptible, it was a very quiet glide through a night that would have been beautiful.

Holicek started to test run the bridge window shutters. One after another in an overhead electric whir, an armoured steel eyelid slid rapidly down over its night black window, sealing it completely to all light, to gamma radiation and thermal neutrons, to heat and stupendous shock. One after another, down and up again, as if the Vindicator was winking to the empty night with all of its blank little eyes in sequence. Back in the TLCP they would be doing just the same.

The entire ship was closed up at Condition 1. All the water-tight and thus smoke- and fire-tight doors in the massive crosswall bulkheads were closed across passageways, the traps were closed over all ladders at every deck. You could still open them and pass through, but with the holding current off, their damped and balanced spring-hinges automatically closed them again and rotated the locking dogs home. Neither of the two killers, fire or water, could spread through the ship. There was just blast, the hammer shock transmitted through air—or even worse, through water—that propagated at the speed of sound in steel right through the fabric of the ship, that sheared and split panels and frames, mounting bolts and machinery shafts. And bones and flesh and blood. You just had to hope the designers had known what they were doing. Closed up, all the external doors and deck hatches sealed the ship from the outside world. No nuclear blast should burst in, no fallout enter the submarine-type closed air system. They could sail away and wash down with the fountaining water jets, and live to fight another day. A survivable system, that was the idea. Well, it had survived. But the Vindicator had never brought its weapons within strike range before. Now it was going to be different.

The little glowing instrument readouts. The corrected inertial compass read 000, due north. The helm setting crept back to centre zero as the helmsman one deck down ended the long and gentle turn. The position readout clocked up 60°00'N 04°00'E. The Vindicator had attained the first firing position.

Boyce really was wearing his automatic pistol in the button-down holster strapped round his waist. He stood there in front of the deckhead high instrumentation to the right of the door through to the CIC, his hands on his hips, his back to the panel and the shoulder level control point. Bedford could see the weight of the firing key in the right shirt pocket of Boyce's shirt. The man was as impassive as if it was a drill.

Captain and First Officer and all ten of the MCC personnel were present, plus Bradford Kylander and Arlene Rimmington. The two civilians were standing in front of the tunnel door that led out of the rear of the C3 box. They each wore a holstered revolver, heavy revolvers, .38 Service-Six Rugers just like Jenninger had carried. Dresher, the USAF major, was waiting with the infantry sergeant and two troopers outside the tunnel door between the massive support struts beneath the tower base. It should have made Bedford furious that Kylander had brought some of his enforcer squad right up to the MCC door, but it didn't matter at all. There were only two intruders inside and watching, and they weren't going to get in the way of the launch.

At the Launch Control Console, PO1 Kenneth Teng was watching the position and heading readouts. "Firing position attained, sir."

"Confirm," said PO3 Kelly Jace next to him. "Heading zero-double-zero. Speed nine knots dead."

The firing position had to be right, exactly as planned. Each missile found its way primarily by inertial navigation and had to start at exactly the right orientation from exactly the right point along the course that the Vindicator was about to follow. Otherwise the missile would be hopelessly lost, it would never find its initial timing control point and would simply automatically abort.

Lister turned and opened the little safe on the wall between the side door to the CIC/MCC Administrative Area and the three-position Launch Control Console. He took out three keys and held them in his palm, looking solemnly at their engraved and coloured identification numbers. He handed one to Lewy at the launch console, and crossed over to where Wigner sat next to Deevers and Seaman Alice Jackman at the Target Control position. He handed one key to her, kept one for himself.

Boyce unbuttoned his pocket and took out his firing key. He just held it in his fist, and the clenched brown fist was the only sign of any tension in him.

"Control keys issued," Lister reported per ceremony.

Bedford took out his own key from his shirt pocket and held it lightly in his fingers. Kylander was looking at him steadily while Rimmington's eyes wandered round the room. Boyce was watching Kylander. All the others were looking at their instruments.

"Okay," Bedford said. Lewy was staring at the key glinting in his brown hand. His was the first key to go in. "Lt. Lewy."

Lewy inserted his key at the control point on the sloping panel in front of him, turned it and locked it. Signal lights came on. "Firing Signal Verifier engaged. Automatic Missile Abort engaged."

Each Fire Lance, as it slid from the loading port at the head of the hoist into the back of a tube on the launcher, received an activation signal for its guidance system. The guidance system then only waited for the solid fuel booster to ignite and fling the missile from the tube, and it would begin its long time-and-route countdown to target. But no firing signal could come through appropriate to the ignition circuit on one of the land attack mode boosters unless the Firing Signal Verifier had been both engaged and clearance locked. And the whole time the engaged Automatic Missile Abort would be instructing the missile to self-destruct immediately on booster burnout thirteen seconds after launch. A successful firing required the cooperation of five officers at separate control points around the MCC.

Bedford nodded to Lister and Wigner. Wigner reached up and inserted her key at one control point on the Target Control console, Lister leaned between Deevers and Jackman and inserted his key at the other. They both turned their keys ninety degrees round. More signal lights.

"Clearance locking keys both engaged and locked," Wigner said.

The two locked-in keys could not be removed to cancel a launch unless both were turned simultaneously; Lewy's launch control key could not be removed while the clearance locking keys were still in place. The firing Signal Verifier was now locked in and would transmit a firing signal to each missile in turn as it was sent out from the launch management computer in the MCC. But the Automatic Missile Abort was still engaged—they could fire the missiles but every one would fail.

Bedford glanced at Boyce, Boyce turned and located his firing key at his control point.

Bedford put his own key into the slot in the control point on his side, left from the CIC door. His hand was shaking, very slightly shaking.

"Firing key engaged," Boyce said.

Bedford turned his key. "Firing key engaged." Only one more step now. "Warren, will you read us the PAC for the first launch?" He and Boyce just had to type in the code, and it was done.

Lister read slowly. "One. Three. Oh."

He tapped in the digits at the little keyboard.

"Six. Oh. Two."

He tapped the last digits in.

"Firing Signal Verifier certifies the PAC," Lewy reported. "Automatic Missile Abort is blocked."

The Permissive Action Code entered into the Firing Signal Verifier corresponded with the first number on its electronic one-time pad, and it instigated the signal which blocked the Automatic Missile Abort. The fail safe ritual was over.

"They ready down on the missile decks?" Lister asked.

"Ready, sir," Teng reported. "Four Fire Lances in each hoist and ready to lift."

Lister looked at Bedford, and his Captain nodded. "Okay, engage the launch management computer."

"Engaged and running," Lewy said. "Port and starboard hoist lifting."

Eight missiles on their fifteen second elevator cradle rise, four to each launcher. Down on the missile storage decks teams would already be running aft with long empty cars to bring up further rounds to the handling spaces at the foot of the hoists.

"Starboard launcher loading. Port launcher loading."

It was all automatic now, pre-programmed. The only way to stop it, to cause a general abort, was to turn both clearance locking keys together or to disengage either of the firing keys. Then the entire complex Fire Lance system would stop, and the firing procedure would have to be run through again from start.

"Starboard launcher elevating and training outboard. Port launcher elevating and training inboard."

"Hoists dropping," Jace said.

"Coming right to the launch point."

The first missile to go had a 250 kilotonne head and was the first of a total of twelve targeted on the underground command complex at Narodnaya-Chobeyu. It would arrive and detonate in two hours and fifty minutes, by which time some of the other missiles would already have destroyed their nearer-sited targets.

"Launch point. First missile gone starboard. Two. Three. Four." On their way, Fire Lances flying out to hell. "First missile gone port. Two. Three. Four."

Drexel sat in the canteen. Not far away at another table sat Raffles with her head in her hands. Gittus and seven of his men were there. A good two dozen men and women, petty officers and seamen, were waiting with their emergency equipment stacked next to them—portable fire fighting gear, cutters and torches and saws, folding stretchers and medic packs. They made up the damage control parties, sitting there quietly and unconcerned. No steel helmets and anti-flash cream needed on this insulated ship—the only protective clothing was flame proof overalls and protective gloves lying ready on neighbouring tables. And respirators, of course.

The only sound, in which the quiet voices were lost, was the unbroken whir and hum of electronic motors as the hoist cradles just forward and outboard of the canteen went end-lessly up and down, as the launchers up on deck lifted and turned, turned back and dropped for reloading, lifted and turned again. Just the heavy electrical machinery noises run-ning through the ship.

He had been exhausted, but he hadn't been able to go to sleep in his cabin right forward there on 2nd platform. Not at first. The big ship had been rolling, with its slowly pitching bow sweeping up and down. Double armoured hull or no, the huge waves had thundered against the bow cheeks. He hadn't been able to sleep for at least a couple of hours. And now it was quiet, hardly a motion—and they'd woken him up.

He had to sit at an empty table in the closed-down can-teen, half awake and wasting his time. There was no need to bring the ship to action stations or whatever the Americans called it—there would be no answering nuclear strikes com-ing in. Not until after the first Fire Lances started to vaporize their targets far away and the crippled shreds of the Soviet command started to realize what was happening. Then was the time to worry. Until then he could sleep, if they'd let him. Right up forward the racket of the launch machinery wouldn't be so bad. In a comfortable bunk he could sleep. He was tired enough.

He looked across at Gittus and his men. Kylander and Rimmington and Dresher were up in the Missile Control Centre; they had taken the sergeant—Hawley, the hulking white protestant bastard—and two privates with them to en-sure the launch went smoothly. Stupid. They didn't even understand the system they ruled and utilized. The launch would go ahead as simply and mechanically as any peacetime practice. They were all good American boys and girls, right from their captain down to the freshest faced seaman male or female. They all believed in it, they were exercising neces-sary deterrence in the defence of what was supposed to be left of the Free World. They *knew* it was so, because that was what they'd enlisted to do, what they'd based their careers and their salaries on. When the Russians behaved like that it was indoctrination, when Americans—or anyone else in Nato—did it, it was free choice.

They hadn't seen what was left of the Free World, any more than Kylander and his team and all their fellow thinkers back in STRACC and CASAL had really realized what was outside their cozy hideaways. They didn't realize that the

Free World—*all* the world—was already a corpse. It was still kicking, but it was dead. As good as.

He was going to go to the toilet. The launch only lasted for twenty five minutes. He would walk out to the washroom and then go on back to his bunk to sleep. Why sit around here? He stood up and walked past the table where Raffles was sitting with her head in her hands.

"Drexel." She looked up at him with awful hollow empty eyes. "You helped with the targeting."

He nodded. "With assigning some of the warheads."

"Why? Why did you help?"

He shrugged. "Better than getting shot."

She looked at her hands. "I should have used my gun and shot Kylander. But I was afraid. I'd have been dead before I could explain to the captain why he shouldn't obey any launch orders that came through. And he wouldn't have listened. He'd have obeyed just the same. Doesn't matter now."

"Doesn't matter at all." He shook his head. "Whether they hit this ship or not, whether we all run south of the equator or not. It doesn't matter a damned bit."

"Doesn't matter." She stared at him this time. "Does it? *Does* it? You know as well as I do. This is a first strike. Unprovoked. Do you know what we're doing? Do you know what those things they're firing do? Not in numbers. In people. Do you know what they *do*?"

"I know." Why did she have to go and open *that* cage in his head? "I had a girl in Washington. I had my family and all my relatives and old friends in my own country. We've just sailed halfway round my country. It's got a couple of dozen officers and civil servants and politicians in a hole in the ground called the British Emergency Government, it appears to have a couple of ancient Sea Kings on an airfield in Cornwall and one or two more at a few other places—and that's it. That's all of it. It really doesn't matter any more."

Raffles looked away, buried her face in her hands again.

The machinery noises went on.

Forty eight Fire Lances gone, still more than half the strike to go. The MCC personnel were quietly monitoring everything. Kylander and Rimmington were watching, just watching. What was going on in Kylander's head?

Boyce was standing with his hands on his hips, Lister had settled in a spare chair next to the door to the CIC/MCC

Administrative Area as if guarding the empty safe. The Fire Lances were going out all the time, two batches of four every two minutes. The whole first launch alone represented a cumulative seventeen and a half megatonnes, another half percent or thereabouts on top of what had already gone into the air, into the dust veil.

"I'll be on the bridge," he said to Boyce, and turned to leave.

Boyce barely moved an eyebrow behind the steel frames of his glasses. Normal procedure prescribed that both the first officer and the commanding officer remained in the MCC during a launch unless the ship was actually under attack. But captains are arbiters of rules.

Gloria Craze had moved to the forward windows on the starboard side. She could see both the port and the starboard launchers, lit up alternately in each other's lurid light. They each elevated their four tubes to forty five degrees and trained round, the port launcher pointing across the beam of the ship over the top of the Rayflex-2 mounting, the starboard launcher pointing out over the ship's side and the sea below. Huge red flames flashed at the rear of the tubes and a missile streaked away, four in fifteen seconds, then the launcher trained round forward and lowered in the shifting flashes and trail flares from the other mounting. The loading ports extended and coupled with the rear of the launch tubes, then they disconnected again and the launcher swung up and round once more. One batch of four Fire Lances from each launcher on a two minute cycle, four missiles every minute.

The solid fuel boosters left flaring red trails of dissipating smoke. They could hear each shrieking departure even through the armoured glass of the bridge windows. The streaking red flares lit up the entire bows and long foredeck of the ship, first a brilliant pink and then a fading crimson. Each trail tore climbing out to starboard for thirteen seconds before the booster cut and fell away and the turbofan sustainer took over. By that time the tail fins and the stub wings were already deployed and the cruise missile was turning onto its initial course. Most of them had to climb. The Norwegian coast was only sixty kilometres away with mountains rising behind, and the majority of the Fire Lances were routed over them, not around to the north or south.

The Norwegian government had once voted, she had heard,

for the stationing of first generation cruise missiles on the territories of other Nato countries, but not on Norwegian soil. Very sensible, very cynical. And once the Soviets had fought their overwhelming way into north Norwegian shoreline positions, the Norwegian Government had called its own ceasefire and threatened to attack other Nato forces if any nukes detonated on its own ground. Very wise. But the Nuclear Winter had got them all the same. And now much more modern cruise missiles would be sweeping almost silently over their mountain ranges at more than one thousand kilometres an hour. From the hills behind the shore, if there was anyone there left alive and with enough interest, the Vindicator must now have been a spectacular sight, bars of red light endlessly stabbing from it up and outwards into the total night.

Lances of fire.

They tore away and lit up the sea. The illumination spread far away over the regular swell, painting it brilliant red with oily black moving shadows in the troughs. The distant water gleamed dully blood red, multiply lit and then briefly lost in blackness again.

She looked round at the faces of the other men and women on the bridge. They were lit by overlapping rose-red glows and carved out of shifting shadows. One, two, three, four overlayed and sliding window-line stencils in the blacked out bridge, the last one fading and then extinguishing. Half a minute of total darkness, and then the same miracle pattern again as four more Fire Lances screamed free.

She went back to the bridge console and stood beside her seat.

"That's sixty now, sir," Holicek said in the briefly returned dark. "More than half of them gone."

One hundred and two missiles in this strike, one hundred and two packages of appalling death. Four more went off, flashing one after another across the ship and streaking away. Four more lances of fire stabbing the dark.

She blinked in the returned night. Their afterimages laced the black space. "You know what this is we're doing? It's an attack. We're launching a first strike. We're starting the war up again."

"Oh I doubt that very much, sir. Our people wouldn't do that. The other side will have started something for sure. Besides, the war hasn't exactly stopped. Ask our aircrew."

She nodded in the renewed sweep of light, in the softened

rocket screams penetrating the bridge. It hadn't exactly stopped. It never would. While it was possible to prosecute the war it would go on. What was the sense of the appalling, the inconceivable loss, if you stopped just short of final victory? That was what was wrong. That was what they all believed, going mad to stop themselves going insane. It *had* to be worth continuing just to prove that it had been worth starting the war. She looked round at them all, perfectly normal men and women just like herself, all turned to demons in the arcing overlapping rose-red hell light.

It was Bedford standing there at the back of the bridge, watching. Like everyone, she'd been so absorbed in the awesome spectacle that she'd failed to notice him enter through the blacked-out door. She didn't say a word. She watched him watching his lances of fire lashing out into the night, into the last and final night. Lances of fire turning the ocean into a sea of sombre blood, putting more burning blackness into the dying world.

Lances of fire.

June 13, 0540–0815

THAT WRAPPED IT up, that was the end of the checks on the second and third launch. Mounted in their computer architectures behind all the instrument panels, the tireless little microprocessors had all the data and would hold it in stasis like some complex concept waiting to map itself magically onto the real world, imposing changes. Everything in the end is reducible to structured data—to *information*. From caveman magic to computerized manipulations, the only change is that the spells you weave describe the world more precisely and so modify it more implacably.

Warren Lister pushed his chair back from the console and looked at Lt. Judy Wigner and CPO Jonathan Deevers, the only two from his so excellent team still working in the MCC. It was time to break.

"The first warhead will be going in on its target now," Wigner said. The wall clock said 0542.

Lister nodded. Now the Soviets knew for sure. "Which target is that?"

"Silo near Kepina, north of Archangel. Hundred kilotonne head."

He sighed. "Only a matter of time now waiting for the response. Wonder how quickly they can get something lined up and thrown at us." A big ICBM or a theatre range weapon would be able to fly over in a matter of minutes, it was the targeting that would be the problem.

Deevers was shutting down his console instruments. "Think they can get an accurate enough fix, sir?"

"That should be easy enough. The Norwegians are probably passing data on our position by now. The only way they can prove a strike launched from inside their economic zone isn't anything to do with them is to pass constant updates on where we are and what we're doing. Otherwise they'd get themselves nuked in response."

"Would they really do that?" Wigner asked.

"Be fools if they didn't." He stood up and made towards the tunnel door.

"There's a rumour going round the ship, sir." Deevers looked from one officer to the other as if he was sure that he had something new for them. "Our strike isn't a response to any new nuking of the States. We're starting it up first."

Lister looked at Wigner.

The lieutenant shook her head. "I haven't heard anything, sir. I've been working here the whole time with you."

"That British guy, Drexel, says so." Deevers shrugged. "And the Army captain, whatever she's called. Someone asked Lt. Craze, and she said it was true. Don't know where she'd get that from, though."

"Well," Lister said. One hundred and two missiles flying— one already arrived. "There's not much sense in worrying about that now. Judy, get Barbara Vogt up here to spell you. She's had two hours sleep, so you take a turn. You as well, Deevers. Let's all try and keep fresh."

"I knew you wouldn't be asleep, sir," she said. "Commander Steetley said you weren't breakfasting in the wardroom, and when I checked with the galley they said you'd ordered something sent up."

He had a pot of coffee and a plate of sandwiches on his desk, and was working at his desktop computer. He looked at her for a moment as if wondering whether he had time for intruders, then glanced at his watch. It would be reading around seven thirty. That seemed to make the decision for him. "Sit down, lieutenant. Yes, over there." He stood up himself and picked up his coffee cup and the plate of sandwiches. He followed her over to the two couches. "What's the problem? You look tired."

She was terribly tired. She realized that she'd dropped onto the couch. Gloria Craze in a daze—stupid turns of phrase coming back from her school days. He looked tired as well, very tired indeed. "Had any sleep since yesterday, sir?"

"Around three hours. The problem?" He hunched forward with cup and plate on the little low table between them. He took a mouthful from a sandwich and waited.

She wasn't at all sure how to begin.

"Lieutenant." He waved the half eaten sandwich at her. "If you wait around long enough the Soviets will get here with their nukes before you get around to saying it. We're sailing on a constant heading due north at a steady nine knots. They can't miss."

"Shouldn't we—zigzag or something, sir?"

Bedford shook his head. "Any warhead they're likely to throw at us won't just drop. It will come in using snapshot radar to correct its aim. It will take its first look on the way down, before atmospheric re-entry, so that it can use attitude control right at the start of its re-entry path to make a course correction, then it will take more looks at us for fine glide corrections while it's on the way down through the lower atmosphere. That's for sure. That's what will have happened to all the carriers and half the rest of the surface Navy the minute the ocean war went nuclear. Subs, too—you put a big water burst down near a boat and you crack its hull." He paused to sip his coffee. "A re-entry vehicle intended for naval targets will spot a thing the size of the Vindicator on flat ocean from hundreds of kilometres out. We couldn't zigzag far enough at full speed to avoid one of those. Only mystery is, where exactly has the counter-strike got to? Our first Fire Lance went in at least two hours ago and the whole strike will have hit by now. So—your problem." He bit at the sandwich.

"It's—" You have to say it, or else go. "It's the strike. Do you know that it's a first strike, a nuclear *attack*? The Soviets haven't launched any strikes of their own since the Freeze set in—around twelve weeks ago now."

Bedford put down the still unfinished sandwich, brushed off his fingers. "Lieutenant Craze, I'm neither blind nor deaf nor stupid. What I don't see or hear or ask for myself I get told, and the rest I can figure out from what I've learned."

"But it means—it means we're starting it. *Starting* it."

"Surprised?" He was sitting with his elbows on his knees and with his fists clenched together in front of him. No relaxed poses this time. "A handful of people with apparently absolute powers like some sort of Roman or medieval hatchetmen—they get themselves flown across the Atlantic in a C-5 all to themselves. A whole C-5. They come on board my ship, and within fifteen minutes they've killed one person and have carried out a summary execution of another who only wanted to avoid any precipitate resumption of the war, and who was just trying to run away anyway. Sure, stealing a Wolfmarine from a US warship in time of war would be a capital offence, but that wasn't why Jenninger and Caufield were shot. Does that sound remotely like the rigorously democratic United States of America we all know from before the war? You said it yourself, the survivors have to go crazy to keep themselves sane.'' He looked at her with raised eyebrows. ''You're surprised?''

''But it's not—it's not—oh! Don't you see? It's not just Kylander and the people he's working for. It's us. You and me and all of us. *We launched the strike.* We did. We've restarted the war.''

''Working on the assumption that the leaders on the other side are thinking—or going crazy—in the same way that ours are, then does it matter who starts it up again? Someone was bound to.''

''Huh. Every time someone doesn't start it—it doesn't start. That just sounds like the old 'I was only following orders.' ''

''Lieutenant, are you accusing me?''

''No sir. Of course not. All of us—not just you.''

Bedford stood up and took his coffee cup back to his desk for a refill. Gloria looked at the picture up by the door—Gayleen Bedford aged 39 and Linda Bedford aged 12, both four years dead. Smiling, they watched the whole cabin from their vantage point on the wall. Did he want them with him, their censure and their approval? How much did he love them, and how guilty did he feel towards them?

Bedford crossed in front of the photograph. He sat down again, placing cup and coffee pot on the little table. ''There won't be any Nuremberg after this war. Not for either side. Not this side of eternity. Every one of us would belong in that court.'' He filled the cup with coffee. ''Lt. Craze, are you at all religious?''

''Me? Religious?'' Impossible. ''I'm a graduate in combined psychology and sociology. I know and can analyse every personal supportive and communal regulatory function religion's been invented for. What kind of a mess would I get myself in if I was religious?''

''A crisis of belief.''

''Exactly.'' And why did he say exactly that? The most fundamental upheavals could occur in an individual's psychic structures, in their patterns of thought and behaviour and belief, at times of extreme stress. And if that end-of-the-world vision visible outside together with the awful responsibility of captaincy at such a time didn't add up to extreme stress, then what did? "Sir, you're not coming down with Moral Majority Apocalyptic Fundamentalism, are you? You haven't contracted Reagan's Disease?" And *that* sounded like her student days.

"The Reagan Doctrine? Is it in my file?" He shook his head, supplying his own answer. "You're one among my at the most three potential confidants on board. Boyce and Andrew Culbertson and you. No one else would be appropriate. Trouble is, I know all three of you too briefly personally. Only half a year. Boyce is an excellent first officer and I rate him highly. He has his limits, probably, but not in competence or intelligence. However, I don't feel myself personally drawn to him. No empathy. Andrew is different. But he's closed himself off. Do you realize he's never once gone up top to look at the dust veil? His way of coping with it—with the loss of his family and what's been done to the world—is to close himself off from it. And the situation, which is the only thing that matters right now and is precisely what I might want to talk about, is therefore an impossible subject with him. Which leaves you."

She shrugged. "That's what I'm here for. Personnel Advisement Officer and all that. I don't have to file and report everything I hear."

Bedford shook his head again, drank from his cup. "Sometimes I think we'd be better off with a good old-fashioned chaplain. Bless us all and consign us to God. Also then I wouldn't even contemplate making a fool of myself by making a pass at you."

"Pardon, sir?"

"I said then I wouldn't even contemplate making a fool of myself by making a pass at you. It's an old term for trying to get you into my sleeping cabin."

"I've met the term before, sir. I read a lot these days—passes the time on board." And wasn't that a stupid thing to say.

He was neither discernibly amused nor embarrassed. To amuse or embarrass could not have been his intention, either. "Are you shocked, lieutenant?"

"Ah—no. Not shocked. Surprised. I always had the impression you were forbidden territory."

"I am. I'm not going to make a pass at you, and I hope to God you're intelligent enough not to try and help me out by making one at me. You're twenty years younger than me, and it is not something I would permit to happen."

She glanced at the smiling wife and daughter, policing, protecting, watching over the man in his isolation.

"However, that is probably the root of the problem why I can't confide in you. At least only with difficulty, I'd expect."

Had he found a way to resurrect his wife and daughter in his mind, reincarnating them as guardian angels appointed to watch over him, to protect and to guide?

"Lieutenant, since midday yesterday—quite suddenly—I've been arranging for people to die. My own aircrew, two Russian pilots, a couple of hundred Russians on a ship and probably around a hundred more in a submarine. And then I've launched one hundred and two Fire Lances—seventeen and one half megatonnes all up. None of them are going on cities or heavily populated targets. Thank God I've been spared that. But they'll kill directly, and they'll kill indirectly as a result of longterm fallout and worsening of the climate collapse. And because of the response they'll provoke. Less than twenty hours from a handful of aircrew to a full nuclear strike going home. That's something of a shock."

He was squeezing his hands together, as if forcing out some kind of anguish that was totally absent from his voice.

"I've spent twenty seven years training and preparing for it. I've been on a Poseidon boat, Trident boats. I was on the Iowa when she was refitted—had her turrets taken out and replaced by magazines for land attack mode Tomahawks. The Tomahawk's before your time—it was the crude little predecessor to our Fire Lance. The whole time I have been perfectly aware of *what* I was doing. I was supporting credible nuclear deterrence. No sane human being can approve of nuclear deterrence in an ideal world, but while the other guy has it, I've always believed, the only way to ensure he doesn't use it is to have it—for real—yourself. And now I've been forced to see with my own eyes what happens when it breaks down—and what couldn't have happened if it wasn't there to break down in the first place. It's now suddenly occurred to me that *deterrence* does not involve shooting back if despite your deterrent the other guy shoots first. That's the coherent war philosophy, but it's not deterrence because the thing it's supposed to deter has already happened. So it can only be vengeance. And vengeance I do not believe in."

She had her listening role again, she should be at ease. Instead she was acutely uncomfortable.

"So. Deterrence is no use after a first strike. If he hits you first after all, it's too late to stop him by hitting him back. And deterrence cannot involve first use—that would be an unconscionable crime. So your deterrence is the whole time just scrap. The Vindicator and its four hundred Fire Lances are just scrap. So first off, the strategic instrument I have actively supported hasn't worked. I've been trying to rescue myself through the conviction that the continued existence of this ship was being used successfully to deter the other side from any resumption of nuclear level attacks. In other words, that deterrence was still valid after all. Now they've taken it away from me and turned it into first use. That is my dilemma."

He'd said it so flat and calm and factually. She didn't know how to respond.

"I assume you can't help me there, Gloria. Your line is observing belief systems, not repairing or replacing them. You've done no clinical psychology?"

"Never interested me. It's just about re-normatizing people."

"And you're not at all religious. Pity. That I could really use. That I could use."

"Are you religious, sir?" He had the token confessional category in his file, but that was all.

"I know what the inside of a church looks like." He separated his hands at last, reached for the coffee cup. "What was it you wanted from me?"

"I really wanted—you've sort of caught me out." Not quite the way she thought the conversation would go. "I wanted you to stop it. Stop the strike somehow. Stop the one that's already happened, I guess." She just looked at her hands.

"It's a little late for that." It was too late, far too late. "It reminds me of a joke. A guy's looking for some small town in the middle of the Midwest. He drives around and gets totally lost. It gets dark, he gets desperate. Eventually he finds a farmhouse, drives up and knocks on the door, tells the farmer where he's trying to get. The farmer thinks for a while, slow and sure like country folk. That's kinda difficult, he says at last. If I was you, I wouldn't want to start from here."

Gloria nodded. "I heard it before."

"It's a very old one. It's probably as old as history. Make a good epitaph for the human race, don't you agree?''

She just looked at her hands. Nice brown hands. That was why he permitted the strike, that was why he went along with it. Like Drexel, in a different way, he thought it was all over and didn't care enough any more. He'd given up. The basic will to live, and all the interactive skills and needs that follow from it—by force or charm or bargaining or politics to keep in with some sort of influence on the world around you so as to keep it optimal for your own survival—the psychological engine that powered him had shut down.

Why not? Why shouldn't it happen to them *all*? Drexel had been on land like Raffles—he'd seen it himself, he'd even helped do it. Bedford had always lived with the prospect of doing it and had now been faced with it being done by himself. Maybe he only found out it wasn't a retaliatory strike afterwards—not that delivering a retaliatory instead of a pre-emptive strike would probably make you feel better about the blood on your hands. Why shouldn't it be too much? Why shouldn't they be allowed quietly and invisibly to turn off their survival motors instead of losing control and killing themselves, or else developing a hysterical self-justifying response. Dammit, oh God dammit to hell—it was too much for any human being. But she still wanted to live! She looked at the Captain sitting solid and real and strong and secure there, sipping his coffee, his wife and daughter smiling from the wall over his shoulder. He looked firmly in command, every inch the same captain. You wouldn't know from outside that his life motor had stopped.

The ship's address speaker clicked. *"All stations alert! Nuclear attack! Ship closing up to Condition One! All stations alert! Nuclear attack!"*

Crossing the corridor in a step and a half, he bumped into a crewman at the tunnel door, pushed the man through the tunnel ahead of him and into the CIC. Boyce was at the OpSum, headset on, the room was three quarters full. Bedford went straight to his dais, sat at his little console, pulling on his headset. He looked at the main CIC plot. It was carrying a 500 kilometre concentric scale with the ship at the centre. Up at two o'clock on the rim were little flashing dots, visibly moving in along the radius. He called up a repeat of the BMD plot on his own embedded console screen.

"Four coming in on oh-six-three," Boyce reported over the open circuit. "First at four hundred sixty at eight-six thousand. Showing re-entry retardation."

Get the defences into gear. "SADIS on Skytop mode. Automatic."

"SADIS on Skytop," repeated Redden, the SADIS Supervisor. "On automatic. Tracking targets one to four."

"Rayflex is slaved to SADIS," reported Jorge LoSecco, the Weapons Control Officer.

"Slave Arrowflash," Bedford ordered. They came in so *fast*. All four dots were well separated from the periphery of the plot—re-entry vehicles no bigger than a man, surrounded now by an impenetrable halo of incandescent plasma as they bored into the denser lower layers of the atmosphere at something approaching Mach 25, 30,000 kilometres an hour. Without atmospheric breaking they would have arrived from 460 kilometres out in less than sixty seconds.

"Arrowflash slaved to SADIS," reported Condillac. Seaman Condillac was seated next to PO2 Iris Mellott, who was monitoring the Rayflex-2 NBMD. Condillac primarily ran the Seastrike, and the two backed each other up with the Arrowflash point air defence system. Only three out of the four operators were present at the weapon consoles—it was almost twenty hours since the CIC first went to Condition 1, and you had to allow the people rotation breaks if they were to continue to do their jobs properly. Loggia, the man for the Mk56 155mm guns, was missing and might not even make it to the CIC before it was all over. This happened fast—so fast!

"First at two hundred kilometres at five-eight thousand," Boyce reported. Four nuclear warheads coming in, and not one of them a firing practice dummy. All of them real.

"Ship externally closed, sir," Kuroda reported over his private Talker circuit. "Damage Control says internally closing up."

He nodded. If they came right in, if they cracked the ship, it *must* be internally sealed into watertight sections and decks. Only the aircraft hangar would be left as one big undivided space, full of aircraft and aviation fuel and air weapons and God help them all.

"All weapons ready to fire," LoSecco reported.

"Firm tracking." Redden. "Firing selection running."

Boyce. "They hit us once each with radar on the way in before hot re-entry. They've all shown re-entry correction manoeuvres."

Zeroing on the ship. As soon as they had slowed enough to emerge from their incandescent cloaks they would fire more radar snapshots so that they could make attitude changes and manoeuvre right on to the ship. Programmed to target on the biggest echo sticking up from the piece of sea they were diving for, they would come in as close as possible before detonating. That was a nice quandary for the programmer. His re-entry vehicles would be able to register the incident homing radars of intercepting missiles, and would be able to predict when the missile was coming in too close to be avoided so that it would kill the vehicle. It could select not to let itself be wasted, but to detonate in full thermonuclear fury a thousandth or a tenthousandth of a second before the missile collided and exploded and smashed itself and its target to useless radioactive debris. But if the nuclear warhead detonated, it would destroy the other re-entry vehicles in what the planners called fratricide—brothers that might otherwise have had a chance of getting through the defending missile screen. That was a tricky problem for the programmer, when to have his warhead waste itself in the interest of its friends, and when to have it go prematurely for broke and burn like a second sun.

Boyce. "First at eighty out, four-oh thousand up. Radar pulse. Radar pulse from the second. They can hit us on the nose."

What he needed was the Skyguard System. The vast long-range Rooftop radar, the Histrike missile—a kinetic collider with a catcher net that intercepted an incoming warhead right outside the troposphere, stratosphere, mesosphere—then the Rayflex-1 and a laser defence as low level in-atmosphere backups. You couldn't put that on a ship. Instead you got the Rayflex-2 shipboard system, with the Arrowflash as a close-in backup. The Rayflex-2 could go up to 40,000 metres with a thirty kilometre lateral range at its maximum altitude, flying at Mach 5.5. It attempted a head-on intercept—coming in from the side at a wide intercept angle was nearly impossible at such high closing speeds. If it realized it was going to miss it blew its fragmentation head—blast and fragments might damage or tumble the target. The Arrowflash could reach 6,000 metres with a ten kilometre lateral range, and only hit a mere Mach 3.75—4,500 kilometres an hour. The next ship in the Nemesis Class would have been given the new Hilite laser to replace Arrowflash. Arrowflash was the oldest missile system on board, but therefore also the most reliable.

"Which radar are we running?"

"Forward SPY-X12." CPO Irene Jablonski at Track Evaluation and Scheduling. "The aft SPY-X12 and both SPY-X10As are retracted. All other radars and antenna retracted."

"Rayflex receiving target instruction. All rounds." PO2 Mellott was one of the ship's real black beauties, Clemence's girl on board. The other three weapon operators were seamen, but the Rayflex had a petty officer. The Rayflex was important.

Boyce. "First at fifty out, three-one thousand up."

Dylong came skidding in, beating the warhead intruders. He stopped to assess the situation then moved in beside Boyce, picking up a headset at the OpSum but neither interfering nor interrupting.

Mellott. "Rayflex launching. One gone. Two. Three. Four. All flying. Reloading." It was a battle of seconds now, with the Rayflexes and their targets closing on each other so incredibly fast. "All rounds firing radar. Tracks separating."

The CIC plot was switched to a hundred kilometre concentric scale by one of the systems operators. Four flashing lights halfway in, four flickering dots going out to meet them. Closing.

Boyce. "Thirty out, two-one thousand up."

"Our Wolfmarines are all warned?"

"Yes sir," Kuroda said. They would all be two hundred metres up from the sea to give them shock correction room, they would have their tails to the ship's position and the potential blast, and they would be flying out and away from their distant patrol positions.

Boyce. "Twenty two out, one-seven thousand up."

Dots and lights closing together. "Warn the ship."

"Nuclear blast imminent! Nuclear blast imminent!"

Drexel had come running with his shirt all unfastened through a series of doors he had to undo and heave open against their heavy return hinges. In the canteen were the damage control parties, Kylander's trio, Gittus and his soldiers, Raffles, and some aircrew. They all went into the shock posture, bent over with their feet wide apart on the green deck and their hands clutching the rims of the anchored tables. A shocking posture, it was, like lots of boys and girls at some mixed boarding school with their arses stuck out awaiting punishment. But Raffles stood up straight. She stood up straight, wide eyed, her head lifted toward the baffled ceiling lights. Stupid woman.

Mellott. "One hit. Two. Third a near miss but it's tumbled. One miss."

Boyce, calmly. "Fourteen out, twelve thousand up. Dive angle increasing."

Mellott. "Rayflex launching. One gone. Radar firing."

Condillac. "Arrowflash instructing. One round."

"Override the auto. Fire three rounds in series." They could afford to fire three for safety's sake and risk wasting two of them if the first made it. The warhead was *so close*, and with Arrowflash you got just one chance at a launch. "Stand by to pull in the SPY-X12."

Boyce. "Radar's lost the near miss tumbler. It's broken up."

Mellot. "Rayflex missed."

Boyce. "Ten out and nine thousand up."

"Pull in the radar when the Arrowflash fires." No sense in losing a radar to the blast each time a nuclear attack came in.

Redden. "All ready, sir."

Condillac. "Arrowflash launching. One. Two. Three."

Boyce. "Eight out, seven thousand and five up."

A nuclear warhead closing to kill.

The shutters were already down when she reached the bridge and the low level lights coming on. Now they sat in the red glow gloom with dim images of themselves reflected in the shuttered glass. Gloria Craze looked at herself seated at the mirror bridge console twice the depth of the bridge away. She didn't *look* terrified. She didn't *look* any more terrified than did the rest of them.

Holicek wasn't trusting the seat. He had joined the others with his feet splayed on the green deck and his hands wrapped white-knuckled round the console's grab rail. She had the BMD plot repeated on a console screen, had been trying to comment calmly for the bridge team, but now the plot had blanked as the radar shut down and retracted. She leaned forward to grab the back edge and side edge handles. The Rayflexes had gone off from the foredeck launcher with tearing screams, the Arrowflashes from the starboard box aft of the bridge with wildcat shrieks. There was no more time. It must come now. Must—

She hit the console. She hung half out of her seat and scratched to keep hold.

Some sort of noise. Some monstrous noise like hell yawning.

She couldn't hold. She let go of the rail and descended hands and head first for the deck. Her elbow buckled, she dropped onto her shoulder, she rolled with her feet tangled up around the footrest. What a mess, what officer dignity. What a dumb thought to have right then.

Bedford's seat and dais and world went on a whooshing ride—*up*, and then *down*. He held himself steady. Boyce stumbled. Dylong caught him and helped him up from his knees, braced against the OpSum. Everyone else was in a seat and clutching a console grimly.

So *that* was what the one metre freedom on the isolation box suspension was like, while a blast wave pushed the ship into the water and then let it bounce out again. Next would come the compression shock put into the sea right below the air burst, radiating through the water, reflecting off the bottom, coming in from the side. He looked round at the tunnel door.

Nothing. No shock. But the tunnel swung and shortened, the footplates slicing over each other and the wall fabric concertinaing. The *ship* moved around the isolation box.

The tunnel straightened out again as the huge return springs pushed against the shock damper pistons. The whole ship moved!

Wait for Damage Control's flood of reports.

Rolling all over the place, writhing around like idiots at an orgy between the tables. God almighty. God almighty. Whoever invented something that could do *that*!

Getting up to his hands and knees. He saw Raffles pull herself into a foetal ball, hands folded round her head. Poor woman, poor bloody woman.

Voices suddenly. And someone yelling, howling hysterically. Then a bull voice above all the others. *"Shuddup there! Man, if I can still hear you you're as alive as I am!"*

What was Villman doing down there in Damage Control? Where were the reports? Boyce and Dylong were working at the OpSum, searching for something inside all the instrumentation and computation of the ship. Time to give the poor bastards around him something to do. Something to *do*. My God, they'd taken a nuclear near miss and were still alive!

Calm yourself. "ASW, how'd the Surtass and sonars take it?"

"Checking, sir." Lt. Anthea Slamon had her headset on, imprinting a groove across her Afro hair. "Bow sonar transponder was retracted. MSP sonar was not deployed. Just the Surtass to worry about."

"The SPY-X12 radar get closed up in time?"

Redden. "Yes sir. Deploy it again, sir?"

"No. Give the fireball a chance to disperse." Electromagnetic bedlam would be reigning outside the Vindicator's armoured shell. To stick a radar transponder out into that would be simply to throw it away. "Reload Rayflex and Arrowflash. Run system check-throughs. Put SADIS back on surveillance mode." Where were the damage reports? He turned to Kuroda. "Ask Villman what in hell he's playing at."

He wanted to know. Were they sinking? Burning? What?

In the dim red light she helped Holicek to his feet and he helped her.

"Okay, sir. Sorry sir, you're shirt's torn."

The front of her uniform shirt was ripped across her stomach, two buttons gone and the fabric torn open. The teeshirt was still whole. She must have torn it on the corner of the console. Which idiot designed a sharp edge? She would be bruised under the teeshirt. She ignored the torn shirt. "You okay?"

Holicek nodded, and grinned.

"Anyone hurt?"

Standing or stricken, they shook their heads where they still hung on to grab rails or chairs around the bridge sides. Gloria looked at herself looking darkly back from a shuttered window. Lived through that one, then.

"Should we take a look out, sir?" one of the observers asked.

"Christ, no! Not until we get the all clear." You didn't take a look outside even though the endless night of the end of the world had been banished for a few brief moments. Because out there, searing and scorching and seething with death, a fearful and terrible sun had been born.

Fleetingly.

• • •

"Damage Control are working through their checks, sir."

"What? Give me Villman direct." He got a click in his headset as Kuroda switched him through. "Bedford. What's going on, lieutenant? I need to take corrective action."

"I'm sorry, sir," Villman answered. "We don't have any systems alarms. Minor damage, sure. Computer peripherals, circuit boxes, that kind of thing. We'll trace those through in time. We can't take a shock like that without some instrumentation outside the isolation boxes crapping out. But absolutely no systems alarms."

"Fire? Water flooding?"

"No sir. No ship damage. The hangar people say a few things flew around in there but they have everything under control. I think—I think we just bounced, sir."

Bedford switched back into the CIC open circuit. "It seems the genius who thought up this ship knew what he was doing after all. Apparently we have no major damage." He got a chorus of gasps in his ears, he could see some of the wire tight tension going out of his people.

Redden, looking around from his console. "We have to get a radar out soon, sir. We're blind."

"I'm aware of that. Stand by with towertop one and both the SPY-X10As." He could afford to lose one of the three towertop radars if it was damaged beyond repair. And if it really came to it, then on balance the SPY-X10As immediately fore and aft of the tower base were fractionally less crucial than the SPY-X12s mounted one each just in from the bridge and the TLCP. And now he remembered what Boyce and Dylong were doing. He shouldn't blank out like that—apart from the fact that the warhead had been real and had kicked the 56,000 tonne ship around like some toy, it was all just like a drill.

Slamon, the ASW Supervisor. "The Surtass took a shake-up, sir. The end fish at one hundred down is okay, but the halfway line is mostly out. Only one hydrophone working. Sonar SCR want to reel it in and replace it."

"Let them." He needed his submarine detection system working—a Wolfmarine screen was good, but it wasn't impenetrable.

Boyce. "We've got an estimate. That was two hundred fifty kilotonnes at six kilometres out. Just a little one."

Just a little one—true, but Boyce was crazy. "Can you

assess when we could risk a radar?'' The SCANs on the distant hovering Skyhooks were still surveying sea and air—even without antennas deployed on the ship to take telemetry of their data—but nothing was looking for further re-entry vehicles. Not that any would be coming in, because the air out there was going to be too hot and roiling and turbulent for another strike to get through for several minutes yet.

Dylong, looking into the OpSum beside Boyce. ''Maybe we can risk a towertop in four or five minutes.''

Dylong was always cautious in his estimates. ''Lt. Redden, deploy towertop one in three minutes.''

''Right sir.''

''And let AOC have telemetry to contact their Wolfmarines and Skyhooks. If we waste telemetry antennas we have plenty more.'' Replacing radiation-flooded wave-guides on a radio antenna mounting was just a black box job. ''Can you give me an estimate on how long we'll be in fallout?''

Boyce. ''Not precisely. We'll have to monitor. But the wind is from due north. On our north heading we'll have passed ground zero in a quarter hour, and then we'll be upwind. Maybe an hour before it's worth using the washdown.''

''Can we use it without icing?'' The air temperature had been well below freezing before the blast, and would be once again long before an hour had passed.

Kuroda. ''Excuse me, sir. AOC say the Wolfmarines are okay.''

Boyce turned at the OpSum, still talking through his headset. ''The ambient out there was minus fifteen. Right now it's sixty eight centigrade and dropping like a stone. The water is at plus three and a half. It we do a sustained washdown it will warm up the outside surface to above freezing—at least at this water salinity. We won't ice up. Pity about all the corrosive salt. There won't be a square inch of paint left on our starboard side.''

A joke on the CIC open circuit so that everyone could hear. That was good, helping them all get back to a perception of routine cares and away from any near panic or shock. A close nuclear attack was an unbelievable thing to have lived through.

Kuroda. ''Sir, AOC says the south position Skyhook is in trouble. The SCAN is wiped out and the Skyhook's control electronics are crapped some. They don't think they can keep it in the air. Also the telemetry is mushy. Ah—correction. They've lost it. It tumbled. It's going down into the sea.''

So the Soviets hadn't completely wasted their time.

The Vindicator had full radar cover again fifteen minutes later.

Opening up the ship to fly out another Skyhook would have to wait until after the washdown—this wasn't an air emergency, so they could keep the fallout and all the clean-down complications it would cause out of the hangar box. After all, the two remaining Skyhooks on station to the north, where the real danger would surely come from, could see for two hundred kilometres at their altitude. Being only one hundred kilometres north of the ship, they extended the safety zone southwards of the vessel to more than four times the twenty three kilometre sea horizon that its towertop radars could reach.

And there were no systems casualties apart from one more Skyhook and every tv set in every cabin. No more private off-duty videos and on-line computer games. But the crew would survive. There were no injuries beyond bruises and lumps on the head, and simple emotional shock. Andrew Culbertson was checking through a little line of people down in his Sick Bay Area, and no medical worries of any description had arisen.

His own desktop computer in his day cabin was alive and well, still showing the log page he had left glowing on the screen when Gloria Craze had turned up to force him into speaking out his own confusion. He could have done better without. He needed a soft-mounted mind, shock resistant like the computer, soft-mounted on his desk and with its innards soft-mounted again.

The only mess in his cabin was on and under the table between the couches. The coffee pot had gone over. He tried mopping up cold black coffee with disintegrating toilet paper, failing with the mess as surely as if it was his spilled belief. He gave up and called the canteen for someone with a rag. He ordered more coffee and some eggs, another attempt at breakfast.

It was 0815 and only fifty five minutes to the next launch. The Vindicator had survived, had proved the impossible true. The Vindicator had survived essentially unscathed, and so he still had his problem. His ship and his problem.

And no answer anywhere.

THE CABIN WAS right forward on 2nd platform, starboard side, and it stank.

Cpt. Danella Raffles lay on the floor of the narrow cabin, her shoulders propped against the lower bunk, her head tipped back, her arms limp and her legs splayed. It was obvious from the way her uniform blouse was rumpled up around her shoulders and her shirt stretched underneath that she had been sitting on the edge of the bunk when she did it, that she had bounced back and then slumped off the edge onto the floor. The whole outboard cabin wall and the underside of the top bunk were spattered with a red mess, under her head and shoulders on the lower bunk a soaking sea of red blood was seeping into the blanket. Her head—the back and half of the top was blown clean away, was completely gone. It was a mercy she was lying face up. But she was *staring*, wide pupils in motionless eyes staring up past them at the deckhead. Her mouth was open, and blood had spilled over her lip and down over her brown chin and throat. RAFFLES was written over the shirt pocket of her uniform. RAFFLES crumpled over the right breast, US ARMY crumpled over the left.

Danella Raffles had shot herself.

Andrew Culbertson wasn't needed to certify the woman as dead, but doctors are expected to inspect such scenes. "Quickest way to do it," he muttered. "She knew what she was doing. Gun in the mouth, angled upwards."

Gloria had picked up the gun. It was one of those huge and heavy Colt .45 automatic pistols, like the one Raffles had worn in the first place, like the one Gittus carried. It had been lying on the floor between the woman's legs.

"That's the popular way to do it back home," said Dresher, the US Air Force major. "That or go for a walk out top.

People've learned not to shoot themselves in the side of the head. Seen too many lingering on for a while after trying that.''

"Where'd the bullet go?" There were cable ducts all over the ship, and Boyce just wanted to be sure. He was talking reluctantly against the stench. "Why'd it make so much mess?"

"No bullet, that." Gittus squeezed into the cabin with them. "Colt .45 Model nineteen-eleven-A-one. Takes a ball round but also takes high density shot." He lifted the pistol out of Gloria's hand, released and pulled out the magazine. "Yep, high density shot. Sabot with sixteen spheres inside. Antipersonnel—the sabot splits open and the spheres spread just like a scatter gun. Makes one hell of a guaranteed mess. Stick it in your mouth like that and you get all sixteen spheres plus the sabot shell. Sure way to get instantly dead." He snapped the magazine back home and put the heavy weapon back in Gloria's hand. "Take your brain clean out of your skull."

"Looks like it." Boyce wrinkled his nose as he turned away. "Who heard the shot? You?"

Drexel nodded. "I was in my cabin. Just across here. Obviously I heard it. When I opened the door there was still blood coming out of her head." He'd thrown up right in the corridor halfway to the washroom. Some unfortunate crewman was back there cleaning it up. "How did she get hold of a gun?"

"Did your soldier boys think to check if the other two had it?" Boyce asked. "Did you search her cabin?" The pillow of the top bunk was pushed aside, and there lay the webbing belt with the webbing holster and ammunition pouch. He reached for it and handed it to Gloria. "Put it somewhere safe, will you? We've got a ship full of people overjoyed to be alive after the nuke came in, but in no time the truth is going to hit them. They'd be standing in line to use it."

Gloria held the gun in one hand and the gunbelt in the other. Raffles had blown her brains to blood red shreds, had finally blown the nightmares and the memories and the truths she knew away.

Culbertson was daring to go closest. "I'm no forensic expert, but look here. Her top incisors are broken out. Maybe force was used. Maybe it just looks like suicide."

"Uh-huh," Gittus said. "The teeth are broken outwards."

"You put the gun up in your mouth with the muzzle behind your top teeth." Dresher paused to demonstrate with his forefinger. "Yeah? And when the thing goes off it kicks out. You can't exactly hold it firm like that. Sometimes it smashes the teeth."

Culbertson shrugged. "You people should know."

"Andrew, can you organize cleaning this mess up? Just put the body over the side, for Christ's sake. We've got enough to do." Boyce looked at the staring face and gaping bloodied mouth, at the careless body. US ARMY on the left breast, RAFFLES on the right. "Anyone remember what her first name was?"

"Danella," Gloria said. "Danella Raffles."

Boyce nodded. "Miserable way to die." He turned and pushed past the others out of the cabin.

Culbertson was already folding the dead woman's limp hands together in her lap. "Anyone know a happy way?"

Gloria pushed the gun into the holster and went out into the clean air of the corridor. She hurried after Boyce and caught him where the corridor split around the ammunition hoists for the Mk 56 mounting, just past the place where a crewman was mopping the deck.

"John, what did you mean? In no time the truth is going to hit them—they'd stand in line to use the gun?"

"Huh?" He shrugged, tall black man under the low corridor lights. "Oh—instant way to go instead of jumping over the side. Go over the side and you have to wait until you drown or get sucked into the screws. Gloria, you all right? You feel okay?"

"What?" There she was, absently rubbing at her stomach with her empty hand. "Oh that's just—I bruised myself when the ship bounced. No, the truth you said. What truth?"

He looked at her, silhouetted against one light with rows of others reflected in his glasses. "You don't know? What do you think our chances are of getting out of this hole? If they can put a two-fifty kilotonne warhead that close to us, they can do it with a couple of megatonnes. That close, two megatonnes would crack us wide open."

"Who says they'll manage that?"

"And if we do get out? What then?"

"Go south. Obviously."

"The dust veil is going south."

The crewman was looking up, was standing up and listening.

"Are you trying to make out we're done for or something?"

"Gloria, do you have a private spaceship parked somewhere the two of us could use?" Then he adjusted his glasses with his middle finger, fleetingly guarding his face with his hand. "Just put the gun somewhere and get to the bridge. The launch is in twenty minutes."

Richard Erwin Bedford came aft from the bridge through the retraction space on 05 level and started down the ladders under the tower base. He had gone to take a long last look at the dim night that counted for mid morning under the veil. It was a flat calm out there on a black sea, wind force three, air temperature −16°C and slowly falling. That on June 13th. Craze and Holicek were waiting quietly on the bridge for the launch, the entire ship was closed up at Condition 1 and waiting. The Vindicator was making 9 knots on 000, due north, was coming right up to the second launch point dead on time—100 kilometres north of the first, 35 kilometres west of the island of Sula at the mouth of Sognafjord. Some Norwegian in an Arctic tent on the crest of a hill, with a battery pack and low-light imager to help him, would just be able to see Vindicator's tower out in the perfectly clear unnatural light, would be passing the ship's position by landline to some lingering signals post, and from there it would route its way to the Soviet command. It was a mystery that no further strike had come in. Maybe they were busy trying to throw all they had left at their guessed targets in the continental United States in a desperate attempt to force a break-off of the sparse but continuous rain of warheads coming in. Which would not happen, not while Soviet warheads were still clearly capable of coming in on American targets. It was all madness, cumulative kilotonnes and megatonnes of madness.

At the bottom of the second ladder Dresher was waiting, along with Sgt. Hawley and two privates. The soldiers wore forage caps and had their assault rifles slung from their shoulders. A ridiculous show of force. He went straight past them through the tunnel door and into the MCC.

He had to push past Kylander and Rimmington waiting inside there, both with their holstered Service-Sixes.

Boyce had the only other gun, an automatic hidden in a webbing holster slung from his waist. He stood there to the right of the CIC door just like last time, just like a drill, his hands on his hips and his back turned to the instrumentation and the control point at shoulder height.

Bedford was carrying no gun.

He nodded to Boyce, to Lister, went to stand in front of his own control point to the left of the CIC door. He turned, looking at Kylander. It was 0908.

Lister unlocked the wall safe between the side door and Lewy's three-position Launch Control Console. He took out the three keys, examined them, gave one to Lewy at his console, crossed over and gave one to Wigner seated at the Target Control position. Just like the last time.

Boyce unbuttoned his shirt pocket and took out his firing key. He held it in a clenched fist. Just like the last time.

PO1 Teng was watching the position and heading readouts at the Launch Control Console. "Attained firing position, sir."

"Confirm," said PO3 Jace next to him. "Heading zero-double-zero, speed nine knots dead."

Just like the last time. Except that last time there was still the sense of intolerable purpose, the sensation of the reluctant executioner turning the key, opening the trap, dropping remote controlled axes on unknown human lives to fend off something even worse, to deter some still more savage mayhem, to save the world from final damnation. Committing a horror to do the ultimate good. This time there was not even that sensation. There was hardly a physical sensation at all. And no sense whatsoever.

He took his firing key out of his pocket and watched Kylander watching him. Kylander almost seemed to know. Rimmington was watching the other people around her as if they were a potential danger to the correct delivery of the strike. But Kylander seemed to know.

0910 and everyone waiting. Kylander stared steadily back at him. Kylander parted his lips. "Captain?"

Lister was looking at him. He nodded.

"Lt. Lewy," Lister said.

Lewy inserted his key at his control point, turned it and locked it. Signal lights came on. "Firing Signal Verifier engaged. Automatic Missile Abort engaged."

Lister leaned between Deevers and Jackman at the Target Control position and inserted his key at one control point above the console, Wigner reached up and inserted her key at the other. They both turned their keys ninety degrees round. Signal lights again.

"Both clearance locking keys engaged and locked," Wigner said.

Bedford glanced at Boyce, an expressionless perfect technician of a first officer. What would happen to him in a situation where he was caught between his duty as a Nemesis System officer and his duty as principle support of his captain?

Boyce turned and located his firing key at his control point.

Bedford turned to his own control point, turning his back on Kylander's eyes. He reached up and located the key.

"Firing key engaged," Boyce said.

Bedford turned his key. "Engaged." He stood waiting, waiting the seconds away. They hadn't come to help him, there were no miracles whirling in on angel wings. He was completely alone and the situation had him trapped, had its claws bedded in his flesh. He could not escape. He could not avoid it. He could not do it, but if he left now they could continue without him anyway. Caught between duty and the devil and the deep black sea. So the Army woman Raffles had killed herself because she couldn't take any more. But for him that would be running from the responsibility. He'd sought the responsibility. He should carry it even if it broke him.

"Warren," Boyce said, "give us the PAC please."

"Permissive Action Code for second launch point," Lister recited. "Two. Three. One."

He watched his forefinger tap the digits into the keyboard. "Two. Five. One."

His finger tapped the keys.

"Firing Signal Verifier certifies the PAC," Lewy reported. "The Automatic Missile Abort is blocked."

Waiting the seconds away, waiting them away. The key is there, turned through ninety degrees. Waiting and wishing them away.

"Sir?" Lister said. "Captain Bedford, sir?"

Bedford nodded at his key.

Lister let out an audible breath. "Lewy, engage the launch management computer."

"Engaged and running. Port and starboard hoists lifting."

Eight missiles on their fifteen second elevator cradle rise, four to each launcher. Eight Fire Lances ready to open up yet more holes in the already dead enemy heartland.

"Starboard launcher loading," Lewy said. "Port loading."

The first Fire Lance into the starboard launcher would also be the first one to fly. Fly all the way with a 250 kilotonne warhead to the underground command complex in the North Urals—the fifth missile to arrive there it would be, telling them their enemy hadn't finished yet, making them join the further madness.

"Starboard launcher elevating and training outboard. Port elevating and training inboard."

"Hoists dropping." Jace said.

"We're coming right up to the launch point."

They hadn't come to take him away. Or to change the world around him. He glanced at Boyce. Boyce was watching everything.

Bedford reached out and turned his key.

"Abort," Lewy said. "We have an abort! How in hell?"

"Systems all running," Teng assured.

"The Automatic Missile Abort is back on. How in hell? How in hell is it back on?"

"Freeze the launch, man!" Lister yelled. "Or the fucking things'll just jump into the sea! Wigner—key out!"

Wigner reached up and grabbed her key—turned it hard over as Lister wrenched the second key round.

"Systems frozen, sir!" Teng called. "Launch has stopped."

"It's the Captain's key." Lewy suddenly sounded more puzzled than alarmed. He turned in his seat. "Sir—your key has disengaged."

They all turned in time to see Bedford take his key out of the control point.

"Captain," Kylander said quietly. "Either restart the launch or give me your key." Kylander had his revolver in his hand.

Bedford still stood with his back to Kylander, turning the firing key over in his hand. Rimmington turned into the tunnel and headed for the door at the end.

Facing Kylander across the MCC, Boyce unbuttoned his holster.

"Don't get yourself hurt," Bedford said. "That's a direct order, John."

Boyce's hand hesitated. Boyce's hand went back to his hip.

Bedford turned half round and looked towards Kylander. Behind the man, Rimmington was stepping aside from the door tunnel, Dresher was following her in with his gun drawn, and the soldiers were crowding at his back.

Kylander was pointing his revolver at Bedford. "The key, Captain. The key."

Bedford looked at his own key in his hand, then at Boyce's sticking out of the control point across on the other side from the CIC door. And through *there*, in the CIC, he was the boss of a ship and not of a missile system, and the only killing he had to organize was in order to defend the ship when it came under attack. That he could cope with.

Dresher started manhandling Rimmington past himself and back into the tunnel between the troopers. "Get Gittus and the rest up here! *Fast!*"

"I'd better take possession of your key, John." Once he could get through the CIC door it was too late for Kylander. He had eighteen crew in there, and only one more door and one deck to go to reach the small arms store outboard of Boyce's cabin. Rimmington would still be running round the C3 box for the canteen in search of the soldiers when he already had Kylander's group boxed in front and back. Just get through the door!

He stepped as if to cross in front of the doorway, he reached out as if to take hold of Boyce's key still sticking out of the control point. In the shadow of his own body he put his left hand on the handle of the CIC door. Kylander wasn't going to shoot him just for reaching for the key—

Kylander fired.

Kylander had fired, and Bedford bounced against the CIC door, fell away again full length onto the deck, and rolled onto his back. He lay there coughing, his left hand clutching a fistful of shirt over his stomach, pulling at the cloth. His firing key dropped out of his right hand onto the deck.

No one moved but the two soldiers. They came in behind Hawley, short rifles levelled.

Lt. Barbara Vogt rose from her console and turned on Kylander. "What do you think you're doing? *What do you think you're doing?*"

Boyce could see blood running out of Bedford's side at the waist. "Vogt! First aid pack." And she was going to jump right at Kylander's gun. "*Vogt!* I said first aid pack!"

Vogt glanced suddenly at Bedford. Then she turned and ran for the pack on the opposite wall.

Everyone moved. Deevers went from his chair straight onto his knees at Bedford's side, reaching over to pull the bloody

shirt from the wound. Bedford wasn't coughing—he was
bubbling in his throat. "Jackman! Here! Help me turn him."

Wigner was already on the phone. "MCC. Get up here
with your team. The Captain's been shot. Yes! The fucking
bastard's shot him. Just get up here."

Lister was looking at Boyce, and Boyce had decided on his
only option. "Lock away the keys."

Lister turned round and pulled the two clearance locking
keys out of the Target Control Console. Boyce pulled out his
own firing key, stooped and swept up Bedford's key, and put
them both in his shirt pocket.

Deevers had got Bedford's ankles crossed, right over left,
had the man's left arm tucked half under his side. He was
pulling Bedford's right arm across his chest while Jackman
knelt nursing the Captain's head in her hands. Vogt dropped
to her knees with the first aid pack broken open, with the
breathing tube ready to push into the man's congested throat.

The CIC door opened. Dylong stared at what was at his
feet. He looked at everyone moving and at Kylander, Dresher,
Hawley and the two soldiers, all in a knot at the opposite
tunnel door, all with guns in their hands and all being ignored.

Deevers and Jackman had Bedford turned on his side and
Vogt was starting to work the curved tube into his mouth.
Now he could vomit or bring up blood from his stomach or
lungs and he wouldn't choke.

Boyce stepped straight at Dylong, pushing him back. Behind in there people were crowding out of their seats.

"Keep your station under control!" He paused, looking
round for Lister. There at the safe, locking it. "As soon as
Culbertson's got the Captain out of the way, start resetting the
systems. We'll come round to the launch point again to
resume." He looked at Kylander across the MCC. "If you're
still here when I come back, I'll blow your guts out, Kylander.
I'll blow your guts out." He went through the CIC door and
slammed it.

Dylong was still yelling at people to get back into their
seats. "Positions! *I said positions!*"

Make them work—and there was work all right. Who
could he spare? The SADIS Systems people. "Stratten!"

Lt. Andrea Stratten was half in and half out of her seat.
"Sir?"

"Take both your operators. Go with Dylong. Joe!" He
fished out his bunch of keys and threw them at Dylong, who

caught them against his chest. "Go down and open the small
arms. Issue yourselves and every man and woman I send you.
If any soldier or civilian shows in the corridor there you blow
them away. Understand?"

Dylong nodded. He went straight out through the forward
tunnel door with Stratten and her two operators.

Boyce marched to the commanding officer's position, picked
up the headset in his hand, punched for the ship's address
channel and spoke into the mike. "All damage control parties
assemble immediately outside first officer's quarters on 02
level. Further orders from Lt. Cmdr. Dylong." He cancelled
the channel. "Kuroda! Ship's Conning Position. All rudders
ten degrees port and hold."

While Kuroda started passing the order, Boyce was already pushing for the bridge channel.

"Bridge," said Craze's voice, small out of the headset.

"Boyce. Get Holicek and two people down to Dylong at
the arms store. They're to take arms for the whole bridge
crew and guard the Conning Position and the bridge."

"Got it. They're already on their way. Defend it against
who?"

"You get down to sick bay. The Captain has been shot. I
want you to let me know as soon as Culbertson can tell how
he is."

"*What?* The Captain has—"

He cut the channel and put down the headset. "Slamon!
I'm circling the ship. Get the Surtass wound in before we tie
a knot in it. And get it deployed again as soon as we
straighten up."

"Sir!" Slamon started immediately passing orders.

Stratten and her operators came back, guns strapped on and
more gunbelts over their arms.

"The damage control teams are already arriving," Stratten
reported. "Dylong's sending one down to secure the engine
and reactor control rooms and pass arms through to the
isolation boxes aft." Which was perfect, perfect. The situation had clicked with Dylong instantly. "He's going to keep
some people there to guard the store. He thought we could
use these up here. One each."

"Good. Pass them out." But he didn't want—couldn't
possibly afford—shooting in the nerve centre of the ship.
Saturating everywhere with weapons to smother trouble would
have to be the answer. "Run down and get another load for

the MCC—Lister, the officers, the CPO in there. Bring them up here but don't go straight through in case those trigger happy bastards are still there.''

''Right sir.'' She pushed her armful of gunbelts at Kuroda. ''Oh, your keys. Dylong gave me your keys.'' She handed them over. ''Do you want M16s up here as well as handguns?''

''Christ no, not in here.''

Stratten left.

Boyce pocketed his bunch of keys and then tapped his shirt pocket where the two firing keys were safe. He watched Kuroda and the two SADIS Systems operators handing weapons out. He remembered to button his own holster closed. And how many people did he have armed? The damage control teams, most of the eighteen CIC personnel, six guarding the bridge and the Ship's Conning Position—around fifty, just about the whole of the small arms arsenal handed out. Not even Kylander and his bunch of paratroops would try to move against that much force. Why didn't the Captain do it himself? Why didn't he do it at least a day ago?

The door to the MCC opened and Wigner looked through. ''They just took the Captain downstairs, sir. He's in a bad way. And Kylander and the others have gone. We're setting up to rerun the launch from the launch point again when we come round.''

''Okay. Tell Warren we're already circling. About ten minutes before we come back at the launch point.''

Wigner closed the door.

Well now he had command of the ship. Think. For Christ's sake, think. The first thing is the ship and the crew. Kylander was jumpy as hell, maybe as jumpy as Jenninger was or even worse—and he was prepared to shoot. So he had to calm the situation down immediately before something happened. Inform the crew, inform Kylander that he's not in any danger as long as he keeps his head down, inform him things are going ahead just the way he wants so that his anxiety is defused. Whatever else, avoid bloodshed on the ship.

Stratten appeared with another five gunbelts. Stopped.

''That's okay. Pass them through.'' He turned to pick up the CO position headset again and pressed for the ship's address. The speakers clicked on and waited for him. Nothing for it. ''This is the First Officer in temporary command of the ship. There has been a shooting incident and the Captain is injured. He is being treated right now by Lt. Cmdr. Culbertson. I have

issued small arms to secure the ship as a precautionary measure. Any attempt at interference in any way in the running of
the ship by any member of Kylander's team is to be reported
to the CIC immediately. Kylander's team will assemble in the
canteen and stay there while the ship remains closed up. They
will not at any time attempt to enter the C3 box, the reactor or
engine space boxes, or the superstructure levels. We are at
present circling to regain the planned firing position, and in a
few minutes we will resume the Fire Lance launch as programmed.'' He cancelled the channel.

That would have to do. For the moment that would just
have to do. Once the strike was completed and no one else
had been shot on board, he could hope the danger of a fight
was over. He would have time to talk to all his senior officers
one by one at their stations and ensure an accurate and
controlled dissemination of information about what had
happened— rumors and guesses would all be even worse than
the truth. The best possible safety measure would be to
disarm Gittus and his little detachment, but until and unless
things calmed down completely and they spread themselves
around in smaller groups and dropped their guard, that would
be impossible without major bloodshed. And whatever else,
he had to secure the internal safety of the ship. Without that
nothing else was possible at all.

So the second strike had to go ahead, and so did the third
in another six hours—otherwise Kylander might feel himself
defeated and too personally threatened, and might start up a
firefight after all. So now the Captain's last act in cancelling
the strike, his effective last order, had to be overturned. That
was a lousy way to have to show your respect for the man
when you took over from his command. That was a lousy
way to try following his wishes. Why hadn't Bedford issued
small arms if he intended to cancel the strike? Why, oh why,
oh why?

ONLY ONE? JUST one single warhead? Were they so exhausted they couldn't dredge up any more not already committed to land targets? Was that all they had left to throw at the Vindicator? It was 1046—they'd replied even before the first Fire Lance from the last launch had vaporized its target. They were getting information through Norway all right, or else they had been planning the strike against the ship anyway.

The CIC plot was still on its five-hundred-kilometre concentric scale. Halfway out to the rim at 2 o'clock was a single flashing light—the warhead coming in on bearing 072 degrees, coming in from somewhere further eastward in the USSR than had the previous quadruple attack. It was already well through its hot re-entry phase, trailing an incandescent plasma trail across a brilliant heaven up there, way above the awful dust veil in the unattainable empire of the sun. Just one warhead coming in.

Dylong stood at the OpSum, but his voice came over the headset on open circuit to Boyce seated at the commanding officer's dais. "Contact at two hundred at six-one thousand."

Kuroda. "Ship externally closed. Internally closed up."

Now he knew how the Captain had felt. You survived in this business by luck as much as anything. It was sheer luck that all three Wolfmarines on search sector station were halfway through their patrol duration and so no relieving or returning machine was closer to the ship on its way out or back, almost certain to be killed by any reentering nuke. It was a lesser good luck that no Skyhook was being rotated and hovering helpless near the ship. It was sheer luck that the Soviets were either so depleted or so loaded with other priorities that they weren't sending over multiple strikes every hour. That, eventually, would start to damage the ship.

LoSecco, Weapons Control Officer. "All ready to fire."

Redden, SADIS Supervisor. "Firm tracking. Firing selection is running."

The SADIS was on automatic Skytop BMD mode, making its own decisions about what weapons to instruct and when to fire them. This time round it had no target selection priority problems. All the isolation boxes were hanging free in their suspension cages with the valves in the shock damper cylinders dedicated to automatic response.

Dylong. "Contact showing course correction manoeuvre."

Zeroing in on the ship. Sheer luck that the CIC personnel were on rotation break changeover when the warhead announced its arrival. Every position in the CIC was occupied, everyone there in case something went wrong and he needed them all. And they were growing tired now—everyone on board was tired. It was probably sheer luck that Kylander had managed to perceive the need for peace on board, that he had not objected to being ordered out of the way with a promise of being shot if he turned up again in any of the places that interested him. Sheer luck that he wasn't so mad he could no longer swallow an insult—whatever else he was mad enough to do—and had taken the continued launch of the second strike as a signal that things were going his way and that he could keep quiet.

The CIC plot switched to the one hundred kilometre concentric scale, with the flashing light of the warhead well in from the edge.

Dylong. "Contact at eighty out, for-five thousand up."

"Radars?"

CPO Irene Jablonski. "We're on the forward SPY-X12. All others retracted."

PO2 Iris Mellott. "Rayflex receiving target instruction. One round."

"Override. Three rounds in series. We can afford to waste them." If it was only one warhead coming in, then it might be a big one, and he wanted to be sure they got it as far out as possible. At the Rayflex console Mellott started running her beautiful black fingers over the keyboard. Lucky Greg Clemence. What a time for a thought like that.

Dylong. "Contact at fifty out, four-one thousand up."

How big was it, how close would it come? It was time for the SADIS to launch the Rayflex intercept. Down below inside the C3 isolation box on 2nd platform Culbertson had

the Captain on the operating table, still trying to patch his
insides back together again after more than one and a half
hours, and expecting to be working for at least as long again.
Why hadn't Bedford neutralized Kylander first? Did he feel
he had to provoke Kylander to have a reason to neutralize
him? Why?

Mellott. "Rayflex launching. One gone. Two. Three. All
flying. Launcher reloading."

Three flickering light points in a line moving out from the
centre of the plot, the flashing warhead contact closing in.
Mach 5.5 meets Mach 7 or 8—seconds only.

Mellott. "First round failed. No radar. Motor cut."

Redden looked round from his Supervisor console.

Mellott. "Second and third round good, radars firing."

Redden was looking at him. He managed not to shrug—
just copying the Captain and harvesting luck. Sheer goddam
luck.

Dylong. "Thirty out, three-nine thousand up. Dive com-
mencing."

"Stand by to pull in the SPY-X12. Where's the dud round
going to fall?"

Jablonski. "Nowhere near us. Four or five kilometres out."

Dylong. "Twenty five out, three-two up. It's got ECM."
Firing pulses to fool the Rayflex radars.

"Warn the ship."

Kuroda started passing the warning on the ship's address.

Mellott. "Second round missed. Rayflex reinstructing."

Dylong. "Twenty out, two-five up."

Condillac. "Arrowflash instructing. One round."

Mellott. "Third round closing."

Dylong. "It's beating the ECM. Sure intercept."

Mellott. "Hit."

Dylong. "Fuck." He grabbed tight hold of the OpSum
handles. "Detonated. Seventeen out, nineteen thousand up."

Jablonski. "Radar is out."

Redden. "Retract it!"

Then it hit. The seat, dais, surrounding CIC seemed to
sweep down, then to sweep up. Behind his shoulder the door
tunnel walls and floorplates creaked and clattered. Everyone
was clutching at grab handles and seats, Dylong was doing a
balancing dance in front of his OpSum and somehow keeping
on his feet.

• • •

Andrew Culbertson had Bedford on the table—had him held wide open with clamps, a living body gaping and pulsing with heat, bits of its insides spread around all over the place still attached to their arterial feeds. He was pouring whole blood into the arm catheters and syphoning it out of the abdominal cavity almost as fast. He hadn't even stabilized the trauma torn by the bullet, never mind starting to sew things back together.

He grabbed the side of the anchored table, the orderlies held on to the wall grips—and the lighted shoebox of the operating theatre flew all over the place. The syphon slipped clear out of the gaping incision and roared, the oxygen mask bounced off Bedford's face.

"Dammit! Do your job!"

The anaesthetist assistant got back off her knees and re-centred the mask. An orderly eased the syphon back into place and it gurgled. Another steadied the swaying transfusion bags. The third picked up the forceps and scissors Culbertson had dropped and dumped them.

Culbertson let go of the operating table's underside rail. He looked at his anaesthetist. "Sorry, Jenny. Sorry."

"No problem, sir." Warrant Officer Jenny Bendix was checking through the respirator functions. "He's still with us."

"Did the radar come in before the blast hit?"

Jablonski. "Yes sir. The housing retracted and the box was closed in time. The antennas are all shot, sir."

Obviously. The flash radiation—gamma and radio frequency, and probably the whole surge of thermal neutrons—got it before it was pulled down into the retraction box. It might still be physically intact, but it was dead until its electronics could be replaced.

Jablonski again. "Sir—Radar SCR have just fired the extinguishers in the box. They say the radome was burning." The plastic streamlining encasing the radar array. "They also have a radioactivity count inside."

"The traps check closed?"

"Yes sir. They reckon it's the array itself, sir. Isotopes produced by the neutron flux. It isn't high-level."

So the mounting would be fire damaged—heated, corroded by toxic fumes, and coated in a mixture of molten carbonized plastic mixed with extinguisher foam. And the whole structure was lightly radioactive. So it wasn't going to be a case of just replacing the antennas in the array but of repairing the thing physically—a major job that couldn't even be started until the ship was well clear of any fallout so that the box could be flushed with fresh air and then cleaned up inside. One main radar clean out. He turned toward Kuroda. "Damage Control report anything else?"

"No sir. No systems casualties. The bounce wasn't quite so bad as last time, sir."

It wasn't, not quite. "Joe, any determination on the warhead yield?"

"Around two megatonnes." Dylong looked around from his OpSum. "We're going to have to wait twenty to thirty minutes before we can deploy any antennas."

A two megatonne warhead—why did it go for a suicide blast that far out when the Rayflex closed, seventeen kilometres away and nineteen thousand metres high? Because it was the only one? And thank God it didn't come any closer with that high a yield. It must have blown a hole right through the dust veil. If the hole wasn't perhaps full of its own filth, the sun might shine for a while. Not that they would see it—they had to stay closed up until they had moved far enough away from the fallout. That they would do at a constant nine knots on the unvarying course due north. There was still the third launch point to make at 1510. At the moment a perfect execution of the ordered strike series was the only way to keep Kylander quiet and to avoid trouble on board. And it was the only way to save his own head when he had to explain sometime why he'd then disarmed Kylander's people and all but locked them up.

Twenty to thirty minutes, Dylong said, before they could risk sticking anything out through the Vindicator's armoured roof, before they could find out what damage had been done to the stationkeeping Skyhooks and to the three patrolling Wolfmarines. And before they could deploy a surveillance radar or start receiving SCAN radar telemetry. The ship was helpless because it was blind. It only had its sonars and its Surtass to listen to the surrounding water, undamaged because the thermonuclear detonation had been too high to put any significant shock energy into the water. At least there was no immediate risk of a follow-up nuclear strike—any warhead trying to re-enter through the monstrous turmoil going on in the stratosphere would just disintegrate.

* * *

It was 1130, nearly forty minutes since the nuclear attack.

"Towertop one is still fuzzed but clearing, sir," Jablonski reported. "Radar SCR say they can make out the sea state right to the horizon now, and they're picking up the Norwegian uplands again."

The electromagnetic pulse effects were lessening rapidly and the radar performance was improving correspondingly. The towertop unit could make out the almost flat calm surface right out to its 22½ kilometre sea horizon, and was picking up the Norwegian hills sticking up from behind the curvature of the Earth. So at least they could see something, by radar if not by eye. Outside a dim grey twilight was filtering through the disturbed dust veil overhead, but it wasn't enough light to see for very far, and it was obscured by a thin mist vaporized off the sea surface into the freezing air—another legacy of the thermonuclear blast. He had been up to the bridge briefly to take a look for himself. It was the nearest approximation to daylight they'd enjoyed for five days. The miserable grey gloom was no approximation to daylight whatsoever.

"Okay," he said. "We'll risk the big radars. Deploy the forward SPY-X10A and the aft SPY-X12. Kuroda, tell the AOC they can wheel their Skyhook out and put it up."

That was the bad news. There had been no telemetry from and no guidance control contact with the three Skyhooks out on station, and the towertop radar had found no trace of them in the air. All three, together with their SCAN surveillance radars, had gone down, electronically crippled by the thermonuclear explosion. Now there were only five Skyhooks left, and it would be impossible to fly more than two of them at once round the clock. Placing them optimally could wait—the first priority was to get one of them three thousand metres up into the air so that it could broaden the radar horizon around the ship out to two hundred kilometres, allowing just enough time to react with an aircraft launch if a low-level air attack came in.

The good news was the Wolfmarines. They'd all seen the flash, but there were no problems on any of the better shielded machines and the crew dosimeters were registering no dangerous exposure levels. The southeast sector Wolfmarine had sealed its heated and ventilated cabin and the pilots had gone onto internal air—the wind was still coming from almost due north and would be sweeping any low altitude fallout towards the machine. There was no sea-level fallout near the Vindicator. The entire decks and upper works had been sluiced with the washdown, but apart from the flight deck crew sending off a SCAN-Skyhook, the entire ship was still sealed and closed up at Condition 1. There had been no minor injuries, no bruises bad enough to require Culbertson's attention. And Culbertson was desperately busy anyway.

Dylong came over from the OpSum, his headset draped round his neck and the lead trailing. A private word. Boyce draped his own headset around his neck.

"If they do that a few more times," Dylong said quietly, "we'll be in trouble. We'll lose our Skytop mode."

Once all four main radars were gone, both SPY-X12s and both SPY-X10As, there would be no other array left with the Skytop surveillance and track facility, multimode or no multimode. And without a Skytop radar mode there could be no warning of a nuclear attack and no sensor for the SADIS Skytop ballistic missile defence function. They would have to wait unknowing until any incoming warhead tore right down on top of them and the towertops and the SPG-X141 fire control radars spotted it and the SADIS went into automatic air defence response. By then only Arrowflash and a prayer would help them—and a blast as big as two megatonnes coming as close as or closer than the first attack would really hurt them.

"Is it your assessment," Boyce asked carefully, "that they let it blow itself so high just to get our radars?"

"It's possible. They got the Protector and the Consolidator some way or other, probably by cumulative damage degrading their defence potential. That would be one way."

It would be slow, but it would work. "We'll have to wait and see, I guess."

Dylong shrugged, from him a very rare embellishment of bare words. "Let's hope we never find out."

Three more nukes like that, and then the one after would make a terrible mess of the ship.

"Sir!" PO2 Hayes was hunched forward in front of his Air Detector/Tracker screen. "Air contact dead astern at one-eight-zero degrees, due south."

Someone combined it immediately on the main plot—a little red arrow down below the center at 6 o'clock, and pointing straight up towards the ship. Something approaching in the air, something that had climbed up over the towertop's intervening sea horizon.

Headsets back on. Dylong was already plugging in at the OpSum.

Redden. "SADIS responding on automatic. Tracking."

Condillac at the Arrowflash/Seastrike console. "Seastrike aft launcher readying. One round taking instruction."

Hayes. "Two contacts. Coming in low around forty metres up off the water. Range forty three kilometres. Three contacts. All closing at Mach zero-point-eight-five."

That's what happened when your Skyhooks were downed. "Kuroda—air attack warning to the ship. Then tell the TLCP to get their people inside off the flight deck."

Hayes. "Four contacts." Four arrowheads on the plot, one behind the other in a diagonal line.

LoSecco. "Seastrike, Arrowflash, one-five-fives, Skyfire taking instruction."

Dylong. "Recommend switching to automatic directed."

"Do it." If Joe Dylong said so.

Redden. "SADIS on automatic directed."

Dylong. "Contacts are Bandits. No IFF. Radar identification—they're Fanners." More of the Yak-236 fighters, the naval strike and air defence aircraft they were assuming were bivouac-based up in the north of Norway. "We can expect an attack from Skimmer Sticks." Those were medium weight air-launched anti-ship missiles, supersonic and nastily packed with survivability and ECM to mess up defence radars. "They should launch at thirty five out, and turn."

Turn or not, the Soviet pilots were committing suicide. Seastrike could chase them for 140 kilometres at Mach 2.8. A Fanner could make a maximum of Mach 1.8—they wouldn't escape.

Time to organize the engagement. "Seastrike takes the Bandits on fire-and-forget. Launch when ready."

Condillac. "Running it, sir."

"One-five-fives and Arrowflash standby to combat missiles."

Loggia, the seaman at the Mk 56 AG console. "One-five-fives loading type two AA shell. Training."

Mellott, turning her seat away from the Rayflex console to the Arrowflash board she shared with Condillac. "Arrowflash port and starboard launchers readying."

"Redden, take direction of combating the missiles."

Redden. "Yes sir. I'd like a fire control radar, sir."

The towertops were multimode and the SPY-X12 looking aft was magnificent, but he could still use a specialist missile and gunnery fire control radar. "Deploy port and starboard number twos." The aft SPG-X141 of each pair mounted on the outboard sides of the elevator box roof.

Dylong. "Bandits turning away. Must have launched. All four turning and heading southeast. Radar sees no missiles."

Jablonski. "A towertop probably won't be able to see a Skimmer Stick, sir." But the SPY-X12 and the SPG-X141s would see them when they came over their horizons in a matter of seconds, low and almost kissing the water.

Kuroda. "Communications say the Bandits are all chattering on their Cracklers."

Condillac. "Aft Seastrike firing. One. Two. Three. Four. All flying."

That was the Fanners dealt with—as good as. But missiles would be coming in from dead astern, and only the aft pair of Skyfire mountings could bear on any targets approaching from that angle. He should bring the ship round thirty degrees across the flight line. The superstructure and foreslope would still afford some protection to the critical foredeck mountings, while one of the forward Skyfires would be able to bear— three Skyfires instead of two. "Pass to the Ship's CP—rudders hard port, bow thrusters port full, assume course three-three-oh."

Kuroda started talking the order through.

Hayes. "Contacts, small and closing. Range two-six thousand."

Loggia. "Fore and aft one-five-five mountings firing."

Two large calibre naval guns, each firing a round every three seconds, and nothing to hear at all. The SADIS moved fast—not that even the highly accurate 155mm Automatic Guns had much chance of knocking down many of the little missiles. They would be weaving supersonically across the flat sea.

Lafon, the man at the Skyfire console. "Skyfire mountings, aft port and starboard and forward port, all ready."

And they would need the Skyfire rotary cannon inside the Arrowflash screen. He could see how many contacts were materializing on the plot. They would *need* the Skyfires. "How many missiles?"

Dylong. "Sixteen. All Skimmer Sticks. Bandits are over our horizon, Seastrike chasing."

Redden. "I'd like semi-active mode for the Arrowflash, sir."

Radar guidance of the little missiles from the ship would make hits all the more certain. "Semi-active mode."

Dylong. "One-five-fives knocked one down. Fifteen coming."

Mellott. "Arrowflash launching. Port all four. Starboard all four. Reloading."

Dylong. "One-five-fives downed another. Fourteen coming."

Too many at once. When they got through the Skyfire mountings would engage them with a stream of solid uranium bullets at sixty rounds a second across a range closing from 1,500 to 500 metres. A Skimmer Stick would cover that distance in one and a half seconds—time for just ninety kinetic bullets, ninety little chances to break the missile apart in the air.

Dylong. "One more downed. Thirteen coming."

Mellott. "Arrowflash ready port. Firing all four."

Kuroda. "Firm on course three—three—oh, sir."

Dylong. "The Arrowflashes are downing them. Ten coming. Nine."

Mellott. "Arrowflash ready starboard. Firing all four."

Dylong. "Two down, seven coming. Six thousand metres." Nine seconds away—no more relaunch time for the Arrowflash. "Two down, five coming."

Lafon. "Skyfire engaging."

Dylong. "One down. Two down. We're hit. Three down. Four."

A sharp rattle far away, like buckshot on an iron door. That must have been hits on the superstructure, if it was audible inside the isolation box.

Dylong. "Attack over."

LoSecco. "Weapons resetting."

"Put SADIS back on automatic." And the Vindicator was hit.

Redden. "SADIS on automatic."

"Kuroda, tell the AOC they should warn the Watchdog on the southeast sector that the Bandits are heading their way."

"AOC already warned them, sir. They're trying to fly underwater."

Jablonski. "The aft SPY-X12 is out."

Christ—another main radar. "Is that the hit?"

Dylong shook his head. "Can't be. The hit was right aft. The Skyfires took four out of the five. I'm sure of that."

"Sir." Anthea Slamon, the ASW Supervisor. "We've got alarms on the port ASW tubes."

That was the hit right aft, then. What was the rattle on the superstructure—the fault in the SPY-X12?

Kuroda. "Damage Control confirms total function alarms on the port ASW tubes. Also the aft SPY-X12 array has lost all power and half the antennas are dead."

Boyce looked at Dylong. Joe Dylong just shrugged.

Condillac. "Seastrike has downed the Bandits. I've got a CCK from every missile." Confirm Contact and Kill—when the Seastrike round was half a second away from hitting it let out a radio chirp, a victory call. The signal was necessary because the missile could be well out of sight over the horizon, and the mother ship needed information on the fate of its targets to permit accurate tactical assessments.

Redden. "Four probables to us. Sir, I'd like to deploy the aft SPY-X10A."

"Okay." And now both SPY-X12s—half the main radars—were out of commission. A mess, a mess.

Kuroda. "One kill is confirmed, sir. Watchdog Eight saw a Bandit go past at two thousand metres and saw the flash as it was hit. It went down."

Dylong was looking at him from the OpSum. "That looked to me like a suicide attack. That was probably the last air strength they have."

"Maybe. Maybe. But what were they doing coming in from the south?" They'd been guessing at a last handful of aircraft stationed somewhere to the north.

"Sir, if I may?" Redden again. "Fifteen out of sixteen Skimmer Sticks downed in a single concentrated attack, plus one and probably three more Fanners. That's really something. I'd like to congratulate our SADIS and the CIC operators."

What do you do, conspire in the diversion or make a slight fool of your officer? Join in grudgingly. "It's a good machine and we're running it well. Kuroda, ask the TLCP if they can see what's happened near the port tubes. And if they know what hit the superstructure and the SPY-X12." He switched his headset through to talk to the Ship's Conning Position. "Boyce. Starboard helm. Come back on to zero-double-zero."

"Starboard helm," said an answering voice. "Zero-double-zero."

He cut the channel and caught Dylong's eye, ready to say
something.

Kuroda interrupted. "Sir, the TLCP are in a mess. They've
got one dead and their hands full. Damage Control has sent
them a backup. There's also a party going aft to take a look at
the port ASW tubes, and Lt. Cole is on his way up to take a
look at the radar." Cole was the radar systems officer whose
speciality was the main arrays.

Boyce nodded. One dead in the TLCP, one more crucial
radar out, and one of the pair of mountings for launching the
Mk 72 ASW defence torpedoes gone. A mess.

Warrant Officer McCune had delayed closing the armoured
shutters over the windows and evacuating the TLCP. Down
on the flight deck he had half a dozen people who had been
readying the SCAN-Skyhook for takeoff, and who were suddenly out in the naked open as an air attack came in. There
was just time to try and hitch the machine back on to the
tractor and haul it into the safety of the elevator box. The
Seastrike launch from the mounting down below the aft end
of the flight deck had been spectacular, four diverging col-
umns of firesmoke boiling up into the dim sky. The muzzle
flashes every three seconds from the Mk 56 Automatic Gun
were brilliant and its voice thunder. Then one of the TLCP
lookouts actually *spotted* the attacking missiles coming in as
specks tailing fire out of the darkness, and McCune told the
flight deck crew to abandon the Skyhook and get the hell out
of there, and started the roll-down door closing to protect the
aircraft inside the elevator space.

The Arrowflashes were coming red-trailed down from overhead and making sudden distant fireballs as they contacted the
Skimmer Sticks, and he ordered the TLCP cleared—himself,
two assistants and two lookouts in a hurry to get through the
door in the rear wall. Sharp stabbing bars of tracer streamed
from the Skyfire mountings and the little things in the air
disintegrated just short of the ship. One made it and burst
blindingly down on the port stern apron below the afterslope.
The last Skimmer Stick was high over the port quarter when it
was stabbed by tracer from all three operating Skyfires. It
broke up and the pieces flew at Mach 2.0, at twice the speed
of sound, straight into the ship. Most of the debris bounced
loud but harmlessly off the armour of the tower and the
superstructure and the elevator box doors, several pieces

smashed through the plastic radome of the SPY-X12 radar up behind the TLCP, something hit the Skyhook down on the deck, and one chunk hit the centre TLCP window before the shutters had a chance to close. It bounced off in fragments instead of penetrating the multiple glass-plastic laminate, it turned the window completely opaque in some grotesque crystal extravagance. A huge circular scab, two laminate layers thick, was split away from the inner surface by the shock of the impact and traversed the short depth of the TLCP to splinter into ricocheting shards against the rear wall beside the access door.

Only two people were still in the TLCP, both leaving in a hurry—McCune, who would have gone last of all, and Seaman Wendy Springer, who had stayed long enough to throw the switches controlling the window shutters. On its way across the TLCP the scab of glass encountered Wendy Springer and went clean through her, taking off her right arm at the shoulder and almost completely severing her neck. The spray of glass splinters that filled the position for a second after the scab smashed apart on the rear wall delivered twenty three separate cuts to McCune, none of them serious but several of them requiring stitches. Most of the blood he was drenched in came from Springer.

The retraction box for the aft SPY-X12 was immediately behind the TLCP. When he heard Boyce was there, Phil Cole clambered out through the inspection door to report on the mess inside. Half the individual antennas in the phased array were wrecked and the support frame was damaged. Replacing the antennas presented no problem, although it would eat up most of the spares—but repairing the support frame would take time. Working flat out with as many people as could squeeze into the place, it would take eighteen to twenty four hours. This was real life—it could not be done twice as fast as was possible, and it would take as long as it took. So the Vindicator was for the moment down to only two main radars, the slightly older and marginally less discriminating SPY-X10As, and would never again have all four in service. The forward SPY-X12 was irretrievable with on-board facilities: the entire array and mounting would have to be replaced.

Boyce hurried back to his cabin to collect his parka, then went through the C3 box between Sonar and Navigation and through the AOC, and down into the hangar on main deck. He hurried aft, counting the aircraft. Only eight F-28s parked on the ship instead of the ten they'd started with, a reduction of their long range air defence. Six Wolfmarines being serviced and one parked out of the way, its fuselage split open and the machine unfit for normal operational use—with the three on patrol that totalled nine instead of the full complement of twelve, an adequate but a reduced anti-submarine capability. And the worst losses among the Skyhooks and the SCAN radars they flew. Now they were down to just four machines. The one left out on the flight deck had been hit squarely by the biggest single fragment of the last Skimmer Stick, its engine turbine shaft. The Skyhook was a total write-off.

The Soviets would know—would *have* to know—that the Vindicator had finally taken some sort of damage, and whatever they had left, a single ship or just a single aircraft, they would have to try to hit the ship again. The Vindicator was just too dangerous to leave alone. And now he could only fly one Skyhook at a time to maintain round-the-clock cover, would only be able to see for two hundred kilometres in any direction. The Vindicator's protective ring was shrinking. He would have to consider rotating the F-28s one after the other on combat air patrol, flying up high so that their radars provided a deeper air and sea surveillance perimeter. But every precious litre of aviation fuel used was gone for ever.

Greg Clemence had worked out the Soviet air attack. In retrospect they had done it just the way he would have tried. With what might have been their last four aircraft from somewhere up near Bodo on the North Norwegian coast, they must have flown south in the radar shadow on the eastern side of the Scandinavian spine, and then crossed over into the deep valley that led into the mountain-screened cleft of Sognafjord. All the way they would have been hidden from any searching radar and protected from the huge thermonuclear blast that had gone off over the Vindicator's position. They had emerged from Sognafjord flat down on the sea and soon enough after the blast to be coming in before the ship had got around to replacing its airborne surveillance radars. Ten minutes sooner still, and the ship would have been completely sealed and totally blind. It made perfect tactical sense.

That it was radars and defence weapons that suffered was inevitable: they were the only things that stuck out through the Vindicator's armoured carapace.

Even in the wind shelter of the flight deck afterslope, the open stern apron was incredibly cold. The air was at −18°C coming straight down through the Nuclear Winter from the Arctic. The parka alone was useless, he should have put on his jacket and even a sweater as well.

The working lights were emergency rigged. Everything damageable portside of the raised Mk 56 155mm mounting and the Seastrike box launcher had been destroyed. It was a miracle that the Skyfire up above the afterslope had survived intact. The important casualty was the port ASW tubes mounting. The quadruple tubes were only four metres long, not much more than the little Mk 72 torpedoes they fired into the water. The mounting was right up against the side of the deck, with black water sweeping by six metres below.

The Skimmer Stick had smashed its high explosive warhead right on top of the ASW mounting. The tubes were split and buckled and useless. Half of the Vindicator's close-in anti-submarine defence had been knocked out. No submarine should slip through the screen provided by the Wolfmarines—but it might. No submarine that did so should be able to approach unheard and avoid being engaged by the Fire Lance in ASW mode, a bare Fire Lance vehicle flying a single Mk 72 torpedo out to anything up to 150 kilometres and dropping it almost straight on top of the target. But it might. The submarine might just happen to be lying right in the Vindicator's path, able to lie silent in the water and just wait for the distance to close. And once it came down to fifty kilometres or less, it could fire a torpedo, and the only thing that would be able to stop that torpedo striking the ship would be one of the Mk 72s intercepting it in the water. And a torpedo-torpedo intercept was not easy, and the Mk 72 had only an eleven thousand metre range, so if the first four missed, then by the time the single surviving set of tubes had reloaded and fired again the attacking torpedo might be very close indeed. And a torpedo could carry a nuclear warhead, and a close water burst was the most likely thing to kill the ship.

It was all a mess, a goddam mess.

When for the first time in your life you put on a pair of glasses, you are most seriously disturbed by the fact that you are looking through a frame, that a ring of metal or plastic or mere lens has insinuated itself between you and the world and has thrown a restricting ligature around the bundle of space that is vision. But you get used to it in time, and once you wear glasses every day of your life you cease to notice the effect. You edit it out of your awareness.

But he was tired, Commander John Ritchie Boyce was tired. He was so tired that he was periodically aware that he was peering out at the world through a metal frame held in front of his eyes. When that starts to happen to a man who has worn glasses for over twenty years, he is terribly tired. And it wasn't just the long hours and the almost total lack of sleep—it was the responsibility and the tension and the worry. And the sudden shock of command.

He sat at the little desk in his small day cabin, forward of the C3 box on 02 level, between Greg Clemence's quarters starboard and the guarded small arms store port. He was taking a break, a blissful pair of minutes organizing nothing at all. He'd just dictated an acknowledgement from the MCC to the latest signal from the Nemesis Direction, and now he sat at his private desk with a facsimile of the signal discarded in front of him.

> ORIG: STRACC NAVCOM NMSS DIR 1019 JUNE 13 0520
> INCOMING: JUNE 13 1230
> NMSS-3 VINDICATOR
> FIRE LANCE COMMAND CODE: DARK MIRROR
> SACI 04

1. This is a Firing Enactment Instruction supplement for strike series as SACI 01, 02, 03.
2. Bring forward launch time for Strike 3 from 1510 to 1400. Launch point as predetermined.
3. Acknowledge this signal SACI 04.

So now they were panicking back home in their bunker under the mountains, snug and warm in the safest place in the entire world. They were panicking as the nasty Soviet responses came falling in over their own heads and on top of all their precious remaining silos and command points. Maybe they should have thought of that first. At least it was nothing other than good news for the Vindicator: if the strike was being brought forward by an hour and ten minutes, then so was the end of the strike—the moment when he could turn the ship away and get the hell out of there before it was altogether too late. He had to hand Kylander's accompanying signal over of course, and there was no point in postponing the encounter. It would be a very brief encounter—he would hand over the advisement and inform him that he was indeed going to comply with the order, and he wouldn't waste another word on the man. What he needed was the time *now* to neutralize Kylander, to disarm him and his band of soldiers, but that was just not possible until they were clear of any immediate threat. If an attack came in while he was halfway through disarming them, the result would be bloodshed on board followed instantly by disaster from outside.

Now he understood why a captain needed a first officer. He was *afraid* to be away from the CIC. Not that Joe Dylong couldn't handle a nuclear attack if it came in, but that he wouldn't be there, wouldn't know and see for himself. He had no one to send on errands around the ship. He was the messenger boy himself, while Bedford lay unconscious in the sick bay after a long emergency operation. Why that had to happen, why Bedford ever let the situation arise, was a mystery.

First things first. The ship is yours. Order the Ship's CP to come up to 15 knots on the same due north course so as to make the firing position in time. It would have to be nine knots again for the launch, cruising like a luxury liner in the middle of a land-locked trap. But then he could bring the ship up to full speed and out out out!

THE SICK BAY itself filled the rear third of 2nd platform inside the C3 isolation box. It held eight beds for the hospitalization of serious cases, five along the aft wall and three against the forward bulkhead between the pair of bed-wide access doors. Bedford, alone in antiseptic seclusion, occupied the corner bed against the rear wall. He wore a white gown and lay in white linen, his face was something between ashen grey and white, his arms lay pallid on top of the unruffled turned-down sheet and the blue loose-weave blanket. Under the bed linen there was a cage placed over his lower body, and the blanket was draped almost undisturbed over it. From an overhead hook hung a plasma bag, from out of the sides of the bedding under the cage on both sides of the bed ran clear plastic drain tubes ending in collector bags. He was breathing shallowly and too rapidly for any normal sleep. He looked like a man who had nearly died.

Andrew Culbertson had time at last. He had stitched WO McCune's more serious lacerations closed, and his little team of orderlies under WO Jenny Bendix had cleaned up the theatre and his office. He had even managed to consume both drink and sandwich that Bendix had conjured for him. The only thing he still hadn't found time for was the shower he so desperately wanted after the hours in the suffocating heat of the theatre, so he was still holding court in his Sick Bay Area in his teeshirt. He was exhausted.

He stood at the foot of the bed, arms folded to combat the overwhelming desire to throw his weight across the shoulders of Boyce and Craze and let them carry him away to sleep. Instead he discussed his patient.

"I was pouring whole blood into him in surgery, but now

he's just on plasma laced with antibiotics. His condition is stabilized—the trauma itself won't kill him.''

"The wound was a mess?" Boyce asked.

Culbertson nodded. "It was a mess. The bullet entered his right side and smashed the lowest sternal rib—which deflected the bullet downwards slightly so that only limited damage was done to the lobe of the liver, mostly by the bone splinters. Except that any damage to the liver is serious. The bullet missed the gall bladder and the stomach, but did some damage to the duodenum—produced some perforation. The colon is torn almost in two right at the junction of the ascending and the transverse colon. The bullet went right across his insides. The jejunum—the upper major part of the small intestine—is repeatedly perforated and lacerated, and is severed completely in two places. There's minor damage to the right kidney but it's probably safe from collapse. The left kidney isn't at all endangered, thank God, and the major blood vessels—the aorta, the vena cava, the renal arteries and veins—weren't touched. That would have killed him outright.''

"You've put him back together?"

"I've pieced most of the perforated and lacerated bits of the intestine together—just a case of trimming the tissue and suturing it closed with a reconnected blood supply. The place where the colon is almost torn in two and the complete severings of the jejunum are a different matter. A bullet doesn't just *tear*. When it's decelerated on impact it dumps its kinetic energy as heat, which causes vaporization of the moisture content of the tissue. The surrounding tissue explodes. A much larger cavity is formed than the hole the bullet itself would have bored—hundreds of times larger. The cavity is widest just inside the entry hole where the bullet has most energy to dump, and gets narrower as it travels on. Gaseous cavitation—that's the correct name for it. It causes profuse bleeding, and the cavity collapses and fills with air, dead tissue, blood, and in this case the contents of the guts. I had to clean out the entire abdominal cavity.''

Gloria Craze had feelings inside her stomach that didn't just come from the vicious bruise she'd taken. She made the mistake of rubbing at it, and it hurt. "The drains," she said. "Therefore the drains.''

"He's got drains attached everywhere—the catheters run through little incisions in the abdominal wall. A drain on the liver lobe, on each site where the jejunum was severed, and at the major tear in the colon. Plus an abdominal cavity drain. He's at least three more operations away from recovery. One to reconnect the small intestine into one piece in a few days or weeks—depends how he responds—and to put in a major drain to isolate the colon. Then he can eventually resume normal feeding, more or less, while the colon damage is given a chance to repair itself. Then later he'll need another operation to remove the drain and reconnect the ileum—the lower small intestine—to the colon. Even without any complications, a third operation will be necessary to remove the plate he's got holding his rib together. Eventually he should be okay.''

They left the bed and went out through the open doorway. The short piece of corridor led to the door of the operating theatre, passing between the foot of the ladder leading to the deck above and the door to the Surgeon's Office on the inboard side. Boyce paused there, his hand on the ladder. Inside the C3 box the ladders really were vertical ladders. "He'll live all right," Boyce said.

Culbertson shrugged. "If you know of a properly equipped hospital ashore complete with a team of surgeons competent to handle reconstitutive surgery necessitated by gunshot wounds, certainly. With just me and my facilities—I don't know. I'm competent to stabilize the trauma so that the recovery process can begin, but it's a long process requiring specialist surgery and intensive care. I'm not a shooting injury specialist. He was shot with a thirty eight, wasn't he? If the same wound had been made by a forty five calibre or one of those high density shot things Raffles used on herself, I'd have lost him. The kinds of injury I expect inside this ship are crushings and lacerations, all grades of flash and contact burns, fractures, blast effect injuries, and toxic chemical and gas exposure. Small arms shoot-outs aren't high on the list of probabilities. I'll do my best. And it's going to take a long time.''

Boyce nodded. "How long before he's conscious?"

"Oh, couple of hours. He's basically sleeping now after the anaesthesia. But he won't exactly be in a state to do anything.''

"I just need to know how soon I can get his advice.''

"Advice?'' Culbertson shook his head. "He isn't going to be giving advice for a couple of days at the least. Gloria, where'd you put that gun Raffles had?''

"In my cabin," Gloria said. "Why?"

"If you suddenly feel like using it on Kylander, tell me first so I can be unable to be found for a couple of hours when they want me to patch him up."

"I'll deal with Kylander," Boyce said. "*I* will. But right now the ship has to stay at Condition One, and I can't assemble enough people away from their stations to be sure I can smother trouble and prevent a firefight when I disarm his group. So it has to wait. And no one—" He looked pointedly at Gloria. "No one takes anything into their own hands." He started up the ladder.

Gloria watched him disappear through the hole in the deckhead. He was still wearing his heavy Colt automatic in its webbing holster.

Andrew Culbertson had already gone into the Surgeon's Office and dropped into his chair. In front of him on the desk was his crumpled up shirt and his wristwatch—things you don't wear in surgery. Gloria went past the desk in the narrow room and sat herself up on the examination couch. The lift made pains stab across her stomach. Culbertson hadn't noticed: he had his elbows resting on the arms of the rotating chair, and was rubbing his face with his hands.

"Well," he said, muffled behind his hands. "How's John coping with having to run the ship?"

"He seems to be following orders okay, doing his duty to ship and country. We're launching the next strike in thirty minutes."

"What?" He removed his hands from his face and peered at his wristwatch. "I thought the strike was at fifteen ten."

"It's been brought forward. Seems the people back in the States think it's a good idea to start firing our nukes at the Soviets again, but don't like it when the Soviets fire back. Suppose they're hitting the same kind of targets as we're hitting—including STRACC and CASAL. Andrew, how can it happen? How can it possibly ever *happen*? Our command people start killing each other in order to resume a nuclear war! They kill Jenninger and Caufield for only being prepared to get ready for it, and then they shoot the Captain for trying to stop it. Isn't life supposed to be *sacred*?"

Culbertson just looked at her, cynicism taking over his tired eyes. "Coming from someone who joined one of the armed services, who accepted a posting on a ship loaded with an arsenal of nuclear weapons instead of resigning her commission, that question seems a little out of place." He held up his hand. "I know, I know. We none of us ever thought it would really happen. Well it has." He slumped down further in his seat, taking on a resigned look. "Life, let me assure you, is sacred to nothing else but itself. There's nothing and no one with any brief to look after it, no instance that's going to step in from outside and rescue things as soon as they get really bad. No amount of wishful belief is going to bring any such thing into existence anywhere outside our own imaginations. Life is sacred to nothing but itself. When it evolves the ability to decide to destroy itself—when it *does* decide to destroy itself—nothing's going to stop it. It ends up destroyed."

Gloria shook her head. It didn't have to be like that while ever there was an individual will to oppose it. "It doesn't have to happen."

"Gloria, you must have noticed." He pulled himself more upright in his chair, a man struggling quietly to keep himself awake. "I don't go up to the bridge or the TLCP. When did I last go out on deck? I've been hiding, Gloria. Down here in the ship where it's safe—water, food, airconditioning, warmth, and no risk from any fallout. This great big armoured ship, unsinkable and defended by the most modern weapons available. I've been hiding away from the world so that I can stay alive. So that it can't reach me. But now I have to face the fact that the ship isn't safe after all. It can go, too. We've taken damage, haven't we? Serious damage to the radars in our missile defence system. And it's been proved that a conventional attack can get through. I've *felt* two nuclear blasts. I'm not safe. We're not safe. The ship can go too."

"Oh, Andrew, that's defeatist. Don't give up. Don't start that. The Vindicator will survive okay. It can take us back south of the equator. The dust veil is transferring south, sure, but the climate collapse in the southern hemisphere has to be less severe, has to last for a shorter time. We can live on board long enough to escape it. We've got two fully operational reactors, haven't we? We'll be safe on board. We'll outlast it."

"Will it be less of a mess down there?" He shrugged, hunching his shoulders and simply dropping them again. Looking somewhere far away, he shook his head. "Will the ship survive?"

The single Skyhook was thirty kilometres due north of the

ship, so there was no triangulation at all on the transmission coming straight down from the Arctic. But in the Electronics Warfare Centre on main deck inside the C3 box, they had managed to work out a rough estimate on the range.

"There's just enough of a drop in signal strength from the Skyhook to the ship," explained Lt. Barbara Spirek, Senior EW Systems Officer, indicating the numbers glowing on the console screen. "Between seven hundred and fifty and eight hundred and fifty kilometres north of our present position."

"And it's definitely a Cracker Box?" He could see for himself as he stood beside her looking at the screen.

"No doubt about it. The carrier and side band characteristics are perfectly clear."

And Cracker Box was a radio communications system fitted to several of the most modern classes of Soviet attack submarine, boats that were smaller than their older rattling nuclear powered designs, boats that were fast and quiet. And therefore dangerous. "And any sub carrying Cracker Box will also be able to fire Skimmer Pole from its tubes?"

Spirek nodded.

Skimmer Pole was the SS-N-100 anti-ship missile, ship or submarine launched—a low level skimmer exactly equivalent to the Fire Lance in its five hundred kilometre range anti-ship mode, and presumably as deadly. Fire Lance could deliver half a tonne of high explosive against a naval target: that would hurt even the Vindicator. And the boat that had just been transmitting was around eight hundred kilometres away in the north, not yet in a position to cut off the Vindicator's escape but easily within range of the ship's F-28 Skycats. He had a single F-28 circling on CAP at 14,000 metres up, and to hell with the fuel expenditure. It provided a less discriminating radar view than the SCAN could produce, but it reached right out to over four hundred kilometres on the surface of the sea. With seven more F-28s on board, he could easily send one north to take a look without weakening his potential air cover in the event of an attack. But sending an F-28 out after a submarine was a total waste of time, and the thing was almost twice as far away as the operational radius of a Wolfmarine. The only thing to do—the only sane thing to do anyway—was to avoid the Soviet boat, was to get out through the IUK Gap again before it came anywhere near.

Barbara Spirek was watching his face in the competing glow of the EW Centre lights and the upwash from the illuminated display console. The man had troubles enough, and now another one was closing in. "I'm sorry, John. I wish I could spirit it away, but I can't. There's a sub up there. No question."

Boyce nodded, his face losing its vulnerability again. Facing facts. "Doesn't matter." He glanced at his watch. "The launch is in ten minutes. Forty minutes from now we turn west and come up to speed and get the hell out of here. That one won't catch us."

Gloria Craze had been back to her cabin on main deck, just checking that Raffles' gun and belt and ammunition pouch were still safely packed away there. The ship was safe. Whatever Andrew said, the ship was *safe*. But just the same, one day they would be going ashore, and then she could use something to defend herself. Raffles had told her what it would be like on land. The darkness and ice might be over by then, but anyone left alive would be starving and wild.

She came forward on the starboard side to the crosswall bulkhead, turned the locking wheel and pushed open the heavy door. It closed and locked itself behind her as she started down the cross corridor that ran past the front of the C3 box on main deck. Around the corner at the other end, also coming from aft on the portside, appeared Drexel.

Instant aggression at the sight of the Englishman, the man who didn't care. The man who helped launch a strike series because he didn't even *care*.

They were both converging on the central companionways leading up and down, routes important enough not to be sealed off by fire traps but by regular steel doors. The ship was still closed up at Condition 1 and the Fire Lances were launching out forward, marching endlessly up from the belly of the ship and streaking away through the frozen daytime night. They met, unavoidably, at the companionway doors. She looked up at him, one of those goddam shabby excessively tall Englishmen. He looked tired. Everyone on board was tired—no real sleep for more than a day and a half, and stress and fear almost the whole time.

David Drexel got in first. "Don't you have something to do at action stations or whatever it's called? Are you spare as well?"

She had a free dispensation to absent herself from the bridge, and had taken advantage of it. The strike was almost over and she couldn't stand the rose-red shifting illumination as the missiles screamed free. She couldn't stand to watch any more lances of fire stabbing into the unnatural winter night. "You're supposed to be in the canteen," she said. "If something happens, no one can do anything for you if they don't know where you are."

"I've been in Kylander's cabin. Kylander is sulking there because your first officer won't let him play in the Missile Control Centre any more. Doesn't like him playing with guns."

"You don't object?"

"Oh—when he wants a briefing I give him a briefing. No one's going to protect me either, if I don't do what he says." He left a little pause to let that sink in, then continued. "Apparently the Russians have been hitting back at our side harder than was expected. Their command structure—what's left of it—was supposed to disintegrate the moment nukes from the ship and from our land based forces came in. Instead it's only coming apart a chunk at a time. It won't last much longer, I'd expect, but they're managing to hit everything we've got—bunkers, silos, even STRACC—as fast as we hit them. Kylander wanted to know why."

"And?"

Drexel shrugged. "So I told him. His people back home have fucked up their attacks—either the strikes themselves, or the data they planned them on. So of course the Russians are hitting back. Just like we would—they can do, so they are doing."

His attitude was utterly despicable. "And you still think it doesn't matter. The whole world is going up again, and you think it doesn't matter. What's *wrong* with you?"

Drexel shook his head at her. "Nothing's wrong with me that isn't wrong with everybody. We're all dead."

"We're not dead yet!"

"We're all dead. You're an educated woman—never heard of the ozone layer? It's a relative concentration of ozone in the upper atmosphere. It has the property of blocking most of the ultraviolet radiation in the light from the sun, ultraviolet that would otherwise get through to the surface undiluted. And ultraviolet kills life. Now ozone is particularly susceptible to chemical degradation, especially by nitrogen containing compounds—and there'll be an awful lot of those in the dust veil, because you get such nitrogen compounds in the smoke produced by combustion. The point is, that when a dust veil as dense and long lasting as this one comes down—and it will come *down*, not disappear—it will deposit a radiation dose of a couple of hundred rems everywhere on the planet, which won't exactly help anything's chances of surviving in the first place. When it comes down, it won't leave much of an ozone layer behind it up there.''

''And this is a new revelation you've just had?''

''A revelation? Good grief, no. It's a standard result of all major to worst-case Nuclear Winter scenarios. Everyone has known this will happen since the mid-eighties. They've just preferred to ignore the fact. Anyway, down comes the dust veil, and we'll be bathed in undiluted UV. And as I just said, UV kills. It kills the plants that form the food base for all animal life, and it kills the animals themselves by destroying their eyes and skins. Didn't I mention this to you yesterday or some time? Thought I had. Anyway, the only thing to do will be to move underground, but for that we'd need incredibly complex systems with nuclear power to drive the light and ventilation for subterranean farms and the like. Think of the lead time in years and the sheer industrial capacity needed to create any such thing. There'll be no years—not even months— and no industry at all.''

''You're crazy! That isn't even certain. It can't be certain.''

''No, it isn't *certain* because there's no one left any more capable of flying and recovering stratospheric balloons to find out to what extent it *is* happening. But unless atmospheric chemistry has suddenly changed at the will of God or Kylander or you or someone in order to protect us, it *should* be happening. And the longer the dust stays up there, the more danger it will do. Of course, the little nuclear war that's going on right at this moment isn't much compared with the big exchanges eighty and ninety days ago, but it isn't exactly going to help. It will extend the climate collapse and extend the consequences.''

''The consequences won't be that bad. Not in the south.''

''There's a circulation divide at the equator, but it isn't an impermeable wall, bloody hell. There isn't going to be any life left on the surface of the land or in the surface ocean waters. The sun will shine again like never before, and there'll just be scorpions and cockroaches and blind fish in caves, and worms at the bottom of the sea.''

"You're crazy! You're a defeatist! You just want us all to give up and kill ourselves!"

"I'm not crazy. I'm a realist. And I've got far too little sense of the dramatic to go and shoot myself. I intend to stay alive as long as I can. The end of the world is quite something to see."

"It's not the end of the world!" She will not believe it, will not believe and give up and let it happen. Will *not*. Life cannot be a machine dictated to by a tyranny of inputs, where if the factual inputs say *stop* it terminates. The will to live must always defeat death. Wherever there is life and the will to keep it burning, there is hope. "It's not the end of the world."

"Look, what's the word? You're the psychologist. You should know the name for when someone completely suppressed the truth about something and hides from it. Come to think of it, you're not exactly the only one. We've all been doing it, haven't we—you and me and my government and your government and every last bloody one of us. We've been hiding and denying the truth about nuclear weapons ever since they were invented. Well now the truth's made itself apparent. And there's no way out at all."

He turned, hauled open the door to the companionway, and disappeared downwards. The door dogged itself closed behind him.

And then the ship heeled. The great big ship perceptibly heeled into a turn. The ship's address clicked on, and spoke with Dylong's voice.

"Launch ended, Fire Lance systems closing down. We're turning hard port and coming onto course two-seven-oh. Increasing speed to thirty five knots. The ship will remain closed up at Condition One."

So at last—they were turning to run due west at maximum speed. Boyce would get them out of it just as Bedford would have done. Drexel could take his vision of the end of the world, and see what it felt like to outlive it. They would get out of this trap, and away from the Soviet Navy and the North Atlantic, and would live. She opened the companionway door and started on the way up to the bridge. Even in such gloom on a dead calm ocean there would finally be something to see—spectacular foam sent boiling from the bows by a hard highspeed turn. Turning for safety and life at last.

·   ·   ·

"So you're awake. How do you feel?"

"Andrew? Can't . . . see a thing."

"Close your eyes. Seeing double? That's just an aftereffect of the anaesthetic. It'll wear off. Just close your eyes and remember how beautiful I am."

"Anaesthetic . . . You operated?"

"I operated, Captain. How do you feel?"

"Fuck awful. I hurt. Stomach. Side. What you do to me, Andrew? What's all this?"

"No, keep your hands still. Just lie still. You've got a plasma drip in your left arm. You've got a cage over your belly to hold the sheet clear. You've got a line of stitches across your stomach as long as your hand. That'll hurt every time you breath."

"Does."

"And whatever you do, don't cough or go laughing at anyone's jokes. You won't burst, but you'll feel as though that's what's happening. You've got a patched up bullet hole in your right side, and your bottom rib is holding together because I screwed every last bit of it back onto a metal strip. You've already got one line of stitches there, and they'll be opening you up again to take the plate out as soon as the rib is properly healed."

"Andrew? What happened . . . ? Some bastard . . . shoot me?"

"Some bastard shot you. Kylander, to be exact. If you have to get yourself shot, why not Kylander? His gun only fires a thirty eight Special into your guts. The others have forty fives. And those assault rifles—they're high velocity— they'd tear you in two. By the way, why did you get yourself shot?"

"Don't know . . . Didn't think he would. Andrew. I feel sick as a dog."

"That's the anaesthetic. It'll wear off. To continue your informational tour of yourself. You've got a whole collection of drains coming out of your sides. Don't pull on the tubes, please. I've plastered them pretty firm, but if you pull the ends free inside I'll—"

"Inside?"

"I'll have to open you up to refix them."

"Inside? What you been doing to me?"

"Repairing you, phase one. The bullet made one hell of a mess of your guts, tore you right up. I've stopped the bleeding, I've stitched up most of the lacerations in there. But you can't fire a bullet through a coiled up mess of intestines and expect to cure it with a kiss and a band aid. Half of your guts aren't connected to the rest of you any more. Putting you right back together is going to require another couple of operations and quite a lot of waiting for things to heal. Meanwhile you're going to be on intravenous feeding. Quite advantageous—get rid of all that surplus fat. Too many eggs for breakfast.''

"Guts are all in pieces?''

"Oh, not *all* in pieces. Not even a first year medical student would get lost in there any more. Don't worry about that. The crisis is over, you're not bleeding and you're on antibiotics. From now on you're just a biology class teaching aid. You know—those little see-through plastic people where you have to put the bits back in the right place. In your case they're already back in the right place, so we don't have to fumble around with them and drop them on the floor. It's all straightforward now, just take a couple of months and an awful lot of patience.''

"Sounds awful.''

"In future you might think twice about tricks like catching bullets. You frighten an awful lot of people like that. No— shut your eyes. Keep them closed. Let yourself go back to sleep.''

"Sleep? What time . . . ? What day?''

"Same day as it was, June thirteenth. Just coming up to fifteen hundred.''

"Strike's due. Are we still firing . . . ?''

"We fired it. STRACC brought it forward an hour. Seems they didn't like the Soviets doing to them what they were doing to the Soviets, or something. Nobody tells me anything down here.''

"The ship? What about the ship?''

"Boyce is in command. We've taken another nuclear attack and an air attack while you've been out. Since then it's been nice and peaceful. Right now we're heading due west for the open Atlantic at full speed. I think we're going to go north of the Shetland Islands—I'm no navigator, but I think so. On a clear day they'd see us go past.''

"Hear us. Thirty five knots. They'll hear us coming all the way.''

"Hear us? Who'll hear us? Don't start playacting you're delirious.''

"On the bottom . . . they'll hear us coming. The submarine.''

"Submarine? What submarine? The only one around here got itself sunk. Poor bastards. At least they'll have gone quickly.''

"You don't go quickly . . . trapped in a holed submarine on the bottom. Andrew, I have—I have to talk to Boyce.''

"No way. He's got his hands full. The ship's at Condition One and in constant danger of attack, and Kylander and his toy soldiers are still armed and skulking around somewhere. John's issued something like forty or fifty people with small arms, but it's going to be hours before he can get away from the CIC long enough to organize putting Kylander out of action. The ship and Kylander—those are his priorities, one and two. Now he knows you've pulled through, you've dropped back to third place. The best thing you can do to help him—or me, or yourself—is get some sleep. You're so weak, if you weren't under a blanket the airconditioning would blow you away. Just relax, lie still, and get some sleep.''

"Sleep? No sleep. Think. I have to think.''

"You just try. You'll sleep all right. You'll sleep.''

BOYCE'S SMALL DAY cabin was almost crowded: himself, Air Operations Controller Greg Clemence, Chief Engineer Officer Orville Steetley, and Chief Navigating Officer Ruth Crimmin— all three commanders and one lieutenant commander. Only the Captain was missing.

They had sandwiches and rolls and paper napkins and cans of Coke; Steetley had conjured up a cup of evil smelling coffee even blacker than himself. Boyce hated Coke, loathed it as representative of all those sickeningly sweet and grossly carbonated drinks—but precisely that enormous sugar content was just what he needed to pick up and keep going. There were paper plates and paper napkins and crumbs on his desk, arrayed around the chart that Ruth Crimmin had brought with her. Displaced to one side against the painted steel wall was a facsimile of the latest signal received, coming in over the Blue Talker cryptographic domain.

ORIG: CASAL NAVALCOM NMSS DIR 1020 JUNE 13 0910
INCOMING: JUNE 13 1615
NMSS-3 VINDICATOR CPT BEDFORD CO

1. Advise communications facility losses at STRACC due to nuclear attacks. CASAL NAVALCOM assuming direction.
2. Advise general attacks continuing. Communication disruptions possible but command direction will be restored. Strikes against Soviet targets with land based weapons continuing.
3. Possible Strike Allocation Command Input within 6 hours.
4. Advise nuclear attacks reported your area: UK, Denmark, Netherlands.
5. British Emergency Government still affording cooperation. He-

licopter deploying to Stromness, Orkney Islands to take off
Kylander team if desired.

So much shit. STRACC was going the way NASCOM had
gone in the major phase of the war, just a little more slowly.
The Soviets were hitting them for hitting the Soviets, and
they were hitting back at the Soviets for hitting back at them.
So much absolute shit. The Soviet command was even wasting warheads on devastated Nato territories surrounding the
North Sea, presumably for ever allowing the Vindicator to
come anywhere near. Norway was right to pass information
to save itself from nukes, but in terms of the catastrophe
overtaking the whole world it was just a waste of time.

And right in the middle of it all the brave and loyal little
British Emergency Government was prepared to stretch itself
possibly as far as it could be stretched, just to get a 'copter up
to Stromness in the Orkneys so as to rescue nice Mr. Bradford Kylander and his butchers. If going ashore to face the
true land version of the incredible Big Freeze with the occasional nuke dropping down on your unprotected head was
exactly being rescued. Maybe their C-5 Galaxy was still
waiting and serviceable, maybe they were going to fly all the
way back to STRACC—or rather CASAL, now. South, due
south, would be more sensible. Ruth Crimmin said the
Stromness had once been something or other to do with
offshore oil, but probably wasn't important enough any more
to have been hit in the war. There would be no one left alive
in the place in current shore conditions, but there might well
be bunkers there full of aviation fuel for visiting helicopters.
Coming out from Stromness, one of their ancient Sea Kings
could reach out across at least five hundred kilometres of
open sea, could reach the Vindicator right where it was
northeast of the Shetlands and wherever it might be for hours
yet on any possible course. But he wasn't going to bother
telling Kylander about it—let him sweat it out on board as
well, goddam it. He'd already refused to transmit a signal for
the man. There was no sense in telling the enemy *exactly*
where they were.

Boyce took a final swig of Coke and placed the empty can
on top of his desktop computer housing. Foul stuff, blew you
up and made your teeth crawl. He looked at the others,
standing round the little deck while he was seated—their
choice, not his.

Orville Steetley was holding his coffee cup folded in his hands, as if the extreme outside cold had mysteriously penetrated into the ship. He spent almost all his time down on 1st platform in the C3 box, in the engine and reactor control rooms, but maybe he secretly longed for the bad old good old days of boiler rooms at steam heat. "We're still heading due west at thirty five knots," he said.

"Worried your turbines and transmissions can't take it?"

"They can take it. No problem. Except, are we going to loiter in the area and wait for this possible SACI and launch a strike?"

Both Clemence and Crimmin looked at Boyce.

The buck, as somebody said, has to stop somewhere. He shook his head. "The fuck we are. This ship is no use to anyone if it's sitting on the bottom of the sea. They've only hit us with two nuclear attacks since we started our launches at oh-three-ten today, and nothing's come over at all for around six hours. Maybe they can't spare anything for us, or maybe they just don't have our precise location any more. Maybe they think we're damaged worse than we are. But their naval units are closing in."

"So we're not staying around?" Greg Clemence said. "That's decided?"

Boyce reached out, tapping the chart. "Up here was a Cracker Box, so that has to be a modern fast sub. Bound to have Skimmer Pole. Now Communications have picked up what Spirek says has to be a Sparker Box way over here just north of Iceland. Sparker Box is carried either by a sub or maybe a destroyer. In either case it will also most likely have Skimmer Pole. And a Skimmer Pole *can* carry a nuke, and it can hurt us even without one. And now there's this new Cracker Box southwest of Iceland, another submarine, again with Skimmer Pole."

"Must be about all that's left of the Soviet Navy," Steetley commented.

Ruth Crimmin shrugged. "Quite an honour for us." She bit into a roll.

Clemence pointed at the chart. "Think this new sub out southwest of Iceland here is the suspected contact we didn't find three days ago? Or could that one have been the boat we engaged over here off the Shetlands yesterday?"

"It *could* have been the one we engaged," Boyce said. "But we'd been travelling damn fast the whole time, and I doubt it could have got ahead of us like that."

Crimmin pointed with her roll. "So it's more likely to be this one southwest of Iceland."

Boyce shook his head. "Be nice if it was, over there and not immediately in the way. But our suspected might be prowling around just ahead of us or even aiming at us right now. If it ever was real."

Clemence nodded.

"The sub we engaged," Steetley said. "Do we count that as dead?"

Clemence frowned. "The Wolfmarine missed the detonation. But they heard machinery noise before, and not after. Either it was hit, or it lay stopped to avoid further attack, and then moved off when our Wolfmarine was gone. No reason to suppose it's still right there in front of us. Unless it is."

Boyce looked at Steetley. "Orville, you were in submarines. Would you guess it was dead?"

"You were in nuclear boats, too. Would you guess it was dead?"

"And," Crimmin said, "there's that sub or surface unit we had way south of us even before the suspected sub from three days back. That's had time to come up behind us. Where's that going to be?"

"The trick for them," Boyce said, "is to close the IUK Gap. We have no other way out except through the English Channel, which would be crazy, a bottleneck like that—they'd close us up back and front. So we have to get out between Iceland and the UK. So—any ideas on a course?"

"Not north of the Faeroes." Steetley was extracting information from his coffee. "With a sub south of Iceland, a sub or surface unit north of Iceland, they'll have Iceland-Faeroes plugged before we get there. They'd catch us."

"Want to try an air strike?" Clemence asked. "Against this unit with the Sparker Box north of Iceland, just in case it is a destroyer. We can reach it okay."

"No." Boyce was eyeing the chart, tracing the choreography of possible movements by the Soviet vessels. If they were talking to each other, they were coordinating so as to kill the Vindicator. "Could cost us aircraft. Let's save the Skycats for use against direct threats."

"We're heading straight for the middle of the Shetland-Faeroes Gap," Crimmin said. "Why not go right on through and then turn southwest?"

"Because it's the obvious choice. Leaves us plenty of sea

room—much better than the Orkney-Shetlands passage the way we came. So that's where any hypothetical sub would wait.''

"Then go back south of the Shetlands again.''

"But that's so narrow. There's been time for a sub to put captor mines between Shetlands and Fair Isle and between Fair Isle and the Orkneys.'' Captor mines lay on the bottom until a ship approached, then the capsule opened and fired a homing torpedo at the ship. "And if our captors can carry nukes, so can theirs. So we're not decided on a course.''

"And we're not staying here.'' Ruth Crimmin shrugged. "We might as well go straight ahead west.''

"If we're not loitering to receive any new SACI,'' Clemence said carefully. "If we're putting our tactical survival above our strategic role—what are your plans once we're out of this box they've put us in? Across to the States? Or due south?''

My plans, Boyce thought. *My* plans. Is that Greg carefully affirming that he won't challenge my command decisions, or is he carefully ensuring that any disobedience of orders—any mutiny—is my business and not his? Tactics I can cope with—strategic decisions I shouldn't have to make. "Can't afford to think that far ahead right now. And I'm not at all happy about the basis for an immediate course decision. I think I'll go talk to the Captain.''

Orville Steetley raised his eyebrows at that. "He's up to it?''

"If he is, good. If not, well okay.''

"You want to talk to him right away?'' Clemence asked.

"No. First I'm going up to the CIC to give Joe Dylong a quarter hour break. The poor guy has to get time for a crap or to get something more to eat sometime. Then I'll go see the Captain.''

"How about a ship's address?'' Steetley suggested. "Just to give the basic situation—speaking for my people down there, who rarely get to see a chart display or a tactical plot.''

"Okay, I'll do that. Anything else right now?''

Crimmin nodded. "Bainbridge says the way she reads the clouds on the SCAN radar, there's another front coming down on us from Iceland. She can't say how bad it's going to be, but it might be bad enough to effect flying operation.'' She looked at Clemence.

"No problem,'' he said. "We can still run the Skycat CAPs and the ASW patrols even if it's a hurricane. Ted

Marcovicci's boys hop up and down off the deck like seagulls. No problem.''

Culbertson was asleep on the examination couch in his narrow office.

"John?" He propped himself up on one elbow, his shirt all crumpled. He rubbed at his eyes with thumb and forefinger. "Guess the operation knocked me out, too. What's the situation?"

"You didn't hear the ship's address?"

"No. Turned it down out here so there was no chance of it waking my patient through there." He nodded at the door behind Boyce.

"Well I'm going to wake him. I need to talk with him."

"I wouldn't advise that. He's in a very weak condition. He has to rest."

"As far as I'm concerned he's still in command on board this ship. I'm representing him while he's incapacitated. If he has any orders for me, I want to hear them."

Culbertson shrugged, swung his legs over the side of the couch, and dropped onto his feet.

Richard Erwin Bedford lay ashen faced on a still completely undisturbed bed. Culbertson cast an eye over the colour of the little trickles of stuff collected in the bags at the ends of the drain tubes. He looked at the plasma bag. It was nearly empty and he might as well replace it right away. He turned to go.

Bedford's eyes opened and looked unsteadily at them. "John?" His voice sounded weak, but the vagueness had gone. "What brings you here?"

"Situation report." Boyce smiled. "Sorry if I woke you."

"Wasn't asleep. Just thinking. How's the situation?"

"Tight." Culbertson left to fetch plasma, and Boyce continued. "We've fired the entire strike series, and now we're heading due west at max speed. Right now we're around one hundred fifty kilometres northeast of the Shetlands. Got it?"

Bedford nodded, a mere movement of his head on the pillow.

"There's a submarine north of us. We picked up its Cracker Box around three hours ago. It must still be at least six or seven hundred kilometres away. There's another with Cracker Box southwest of Iceland, and either a destroyer or a sub with Sparker Box just north of Iceland. I figure those last two guarantee we don't go out north of the Faeroes. But I'm worried about the unknowns.''

"The sub contact we had. Or didn't have. The sub contact. And the ship or sub that transmitted from somewhere south of us. Four days ago, that was. Right?"

"Right. I have to guess they're around somewhere. But where do I guess they'll be?"

"Easy, John. Easy. Where do you least want them to be?"

"Right in front of us, stopping us going through south of the Faeroes.''

"So that's where you assume one of them has to be. If it exists at all.''

"Right where we're going. Okay—we should be able to win any conceivable engagement, but we can take damage. That accumulates. What do you think of cutting the corner again for a move southwest—going through south of the Shetlands, back the way we came?''

"Bad option. Any sub that's now north of the Shetlands has had time to go south and maybe lay captor mines. The water's shallow enough there, isn't it? We'd only hear them as they came in, and the channels are so narrow they'd have a real chance of getting close. If they were nuked they could cripple the ship.''

"That's what we already figured—*if* a sub is there and *if* it has captors. What do you think about turning south and slipping through the English Channel? At least that way the three units we actually know about would never come anywhere near us.''

"No good that way, John. All the way down the North Sea, then through the Straits and right along the Channel west before you even begin to get sea room. You need a thousand kilometres of empty ocean all around you, and all of it too deep for a sub to lie waiting on the bottom. You need that as soon as you can get it. They might have put captors in the Channel, there might be something coming the same route up to get at us. That's no option.''

"You're making any avoidance of combat sound kind of hopeless, Rick. Did you just maybe have a recommendation?''

"If you just come out through between the Shetlands and the Faeroes and only then turn southwest, the sub southwest of Iceland—that's right? The sub southwest of Iceland might still be able to come down and run right into you if it happens to pick the right course. Turn a little south right now, say two-four-oh degrees or something. I don't have a chart and I couldn't see it straight even if I did. You'll have to work it out. Come around forty or fifty kilometres north of the Shetlands, not through the middle of the gap. Then turn southwest and go straight back the way we came. Close in past the Hebrides and then out into open ocean. At max speed you'd be clear in fifteen to twenty hours.''

Culbertson returned and started exchanging the almost empty plasma bag for a full one.

"What about the sub we engaged late yesterday? That course would take us kind of close to their last position. Suppose they're still there?''

Bedford said nothing. He watched Culbertson changing over his life-supporting plasma drip.

"Suppose the sub's still there, Rick?''

"It doesn't matter,'' Bedford said, very quietly. Then he looked back at Boyce. "If they're still there, it's because the boat has a hole in it and is mostly full of water. Any poor bastards still alive in it might even hear us go past, but they won't be able to do a thing about it. And if it doesn't have a hole in it, it's not there. They'll be somewhere else looking for us, but they won't be right there any more. They'll have got the hell out of there.''

Bedford closed his eyes.

"Okay, Rick. Thanks.'' Damn yourself for straining the man at all. "That's fine. I don't need to bother you any more right now.''

"That's no bother, John.'' The voice sounded flatter, weaker suddenly.

"Sure. Just one little question, Rick. How do you feel?''

"How do I feel?'' Bedford's eyes opened again. "Fuck awful.''

Boyce grinned. And left.

Culbertson stuck a thermometer in Bedford's mouth, took his pulse, waited, read the temperature. He shook the thermometer.

"Andrew? How'm I doing?''

"Fine.'' Culbertson pocketed the thermometer. "No fever, pulse is stronger and regular. You'll be on your feet in a month—with a little bag plumbed in to your guts, of course—and healed completely in three months.''

"Huh.'' Bedford looked away across the sick bay. "It's not so easy telling flat lies, is it?''

"I'm not lying. You'll pull through."

"It's not you I'm talking about."

There'd been enough time for the people taking Condition 1 rotation breaks to get back to the MCC. Warren Lister had his whole control team there, and with Boyce joining them the place was full. Boyce put down the phone at Vogt's Guidance Control position, cutting the connection with the bridge. He looked again at the screen, at the signal text pushed out of the Dark Mirror and Shadow Glass cryptographic facility.

> ORIG: CASAL NAVALCOM NMSS DIR 1021 JUNE 13
> 1040
> INCOMING: JUNE 13 1750
> NMSS-3 VINDICATOR
> FIRE LANCE COMMAND CODE: SHADOW GLASS
> SACI 05

1. This is a Strike Allocation Command Input for strike series preparation.
2. Firing Enactment instruction in 5 hours from this transmission.
3. Single launch point at 60°00'N 02°00'E.
4. List of TLF PD-targets and Supplementary Target Coordinates appended.
5. Acknowledge this signal SACI 05.

Lister turned to CPO Deevers at the Target Control position. "Targets still coming through?"

"No sir." Deevers shook his head. "List just ended. Ninety targets in total, one strike."

"Huh," said Barbara Vogt. "That'll just about empty us."

Lister shrugged and then looked round at his team. "Okay, tell the people down below we're back in business. Ask Milgrom and Stothers to come up here." He turned to Boyce. "We can get a ninety strike ready to go in five hours. No problem at all."

"No," Boyce said. "We ignore it."

"What?" Lister didn't quite believe him. "We *what?*"

"We can't, sir." Lewy already had a phone in his hand. "It's on Shadow Glass encryption. That's the correct Nemesis domain for an SACI for CASAL."

"The instruction's legitimate," Wigner said.

"We ignore it."

Warren Lister was at a loss in the middle of his own little MCC kingdom. "Why?"

"Where's the position?" Boyce glanced back at the signal on the screen. "Sixty degrees north, two degrees east. That's around one hundred and something kilometres west of our first firing position. Yes?"

"Yes," Vogt said. "South of here, about halfway between the Shetlands and Norway."

"So still inside this box. And the FEI is due in five hours, and even if the strike runs immediately it's going to be five and a half hours before we turn away again to break out." He shook his head. "It'll be too late to break out."

"That means—" Lister had to start again. "That means you're deliberately disobeying an order to launch."

Boyce merely took off his glasses. He rubbed his eyes with the fingers of his left hand, then looked at his glasses as if inspecting them for dirt.

Silence in the MCC.

Gloria Craze came in through the tunnel door from outside the C3 box aft. She stopped, confronted by the soundless tableau. Boyce was standing there with his glasses in his hand. He *never* removed his glasses anywhere outside his own cabin, and then only in relaxed moments such as they hadn't had since the peacetime voyage from San Diego to Honolulu. His glasses were his personal armour—he looked so terribly vulnerable without them. And so tired.

Boyce rubbed his eyes gently again and put on his glasses. He looked at Gloria.

"You wanted me down here?" she asked.

"We've just received a Strike Allocation Command Input." He waved at the readout screen. "On Shadow Glass from CASAL. Seems STRACC is still out—presumably permanently. They're shooting what's left of each other to pieces."

Another launch, another pointless murder of the dying and the all but dead. "So?"

"It means turning south and staying the wrong side of the IUK Gap for at least another nine hours—it will be five and one half hours before the strike is over and we can turn away. By then the Soviet units will have closed us in. They'll be able to engage us and give fixes on us for nuclear attacks."

Was he going to ask her, then, how the crew would react to the announcement of their death sentences?

"They must know that at CASAL. But we'll be empty, we'll have just six Fire Lances left on board. So they're expending us. Sacrificing us."

She waited. Lister waited. Everyone waited.

"And since there's no American People left to defend any more, I don't feel like getting expended. We're ignoring the order."

She could hardly believe it. So—John Ritchie Boyce hadn't given up yet. Someone who mattered hadn't given up, wanted nothing more to do with the madness of nuclear strike and counterstrike in a world all but totally destroyed. Someone else also wanted to stay alive.

Lister sat down in the only spare chair next to the Launch Control Console. "You're crazy. They'll court-martial you. That has to be a capital offence in time of war. You're crazy."

"Warren," Gloria said. "*Who* is there going to be to court-martial anyone? Outside of CASAL—and STRACC, if anyone's still alive in there—the Captain down in sick bay is the most senior US Navy officer left in this world."

Lister just shook his head. There was a further silence. The deck moved slightly, gently, a sea motion under the ship.

Wigner chose to break the continuing silence. "What's the weather like out there?"

"Temperature still at minus eighteen," Gloria answered. "Wind's coming round to west and clouds are coming up. The swell's rising. Bainbridge is right about the weather coming." And then the silence resumed. She looked at Boyce. "You wanted me down here?"

Boyce nodded. "A signal's come in for Kylander as well, presumably about the strike. I've asked Communications to sit on it for a while. Question—do I let Kylander have a signal and then let him find out we're ignoring the strike, or do I tell him straight out, or do I try to keep him uninformed? These people, those in Communications, those on the missile decks—even though we're staying closed up for at least another half a day, they all have to go to the washroom. People meet people. Kylander will hear about it sooner or later. What's the best way to handle his psychology?"

"I don't know his psychology." She shrugged. "He isn't in my file. But the first thing I'd do is make him harmless. To hell with whether the Soviets *might* attack."

Boyce nodded once, then lifted his head—a decision irretriev-

ably made. "Warren, you've got something to organize after
all. We want Kylander and all his people disarmed simultaneously, with odds of at least three to one to smother trouble."

Kylander's cabin was on main deck, portside and outboard of
the C3 box. Bradford Kylander wasn't in the least surprised.
He was sitting on his bunk talking with Arlene Rimmington,
sitting beside him, and with Major George Dresher, who sat
in the chair. When the door suddenly opened and Boyce and
Chief Warrant Officer Kusatsu strode in, guns in their hands,
accompanied by two crewmen carrying rifles and backed up
by still more in the corridor outside, he wasn't at all surprised. It was due. Boyce made the demand, and Kylander
nodded, and he and the others surrendered their weapons
without protest. The warrant officer handed them out through
the door. Boyce holstered his Colt automatic, the seamen put
up their M16 carbines.
    "As a matter of interest," Boyce said, no expression at all
on his face. "We're ignoring a signal instructing us to turn
around and launch another strike, because complying with it
would get us sunk. You as well. We're heading out west
through the IUK Gap into open ocean, trying to outrun Soviet
units that are closing on us. The course we're taking will keep
us in helicopter range of the UK for several hours. There's a
possibility of a machine coming to take you off. If it material-
izes I'll put you and your troops on it. Glad to get rid of
you."
    Kylander nodded. That would have been his contingency
escape route, just as planned back in the States. "And until
then we're all to be locked in our cabins?"
    Boyce tapped the door at his back. "No locks. Besides."
He sneered. "People like you would only mess on the floor."

MOST POSITIONS IN the CIC were occupied, Boyce was there, Lt. Cmdr Dylong was there. It was 2025, and Boyce was sick of Condition 1. They were sixty kilometres northwest of the Shetlands on course 240° at 35 knots, taking Bedford's suggested way out. The sea state outside was moderately high with regular marching waves, it was snowing again with a force 7 blowing from the southwest fine on the port bow. The Vindicator was moving regularly but not sharply. The temperature had climbed to—14°C and was holding steady, the wind was rising as the front came in: the low pressure centre would pass well north. In fifteen minutes he would turn the ship on to 225°, heading down southwest to pass the Hebrides outside of surface radar range, and leaving the Iceland-UK Gap for the safety of the open ocean. The worst danger was almost over, and they would be in a wide and empty North Atlantic in twenty four hours. Where to then? South, most probably south. They still had ninety six nuclear-armed Fire Lances on board—those should surely buy them sanctuary somewhere.

Somewhere.

CPO Cavanee, the Sonar Track Operator, looked round from his console. "Sir, I'm picking up something on the hydrophones." He turned back to his instruments. "Triangulating with hull line arrays and Surtass."

Dylong beat Boyce over to the ASW consoles. "Stacey, systems on." PO2 Stacey, a bearded black man, started throwing switches on the No. 1 Operator position.

"Jastrow," Boyce said. Seaman Belle Jastrow was No. 2 Operator. "Get Slamon back in here."

"I've paged for her," Kuroda said.

"Got it." Cavanee had a mess of data on his screen. "Twenty two thousand metres on bearing two-seven-oh. Right on our port beam, sir. Got an inclination angle. Ah—that puts it deep, four hundred forty metres plus. Near or on the bottom.''

"What is it?" Dylong was leaning over his shoulder. "What have you got?"

"It's the sub," Boyce said. What else could it be right there? "Goddam it, it's the sub. The one our Wolfmarine hit. It's still there." He turned. "Kuroda, ship's address. ASW attack warning!"

There was a suction of snapping breath all round the CIC. The rest of them could only sit there while the ASW consoles fought the action. *"Warning!"* the speakers yelled. *"ASW attack! Warning! ASW attack!"*

Boyce looked round at the CIC plot—Stratten and her people had already got it up there. Dylong went back to the OpSum to call up displays. Boyce turned to Stacey. "Target on the position, Fire Lance ASW mode attack. Jastrow, start loading the starboard tubes." He needed a Fire Lance vehicle to deliver a Mk 72 torpedo right on top of the submarine, he needed more MK 72s ready in the tubes on the stern to launch against any torpedo that came in. He needed the four port tubes as well, but they were wrecked and that was that.

Lt. Anthea Slamon, ASW Supervisor, came running to her position between Cavanee and Stacey, pushing past Boyce to get to her seat.

"Figured it, sir," Cavanee said. "It was external torpedo tube caps opening. And I think—They're firing. They're firing."

"Deploy bow sonar into dome." Slamon looked up at Boyce. "Suggest we use the bow sonar—if there's a big shock the dome will rupture anyway. That way we keep the MSP sonar safe inside the hull."

"Okay." He hurried back to the commanding officer's dais, he slipped on his headset while climbing into the chair. Everyone put on their headsets.

Cavanee's voice. "Red Whale has launched four. Two running deep, two climbing steeply."

Dylong. "Those are missile busses. Expect Skimmer Poles."

"SADIS on automatic," Boyce ordered. "Clear Arrowflash and Skyfire."

Redden. "SADIS on automatic. Arrowflash and Skyfires clearing."

Two missile busses coming up, two lethal air cruise missiles about to come in from a mere twenty two kilometres away. At least they were subsonic and would take a full minute to fly to the ship, allowing time to knock them down. The sub had waited as Vindicator came almost right down on it, thundering through the water at 35 knots, and had launched its attack exactly as the ship passed by at the point of closest approach. "Pre-instruct the port Arrowflash. Two rounds."

Condillac. "Pre-instructing, two rounds."

LoSecco, Weapons Control Officer. "Suggest semi-active mode."

External radar guidance to improve the chances of a hit. "Semi-active mode."

Cavanee. "Two breaking surface."

PO2 Hayes at the Air Detector/Trackor. "Two contacts. Airborne. Two missiles. SADIS tracking."

Dylong. "They're Skimmer Poles. Their radars are coming on."

Condillac. "Arrowflash instructed."

Stacey. "Fire Lance round instructed and loading. Torpedo instructed to search for a bottom target."

"Fire when loaded." One more torpedo had to kill the sub.

Condillac. "Arrowflash launching. One. Two. Both flying. Radars coming on. Guidance locking."

Why didn't the boat fire four Skimmer Poles? Why two torpedoes? Because the bottomed and crippled sub just happened only to have those four weapons loaded in its tubes, and all its auxiliary engines were out and there wasn't enough battery power for the winches to change the ready salvo? Or because the torpedoes just happened to carry nukes and the Skimmer Poles just happened not to? "The torpedoes running. What do you have?"

Slamon, her hair cleft in two by the band of the headset. "Two torpedoes coming in, running deep—three hundred metres. Speed fifty four knots. Both firing sonar. Ah—the Mk 72s are ready to launch. We're selecting two rounds in series for each target, instructing now."

Dylong. "We should launch immediately. They have to circle around our stern."

"Okay. Launch seventy twos and reload." Reloading would take four minutes—the attacking torpedoes would come almost seven thousand metres closer in that time.

Stacey. "Fire Lance round gone. Flying. Course true."

Condillac. "Arrowflash closing."

Dylong. "One hit. Two hits. Both missiles downed."

Easy, simple. One danger swept out of the way. Easy.

Jastrow. "Mk 72s gone, curving aft. Tubes reloading."

Dylong. "The attackers are Red Runners, types three or four. They can probably take avoiding action."

And the Red Runners might survive the first pairs of intercepting Mk 72s and come closer and ever closer. Boyce pressed the channel to the Ship's CP. "Both inboards zero pitch and stop. Close tunnels. Outboards maintain full ahead." Making distance, still making precious distance. "All rudders hard starboard, bow thrusters full power. Come round ninety degrees and straighten."

And they reacted immediately up there. The ship heeled into a sudden turn.

Dylong. "That's the wrong manoeuvre. We should turn to port, bow on to the shock."

From the intercom board on his console he noticed that Dylong was sending his voice over the private consultation channel. He switched into the same. "No. They're too close and we'll run right down on them. Also our next salvo of seventy twos would never circle around us in time."

A brief pause from Dylong. "Agreed. This manoeuvre."

"Are the isolation boxes freed?" And back on open circuit.

"They're freed. Shock dampers switched to automatic response."

Stacey. "Fire Lance has split. Torpedo hit the water."

Cavanee. "It's running. Sonar firing." As if the people on the sunken submarine weren't as good as dead already, they'd called down a final execution by attacking the Vindicator. "The intercept seventy twos are closing on the Red Runners. Dividing in pairs. Red Runners are starting to corkscrew."

The Mk 72s were fast and agile and accurate, and clever enough not to lock on to each other instead of their designated targets. But a head-on intercept of torpedo against torpedo wasn't easy, even though the Red Runners would be five or six times the size of the Mk 72s. The 72 was clever enough to select for a proximity detonation if it found itself missing, but the warhead was small and its effective radius would be squeezed right down by the pressure of 300 metres depth. The Red Runners were corkscrewing, and the 72s really could miss.

Jastrow. "Starboard tubes reloaded. Ready to launch."

Cavanee. "One seventy two detonated. Two. Red Runners

still coming. Three detonated—direct hit. Fourth detonated. Wide miss. One Red Runner still coming.''

"Launch all four of the seventy twos.''

Jastrow. "Launching. All four gone. All four running.''

"How is the Red Runner coming?''

Slamon. "Still running level at three hundred down. It looks like it isn't going to rise. Looks like it must have a nuclear head.'' Armed with a thermonuclear warhead, the weapon didn't need to come up to hit the ship directly. The deeper it ran, the less of its precious blast energy broke clean through the surface and into the air, the more was pumped at the target through the dense transmitting medium of water.

Dylong. "It's nuked, all right.''

Kuroda. "We've straightened up on heading three-three-oh degrees. Speed seventeen and one half knots. Both inboards stopped and tunnels closed.''

At least he would be able to save the inboard screws, save half the Vindicator's drive and escape speed. At least that much.

Cavanee. "Our torpedo detonated. Looks like it hit the Red Whale. Yes, sonar confirmation—contact detonation on the Red Whale.'' So the submarine was finished for good. It would be firing no second salvo. "Red Runner coming in dead astern. Three thousand five hundred out, three hundred down.''

"Have the AOC ordered their Skycat clear?''

Kuroda. "Yes sir. It's broken off the CAP and is running northwest.''

Cavanee. "Red Runner at three thousand. First seventy two at one thousand.''

"Warn the ship.''

Kuroda started passing the warning on the ship's address.

"Pull in all radars. We'll take no chances. Slamon, pull in the bow sonar as soon as you think hydrophones are enough.''

Slamon. "Okay, sir. Sonar transponder coming in now.''

Cavanee. "Red Runner at two thousand five hundred, and corkscrewing. First seventy two at one thousand six hundred.''

He looked round the CIC. Dylong was standing with feet splayed and hands grasping the OpSum handles. Everyone else but the ASW team was hanging grimly onto seat and console. What's this going to be like, a nuclear blast in the water? What's this going to be like?

Cavanee. "First seventy two missed, detonated. Red Runner at two thousand, second seventy two at one thousand seven hundred.''

The Soviet torpedo was good, very good, spiralling erratically through the water.

CPO Irene Jablonski. ''All radars retracted.''

Cavanee. ''Second seventy two missed, no detonation. Red Runner at one thousand eight, third seventy two at one thousand four.''

The torpedo was good. It was far too good. *What's this going to be like?*

Cavanee. ''It looks better this time. I think—''

They didn't swoop. They plunged!

A huge thundering noise. A sudden jarring crashing. A flying feeling, slamming impact, the world waltzing on tumbled gimbals—

He was on the deck with the headset dangling free beside him. He hauled himself up. People were lying everywhere, were struggling to rise. But in shallow ocean a second shock wave would come bouncing back off the bottom, taking a slightly longer path to the ship. ''Wait! There's the bottom shock!''

Crouching on your hands and knees and—

Up and swooping! Jarring as the shock dampers locked at full compression. *Down*—and a slamming solid stop. Clattering of the floor plates settling in the door tunnel. A sickening oscillating feeling as the isolation box came back to its neutral resting position. A creaking from the concertina walls of the door tunnel.

Then it stopped.

And then there was no sound except the alarm buzzers. A chorus of them.

He scrambled back into his seat, pulling the headset on. The others were doing the same. Stratten was standing up, stretching, throwing switches high on her console. Both SADIS Systems operators suddenly fell to frantic activity. The weapons operators were throwing switches, Slamon's ASW team.

The buzzer chorus stifled, one by one.

Joe Dylong got to his feet beside the OpSum. Even he looked scared. Kurado was sitting on the deck in front of his Talker console, frantically talking into his headset mike and glancing repeatedly back at Boyce.

Boyce selected the open circuit. Say something, say *something* to help them all. ''I think we hit the buffers with that one. With both shocks." He looked round for anyone incapacitated by injury. No sign of casualties.

The last buzzer cut.

"CIC damage reports," he snapped. "SADIS?"

Stratten, still punching at her console board. "SADIS operating. We have fourteen computer systems alarms, but the first backups are on line and holding. We have full SADIS functions."

An incredible jolt like that was no good at all for electronics, not even when soft mounted. But the SADIS was operating. Without the system it would be impossible to defend the ship against surface or air attack—human responses were just too slow to keep pace with modern missiles. "Okay. Deploy radars again." A water burst down deep should leave no lingering electromagnetic danger for radar antennas. "Weapons?"

LoSecco. "CIC consoles all functioning with SADIS backups. Our alarms were slaved system alarms from the Weapons SCR. They're checking. Looks like some of the stern mountings are in trouble."

"Okay." Dammit, goddam it. "ASW?"

Slamon. "Consoles okay. Slaved alarms from Sonar Control Room. The Surtass is dead. Our hull line arrays are probably all out. The MSP sonar was protected and is okay. The bow sonar dome appears to be ruptured. They'll have a new Surtass line ready to pay out as soon as the dead one is jettisoned and we're underway again. Right now we're deaf in the water, sir."

"Okay." He switched to the consultation channel linked to the OpSum. "Any comments?"

Dylong's voice came over the headset while the man looked round at him from the OpSum. "That was a medium yield warhead at sixteen hundred metres. All externals will be dead. We'll be lucky if the hull's held."

It had to have hurt the Vindicator—not even a Nemesis ship could take that without injury. "Any possible danger from the Red Whale now?"

"If our seventy two didn't finish them right off, their own torpedo certainly did."

"How come our Wolfmarines didn't pick up the boat? Any ideas?"

"They're doing spaced sonar dips. A smallish boat down on even bottom—they'd miss it unless they were close. Assuming it was immobilized by our 'copter yesterday, there'd be no machinery noise to hear at a distance. And they wouldn't notice it with the Magan unless they flew right over it. Would have been pure luck if the screen had picked it up."

"Okay." Maybe he should have sent a Wolfmarine to locate the suspected wreck, and to blow it apart with torpedo attacks as a precaution. Maybe he'd made a mistake—but it didn't matter now. "Take over the supervision and get the functioning weapon systems patched in. Get the ship fit to defend itself." He switched from the consultation channel to the shielded Talker channel. "Damage reports?"

"Systems alarms on rudders, screws, transmission trains." Kuroda was back in his seat at his Talker board, glancing at the pad where he'd made notes of what Damage Control had told him. "Neither outboard screw is turning. They're checking through with Engine Control. The reactors and main turbines are good. No power interruption. One electrical generator is out and the people there are assessing. Nineteen shock dampers failed on the Service Equipment Space isolation box right aft, but the box is still properly suspended—no support spring damage. It looks like the aft Seastrike and the aft KM 56 one-five-five are out. Don't know why yet. Some ready rounds broke loose in the aft one-five-five magazine, but they came from the unfused rack and there's no explosion risk. Something's happened to one of the aircraft in the hangar, but no explosion or fire. Four box-cells in the underhull aft are fully flooded, but the box-cell walls and the inner hull appear to be holding. No reports of water inside the inner hull. Seven more cells in the underhull are flooding slowly, all aft."

A mess, the Vindicator was suddenly in a mess. But a water burst like that would have smashed the innards of any other ship and torn its hull wide open. "Any indication that the hull flooding is spreading?"

"No sir. But they also think the starboard inboard tunnel may have been cracked open. The pressure meter inside took so much of a kick that it's failed."

And that was the worst. If the rudders and all of the screws were out, if the Vindicator was immobilized—they were dead.

The phone back in his office was buzzing incessantly. He sent WO Jenny Bendix to answer it.

He looked at Bedford again. They'd tried to hold him

safe—Culbertson himself, Bendix, and two seaman orderlies—
they'd tried. But they'd been thrown around like dolls, and
the isolation box had hit the stops and Bedford had been
bounced almost right out of the bed. What it had done to his
insides was anyone's guess.

He had the blanket thrown back and was examining the
dressing taped over the main incision. Bedford had yelled
when he touched it, so he just peeled off the sticky tape and
folded back the gauze pad. It was bloody, and blood was
oozing quickly out of the wound—the stitches had torn in the
middle of the incision. He sent an orderly for the sewing kit:
it wouldn't do to have the patient progressively gaping open
again.

The other orderly started mopping the blood running off the
side of Bedford's stomach. Culbertson stepped back from the
bed for a moment.

"Andrew?" Bedford got out through clenched teeth. "What
was that?"

"That was a water burst, a nuke in the water. We just
nearly got ourselves sunk by a submarine. You took one hell
of a shake-up."

"My guts hurt like hell."

"You're okay." He was looking at the drains coming out
of little secondary incisions in Bedford's side and leading
down over the edge of the bed. "Some stitches have torn but
you're okay." Blood was trickling in the abdominal cavity
drain—the incision must be bleeding inside as well as out.
"We'll have to stitch you up tight again, but you'll be fine.
It'll just hurt, so hang on to your bed."

Bedford tried to grin, and looked ghastly.

Warrant Officer Bendix came hurrying back. "Casualty
reports. There's fractures and fall injuries—couple of dozen.
They're already bringing them down."

Culbertson nodded. And now the blood trickle in the abdominal drain was slightly stronger. If the inner muscle layers
of the incision had torn, he'd have to open Bedford up again
on the operating table and put in new sutures. "Okay, let's get
ready for them. We'll need the theatre."

Now he had the full picture, fifteen minutes after the blast
had hit.

The aft Mk 56 155mm Automatic Gun was out. The turret
had apparently lifted clear out of its ring, severing the power

and control cables. It had settled back perfectly again, but it was dead. The aft Seastrike launcher was also temporarily out, with a drive chain on the missile hoist torn. In the hangar, the F-28 parked nearest the stern had bounced too hard with the shock wave and its undercarriage had collapsed. The aircraft was a write-off for the forseeable future.

The outer hull had been ruptured under the stern just forward of the fallaway where the steep sternslope evened out into the flat bottom of the ship. The massive outer wall of eleven box-cells had been split open and they were now all completely flooded—which meant that a mere 540 tonnes of water had been taken in, which was no reason in itself to worry. The damage to the hull had to occur right there, of course. The pressure wave coming in from dead astern didn't transmit perfectly from one medium to another, from water to the Vindicator's steel, so although some energy was pumped straight into the stern of the ship as the shock wave hit, some residual energy was reflected downwards under the vessel. The underslope of the stern acted like a wedge, partially reinforcing the oncoming shock wave. And then the concentrated wave reached the point where the underslope and its focussing effect ended, and the flat bottom of the hull continued forward—at which point the excess energy in the wave front was released, with the result that the loading on the ship's hull peaked dramatically. If it was going to fail, it had to fail there.

But the ship was still basically sound, flooded box-cells in the hull structure didn't matter much. What mattered was that the starboard tunnel had also split, right down at the bottom of the underslope. The starboard inboard screw wouldn't turn.

Both outboard screws had gone. Exactly what state they were in was still not clear, but neither would turn and both transmissions had lost all pressure and response. All three rudders were gone as well, their drive mechanisms ripped out of the bearings by the pressure on the huge rudder blades. That didn't really matter. The ship still had both bow thrusters serviceable and could steer clumsily but adequately, while both inboard screws together would have driven it through the water at 17½ knots. But the starboard inboard wouldn't turn, only the port was operable. The maximum speed the ship would be able to make was 8½ knots, the bow thrusters compensating steadily and balancing the off-line thrust of the single screw so that the ship could maintain a straight course through the water.

At the moment he was running the port inboard at dead slow, giving just enough push to move the ship so that they could pay out a new Surtass line to give them hydrophone sensors again—so that they could listen to the surrounding sea. All the hydrophones in the hull line arrays were dead, and Jason Hosky's Sonar Systems people were working as fast as they could to replace as many as they could. The ruptured dome of the bow sonar had torn free as soon as the Vindicator had started to move—the sonar transponder was functioning perfectly, but it couldn't be pushed out clear of the hull any more without being overwhelmed by slipstream noise, making it useless. At least the MSP sonar midships was still intact.

The real miracle was that the reactor systems and the main turbines were functioning perfectly as if nothing had happened, that all service machinery was still in operation except for just one auxiliary generator with a broken shaft. Whoever had designed the system, whoever had invented the isolation boxes—they were geniuses beyond praise. But full power was no use without screws to drive the ship. At least three Soviet units were closing in, and if the Vindicator could make only 8½ knots they would catch the ship. And then one way or another, conventional and called-in nuclear attacks would go on wearing down the ship's defensive capability, just as had already been happening. However many Russians they sank or blew to hell in the process, eventually the Vindicator would go down.

The Talker channel light blinked on his little intercom board and Kuroda's voice spoke direct into his ears. "The Surtass line is fully deployed, sir. Damage Control say they're ready with the cameras aft, and a diver's standing by."

Boyce nodded. They would lower cameras and lights over the side to look at the outboard screws and the rudders, and could pass another camera through from inside the hull into the starboard tunnel. The tunnel hadn't even been opened now that the screw wouldn't turn—it would just increase drag and further worsen the effect of the off-line thrust from the port screw.

Dylong came over from the OpSum, wearing his head-set round his neck with the plug lead dangling. Boyce slipped off his own headset and looked at Dylong's stony face.

"Casualty count is twenty six bad enough to take down to sick bay," Dylong said. "Mostly fractures and serious-looking concussions. Six cases are bad. A fractured pelvis and hip, one crushed shoulder, two compound leg fractures, a crushed chest someone got when the F-28 collapsed in the hangar, and a fractured skull with suspected cerebral bleeding. That's Holicek from the bridge. Craze wants to know if she should stay up there to hold things together, or go and help Culbertson."

"What's there to do on the bridge?"

"The ship's CP is okay, we're okay here. The bridge only has to fill lookout duty, and there's another PO left up there to run that."

"Okay, let her help Culbertson." And Dylong started to turn back to his OpSum. "Hold it, Joe. Hold it. What's your assessment of our position?"

"If we get the starboard screw turning within an hour." Dylong shrugged. "Maybe we'll be able to run fast enough only to have to take on the Soviet Navy one unit at a time. We still have all our close-in weapons operational except for one of the one-five-fives and one Seastrike, and the Seastrike will be back in action in a couple of hours. We will have the Rayflex. We have nine Wolfmarines and seven Skycats. We could be okay."

"And if we don't get the starboard screw turning?"

Dylong looked past him somewhere. "Then I'd rather be on the other side. Can we make the British coast, maybe?"

Boyce just shrugged. The British coast would be no sanctuary—no shoreline anywhere in the northern hemisphere offered anything better than a delayed death. "What do you think about sending a signal?"

"No problem. That water burst has told everyone with a hydrophone for a thousand kilometres where we are, so giving them a signal fix can't hurt us."

Boyce nodded. Dylong went back to his position and plugged in.

Why did the sub have to be there after all, with its fore and midship sections where the sonars and crew and torpedo tubes were still intact, crippled and doomed but still able to avenge its own death by firing a salvo at the Vindicator as it went past? Why did they all—including the Captain—have to be wrong in the assumption that either it wasn't there at all, or it was a competely lifeless wreck? And why did the port

Mk 72 torpedo tubes have to be out, why did the Soviet air attack have to manage to do that? If both sets of tubes had been serviceable he could have launched a second salvo right after the first. The second attacking torpedo would have been taken out two or three times as far away, a quarter or a ninth the destructive energy hitting the ship. Then even the outboard screws and the rudders might have survived. Why, goddam it, why?

He put on his headset again and punched for a connection.

Lt. Elise Caro answered. "Communications."

"Boyce. I want to transmit a signal immediately on Blue Talker. To Naval Alternate Command, CASAL." The briefest situation report and a request for advice and assistance would do. Assistance, of course, was a dream.

"On Blue Talker to NAVALCOM, CASAL. Ready for the text, sir."

Culbertson and his team had been running around for almost an hour and a half like a parody of some emergency admissions centre. No burns—thank God there were no burns. The simple concussions he'd cleared and sent back to their cabins, the basic fractures he'd set and splinted and had carried away. One multiple fracture he'd retained in a sick bay bed.

The remaining six beds were filled by patients in various stages of half-treatment. He would still have to operate on the compound shin fracture. The compound thigh fracture had been a mess—the bone had only nicked the femoral artery but it had severed the vein, and the woman was lucky to be alive. The hip and pelvis case required an operation fast, and the crushed shoulder would have to be operated on before much longer in order to sort out the bones and protect the heart, the lung and the subclavian artery—according to the ultrasonic scan a splinter from the clavical was pressing into the artery. Reyhook, the aircraft technician with the crushed chest, required a major operation right away and would probably die during the course of it all. And then there was CPO Holicek with a severe fracture of the back and base of the skull and showing all the symptoms of profuse cranial bleeding. Even if Holicek lived he would be crippled, but his chances of life were minimal.

Culbertson needed another two doctors, another three. He was faced with having to decide who he could save and who he should simply and callously scratch. And now the Captain.

The main dressing was soaked with blood again, and blood was running out of each of the abdominal drains as fast as they pumped it into him. All the major lacerations must have opened up again. Bedford, too, needed an emergency operation.

"Right, Captain. You're next." He turned to the nearest orderly. "Tell Jenny the Captain is ready for theatre if we're clean in there."

"We're clean, sir." The orderly left.

"Andrew." Bedford's voice was as thin as a sick child's. "Don't operate on me. Take one of the other casualties. They're emergency cases. I'm not deaf or blind. I know what's going on. Take one of them."

"No way. You're dying right here in your bed. You're bleeding internally—very badly. You're just filling up with blood in there. I can't pump it into you as fast as it's pouring out again. The wounds have to be closed properly, so an operation."

"No, Andrew. No operation."

"Don't be pig-headed. You feel cold already? Cheeks feel icy? You're starting to die from loss of blood."

"The other cases are dying."

Culbertson looked at the human wrecks immobile on the other sick bay beds. "Two of them can wait. Two of them aren't quite as critical as you, and the two who also need an immediate operation are most unlikely to survive it. You will. So you're first."

"No, Andrew. I said no. The casualties are all my fault. I told Boyce where to take the ship. I brought us right down on the sub. It's my fault."

"Huh. Anyone can make a mistake."

The orderly came back with Gloria Craze, the two of them towing the newly covered theatre trolley to the side of the bed. They started hauling up the drain bottles full of blood so that they could move him.

"Andrew."

The orderly got an arm under Bedford's shoulders ready to lift and Craze took hold of his legs.

"Andrew, it wasn't a mistake." Bedford somehow managed to force his head up and put every ounce of his remaining energy into his failing voice. *"It wasn't a mistake."*

"What?"

"It was no mistake, Andrew. I knew the sub had to be there. It just had to be there. So I brought us right down on it."

Both the orderly and Craze had paused and were looking at Culbertson. And Culbertson didn't know what to do.

Bedford laid his head back on the orderly's arm. "Look after the other casualties, Andrew. That's an order."

The Vindicator was wallowing cumbersomely in a rising storm sea, lying stopped with the bow thrusters keeping its head to the wind so as to minimize the motion of the vessel. Boyce sat in the CIC and held his headset loose against his ear, listening while Orville Steetley delivered his report in person. The situation was that serious.

"The starboard outboard screw has lost two blades and the rest are deformed, the shaft bearings are smashed. The port outer is displaced on its shaft. Even if we could get the transmission working again the screw would just shake itself free. The shaft head must already be fractured. The centreline rudder is useless but won't interfere with manoeuvring. The starboard rudder has vanished, and the port is loose on its bearings and unserviceable."

"And there's nothing we can do about the starboard inboard?"

"Not in the open sea. I think the screw is serviceable okay—the damaged blade should hold. But we can't turn it until we've cut free the chunk of the hull that's sticking up into the tunnel. That's forty centimetres of steel laminate, ten-centimetre section ribs, and a ten centimetre inner sheeting. Half the bottom wall of the tunnel is stove in. We'd have to cut through the whole mess along something like twelve to fifteen metres to free the screw. I think—I *think*—the underwater torches we have on board could do it. I think our divers could handle it. But they can't go down in this sea at all, and it would take twenty four to forty eight hours anyway."

Hopeless. Utterly hopeless, in a situation where they had almost no time at all. "What's you recommendation?"

"Well—ignoring the threat from the Soviet units, I'd say get to some sort of sheltered water where we can put down an anchor and sit there for a couple of days to try and free the screw. The UK and Ireland and all their offshore bits and pieces must offer some sort of suitable place. But with the tactical situation—for all I know we're better off limping into the open sea. But if we do that we'll stay crippled until we get back to some shore somewhere."

"Okay. At some stage I'll be needing you and Greg for a consultation."

"Like can we hold the ship at all?"

"Like exactly that."

There was a brief pause at Steetley's end. "Pity of it would be that she's in perfect internal condition. Could keep us alive for months—a year or more if we conserve reactor power. She just can't move fast enough to get out of trouble. Where in hell would we go if we decided to get off the ship?"

"That would be the question. Okay—thanks, Orville." He cut the channel. He stared across at the CIC plot with its hollow tracery of coastline markings. Where could they possibly go?

"Sir?" Kuroda had come up to speak to him directly. "Cmdr. Culbertson wants to speak to you from sick bay. I have him on line two for you."

"Okay." Boyce picked up the headset again and switched in the channel. "Andrew, how are the serious cases? How are you making out down there?"

"I'm going to lose Holicek. There's nothing I can do for him. I'm probably going to lose Reyhook—I'm certainly going to lose either him or the Captain right away. I just have to decide which one to operate on. The one I leave is going to die while I'm operating on the other."

"Why do you have to operate on the Captain. The shock we took?"

"Right. His wounds have opened up again and he's losing blood at least as fast as he was before I ever got to him. Without an operation he won't last more than another hour.

"Andrew, I'm not competent to make medical decisions, and I can't perform a parallel operation for you. I can't help you with that one. I'm sorry."

"You don't have to help me. The Captain refuses to be operated on. He's even started to order me to take the other cases instead. But you have to come right down here, John. There's something I just can't handle."

"Andrew, I've got a ship here that's all but sinking. I've got my hands full with—"

"For God's sake, John. I can't handle this one."

"Okay. In a few minutes." He cut the channel and put down the headset. What in hell could the panic be? He called across to Dylong. "Joe, it's all yours. I'll be in sick bay. As soon as Steetley's people have their gear back on board, make as much speed as we can. Course southwest until we think of something better."

Dylong nodded.

Bedford was white, a deathly and ghastly white. The reason was obvious: blood was running in the tubes that punctured his side and was gathering in the drain bottles that stood on the deck beneath the bed. The level of the blood tipped slightly in unison in all the bottles as the ship rolled irregularly on the cross swell of a stormy sea. So much blood—and if that amount was now pouring out of him, there was much more pooled inside, and he was dying. The single bottle of whole blood drip-feeding into the center of his arm could never keep pace.

Boyce and Gloria Craze stood beside the bed, their backs to the rest of the sick bay and the couple of orderlies supervising the remaining serious cases. They were setting up a ventilator for Holicek there, to keep the man alive now that his brain was losing control over his breathing.

Boyce shook his head. "I don't believe you, Rick. Cut the crap. Andrew's operating on another case, and he says you'll be dead within an hour. He takes orders from you, I take orders from you. So you pass on an operation and you die. It's a charitable way of committing suicide, giving someone else a chance, and I hope I'd have the sheer guts to do it that way." And there was no point in talking to the man about *that* aspect at all, because it was too late to reverse his decision to kill himself. "But cut the crap, Rick. We do what you tell us without it."

"I knew the submarine was there, John." His voice had weakened to a whisper now. "I brought us right down on it. You asked me where to go and I told you. I'm sorry, John. I've crippled the ship for you."

"You couldn't know it was there. And you sure as hell couldn't know it was alive enough to hit us. That's crap."

"I knew it was there, John." There was still enough life flickering in Bedford to put an intensity into his voice. "I *knew*, I've had enough time to think about it. Figured it right through. I had to stop the ship. You're a good first officer, John. You'd keep the ship alive whatever comes in. You'd carry out the orders they send you. You'd launch all the strikes for Kylander and the people back home. Do that because you're such a good first officer. I would, too. Did, didn't I? I launched the first strike. So I had to stop the ship.''

"Rick, this is crazy. You just have to tell me what to do. I do it. It's your ship.''

"Had to stop you firing strikes again. It's all madness. Tell me—what did we think we were obeying, John?''

"The Government—who else? The orders of the Government, represented through the military command.''

"What Government, John? The one you and I enlisted under, took our oath of allegiance to, served and defended in the name of the people—it doesn't exist any more. Not one of its senior members is still alive. Its successors have appointed themselves. Guess they had to—no people left any more to vote them in. The democracy elected government of the people doesn't exist any more. There isn't any *government*, just something that runs what's left of the machinery. There isn't any democracy. What were we obeying, John? What were we defending?''

"Democracy still exists. What about Australia and New Zealand? In the north we have this mess, but afterwards we'll have democracy again if we keep the ideal alive.''

"No, John. Australia and New Zealand are going to be in the same mess. The dust is moving south. Dark, cold, no crops, no industry, fallout. They'll get the same mess. Only total dictatorships will even have a chance of holding anything together long enough to survive. There'll be no more democracy for as far ahead as you can look. Go talking of it and they'll purge you, John. Maybe the catastrophe will never end. But if it does, there's going to be so few survivors in such a mess, they won't give a shit for democracy and they won't have time for individual rights. Just survival of the group at any cost, or the group dies. We've killed democracy. We've defended it to death. Don't know if it's true that the Soviet Union didn't really start it. But it started so small, and we've made this out of it. We've defended ourselves to death, John. Us and everyone.''

Boyce shook his head again, trying to fight back the irrational thought that it might really be true, that Bedford could somehow have known exactly what would happen to them on the course he'd suggested. But that was impossible. "That's your vision of an Apocalypse, Rick. It isn't mine. Some of us are going to survive. The world isn't dead yet. Some of us are going to survive, and I'm going to try and make sure this ship and its crew are included in the survivors.''

"No, John. The ship has to go. The Soviets are closing in, aren't they? The ship's too crippled to escape. Sorry I did it to you. But I had to stop us firing strikes. We can't go on killing the world. Had to stop you, John. Had to stop you.''

"But that's not so, sir!'' Gloria almost reached out as if to shake the man, but pulled her hand back again. "There wasn't any need. Just a few hours ago—'' And Boyce's hand closed around her arm. "Around eighteen hundred, a new strike order came through. And John—'' His hand clamped her arm so tight it *hurt*.

She stopped. She looked at Boyce, she looked away at the draining bottle of whole blood dangling from the hook. She looked at the blank metal wall. Boyce didn't want the Captain to know, didn't want Bedford to realize that he'd crippled the ship and killed them all for no reason at all. Out of respect, or love, or plain humanity, he was going to let the man die in peace.

Richard Erwin Bedford, Captain in the United States Navy, closed his eyes. His voice seeped out like the whisper of sand in an hour glass. "John? Can you ask Andrew to give me something for the pain? My guts hurt like hell.''

"Sure, Rick.'' He was trying to keep the soundless howl from bursting through his house of thought. "Sure.''

Boyce walked out of the bed area towards the tiny operating theatre, but the theatre door was closed of course. He turned into Culbertson's narrow office. The place was a chaotic litter of empty wrappings torn off sterile dressings, discarded towels, tubs rigid with the leftovers of rapid-setting plastic for putting casts round broken limbs. Containers, jars, ampoules and wrappers were strewn everywhere. Culbertson's shirt had been dumped on the chair. He shook it open and laid it carefully on top of all the junk covering the desk, then sat down in the chair. He sank into it, he leaned back and stretched out his feet under the desk, ploughing furrows through the litter on the deck. He took off his glasses and put his hand over his eyes.

Gloria came in and walked past him, scuffing through the mess underfoot. She brushed sterile garbage aside on the couch, and lifted herself up to sit on the edge. She looked at him, collapsed there in the chair, one hand over his eyes and the other holding his glasses delicately by the double bars of the nose bridge. "John?"

No response from him.

"John? Andrew's stuck in theatre, but an orderly's giving him something for the pain. Andrew said the operation would take at least a couple of hours, and he had no expectation of finding the Captain alive when he came out. Has he really done that to us? Has he?"

Boyce removed his hand from his eyes. He stared naked faced at nothing at all. "If he says so."

There was a long pause in silence except for the sigh of the airconditioning, in a ship still alive but almost immobile, with hunters coming down on its heels.

"John? Has he really done that to us? Are we finished—really finished now?"

Boyce blinked at her. "We're finished. We might still haul ourselves out of this hole. Maybe. But we're finished. We're all dead. We were right from the start. Whatever happens, we're dead." He was silent for a moment, and then muttered to himself. "Nothing happens without the Captain."

"Pardon?"

"Nothing happens without the Captain. Not on a Navy ship. That's the way it has to be. Seems he can't even kill himself without taking the ship with him. And we might have got away. I don't know what good it would have done us. There was nowhere to run. But we might have lasted a little longer. Maybe."

"John—we can't be finished. There has to be something we can do. There has to be!"

"I can't roll the world back and unmake the war. Can you?"

He blinked at her, and then put his glasses on again.

He pulled himself erect, feet scraping litter on the deck. He was a first officer once more, facing a situation that was merely impossible but not yet over. He planted his hands firmly on the arms of the chair, asserting his self control. He was no longer vulnerable and helpless any more, he was the man she had never quite liked and who now had to decide how and when they were all going to die.

Cmdr. John Ritchie Boyce stood up. He looked at his wristwatch. "It's twenty two fifty. I sent a signal almost two hours ago. Maybe there's a reply come in. Maybe they've called a ceasefire, for Christ's sake. I'll be in Navigation. I have to look at the charts.''

He turned and left.

He left Gloria Craze sitting on the edge of the couch in the tiny surgeon's office, an office littered with all the things that human beings really need when they go to war.

June 14

THERE WAS NO signal from CASAL and nothing from STRACC. There never would be again.

At 0200 the British helicopter landed in the pitch dark in a snowstorm on the flight deck. It was another near museum piece kept in perfect condition by dedicated maintenance, a Boeing-Vertol Super-Chinook 360 with all-composite airframe and twin rotors, coming out from Stromness to almost its full action radius. The big machine could shunt almost seven tonnes of internal load around the sky. Daring to set it down on the Vindicator's deck in near zero visibility in a violent wind and sea state, the pilot was either a genius or a lunatic. Or else he had no idea how impossible it was—the Chinook was an army machine, after all.

The Vindicator had been heading on course 186°, almost due south, for three hours at a bare 8 knots. The Orkneys were still one hundred and fifty kilometres away—nine hours sailing time—and the Soviet units would have come up into combat range long before then. Boyce wanted to get in among the islands. They would effectively screen the ship from sea skimming missiles because the Soviet guidance radars were not up to the task of weaving between coastlines while looking for a ship. The Skyhooks and the less discriminating but higher flying radars on the Skycats would still be able to provide a warning screen reaching out to half a thousand kilometres, while the Wolfmarines could run an anti-submarine patrol right around outside the circuit of the islands. It was the only thing that made sense as a plan. If they could stay alive long enough to get the second inboard screw turning again, they could risk a breakout and head southwest for the open ocean and the far south. That, at least, would postpone it all.

There was a fuel dump that was still useable at Stromness in the Orkneys, and nothing else but ice and snowdrifts. The Chinook had come north to the islands from an open field above Tyneside, skirting the heavily nuked Scottish lowlands. Since then it had lost all radio contact with its direction base.

Boyce decided to put Kylander's team and all of the injured into the Chinook, along with several of the half-redundant Fire Lance personnel and a handful of the air maintenance crew kitted out with winter clothing, blankets, rations and emergency stoves. Their job was to secure the fuel dump at Stromness so that it could be used to extend the life of the Wolfmarines. He was possibly condemning them to death by sending them ashore, but at least it wouldn't be by fire or drowning. The Chinook pilot made it clear he wouldn't be returning, but would be heading south again with Kylander and the evacuated injured. There was still some sort of medical care to be had somewhere in the British Isles, and nukes were coming in sporadically, and since he commanded around ten percent of the helicopter lifting capacity still operated by the British Emergency Government—if it still existed—he and his machine would be needed down there. Ted Marcovicci did most of the hurried liaison with the crew of the Chinook, and said he had never before seen young men who looked so old.

David Drexel caught Kylander as he was throwing things together in his cabin. "Armageddon! Hah! Apocalypse and Armageddon! You've done it brilliantly, haven't you? *If* you accept that our side is good and the other side is evil—*if* you accept it. Then this isn't Armageddon. It's Ragnarok, Götterdämmerung, when the gods and the forces of evil fight the last battle and totally destroy each other. The Dusk of the Gods. That takes place in the dark. It's not the end of evil, it's the end of the world!"

Kylander was completely unimpressed by the Englishman's incomprehensible outburst. "I have a flight ashore. The UK. Your country. They're nuking it, but not yet up here in the north. Want a seat on the floor?"

Drexel nodded.

The Chinook left with almost sixty people crowded on board, along with their jumble of scavenged supplies. It made Stromness, set down the Vindicator's shore party and refuelled, then headed south towards the Scottish mainland.

• • •

The first attack came at 0300, sooner than expected. A submarine came in to within two hundred and fifty kilometres west of the ship and launched a salvo of SS-N-100s, Skimmer Poles. The missiles approached fairly high off the sea, searching with their radars and shouting their presence everywhere, and chirruping to each other one by one as they found the ship. The Skycat on CAP managed a chase intercept and brought down two with AIM-320s. Arrowflash took out all but one of the rest, and the Skyfires knocked that one into the water just short of the ship. The half-tonne high explosive warhead went off on impact with the sea, merely shaking the Vindicator slightly. Lighter debris flew on and damaged the starboard forward Skyfire and demolished the starboard Arrowflash launcher. Once again, it was the exposed weapon mountings that were the casualties.

The Wolfmarines crowded to the launch point of the Skimmer Poles, but by then there was no more submarine to be found.

At 0612 three re-entry vehicles came plummeting down out of the northeast. The Rayflex eliminated two, Arrowflash the third. It went off as a suiciding nuke four thousand metres out, giving a three hundred kilotonne yield. The ship bounced. The shock dampers on the aftermost isolation box had been damaged by the water burst during the submarine attack of the previous day, and the box crashed into its buffers. Inside the box were the ship's service equipment generators and systems, and through it went the drive transmission trains to the screws. Another generator failed, which meant putting non-essential areas of the ship on emergency power only, but that wasn't the tragedy. The transmission trains were torn apart. Not even the port inboard screw could turn any more.

That was the end of the Vindicator.

The air burst brought down the Skycat on CAP, sending it streaking down towards the sea with its on-board electronics wrecked. The pilot ejected almost one hundred kilometres away and one of the Wolfmarines on ASW patrol picked him out of the huge tumbling storm waves, homing direct on his emergency beacon. He was in a mess but alive—his survival suit would have protected him from the water for thirty minutes even in the Arctic. There were still six of the F-28 Skycats left, still enough to fight off any approach by a

surface unit, but there wasn't any point any more. It was
nuclear attacks and submarines that mattered, and the great
armoured ship was now drifting helplessly on the hugely churning sea. The wind might even drive the Vindicator onto the
Shetlands to wreck, given time.

Boyce started ferrying people ashore to Stromness, where
most probably nothing but ice and cold and eventual starvation awaited them. He had the Wolfmarines fuelled exclusively from the ship, and got Clemence's people trying to
arrange to somehow lash one of the 1,000 kilogramme external fuel tanks from the Skycats to the underbelly of each
machine for whenever the final trip came: with enough fuel
available they might still be able to use the helicopters ashore,
if they could keep them from freezing up. On each ferrying
trip they squeezed eight people into the tiny cabin of each
machine behind the pilot seats, piled up with bags of stores.
Every trip of 100 kilometres there and 100 kilometres back
took one and one half hours with turn round time. He wasn't
going to get everyone off that way.

He had a team plundering the galley stores for useable
food, picking out anything with a high energy content, some
of it stuff they could heat quickly but mostly stuff they could
eat cold—cooking fuel should be saved for melting snow and
then boiling up the water to purify it as best they could. All
the survival ration packs were helicoptered ashore, of course,
plus anything else useful they could dig out—vitamin supple-
ments by the box full, medication supplies thrown together
out of Culbertson's pharmacy, blankets, metallized plastic
emergency blankets, fire blankets, surplus clothing and winter
issue. And ammunition for the small arms, in case sometime
they had to fight in order to survive.

They could only survive a few days. They had no tents.

Another Skimmer Pole attack came in, dead on the ship's
immobilized position and giving next to no radar warning.
Arrowflash and the Skyfires downed all but one, which punched
a hole through the bow into the anchor chain tiers. He didn't
even bother sending the precious helicopters to look for the
submarine. It wouldn't risk coming in to fifty kilometre torpedo range to attack the ship with nuclear-tipped weapons.
Not yet.

At 1200 the Wolfmarines took off for the last time and

headed south with fuel tanks strapped to their bellies, disappearing into the noonday night. The storm front had cleared, the sea state was improving as the wind dropped. The air temperature was −11°C. Only the dust veil was shutting out the sun. Maybe it always would.

Half the crew got away. The rest went over the side into the inflatable life rafts. Despite the frenzied scramble to strip the ship of what little they could use, it was an orderly departure. They piled the rafts with stores and lashed them together in strings. The rafts were each fitted with an outboard—life raft design had been getting better all the time—and the boats in each string could conserve fuel by taking it in turns to drive them slowly south. With the motors and with paddles and with an abating wind they could make it, somehow. Probably.

The boat flexed as it swept up and down the waves, first the roof fabric stretching and the floor buckling as the side tubes kinked over a crest, then the roof crumpling and the plastic decking grids bowing as the life raft went down into the bottom of a trough. Twenty inflatable boats in four strings keeping company on a desolate dark sea, ten or eleven people in each, half the crew of the Vindicator.

Boyce pulled his parka closed, clumsy in his gloves, and turned to the side flap, unclipping it and opening it to let in the wind, to let in the even colder, the bitterly cold, air of the permanent winter night outside. Black salt water lapped right in front of him against the rubber side of the inflatable, slopping the loops of the nylon recovery rope strung around the boat's rim. A rime of splash-ice was building above the rope, but that didn't matter. He could hardly see a thing at first, just water everywhere and a dimly orange chain of inflatable rafts rising up from the end of his own and over the crest of a black wave, the dome of the highest boat silhouetted against the faint gloomy grey of the sky. He waited until his own raft lifted in turn on the great sliding waveslope.

There! There was the Vindicator back in the north behind them. It had turned head to the bitter westerly wind, the superstructure and tower and the higher length of the flight deck aft acting like a monstrous weather vane. Such a pity about the Vindicator—it had taken four nuclear attacks, three air bursts and one water burst, and was still afloat. Any ordinary ship wouldn't have existed after a single such attack.

The Vindicator wasn't the prettiest ship, and was now nothing more than a distant black shape barely visible standing up against the velvet darkness of the horizon. It wasn't the prettiest ship, but given better luck and the motive power to move it, the mightily armoured giant might have kept them alive whatever happened to the world. Might have. It had to be ill-luck and nothing else—the Captain couldn't have known the sub was still there and still dangerous and still waiting for them. Bedford might have convinced himself it would be, but he couldn't really have *known*.

If they had never been sent north, if they'd been allowed to miss the war entirely. They should have stayed in the hopeful safety of the south. Which was illusory, and which didn't matter now.

The life raft led the way into another wave trough, and the Vindicator was lost from sight.

He closed the flap on the fierce cold and settled back in the merely freezing interior of the flexing boat. They had a dim little light up on the centre inflated ceiling rib. They were all taking it in turns to steadily revolve the hand generator: there was battery power for rescue lights and radio transceivers, but that had to be conserved—and the exercise would be good for them. It would be long hours—very long, and very many of them—before they reached the islands over eighty kilometres south.

There were eleven of them huddled in the shadowy dimness of the roofed-in raft, lying on the floor gratings among a jumble of bags and boxes, with just the rubberized fabric skin of the boat between them and the deep dark sea. Gloria Craze was wrapped up in a muffling parka, wore boots, wore boat trousers over her uniform pants, wore a jacket and sweater. She was clumsy and cold. It would be even colder on land—much, much colder if they ever managed to get away from the edge of the sea. And maybe nuclear strikes were still coming in there as they finally destroyed each other totally with the last dregs of their arsenals, the war ending at last but not quite over yet.

She was wearing the gun she had stowed safe in her cabin, the one Raffles had used on herself. It was a strange weight on her hip, made her feel not so much safer as awkward among this jumble of stores and silent shadowed people. They moved up and down around her as the boat rode the waves. Chief WO Kusatsu and PO1 Rutledge were sitting at

one end under the curve of the roof hunched over a compass
and a chart, checking the course. Dead reckoning and regular
radio fixes from the people shivering ashore, plus the skills of
Ruth Crimmin's team, were the only navigational aids left to
them. There wasn't even a single computer. But Boyce would
get them there, that was certain. But what then? The gun, she
told herself—the gun would be used, if at all, to help her
survive. Only that.

Kusatsu, really only supporting Rutledge, looked across to
where Boyce half lay against the side of the raft next to the
entrance flap. "Think we'll really make it ashore, sir? It
seems a long way in these little things."

Boyce almost shrugged, and hoped the movement was
hidden inside the bulky quilting of his parka. "We'll make it.
Eighteen hours, twenty four hours. Depends on how much
wind we have to compensate for. If they don't send a nuke in
before we're clear, we'll make it."

"I'm thinking, sir. These rafts are kind of heavy to haul
around, but if we could drag them inland we could use them
as shelters. Be as good as tents."

"That's an idea. Would give us a start." John Ritchie
Boyce nodded. "That's a good idea." It was better than
nothing. It would delay things a little longer. He felt the life
raft gliding up and over and down. It would delay things a
little longer.